DC Super Hero Girls™

AT METROPOLIS HIGH

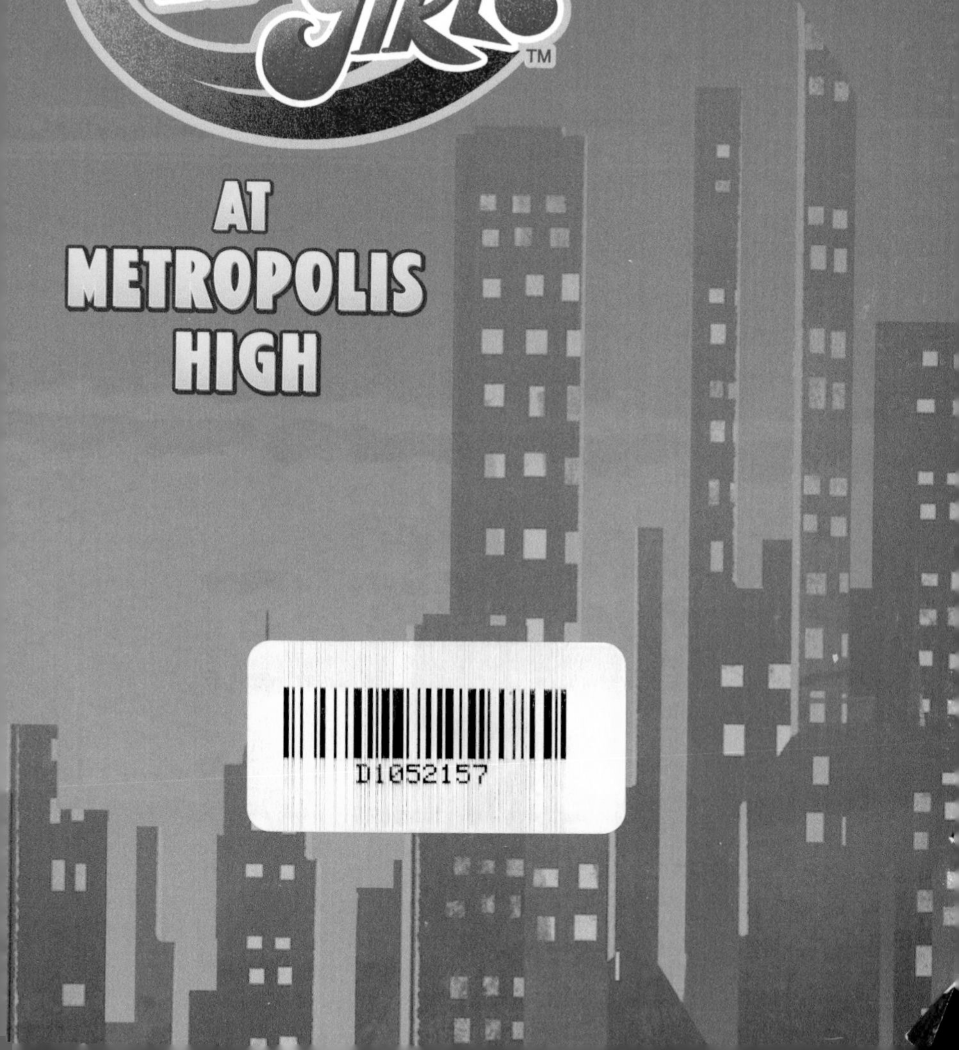

written by
AMY WOLFRAM

art by
YANCEY LABAT

colors by **MONICA KUBINA**

lettering by **JANICE CHIANG**

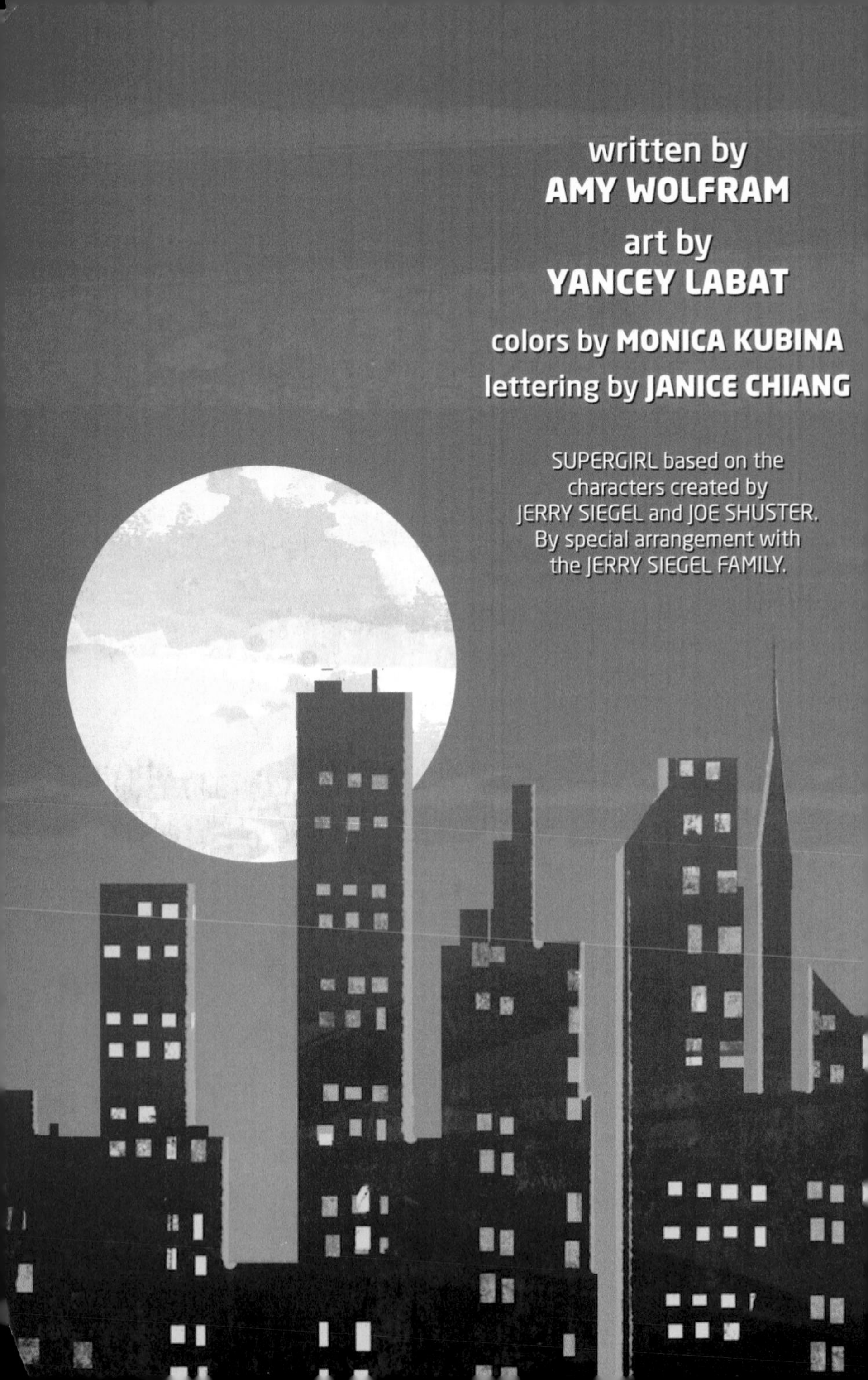

DC Super Hero Girls™

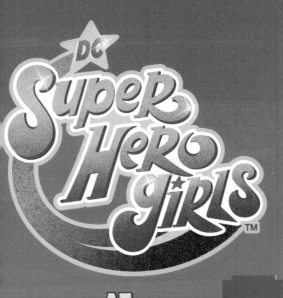

AT METROPOLIS HIGH

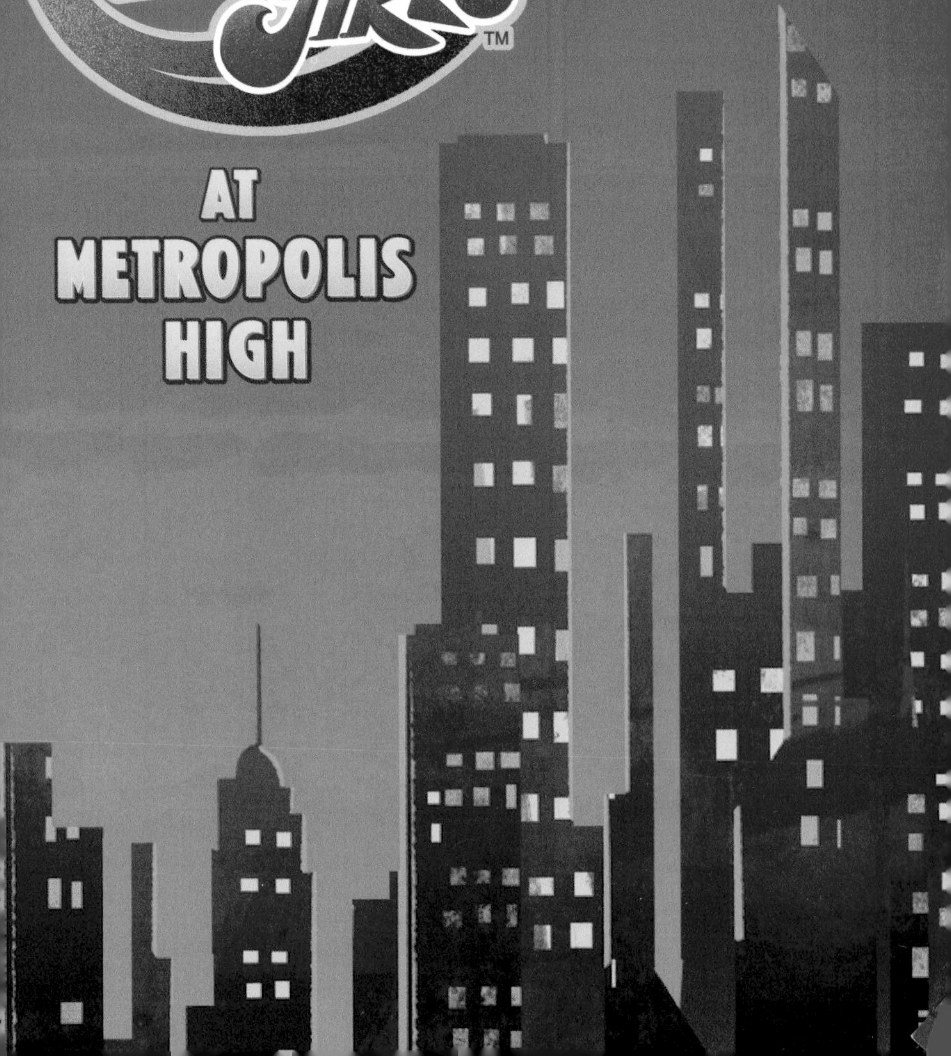

KRISTY QUINN Editor
DIEGO LOPEZ Assistant Editor
STEVE COOK Design Director - Books
AMIE BROCKWAY-METCALF Publication Design

BOB HARRAS Senior VP - Editor-in-Chief, DC Comics
MICHELE R. WELLS VP & Executive Editor, Young Reader
JIM CHADWICK Group Editor

DAN DiDIO Publisher
JIM LEE Publisher & Chief Creative Officer
BOBBIE CHASE VP - New Publishing Initiatives & Talent Development
DON FALLETTI VP - Manufacturing Operations & Workflow Management
LAWRENCE GANEM VP - Talent Services
ALISON GILL Senior VP - Manufacturing & Operations
HANK KANALZ Senior VP - Publishing Strategy & Support Services
DAN MIRON VP - Publishing Operations
NICK J. NAPOLITANO VP - Manufacturing Administration & Design
NANCY SPEARS VP - Sales

DC SUPER HERO GIRLS:
AT METROPOLIS HIGH
Published by DC Comics.
Copyright © 2019 DC Comics. All
Rights Reserved. All characters,
their distinctive likenesses, and
related elements featured in this
publication are trademarks of DC
Comics. DC ZOOM is a trademark
of DC Comics. The stories, characters, and incidents featured
in this publication are entirely
fictional. DC Comics does not read
or accept unsolicited submissions
of ideas, stories, or artwork.

DC - a WarnerMedia Company

DC Comics, 2900 West Alameda
Ave., Burbank, CA 91505
Printed by LSC Communications,
Crawfordsville, IN, USA.
9/6/2019. First Printing.
ISBN: 978-1-4012-8970-6

PEFC Certified
This product is from
sustainably managed
forests and controlled
sources
PEFC/29-31-337   www.pefc.org

Library of Congress Cataloging-in-Publication Data

Names: Wolfram, Amy. | Labat, Yancey C., artist. | Kubina, Monica, colourist.
| Chiang, Janice, letterer.
Title: DC super hero girls : at Metropolis High / written by Amy Wolfram ;
art by Yancey Labat ; colors by Monica Kubina lettering by Janice Chiang.
Other titles: At Metropolis High
Description: Burbank, CA : DC Zoom, [2019] | Series: DC super hero girls |
"Supergirl based on the characters created by Jerry Siegel and Joe
Shuster. By special arrangement with the Jerry Siegel Family."
Identifiers: LCCN 2019019080 | ISBN 9781401289706 (paperback)
Subjects: LCSH: Graphic novels. | CYAC: Graphic novels. | Women
superheroes--Fiction. | High schools--Fiction. | Schools--Fiction. |
Clubs--Fiction. | BISAC: JUVENILE FICTION / Comics & Graphic Novels /
Superheroes. | JUVENILE FICTION / Comics & Graphic Novels / Superheroes.
Classification: LCC PZ7.7.W6 D3 2019 | DDC 741.5/973--dc23

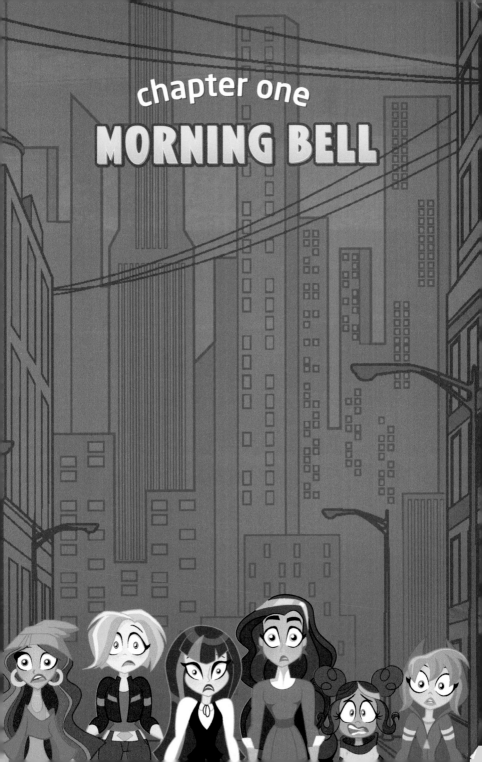

chapter one

MORNING BELL

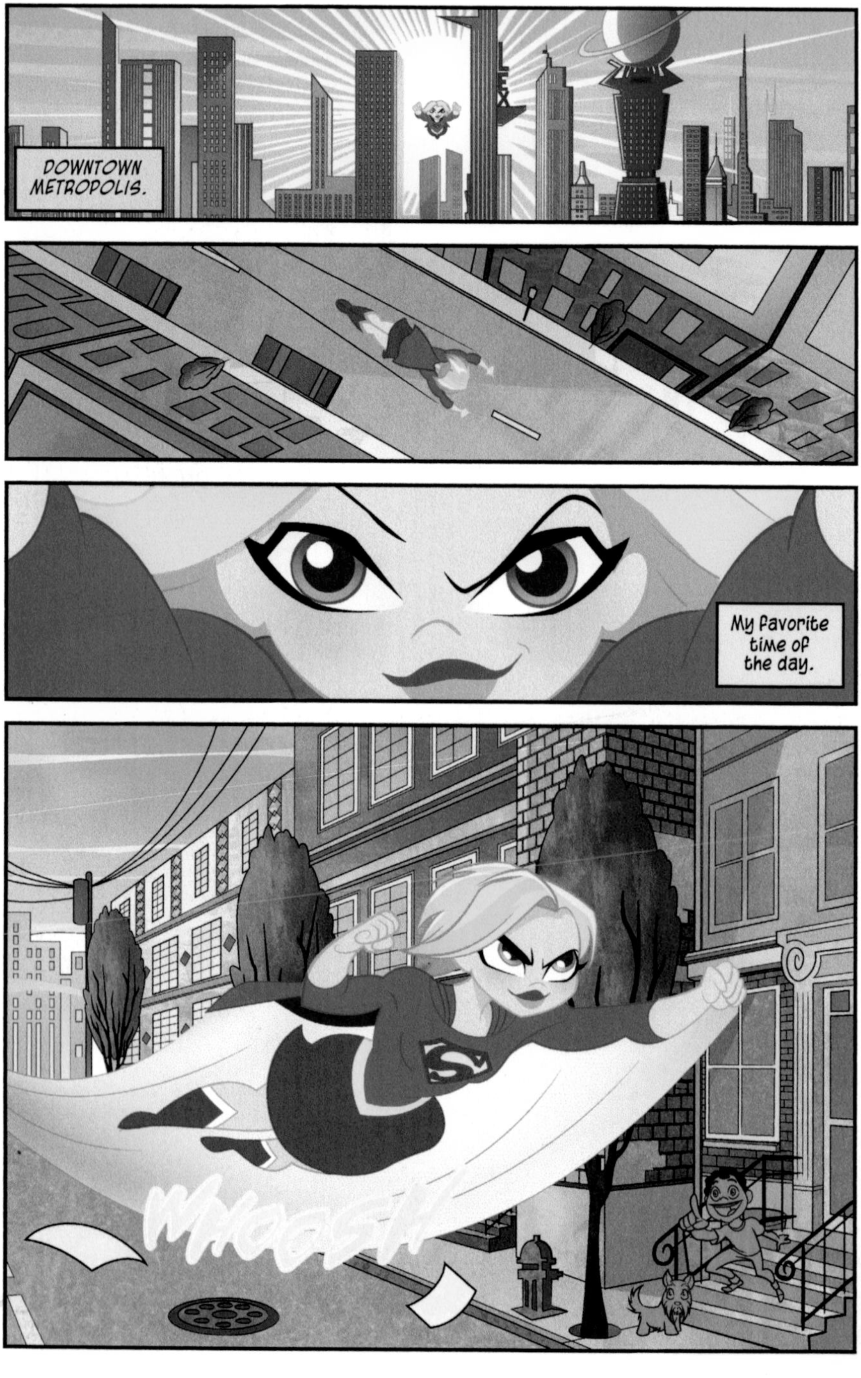
DOWNTOWN METROPOLIS.
My favorite time of the day.
WHOOSH

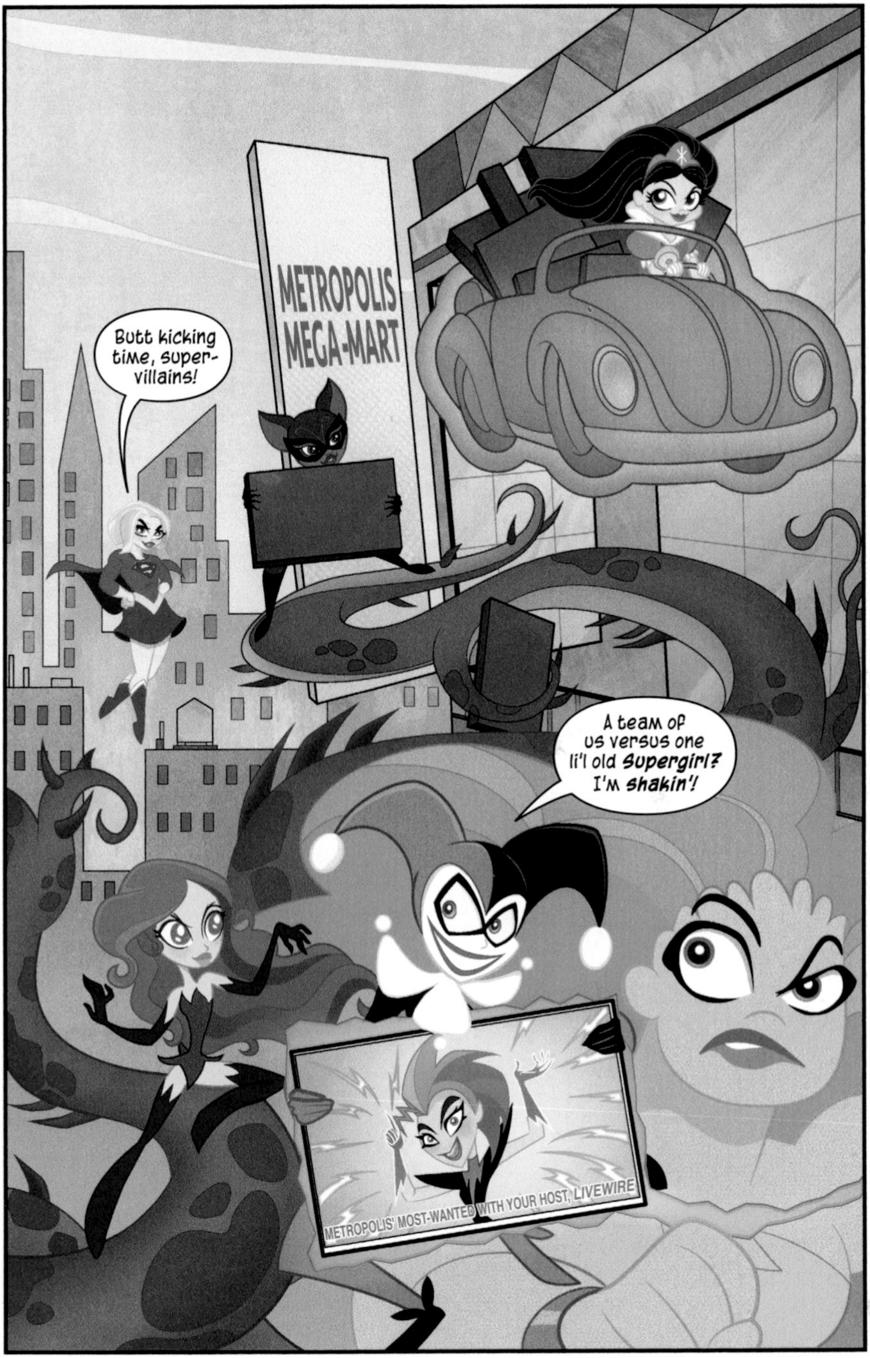
METROPOLIS MEGA-MART
Butt kicking time, super-villains!
A team of us versus one li'l old *Supergirl?* I'M *shakin'!*
METROPOLIS' MOST-WANTED WITH YOUR HOST, LIVEWIRE

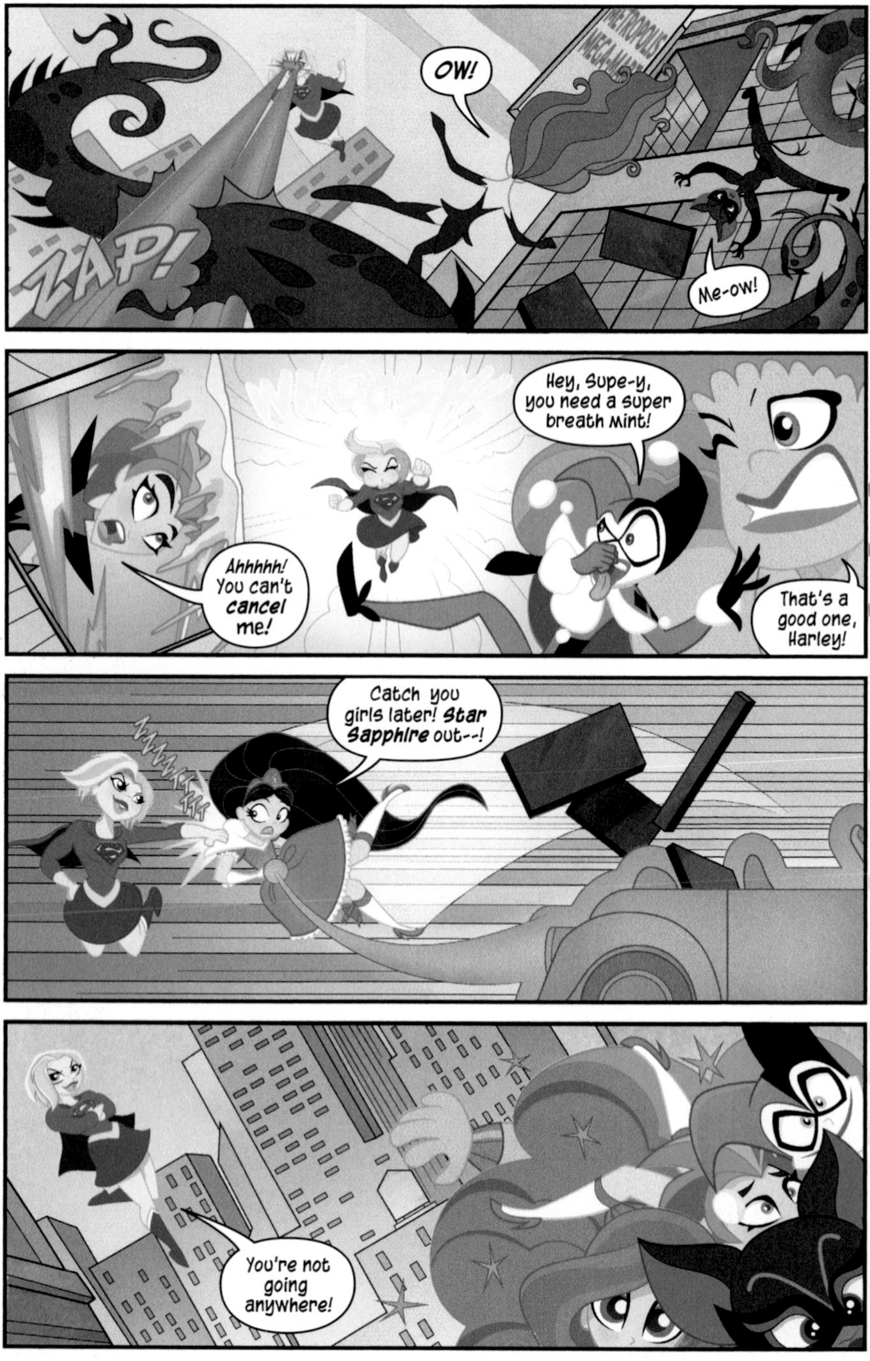
METROPOLIS MEGA-MART
ZAP!
OW!
Me-ow!
Hey, Supe-y, you need a super breath mint!
Ahhhhh! You can't **cancel** me!
That's a good one, Harley!
Catch you girls later! **Star Sapphire** out--!
You're not going anywhere!

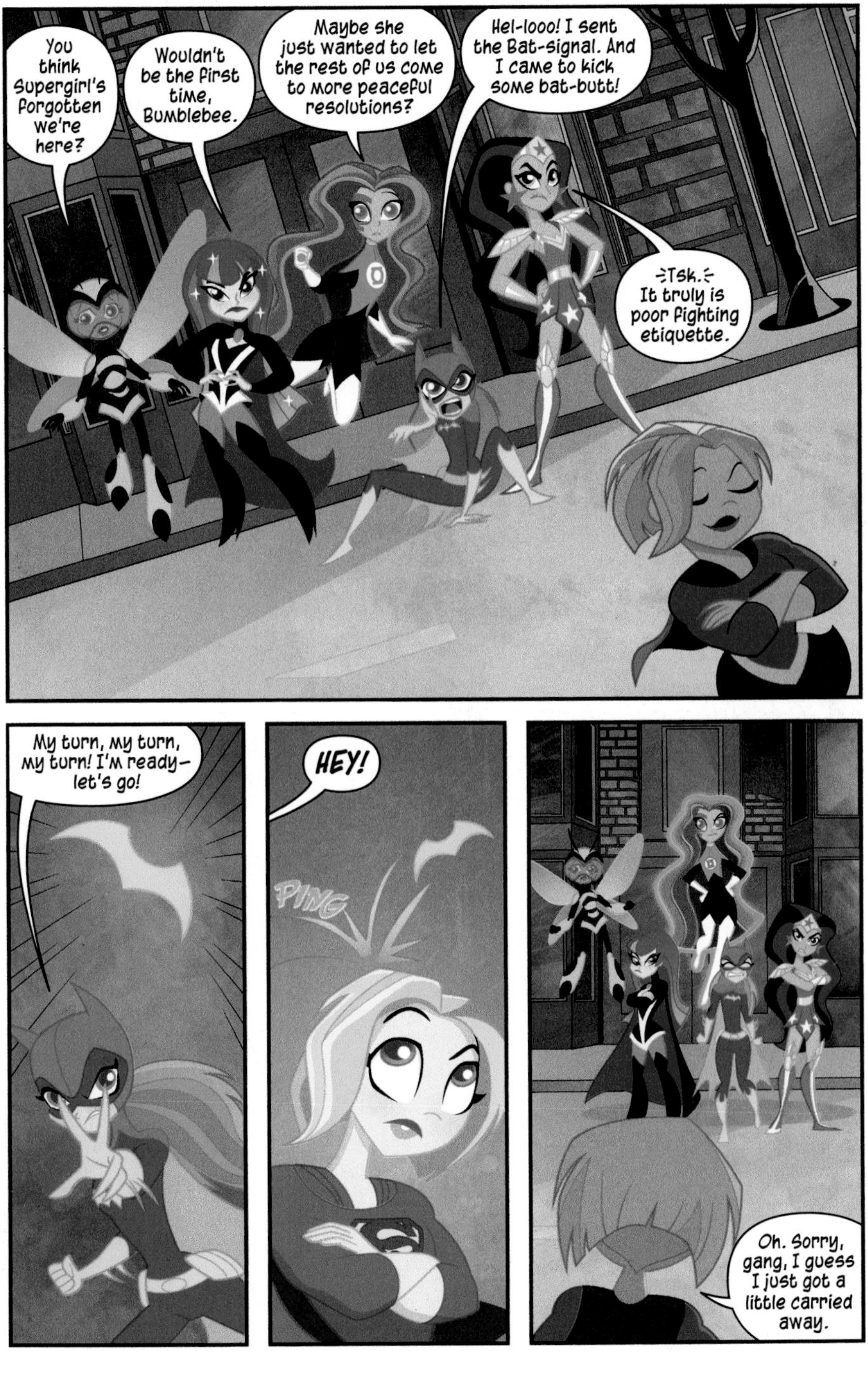
You think Supergirl's forgotten we're here?
Wouldn't be the first time, Bumblebee.
Maybe she just wanted to let the rest of us come to more peaceful resolutions?
Hel-looo! I sent the Bat-signal. And I came to kick some bat-butt!
Tsk.
It truly is poor fighting etiquette.
My turn, my turn, my turn! I'm ready—let's go!
HEY!
PING
Oh. Sorry, gang, I guess I just got a little carried away.

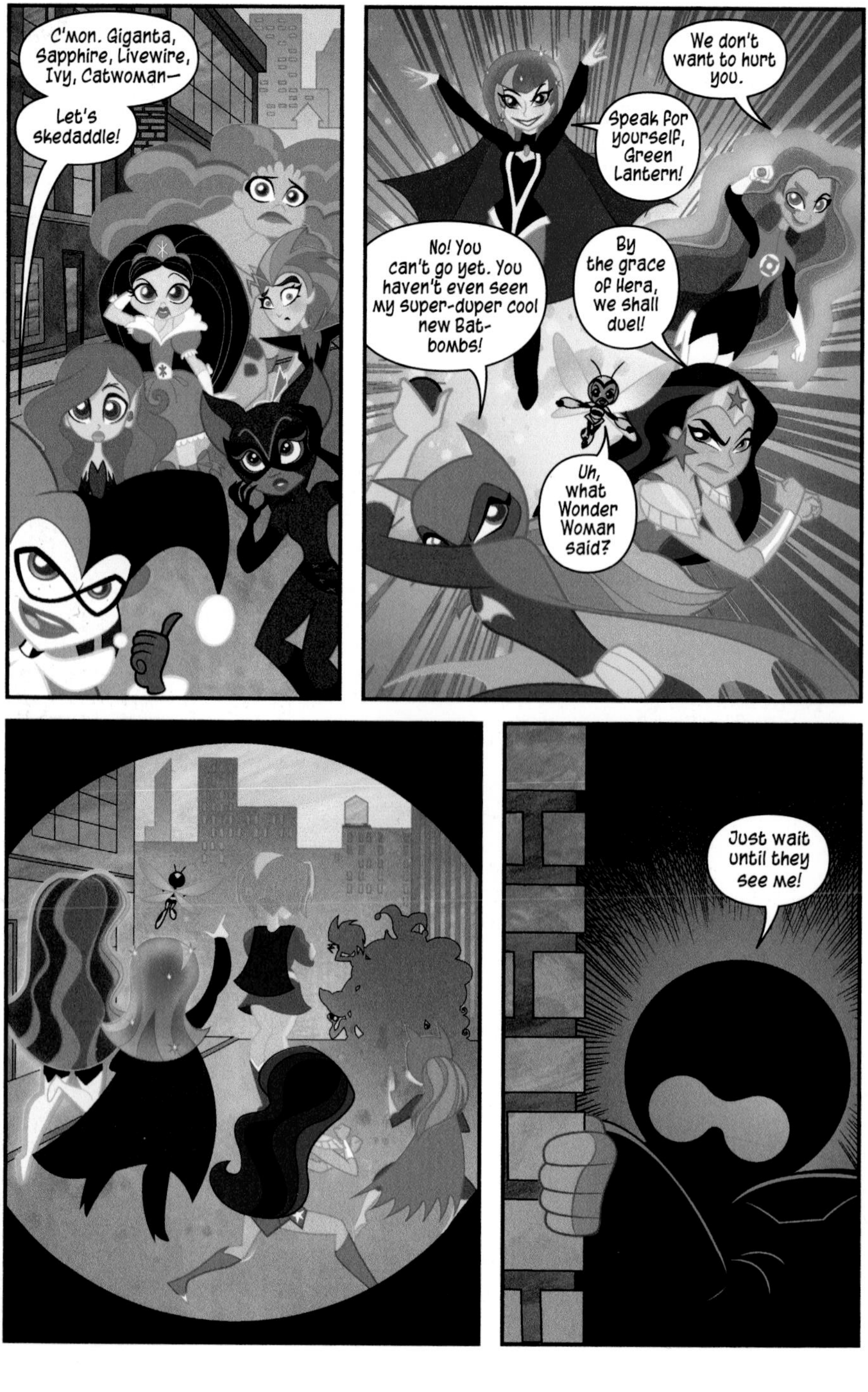
C'mon. Giganta, Sapphire, Livewire, Ivy, Catwoman—
Let's skedaddle!
We don't want to hurt you.
Speak for yourself, Green Lantern!
No! You can't go yet. You haven't even seen my super-duper cool new Bat-bombs!
By the grace of Hera, we shall duel!
Uh, what Wonder Woman said?
Just wait until they see me!

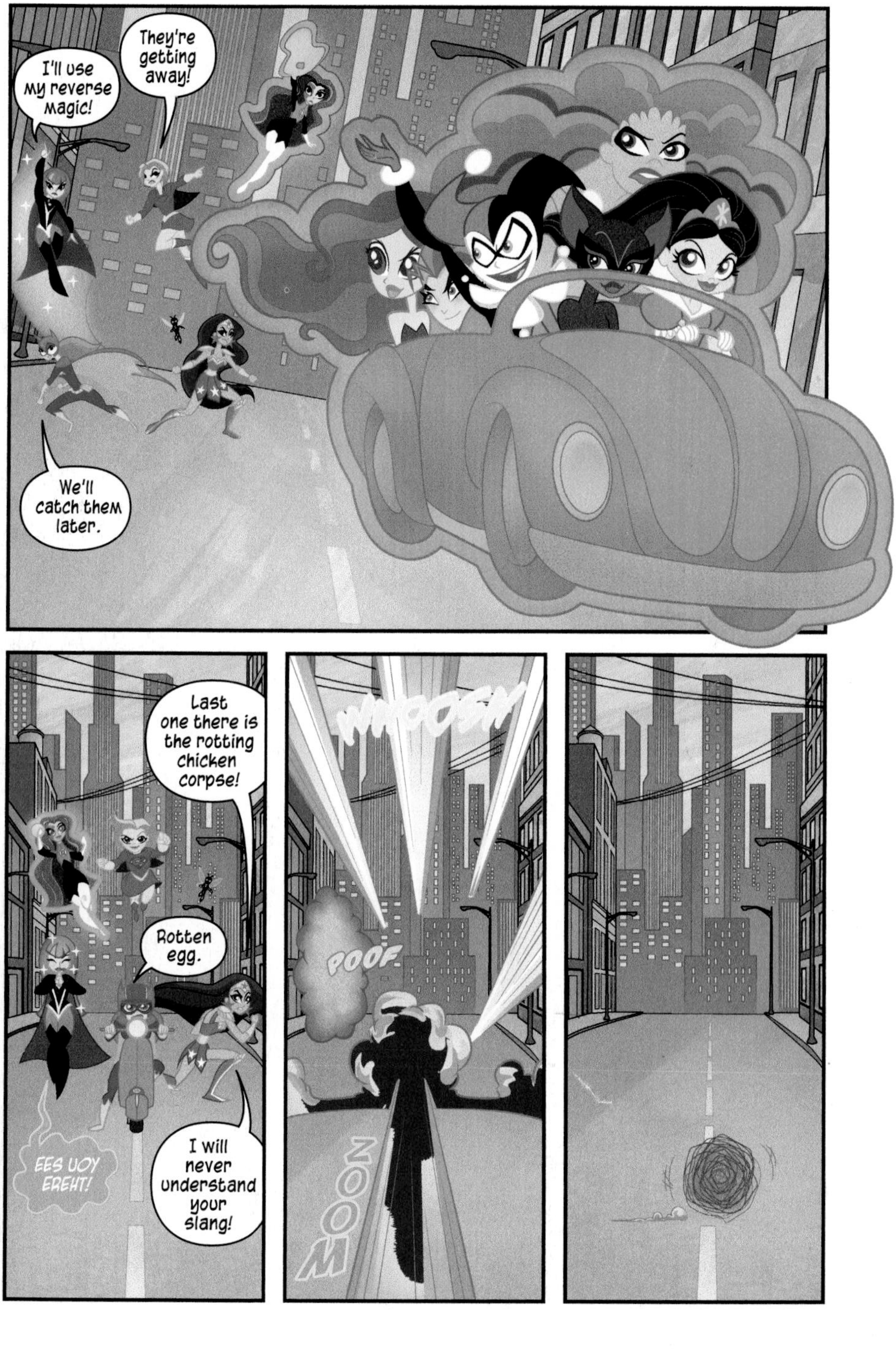
I'll use my reverse magic!
They're getting away!
We'll catch them later.
Last one there is the rotting chicken corpse!
Rotten egg.
EES UOY EREHT!
I will never understand your slang!
WHOOSH
POOF
ZOOM

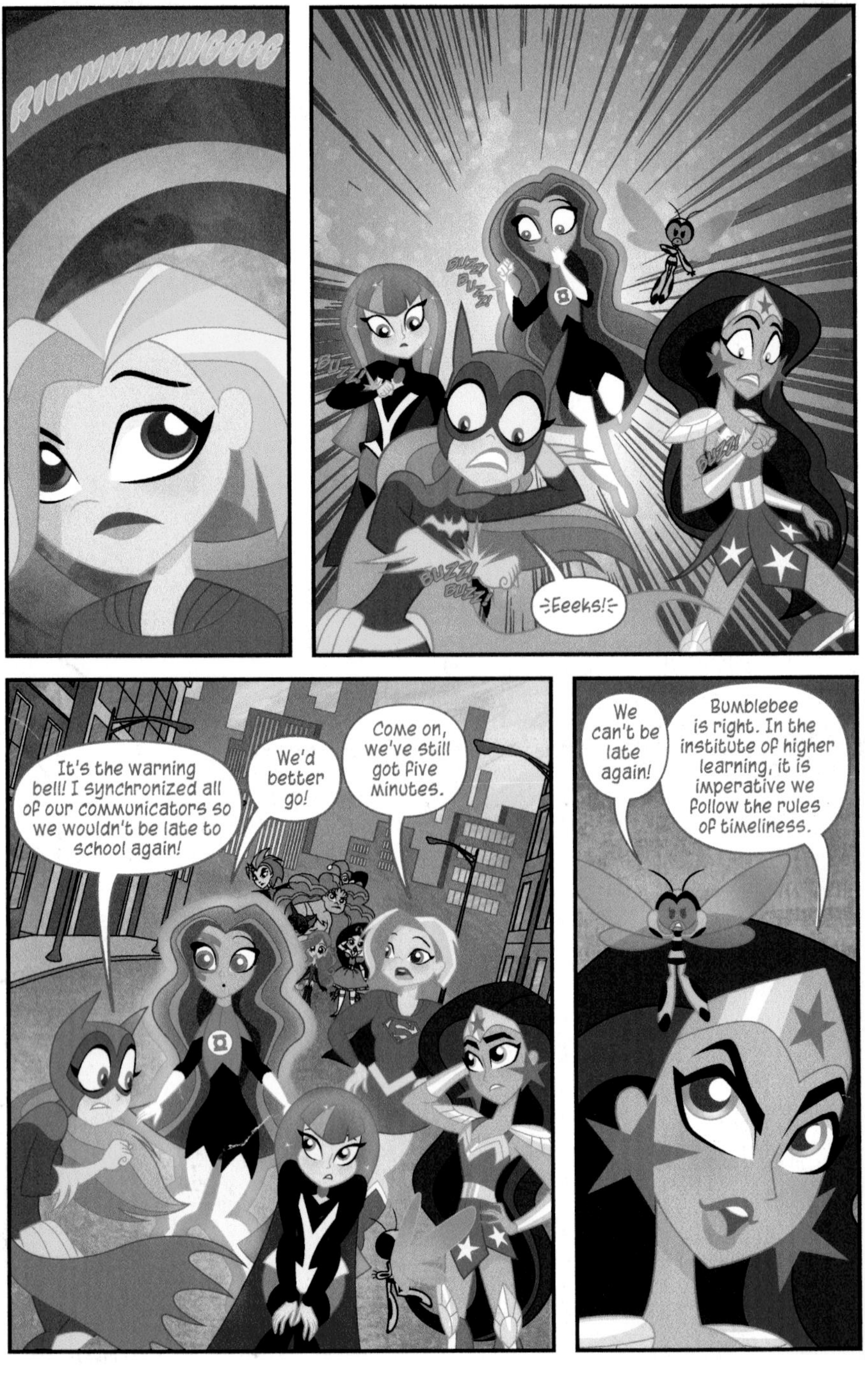
RIINNNNNNNGGGG
BUZZ! BUZZ!
BUZZ!
BUZZ!
BUZZ! BUZZ!
Eeeks!
It's the warning bell! I synchronized all of our communicators so we wouldn't be late to school again!
We'd better go!
Come on, we've still got five minutes.
We can't be late again!
Bumblebee is right. In the institute of higher learning, it is imperative we follow the rules of timeliness.

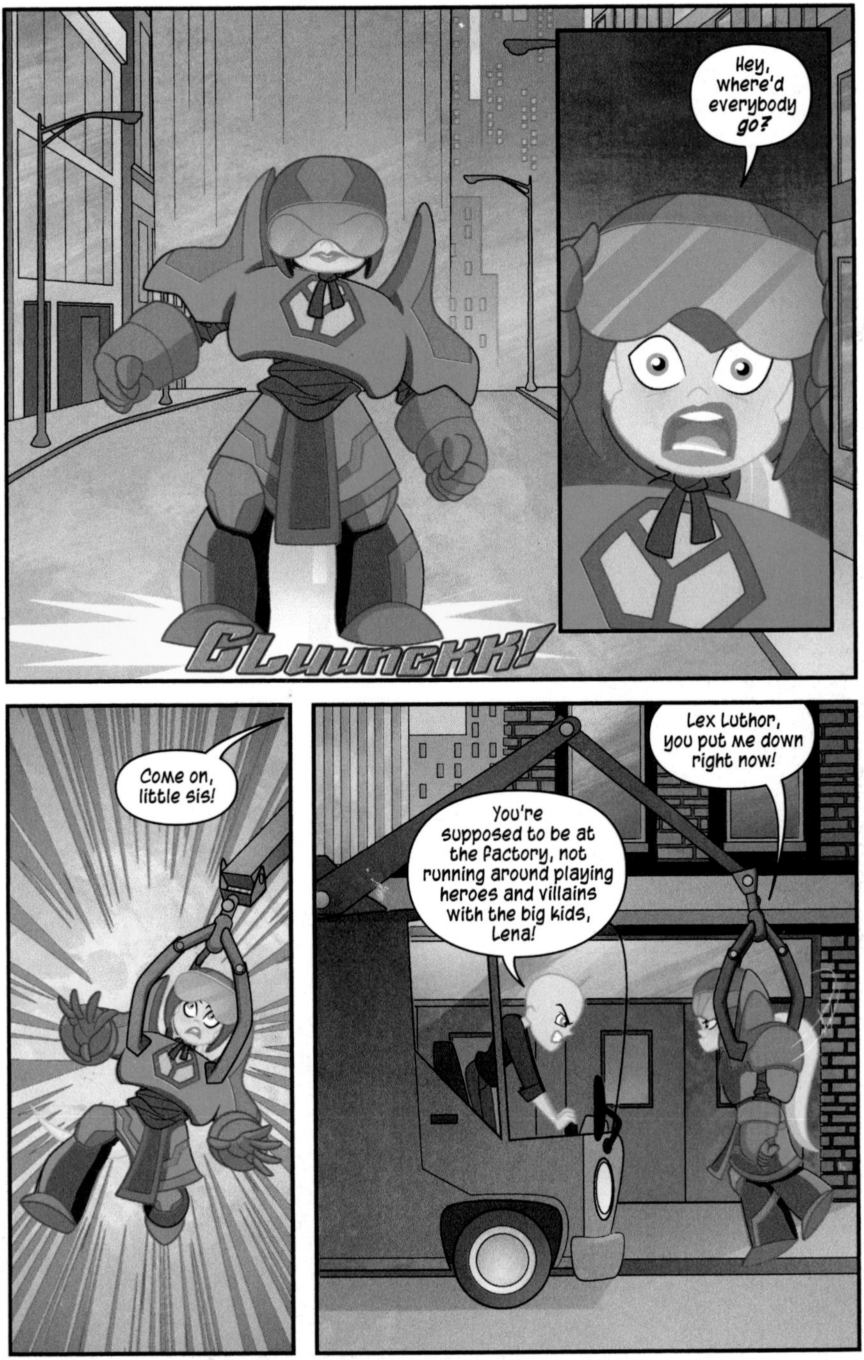
CLUUNCKK!
Hey, where'd everybody go?
Come on, little sis!
Lex Luthor, you put me down right now!
You're supposed to be at the factory, not running around playing heroes and villains with the big kids, Lena!

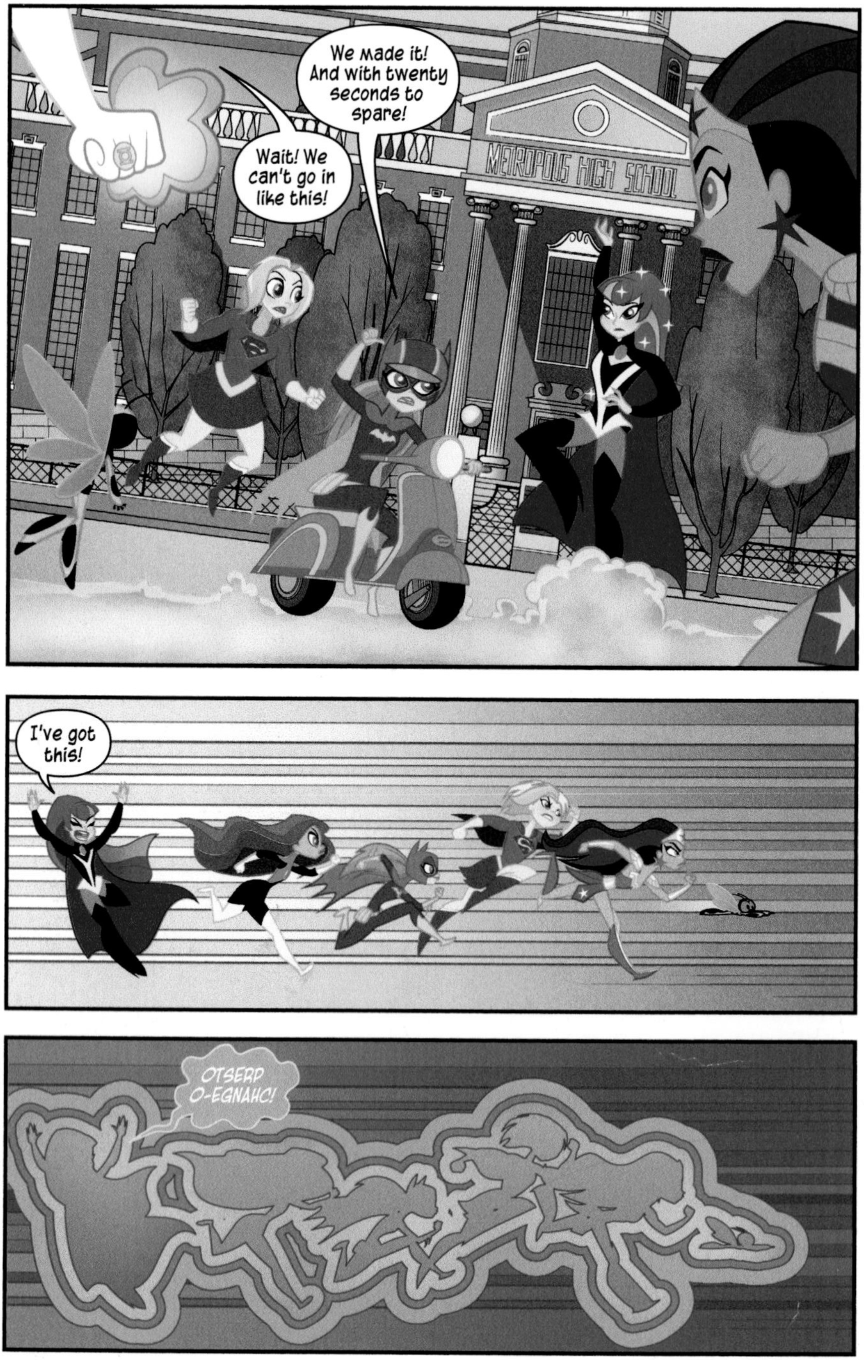
We made it! And with twenty seconds to spare!
Wait! We can't go in like this!
METROPOLIS HIGH SCHOOL
I've got this!
OTSERP O-EGNAHC!

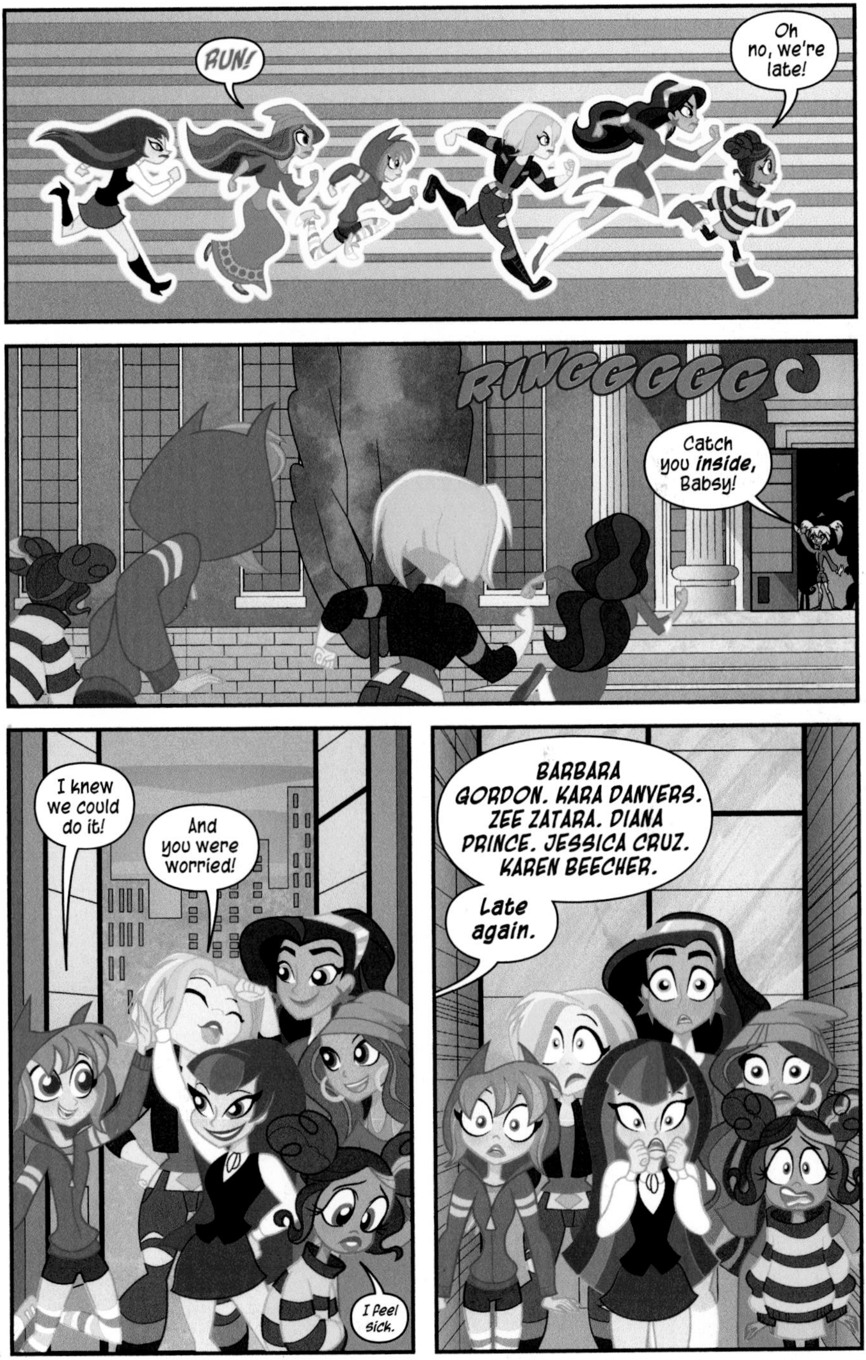
RUN!
Oh no, we're late!
RINGGGGG
Catch you inside, Babsy!
I knew we could do it!
And you were worried!
I feel sick.
BARBARA GORDON. KARA DANVERS. ZEE ZATARA. DIANA PRINCE. JESSICA CRUZ. KAREN BEECHER.
Late again.

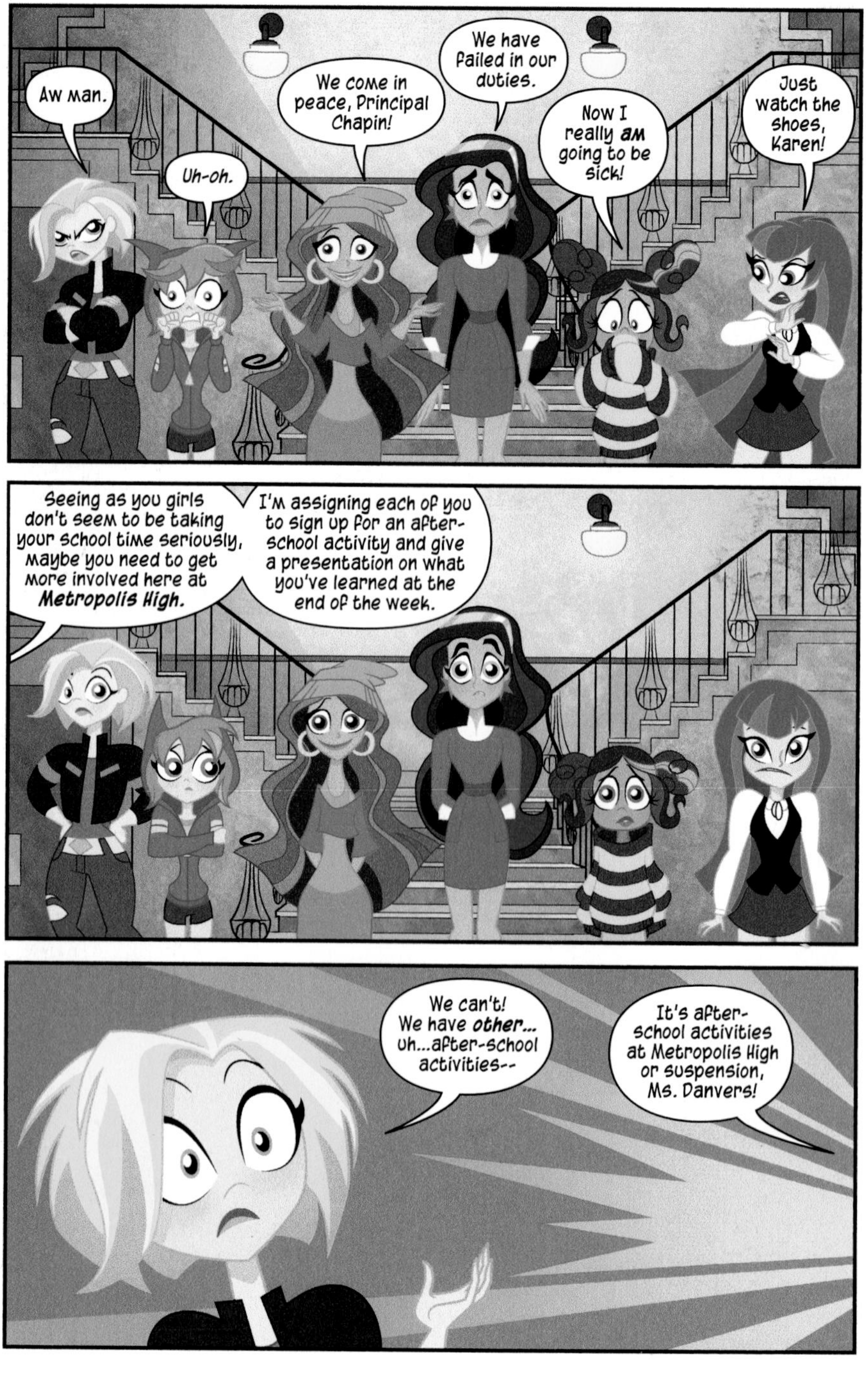
Aw man.
Uh-oh.
We come in peace, Principal Chapin!
We have failed in our duties.
Now I really **am** going to be sick!
Just watch the shoes, Karen!
Seeing as you girls don't seem to be taking your school time seriously, maybe you need to get more involved here at ***Metropolis High.***
I'm assigning each of you to sign up for an after-school activity and give a presentation on what you've learned at the end of the week.
We can't! We have ***other...*** uh...after-school activities--
It's after-school activities at Metropolis High or suspension, Ms. Danvers!

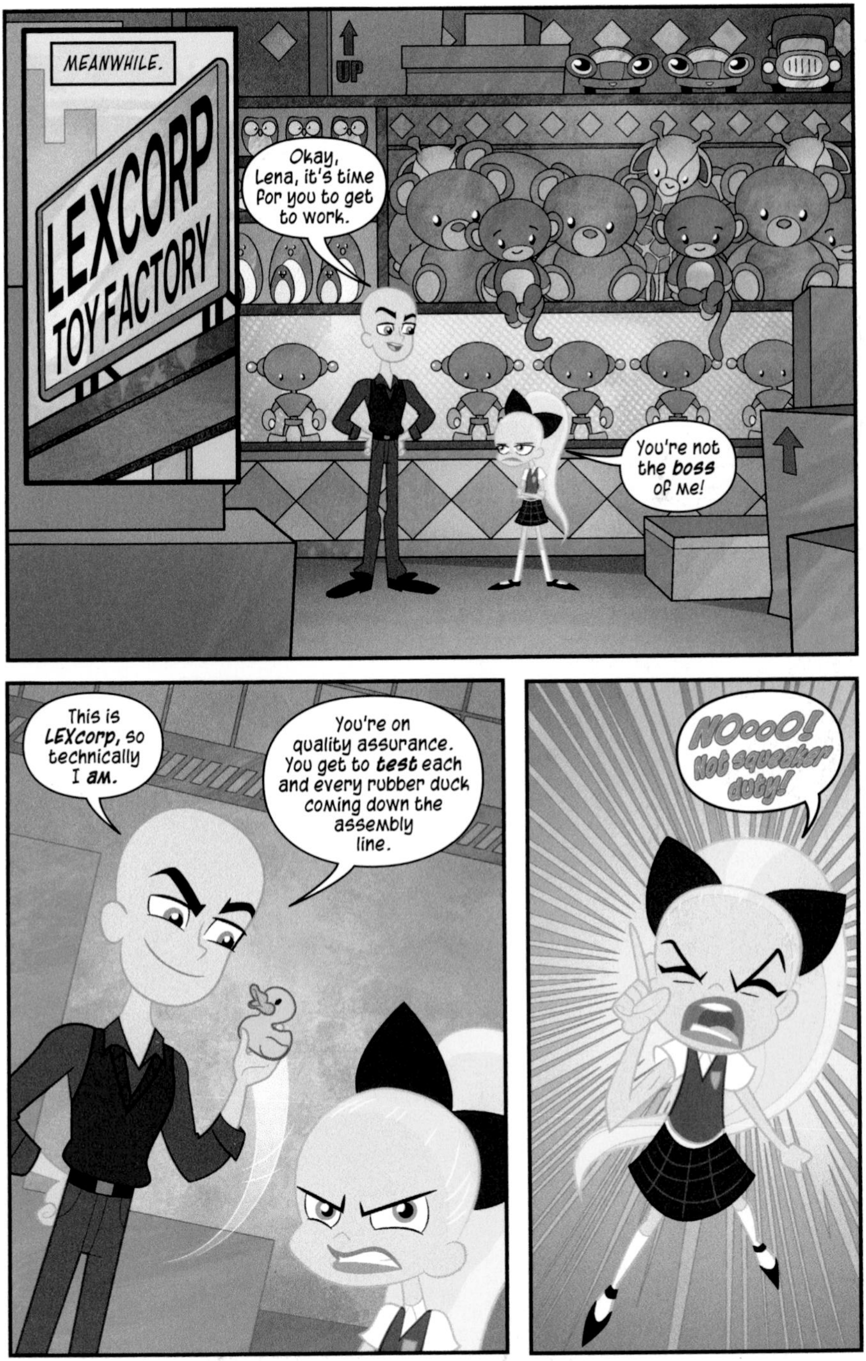
MEANWHILE.
LEXCORP TOY FACTORY
UP
Okay, Lena, it's time for you to get to work.
You're not the boss of me!
This is LEXcorp, so technically I am.
You're on quality assurance. You get to test each and every rubber duck coming down the assembly line.
NOoooO! Not squeaker duty!

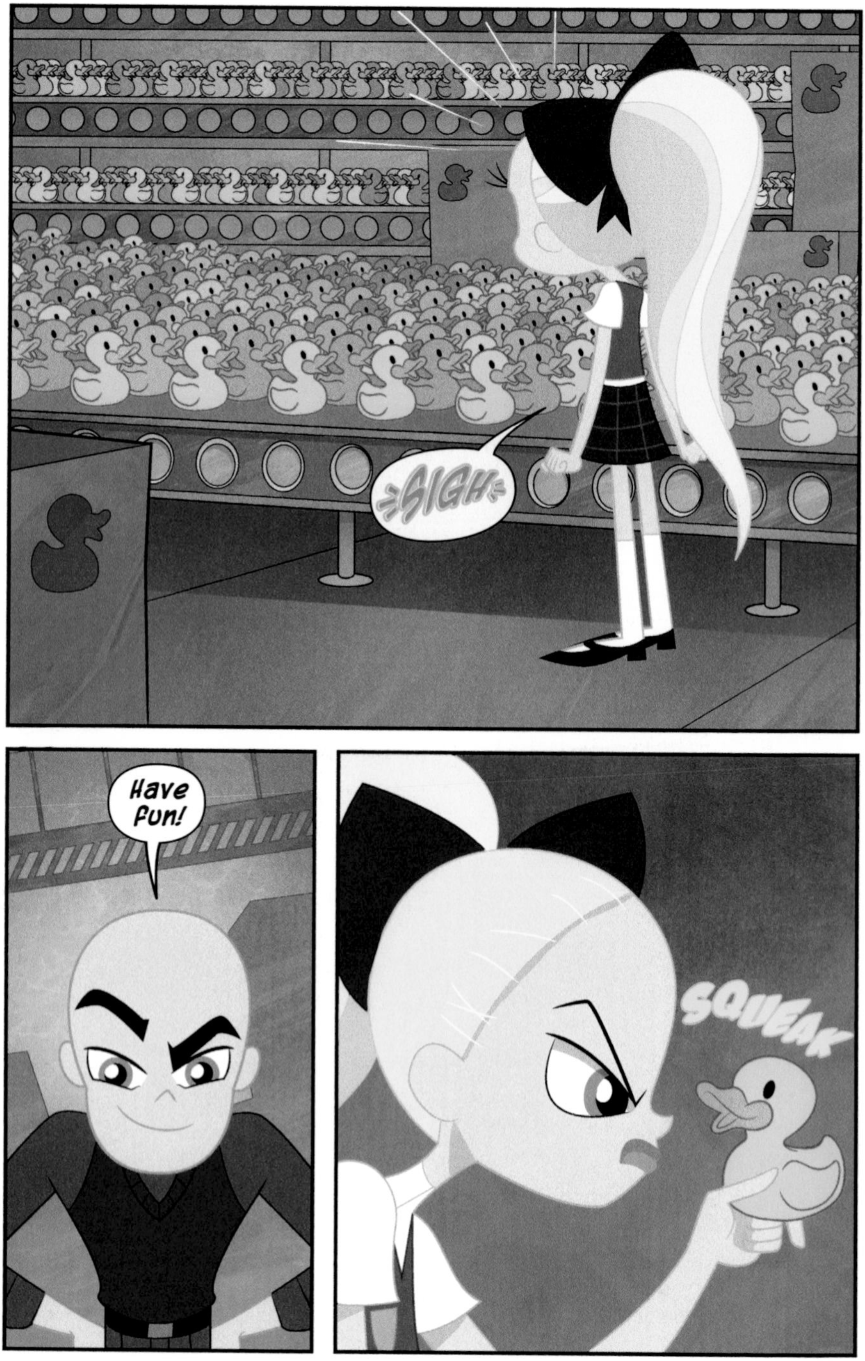
SIGH
Have fun!
SQUEAK

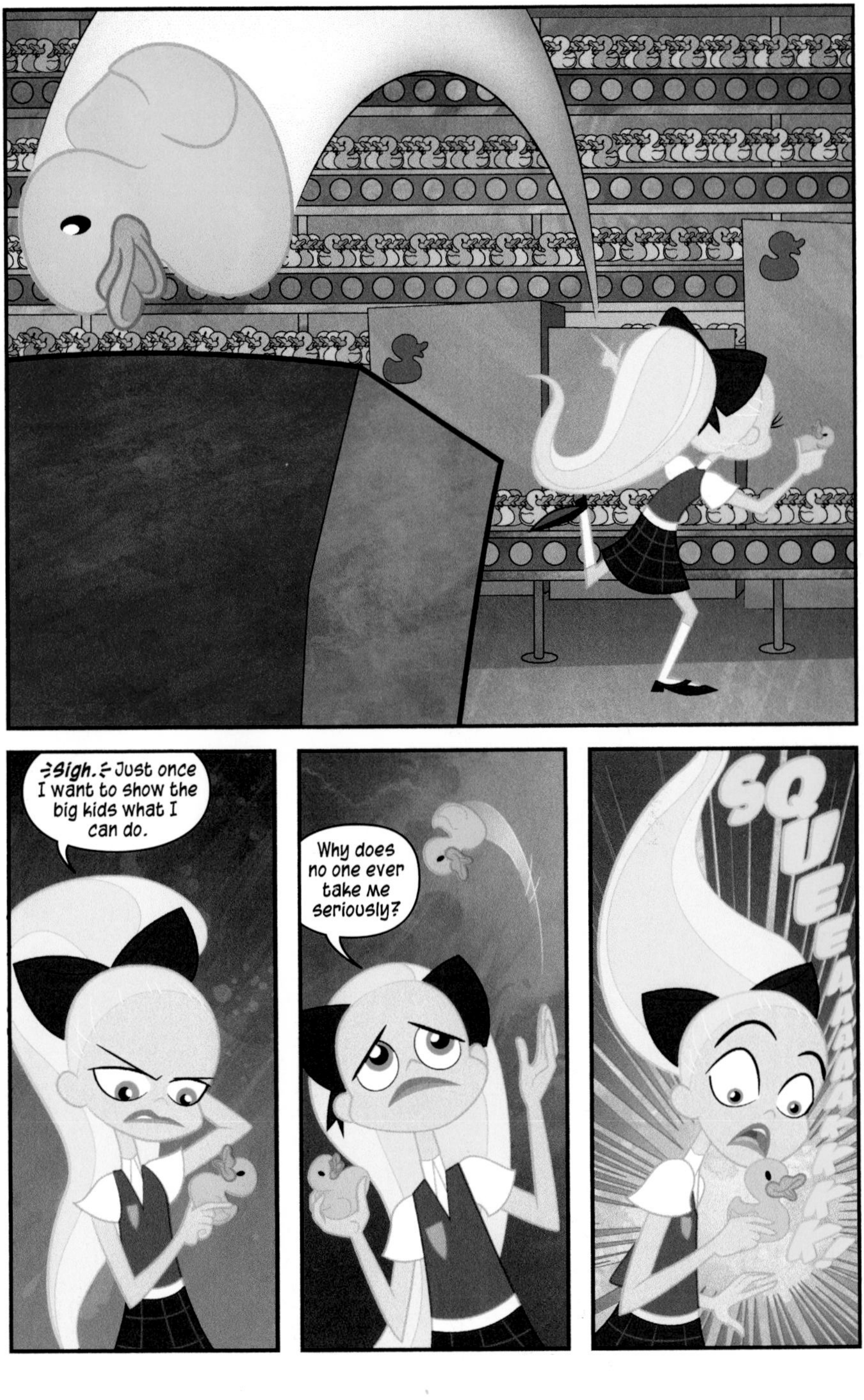

Sigh. Just once I want to show the big kids what I can do.
Why does no one ever take me seriously?
SQUEEEAAAAAKKKK!

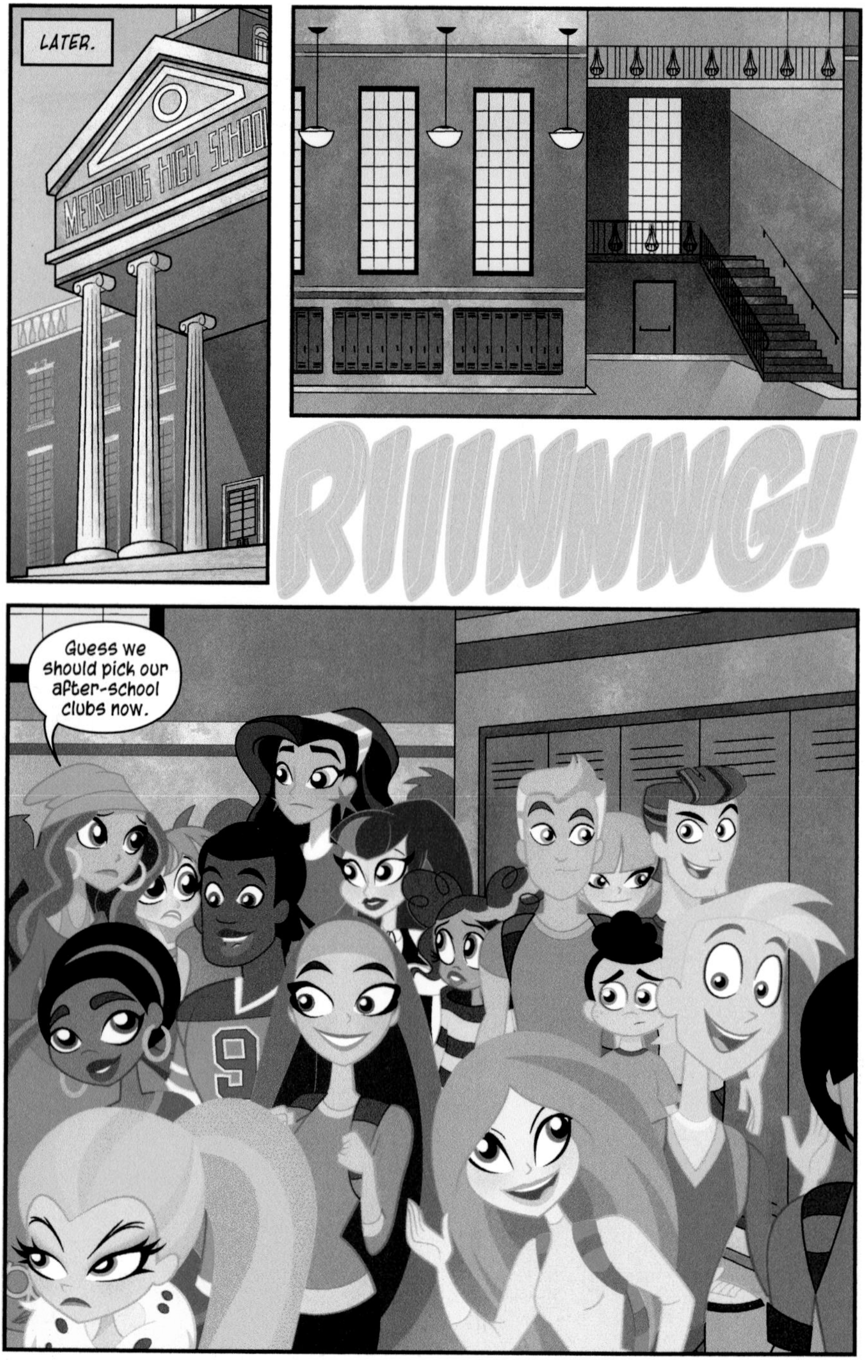
LATER.
METROPOLIS HIGH SCHOOL
RIIINNNG!
Guess we should pick our after-school clubs now.
9

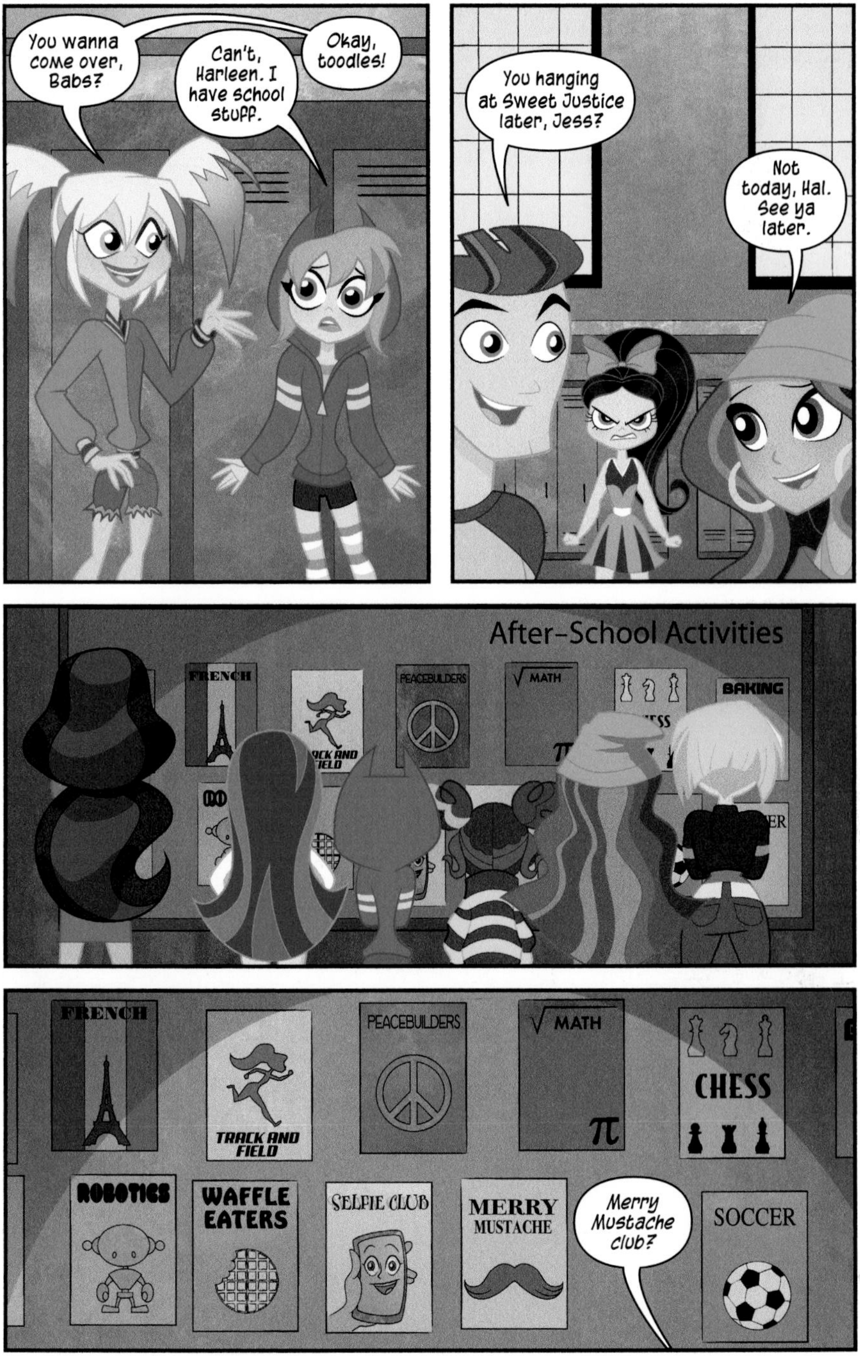

You wanna come over, Babs?
Can't, Harleen. I have school stuff.
Okay, toodles!
You hanging at Sweet Justice later, Jess?
Not today, Hal. See ya later.
After-School Activities
FRENCH
PEACEBUILDERS
MATH
BAKING
FRENCH
TRACK AND FIELD
PEACEBUILDERS
MATH
CHESS
ROBOTICS
WAFFLE EATERS
SELFIE CLUB
MERRY MUSTACHE
Merry Mustache club?
SOCCER

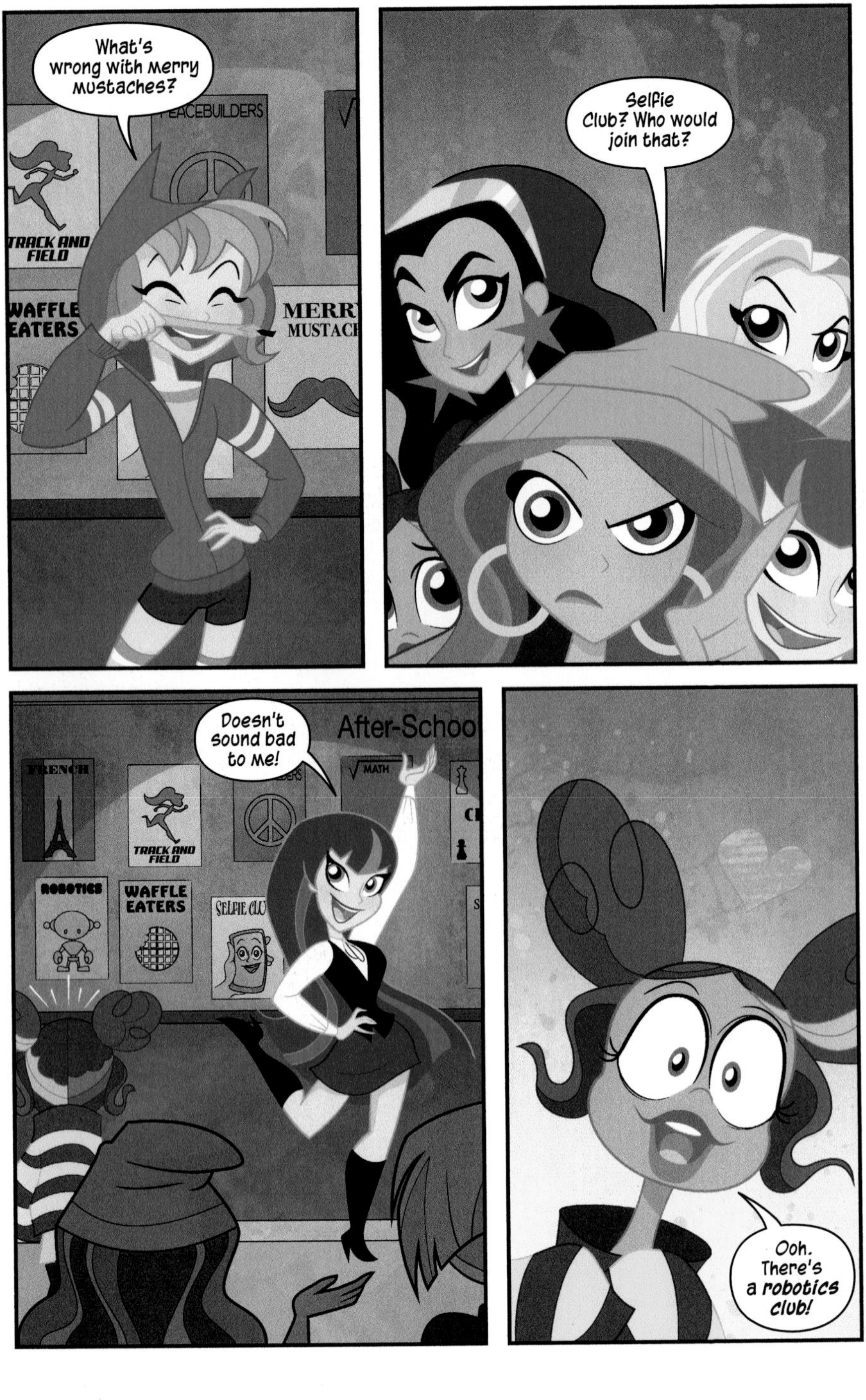
What's wrong with Merry Mustaches?
PEACEBUILDERS
TRACK AND FIELD
WAFFLE
Selfie Club? Who would join that?
Doesn't sound bad to me!
FRENCH
TRACK AND FIELD
MATH
ROBOTICS
WAFFLE EATERS
Ooh. There's a *robotics* club!

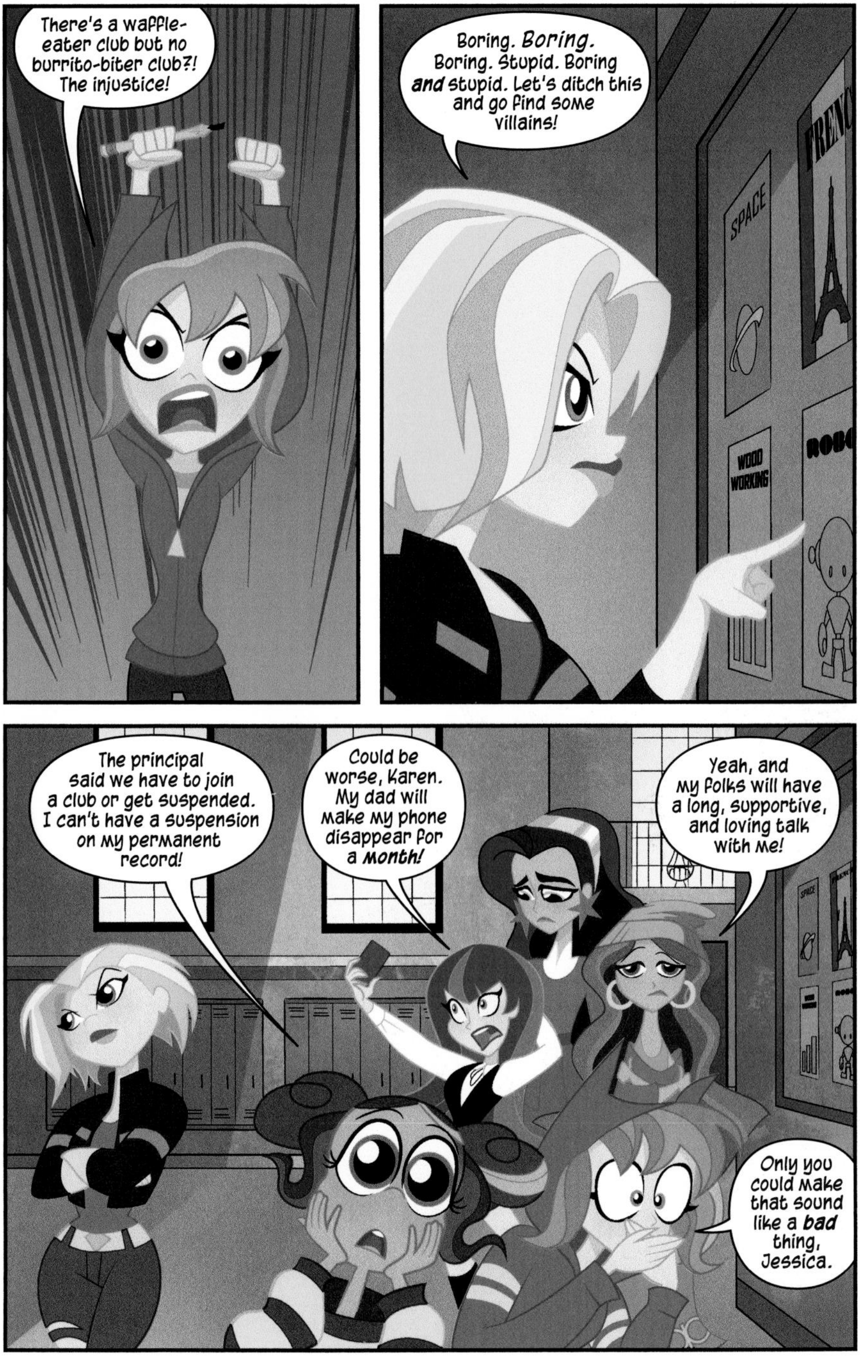
There's a waffle-eater club but no burrito-biter club?! The injustice!
Boring. *Boring.* Boring. Stupid. Boring *and* stupid. Let's ditch this and go find some villains!
FRENC
SPACE
WOOD WORKING
ROBO
The principal said we have to join a club or get suspended. I can't have a suspension on my permanent record!
Could be worse, Karen. My dad will make my phone disappear for a *month!*
Yeah, and my folks will have a long, supportive, and loving talk with me!
Only you could make that sound like a *bad* thing, Jessica.

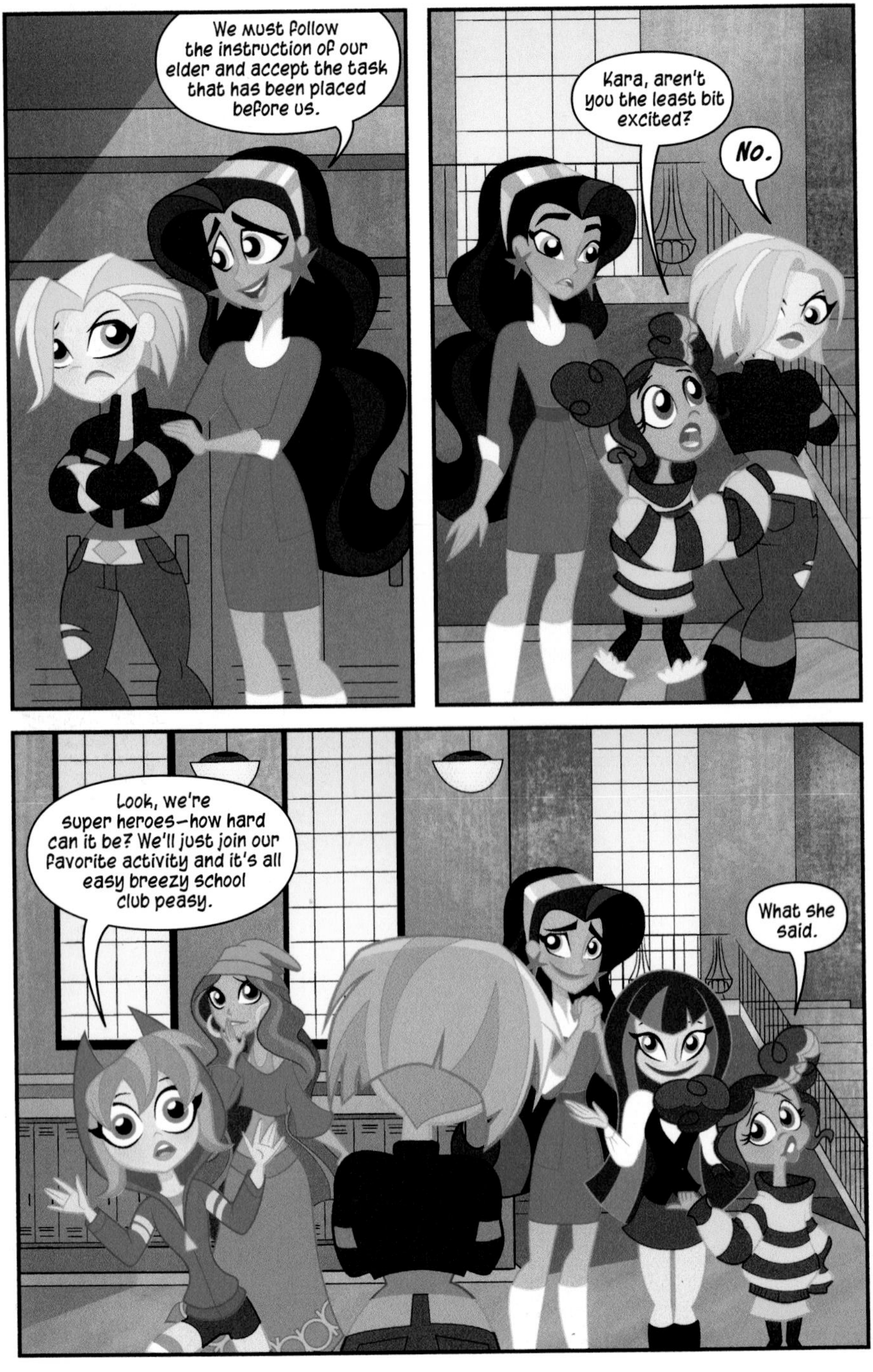
We must follow the instruction of our elder and accept the task that has been placed before us.
Kara, aren't you the least bit excited?
No.
Look, we're super heroes—how hard can it be? We'll just join our favorite activity and it's all easy breezy school club peasy.
What she said.

Okay, but this can't get in the way of our superheroing.

Abracadabra Club!

Peacebuilders!

Greek!

Yay! Robotics!

Oooh Detective Club! I wonder if we get to wear hats? I hope we get to wear hats! ⊰Squeeeeeal!⊱

After-School A

FRENCH

PEACEBUILDERS

√ MATH

π

CHESS

ROBOTICS

TRACK & FIELD

WAFFLE EATER

MERRY MUSTACHE

SOCCE

Yeah, easy peasy...

chapter two

JOIN THE CLUB

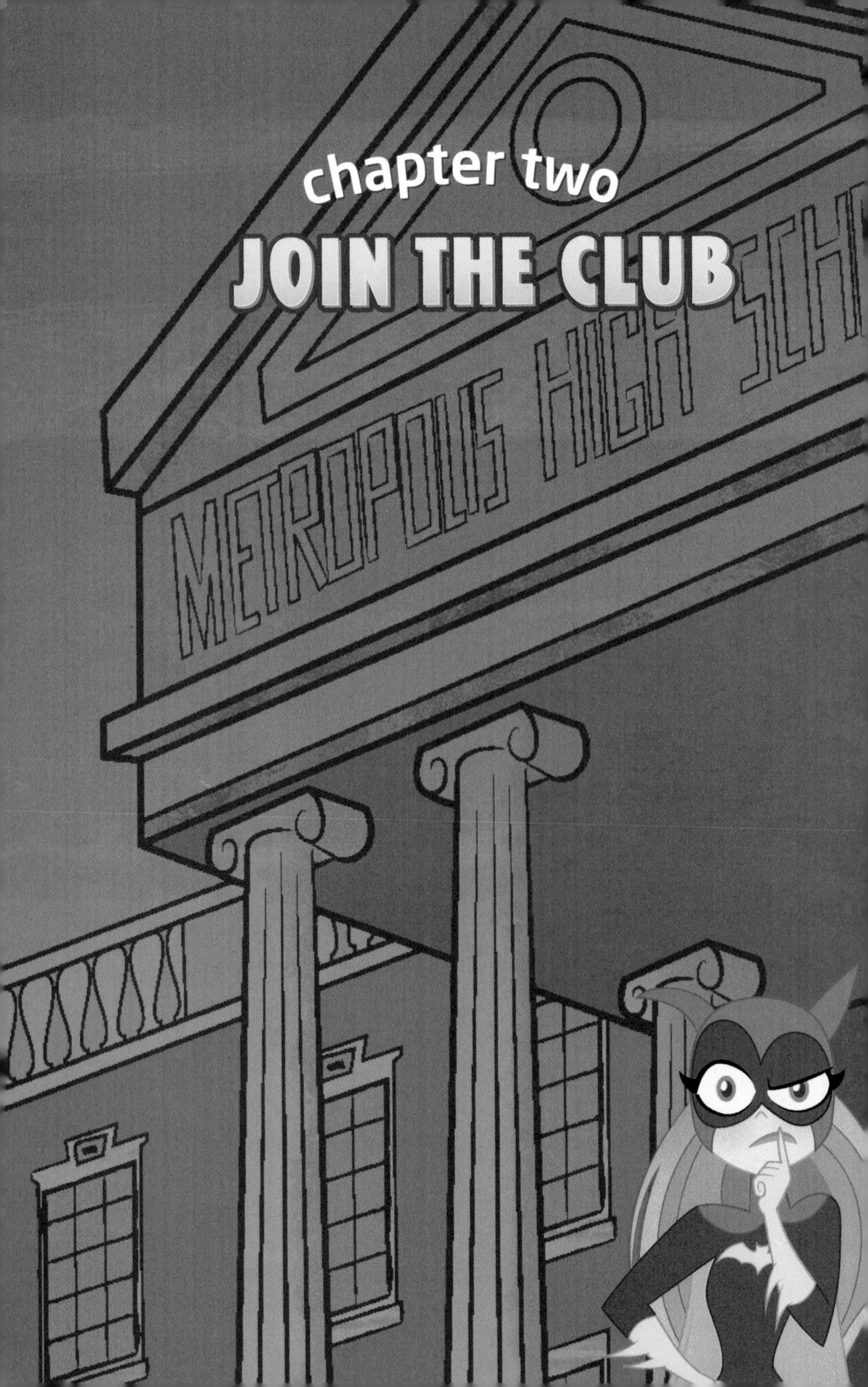
METROPOLIS HIGH

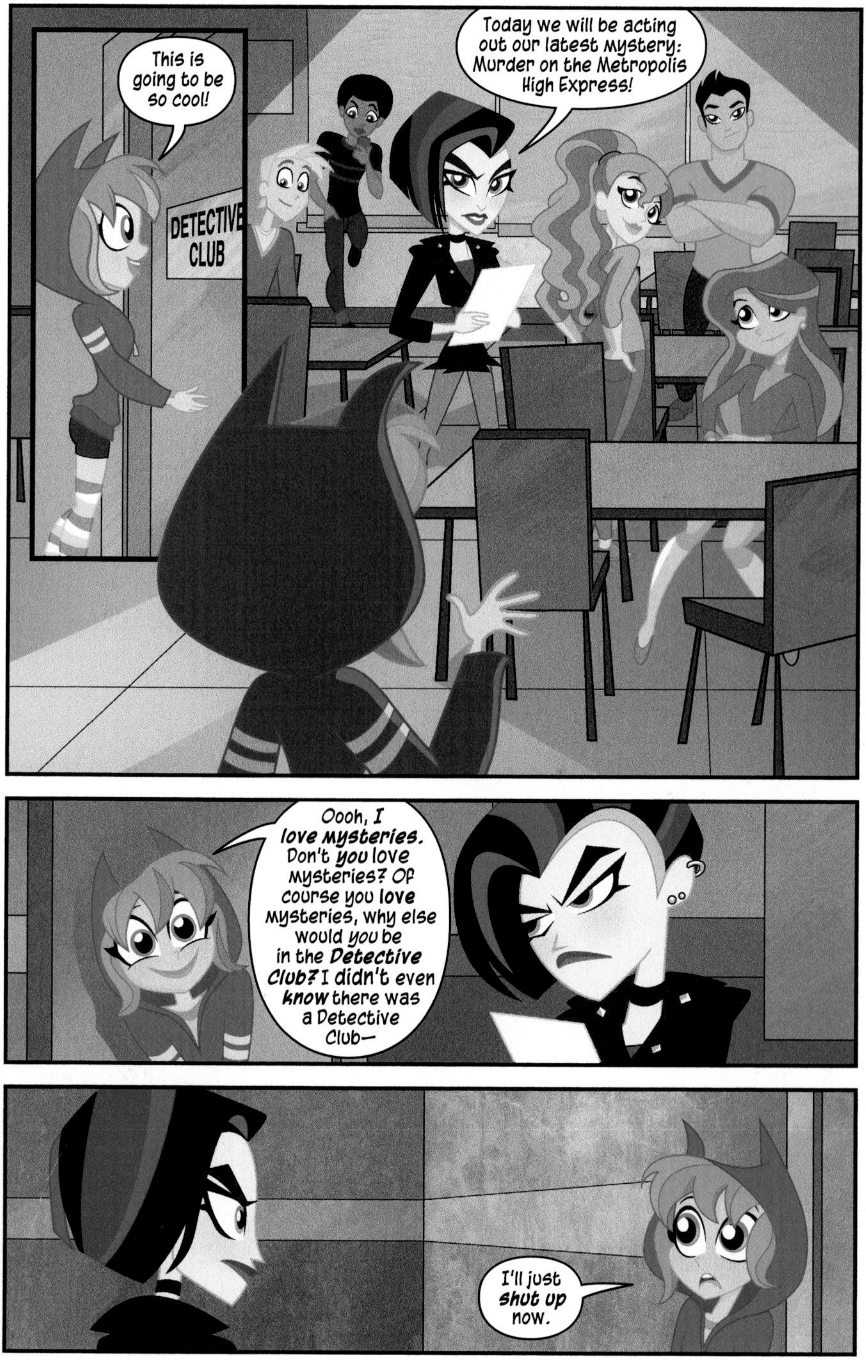
This is going to be so cool!
DETECTIVE CLUB
Today we will be acting out our latest mystery: Murder on the Metropolis High Express!
Oooh, I love mysteries. Don't you love mysteries? Of course you love mysteries, why else would you be in the Detective Club? I didn't even know there was a Detective Club—
I'll just shut up now.

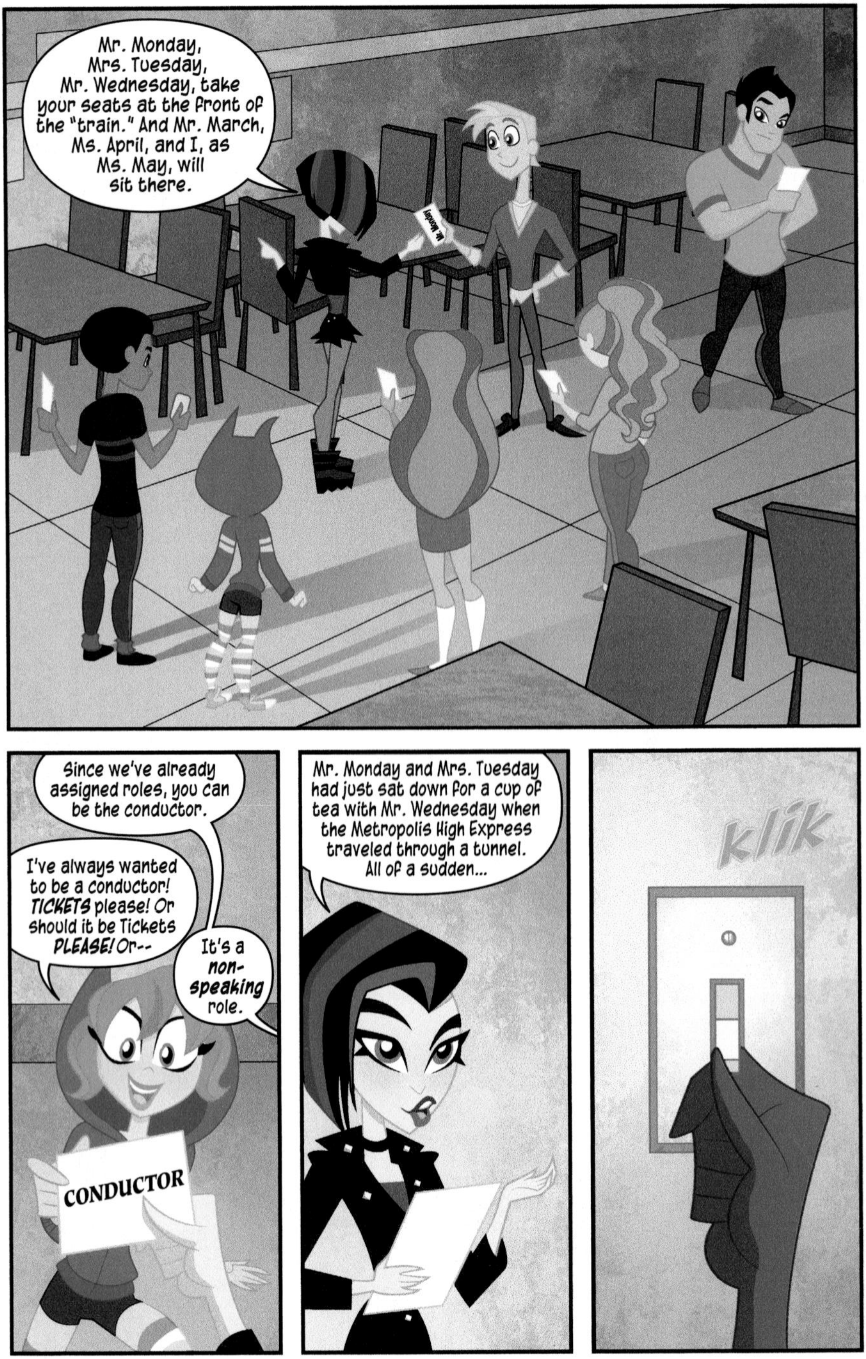
Mr. Monday, Mrs. Tuesday, Mr. Wednesday, take your seats at the front of the "train." And Mr. March, Ms. April, and I, as Ms. May, will sit there.
Since we've already assigned roles, you can be the conductor.
I've always wanted to be a conductor! TICKETS please! Or should it be Tickets PLEASE! Or--
It's a non-speaking role.
CONDUCTOR
Mr. Monday and Mrs. Tuesday had just sat down for a cup of tea with Mr. Wednesday when the Metropolis High Express traveled through a tunnel. All of a sudden...
klik

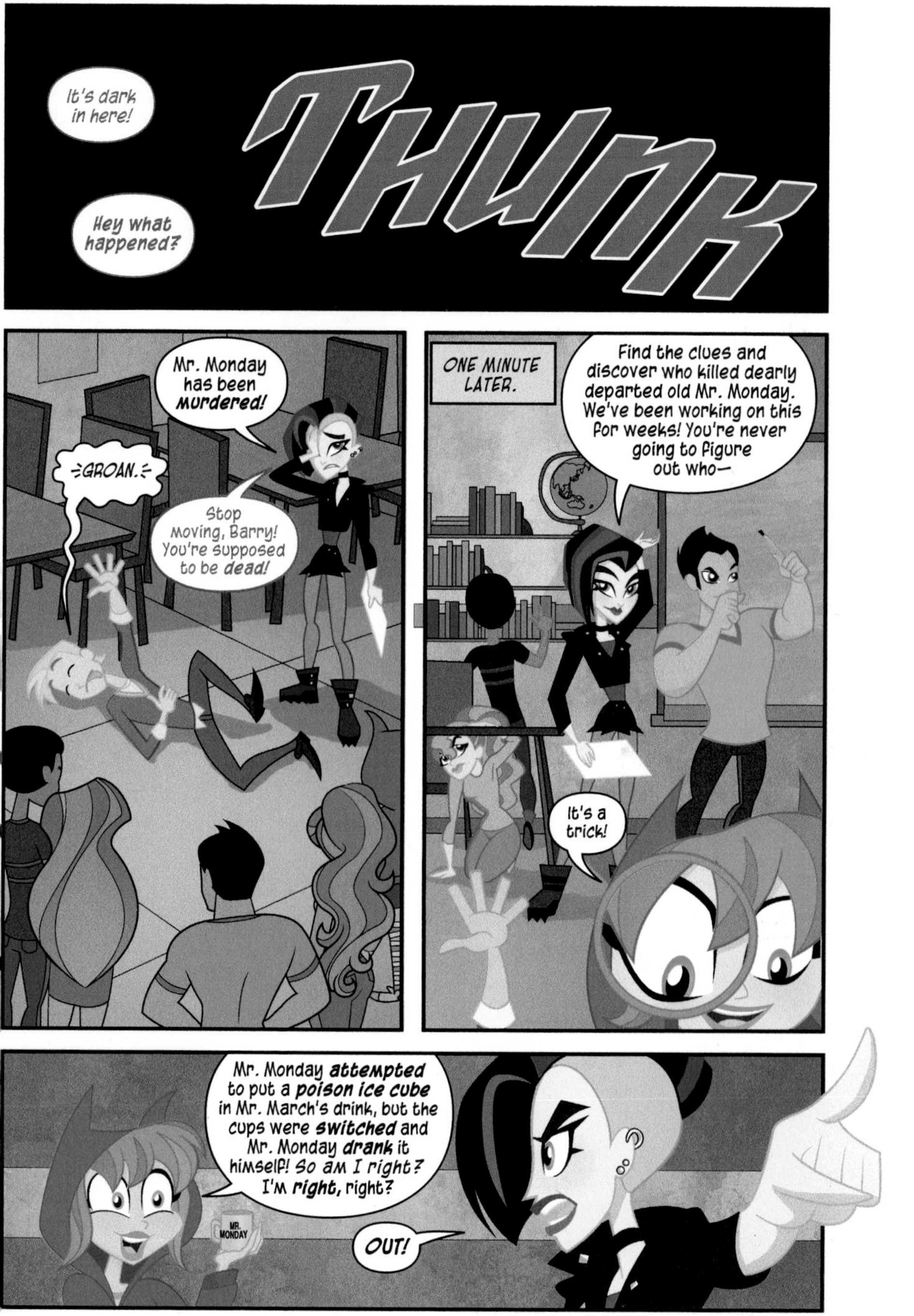
It's dark in here!
Hey what happened?
THUNK
Mr. Monday has been murdered!
≈GROAN.≈
Stop moving, Barry! You're supposed to be dead!
ONE MINUTE LATER.
Find the clues and discover who killed dearly departed old Mr. Monday. We've been working on this for weeks! You're never going to figure out who—
It's a trick!
Mr. Monday attempted to put a poison ice cube in Mr. March's drink, but the cups were switched and Mr. Monday drank it himself! So am I right? I'm right, right?
MR. MONDAY
OUT!

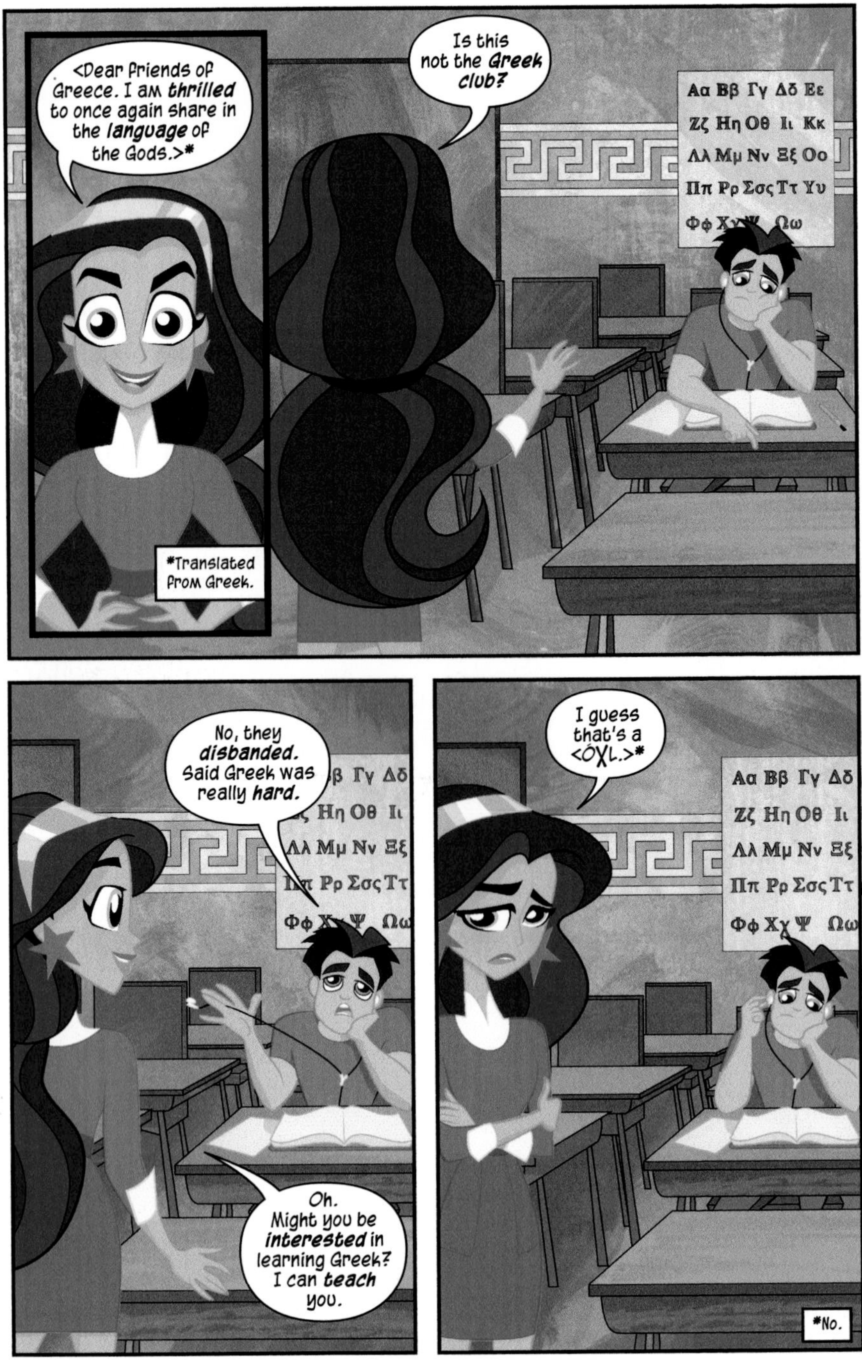
<Dear friends of Greece. I am **thrilled** to once again share in the **language** of the Gods.>*
Is this not the **Greek club?**
Αα Ββ Γγ Δδ Εε Ζζ Ηη Θθ Ιι Κκ Λλ Μμ Νν Ξξ Οο Ππ Ρρ Σσς Ττ Υυ Φφ Χχ Ψψ Ωω
*Translated from Greek.
No, they **disbanded.** Said Greek was really **hard.**
Oh. Might you be **interested** in learning Greek? I can **teach** you.
I guess that's a <ÓXI.>*
*No.

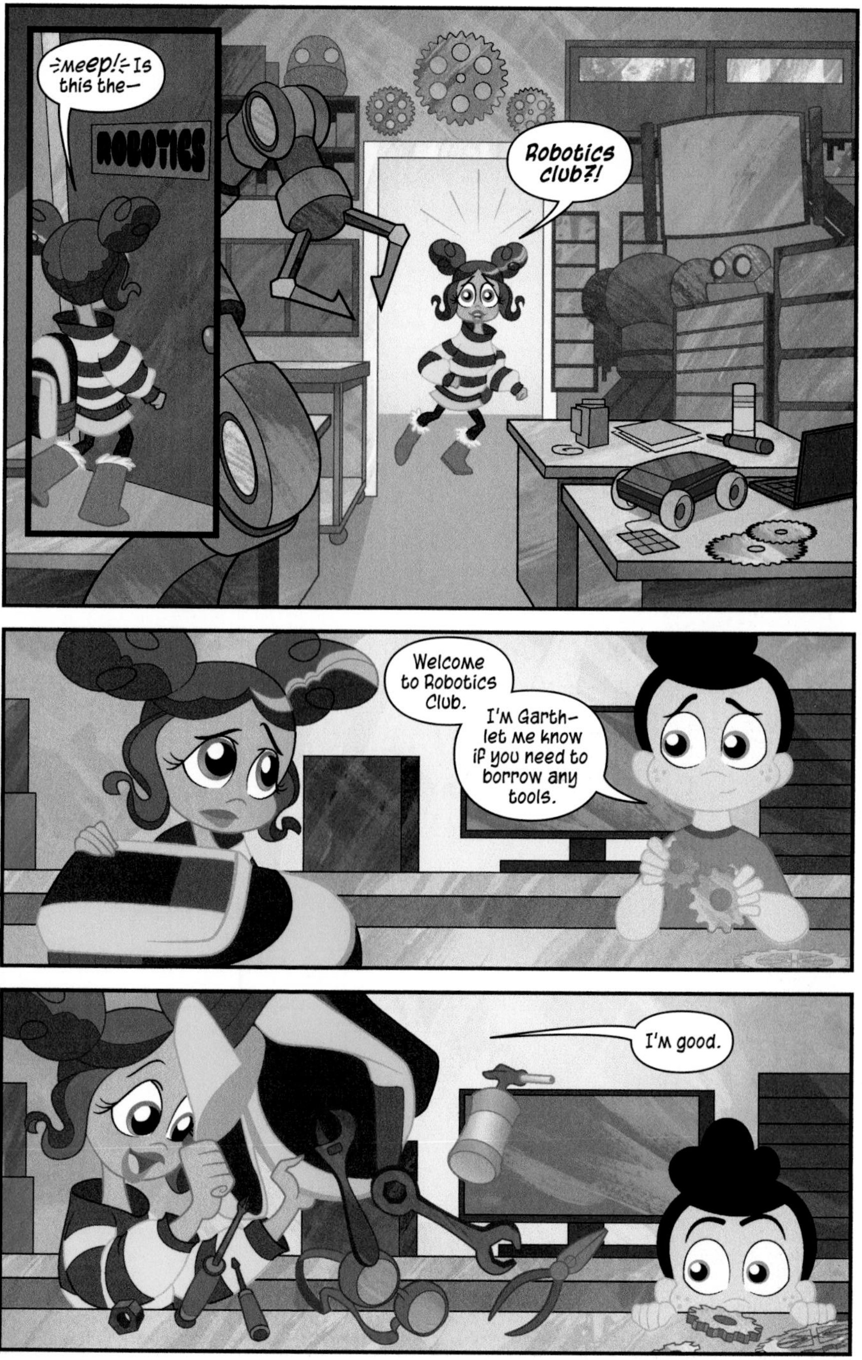
meep! Is this the—
ROBOTICS
Robotics Club?!
Welcome to Robotics Club.
I'm Garth—let me know if you need to borrow any tools.
I'm good.

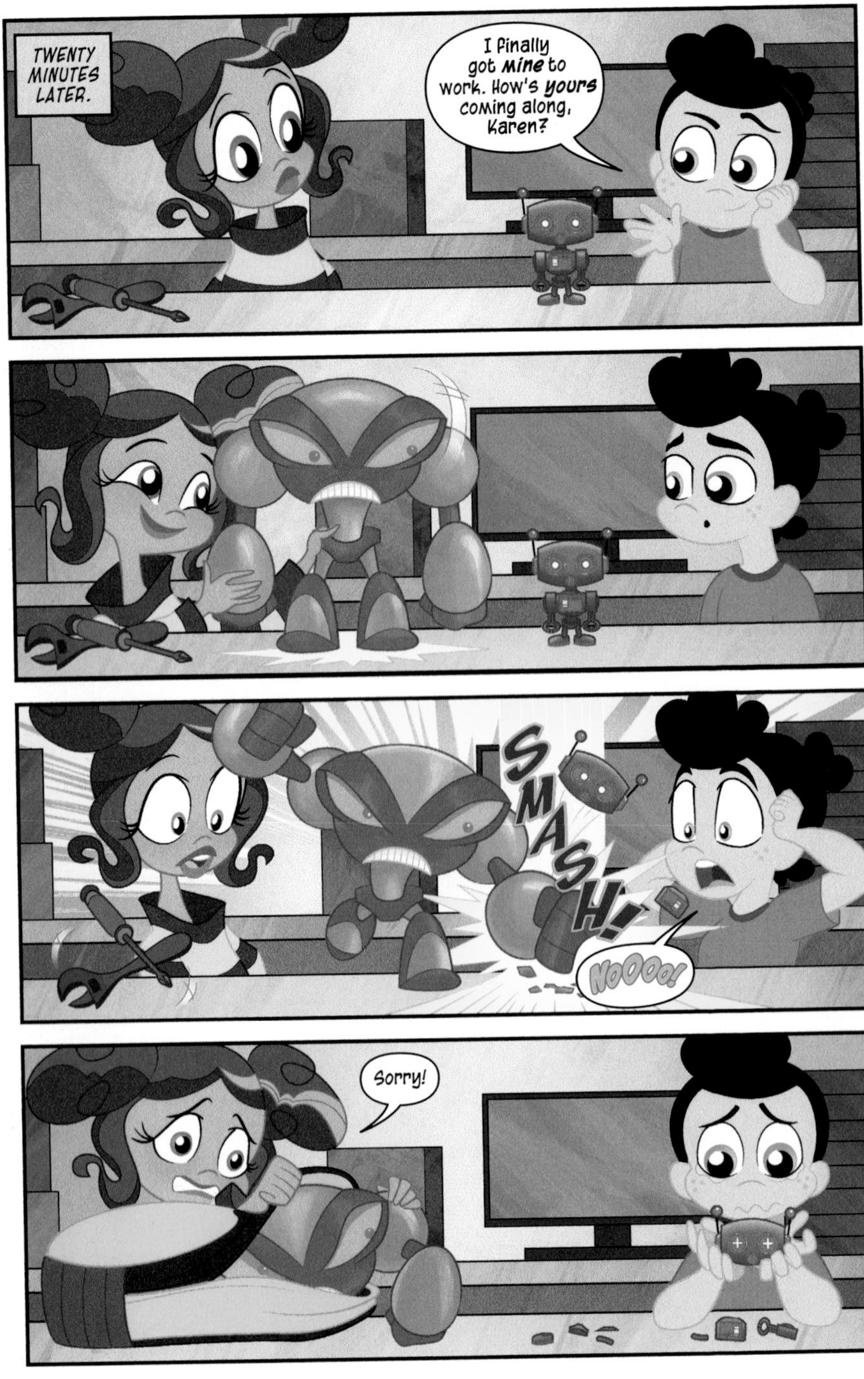
TWENTY MINUTES LATER.
I finally got mine to work. How's yours coming along, Karen?
SMASH!
NOOOO!
Sorry!

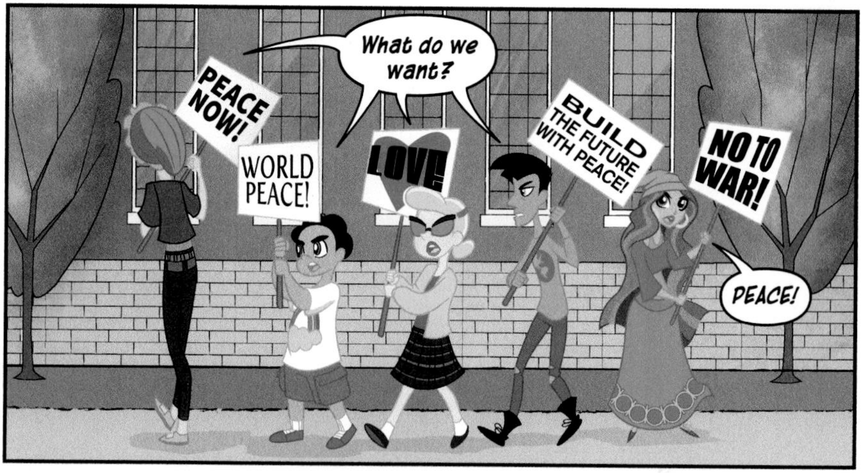
PEACE NOW!
WORLD PEACE!
LOVE
What do we want?
BUILD THE FUTURE WITH PEACE!
NO TO WAR!
PEACE!

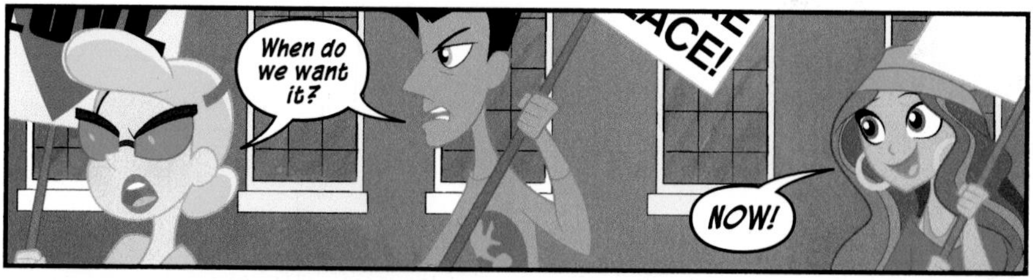
When do we want it?
NOW!

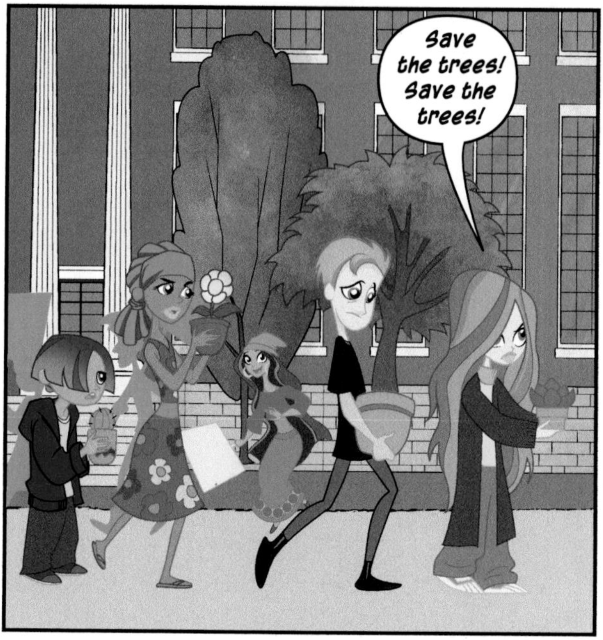
Save the trees! Save the trees!

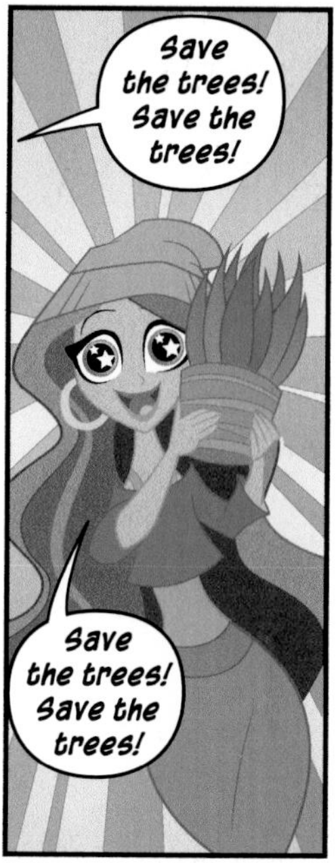
Save the trees! Save the trees!
Save the trees! Save the trees!

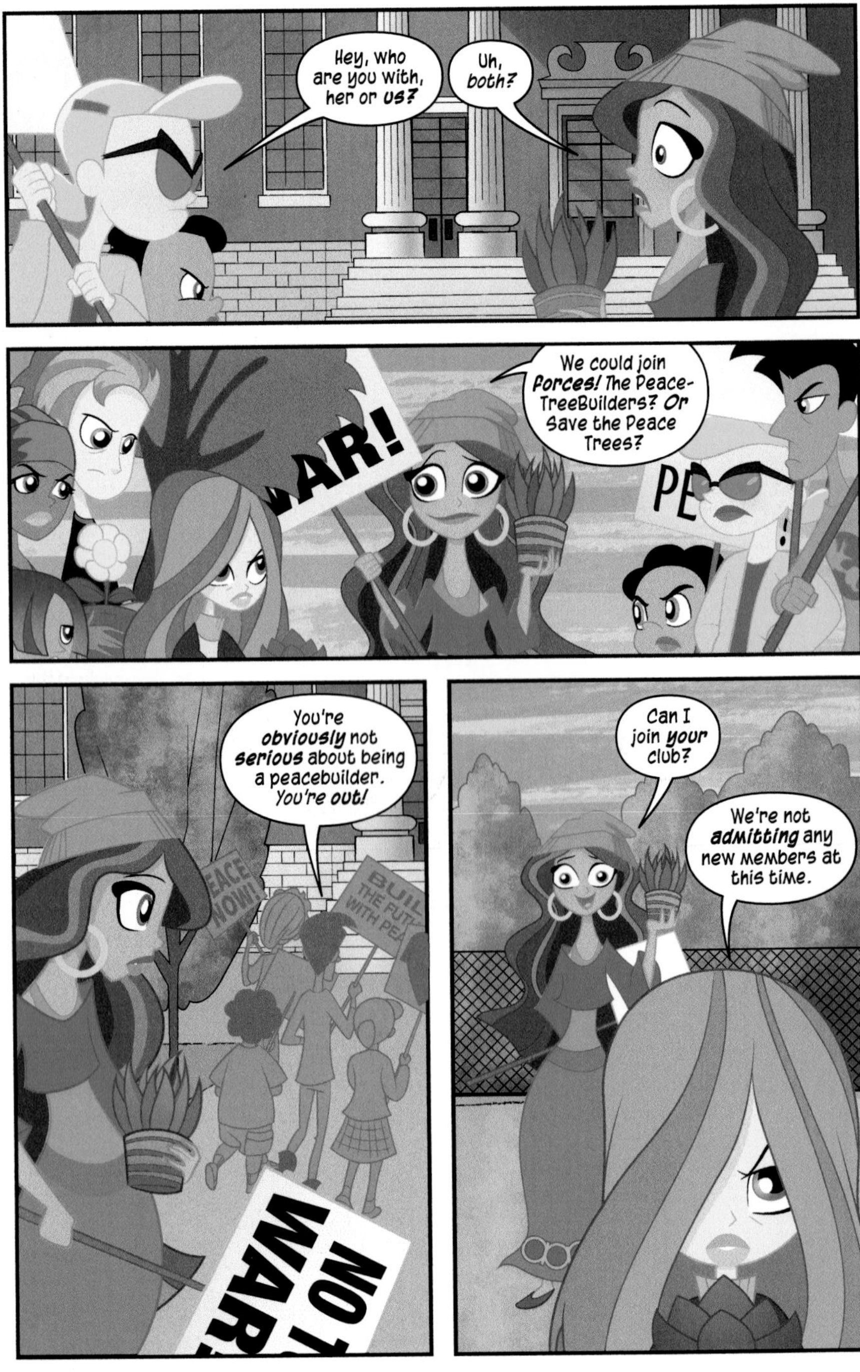

Hey, who are you with, her or *us?*
Uh, *both?*
We could join *forces!* The Peace-TreeBuilders? *Or* Save the Peace Trees?
...AR!
PE
You're *obviously* not *serious* about being a peacebuilder. You're *out!*
EACE NOW!
BUIL THE FUTU WITH PEA
NO T WAR
Can I join *your* club?
We're not *admitting* any new members at this time.

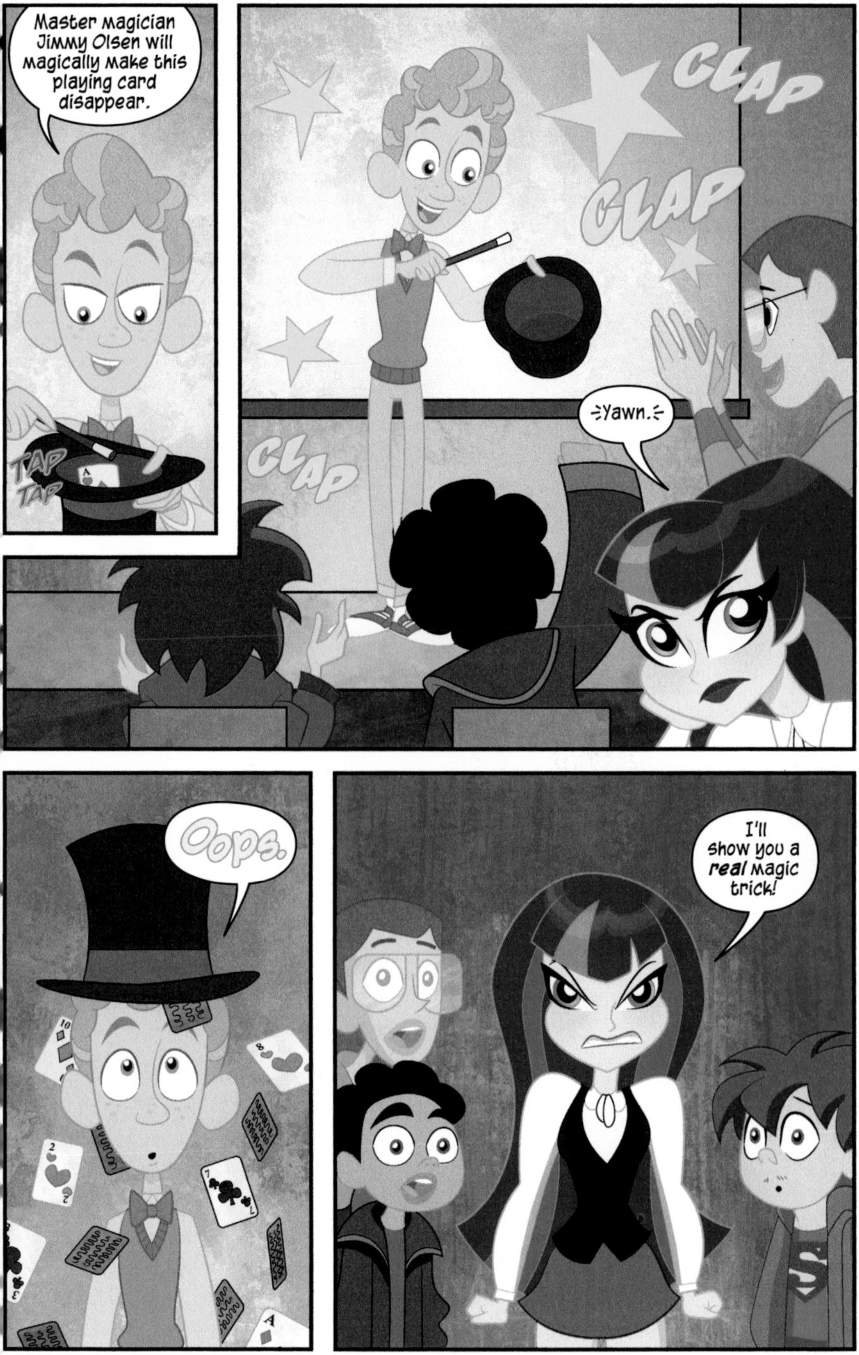
Master magician Jimmy Olsen will magically make this playing card disappear.
TAP
TAP
CLAP
CLAP
CLAP
Yawn.
Oops.
I'll show you a *real* magic trick!

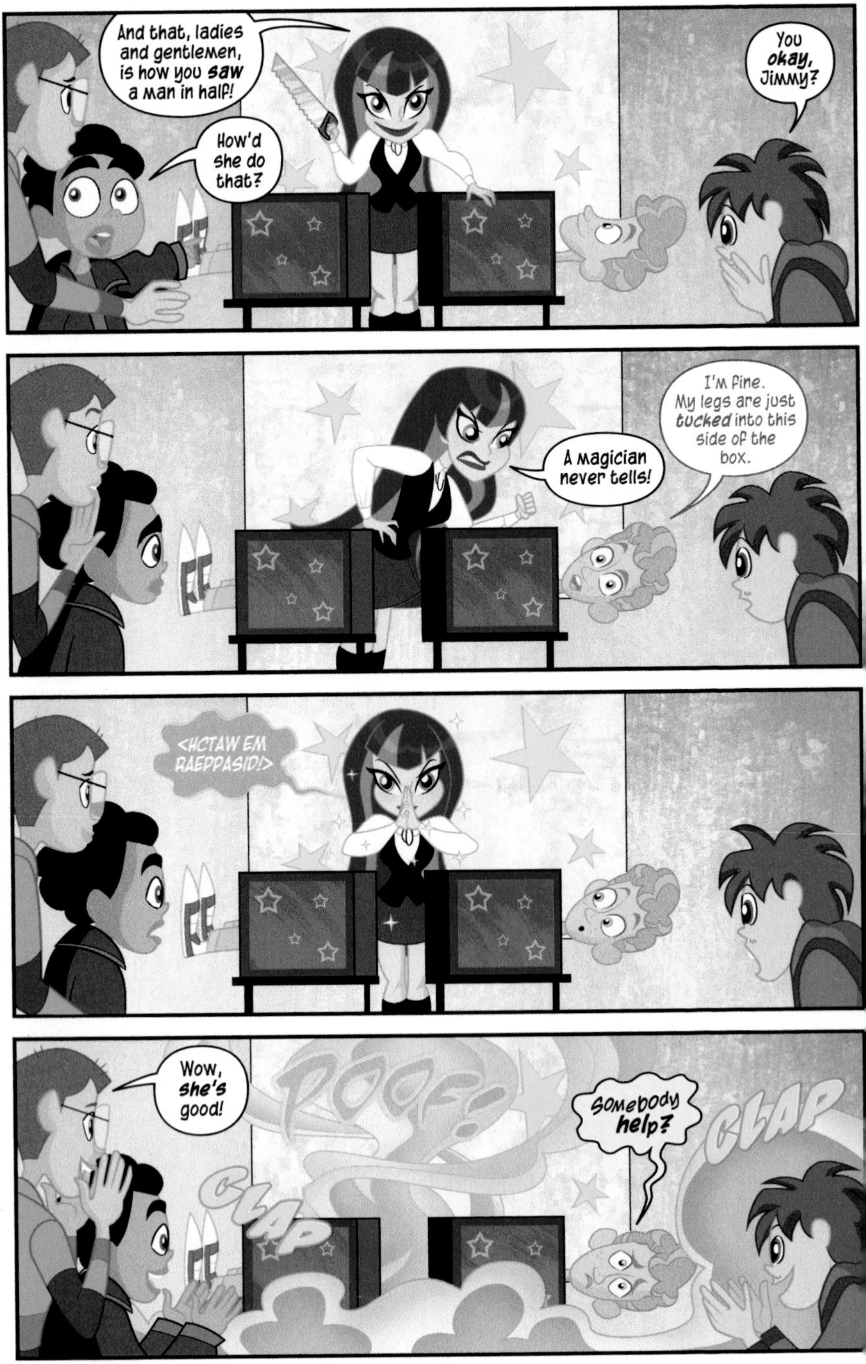

And that, ladies and gentlemen, is how you **saw** a man in half!
How'd she do that?
You **okay,** Jimmy?
A magician never tells!
I'm fine. My legs are just *tucked* into this side of the box.
<HCTAW EM RAEPPASID!>
Wow, **she's** good!
POOF!
CLAP
Somebody **help?**
CLAP

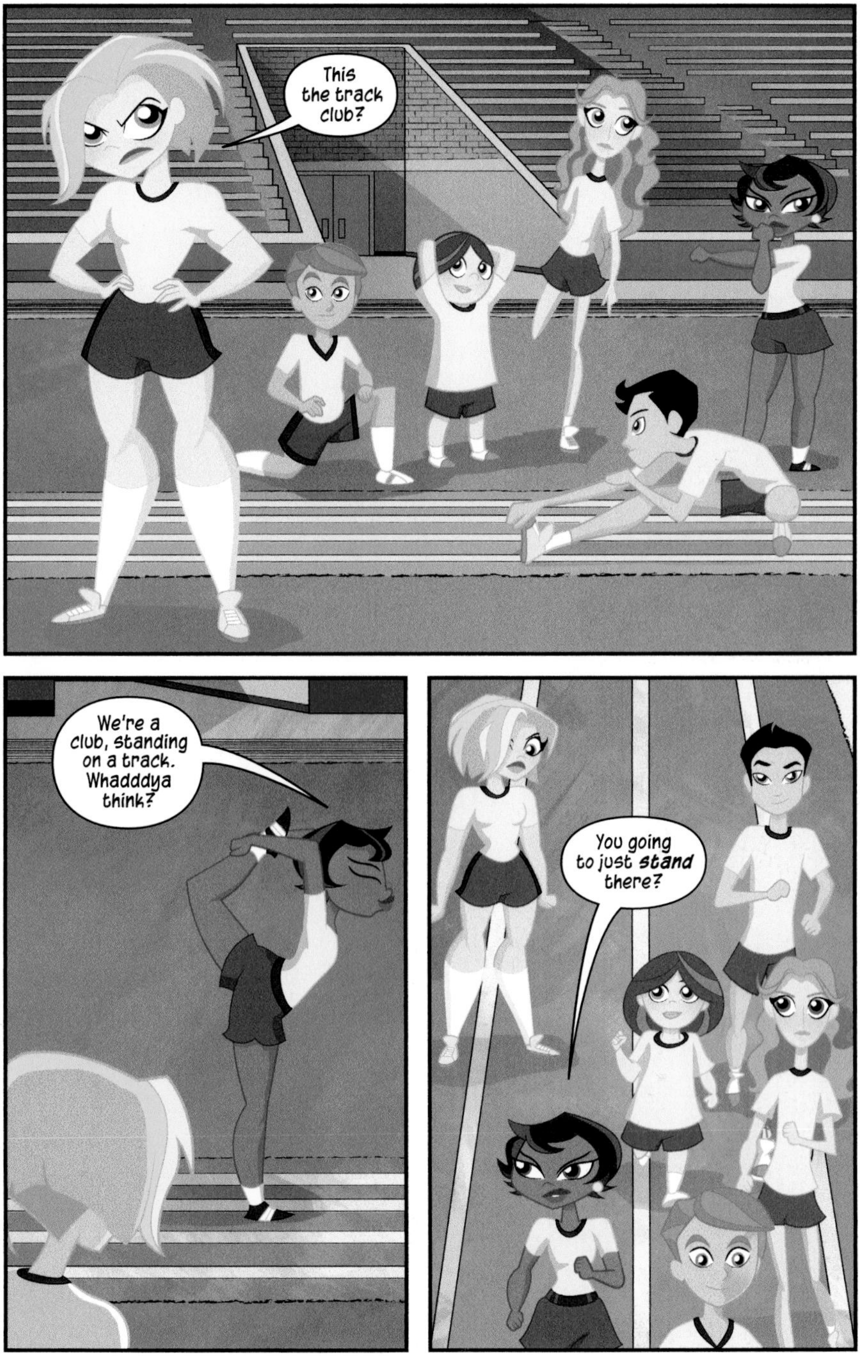
This the track club?
We're a club, standing on a track. Whadddya think?
You going to just stand there?

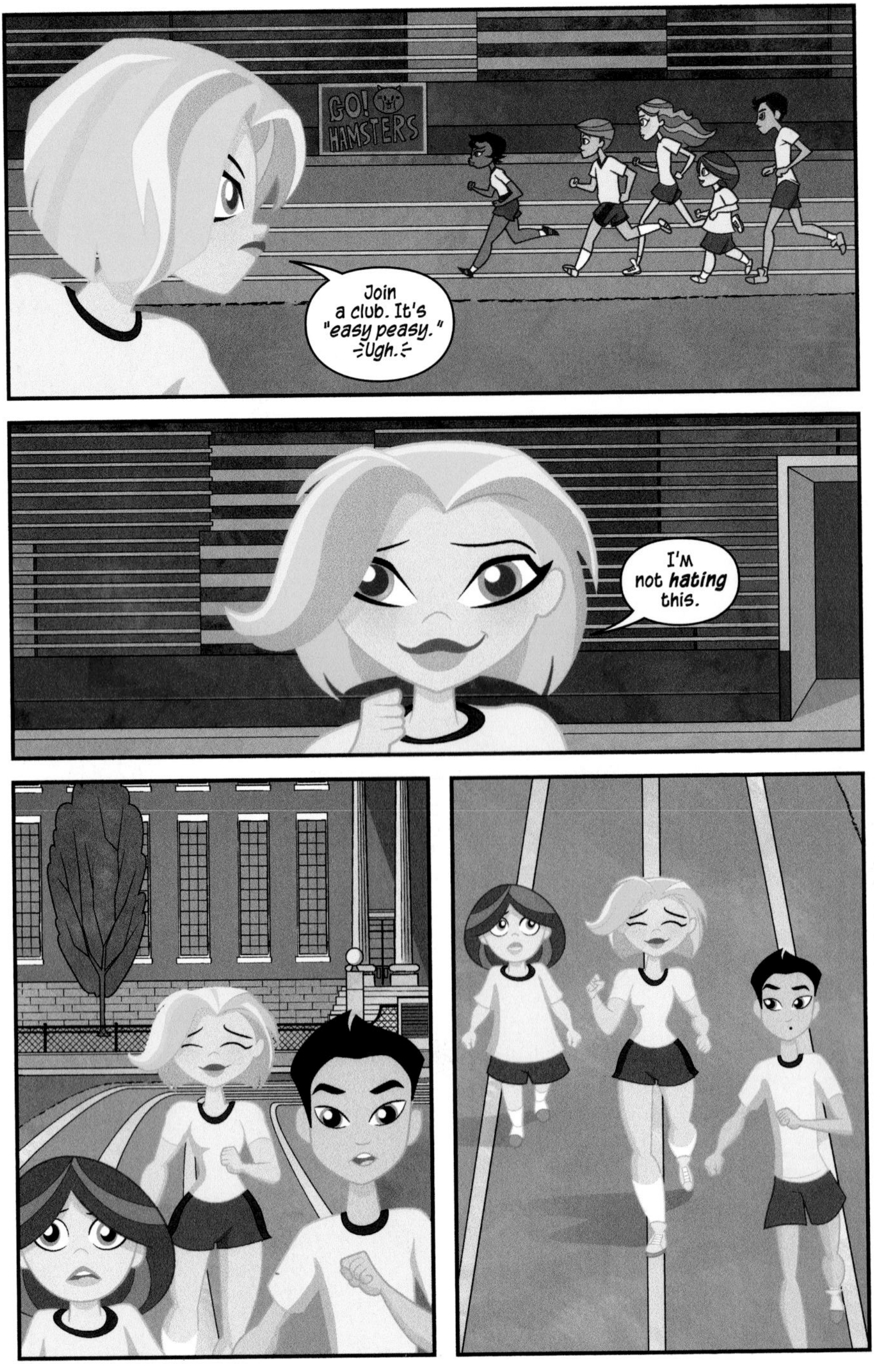
GO! HAMSTERS
Join a club. It's "easy peasy." Ugh.
I'M not *hating* this.

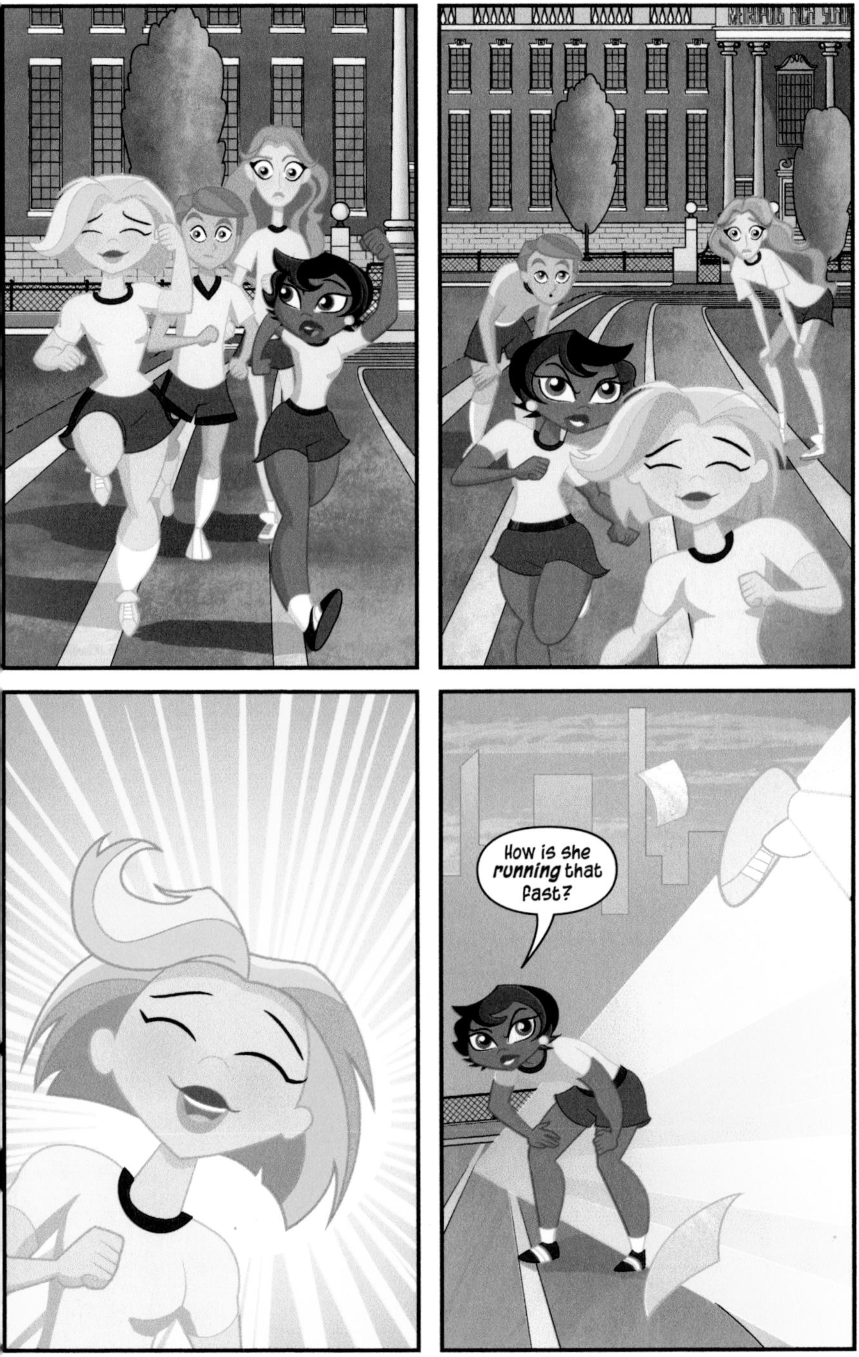
How is she *running* that fast?

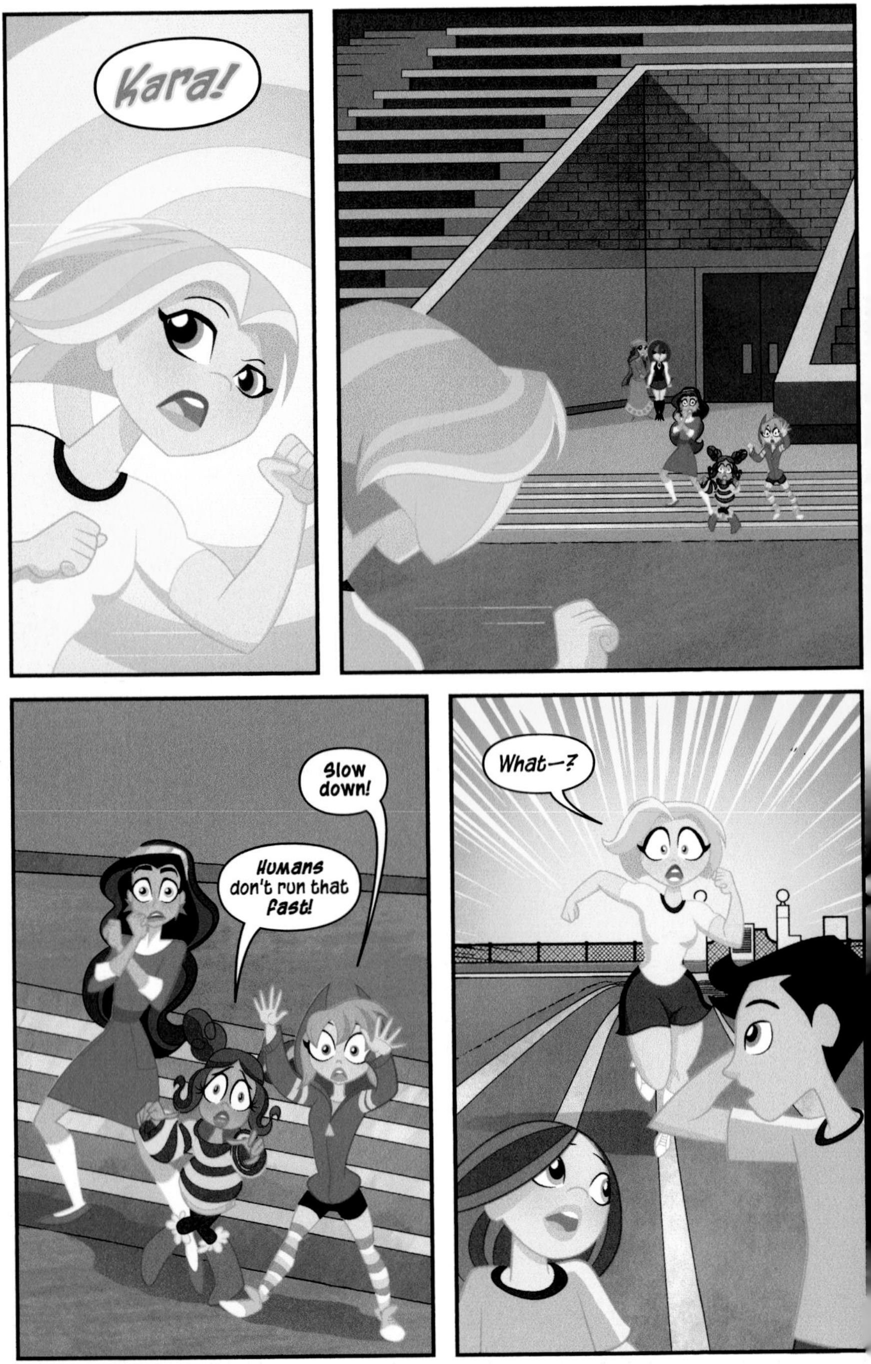
Kara!
Slow down!
Humans don't run that fast!
What—?

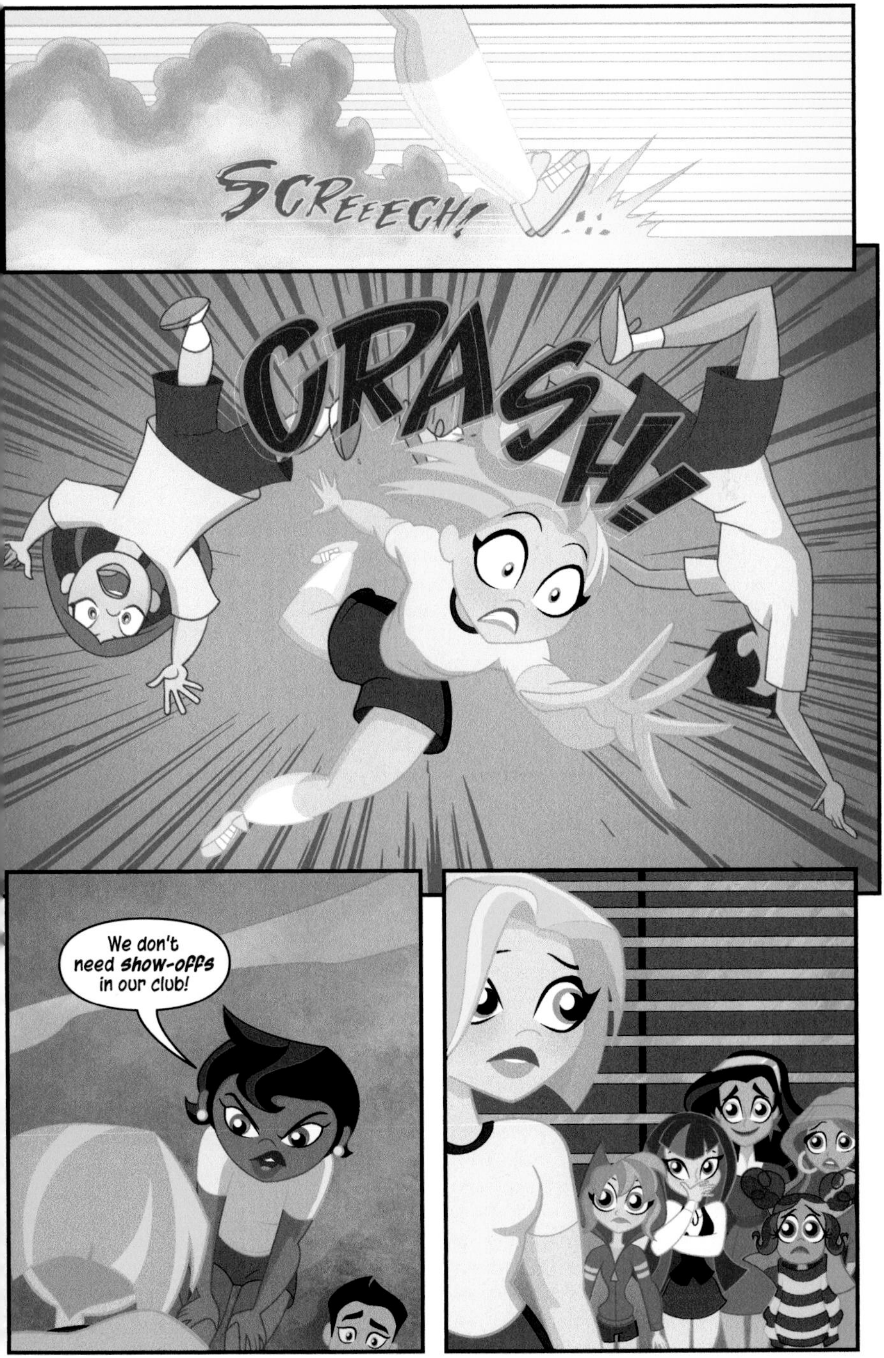
SCREEECH!
CRASH!
We don't need show-offs in our club!

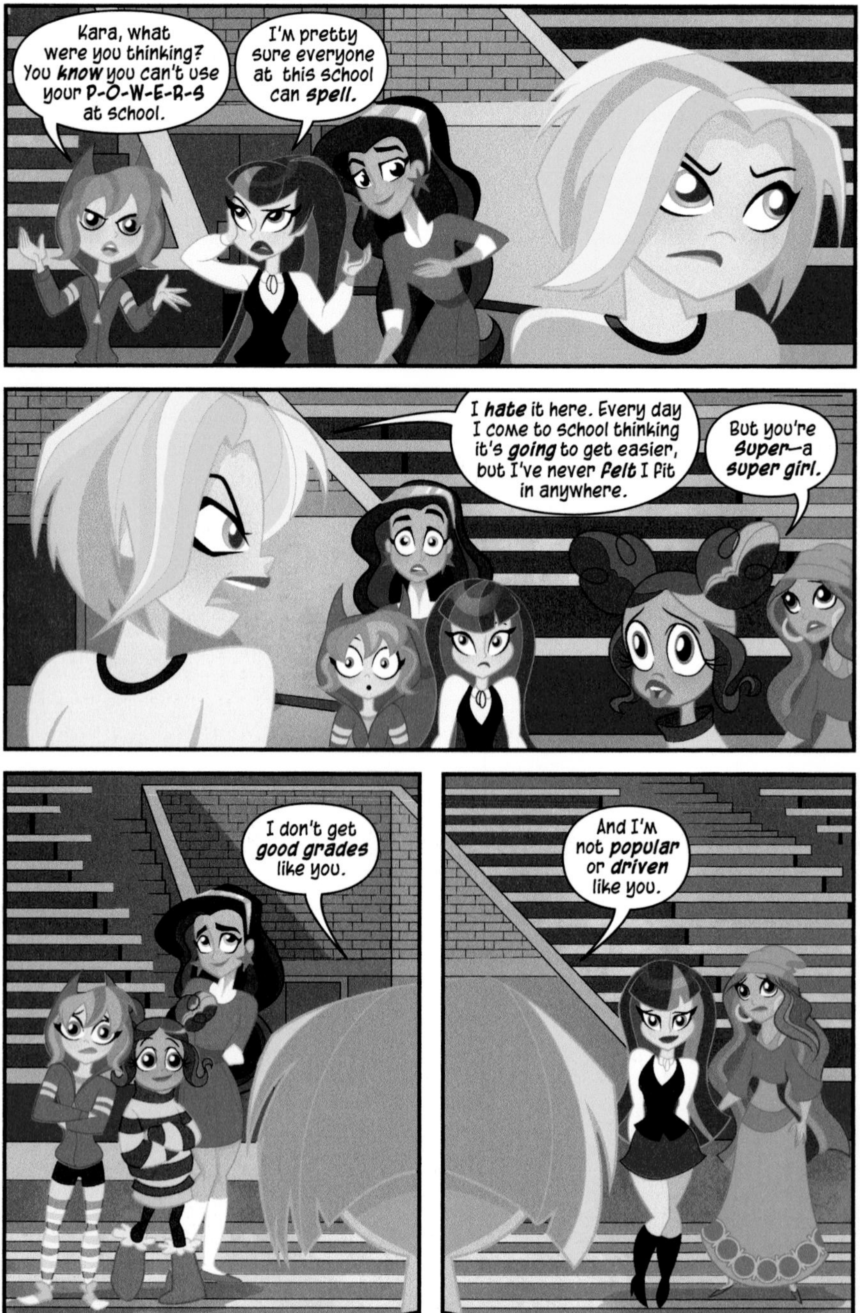
Kara, what were you thinking? You **know** you can't use your P-O-W-E-R-S at school.
I'm pretty sure everyone at this school can **spell.**
I **hate** it here. Every day I come to school thinking it's **going** to get easier, but I've never **felt** I fit in anywhere.
But you're **Super**—a **super girl.**
I don't get **good grades** like you.
And I'm not **popular** or **driven** like you.

But out *there* on the track, for a brief moment I *forgot* about all of that. And I can't even join the track club because I'm *too* fast.

We all got *kicked out* of our clubs, too!

I got rejected by *two* clubs.

I *broke* a robot.

I *refuse* to work with *amateurs!*

I could teach you all *Greek!*

NO!

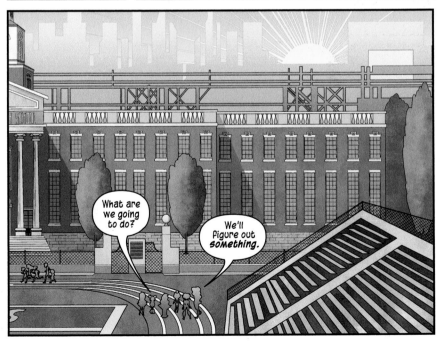

What are we going to do?

We'll figure out *something.*

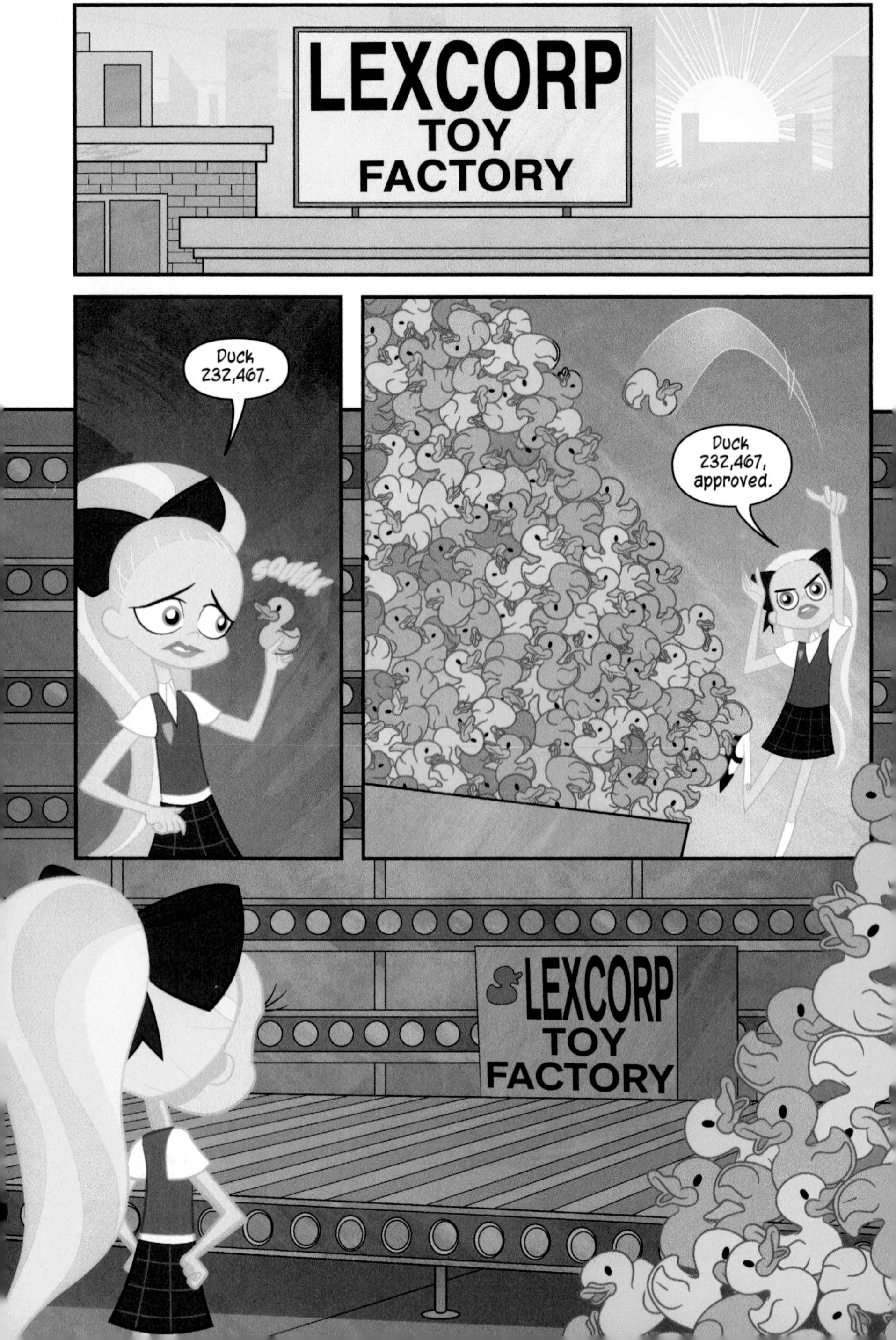
LEXCORP
TOY
FACTORY
Duck 232,467.
SQUEAK
Duck 232,467, approved.
LEXCORP
TOY
FACTORY

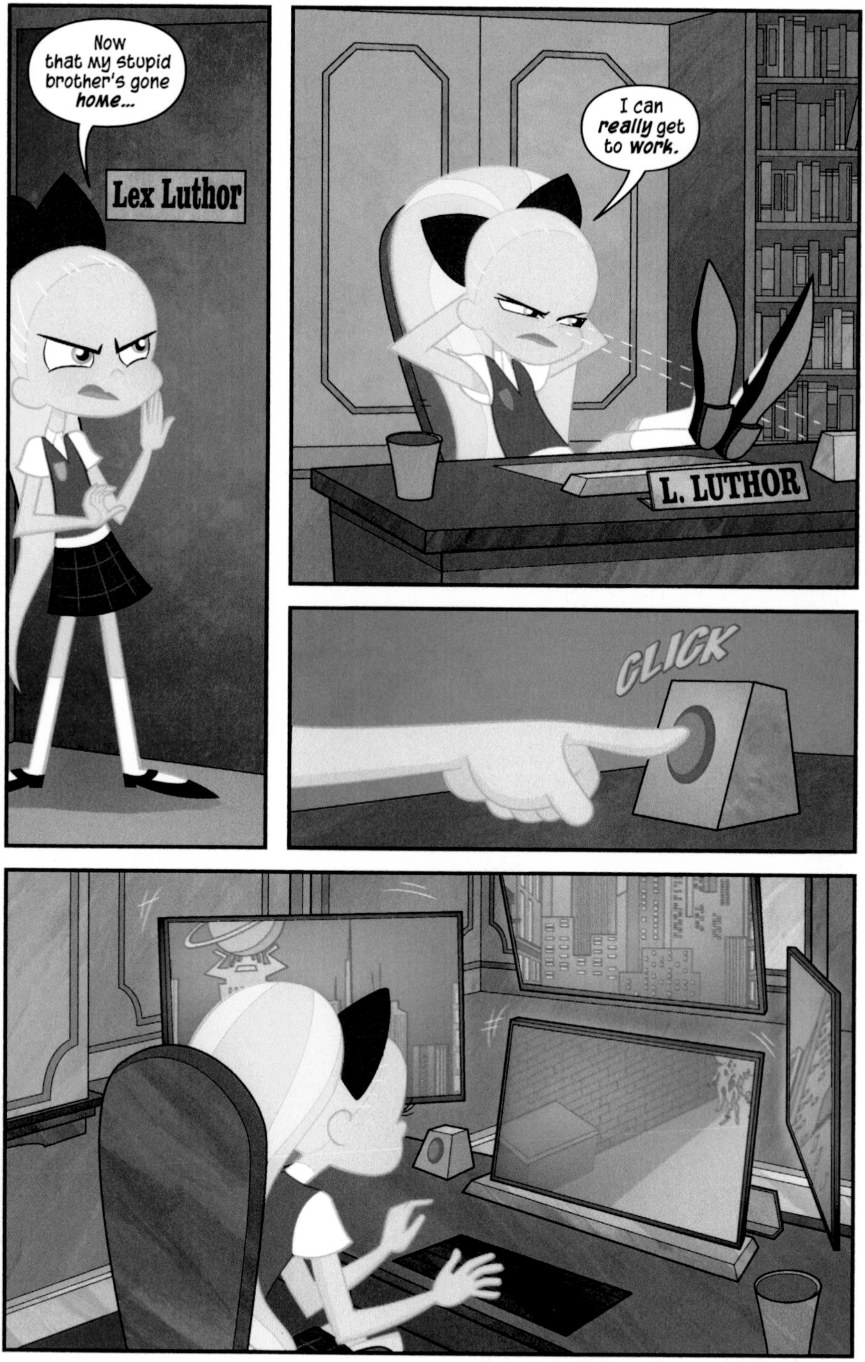

Now that my stupid brother's gone *home...*
Lex Luthor
I can *really* get to *work.*
L. LUTHOR
CLICK

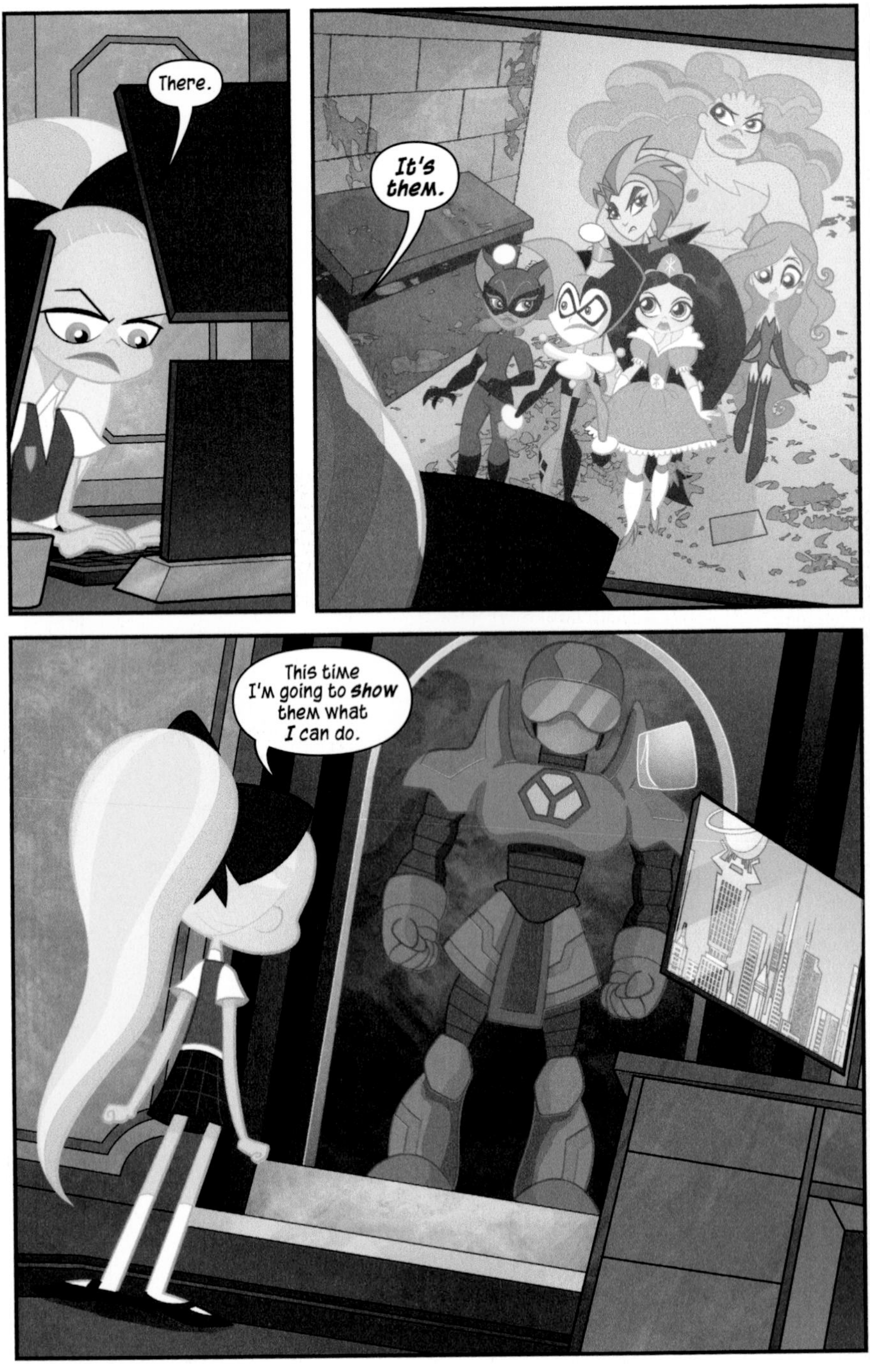
There.
It's them.
This time I'm going to *show* them what *I* can do.

chapter three

TRY, TRY AGAIN

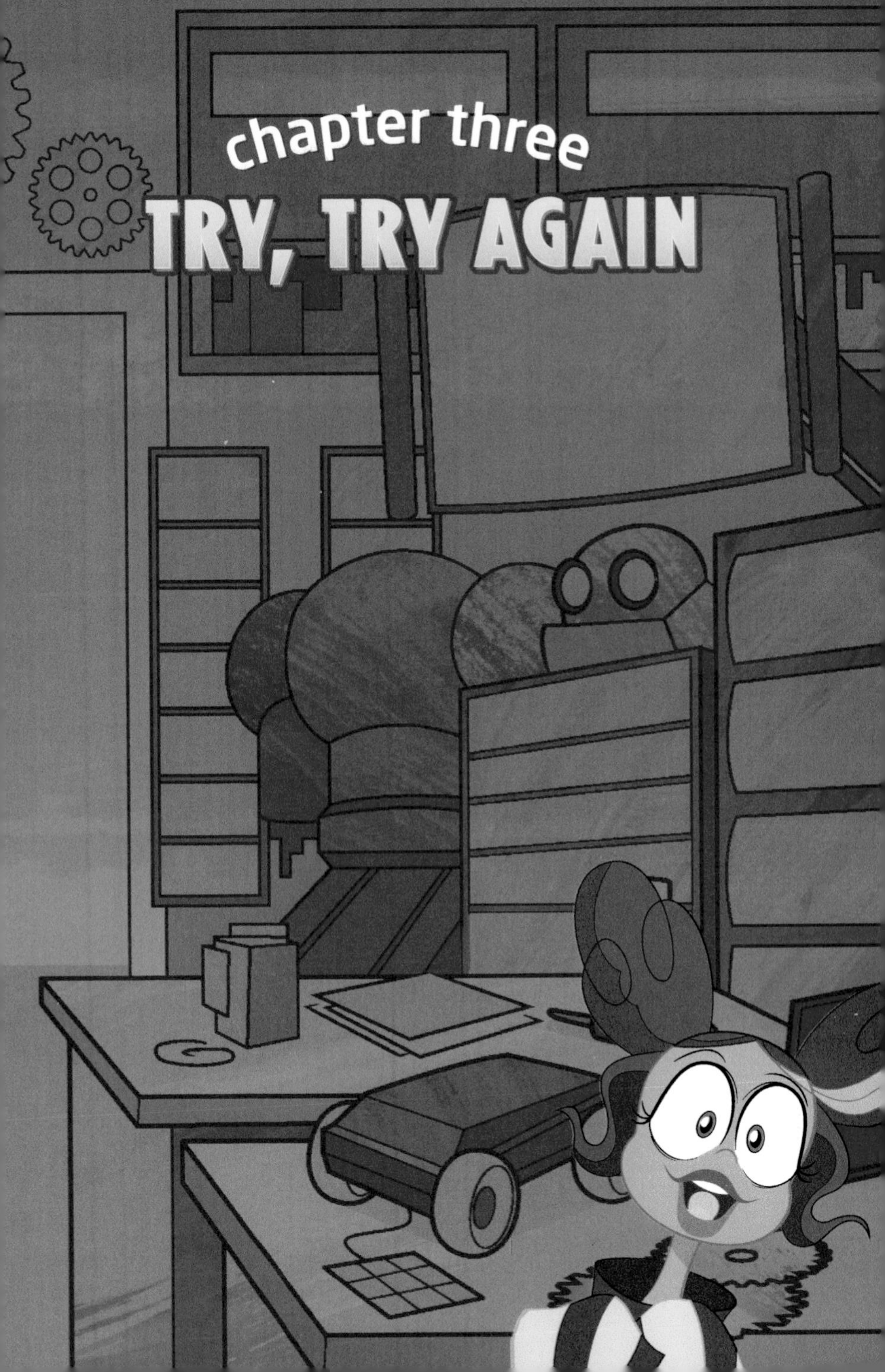

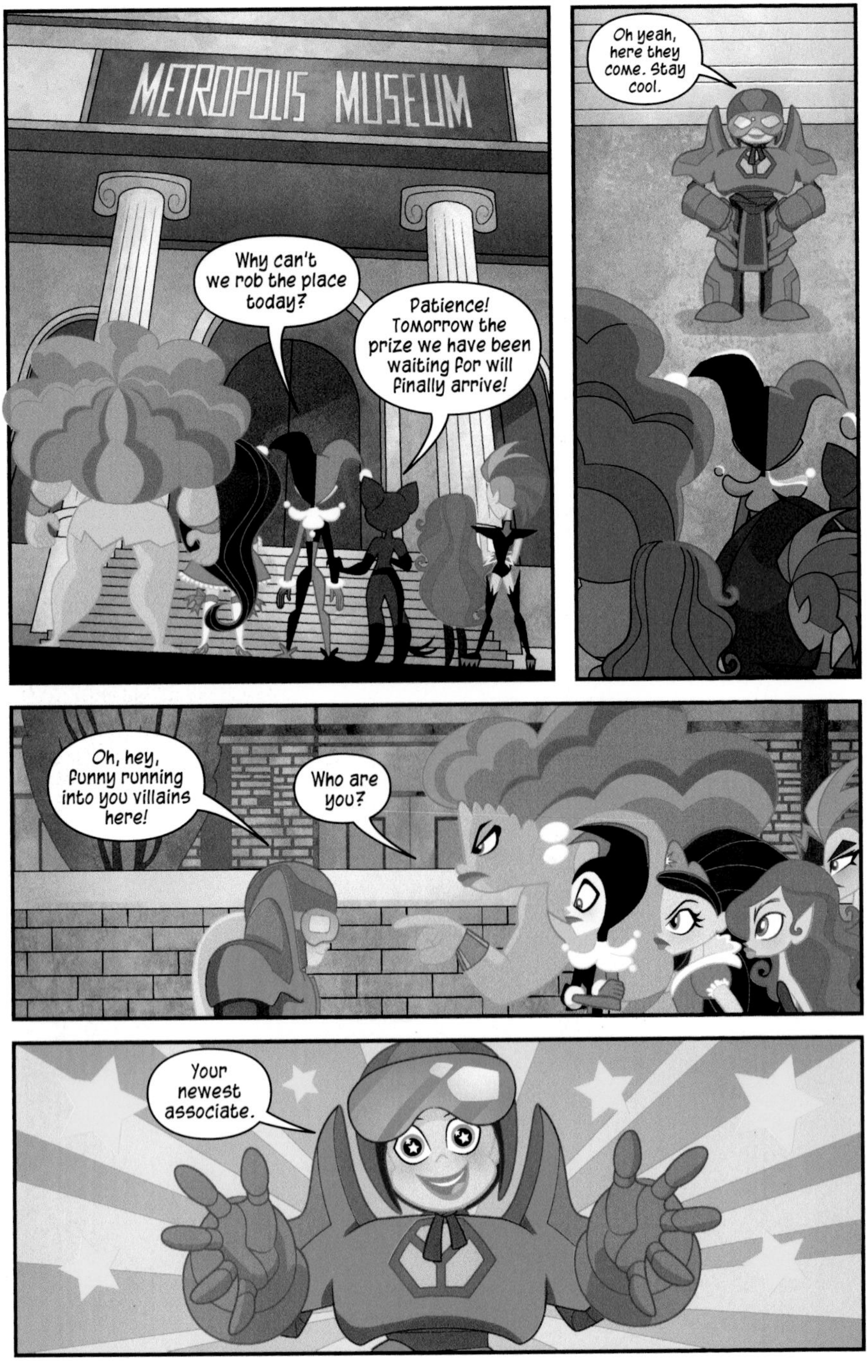
METROPOLIS MUSEUM
Why can't we rob the place today?
Patience! Tomorrow the prize we have been waiting for will finally arrive!
Oh yeah, here they come. Stay cool.
Oh, hey, funny running into you villains here!
Who are you?
Your newest associate.

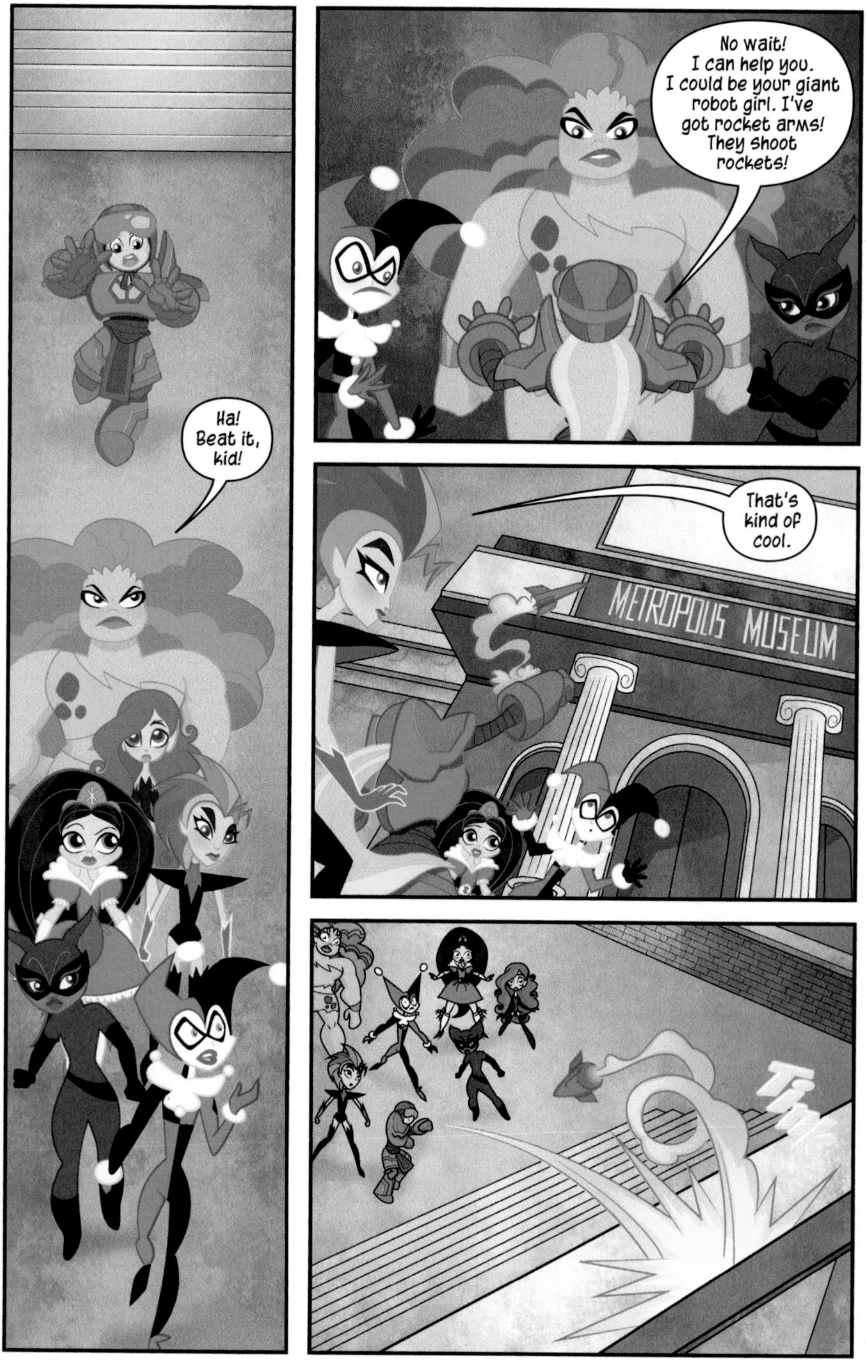
Ha! Beat it, kid!
No wait! I can help you. I could be your giant robot girl. I've got rocket arms! They shoot rockets!
That's kind of cool.
METROPOLIS MUSEUM

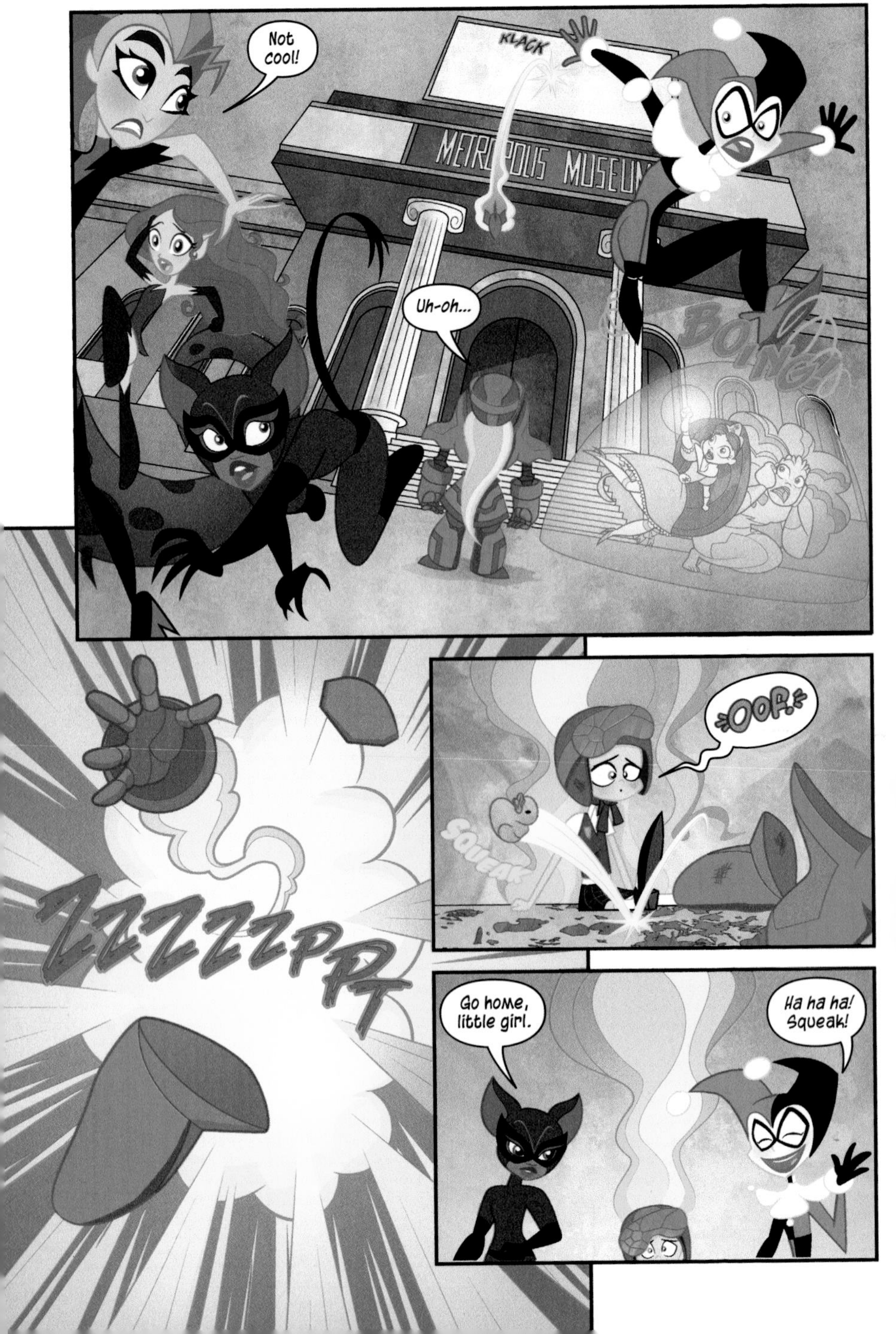
Not cool!
KLACK
METROPOLIS MUSEUM
Uh-oh...
BOING!
ZZZZZZPPT
OOF!
SQUEAK
Go home, little girl.
Ha ha ha! Squeak!

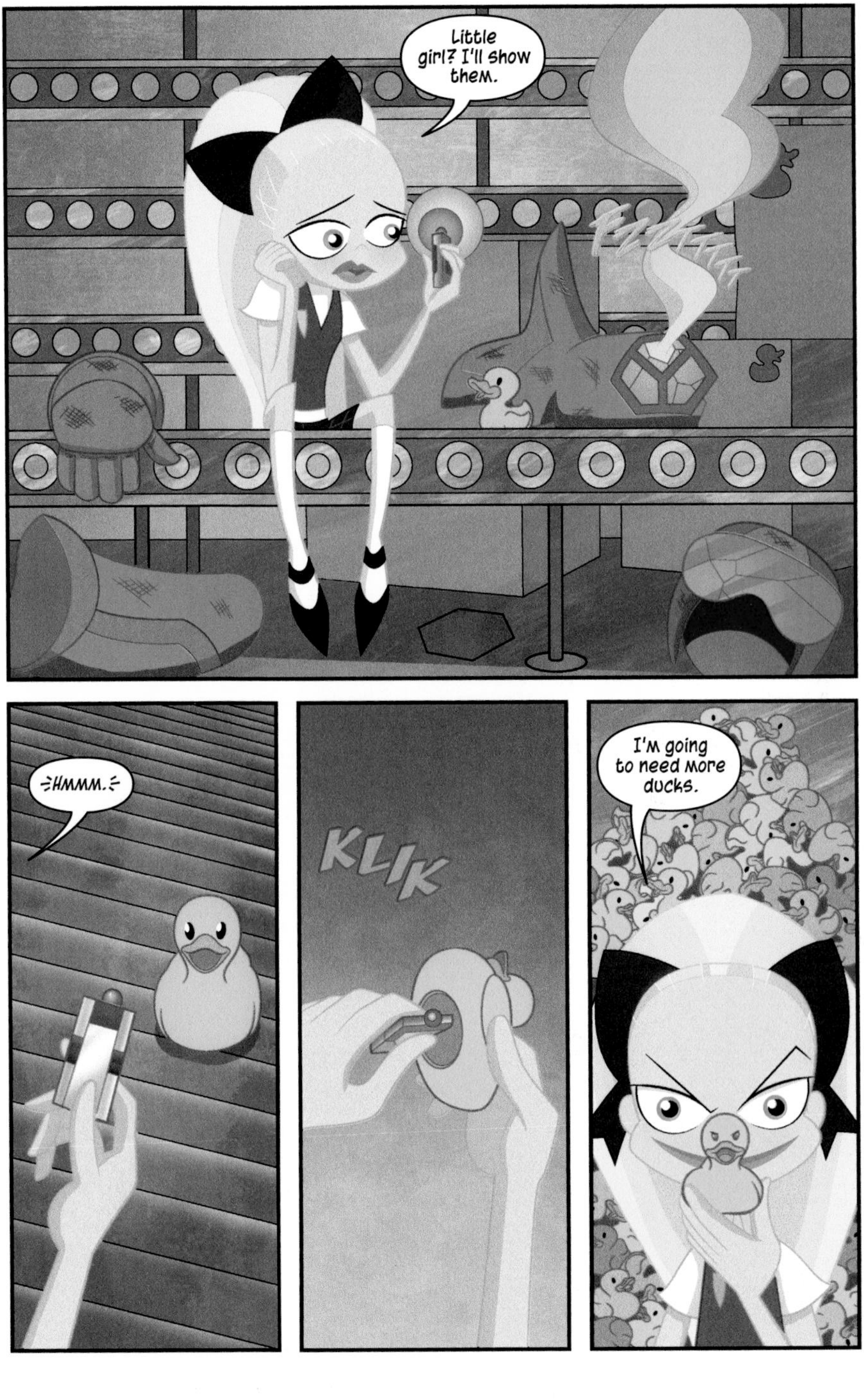
Little girl? I'll show them.
FZZTTTTTT
HMMM.
KLIK
I'm going to need more ducks.

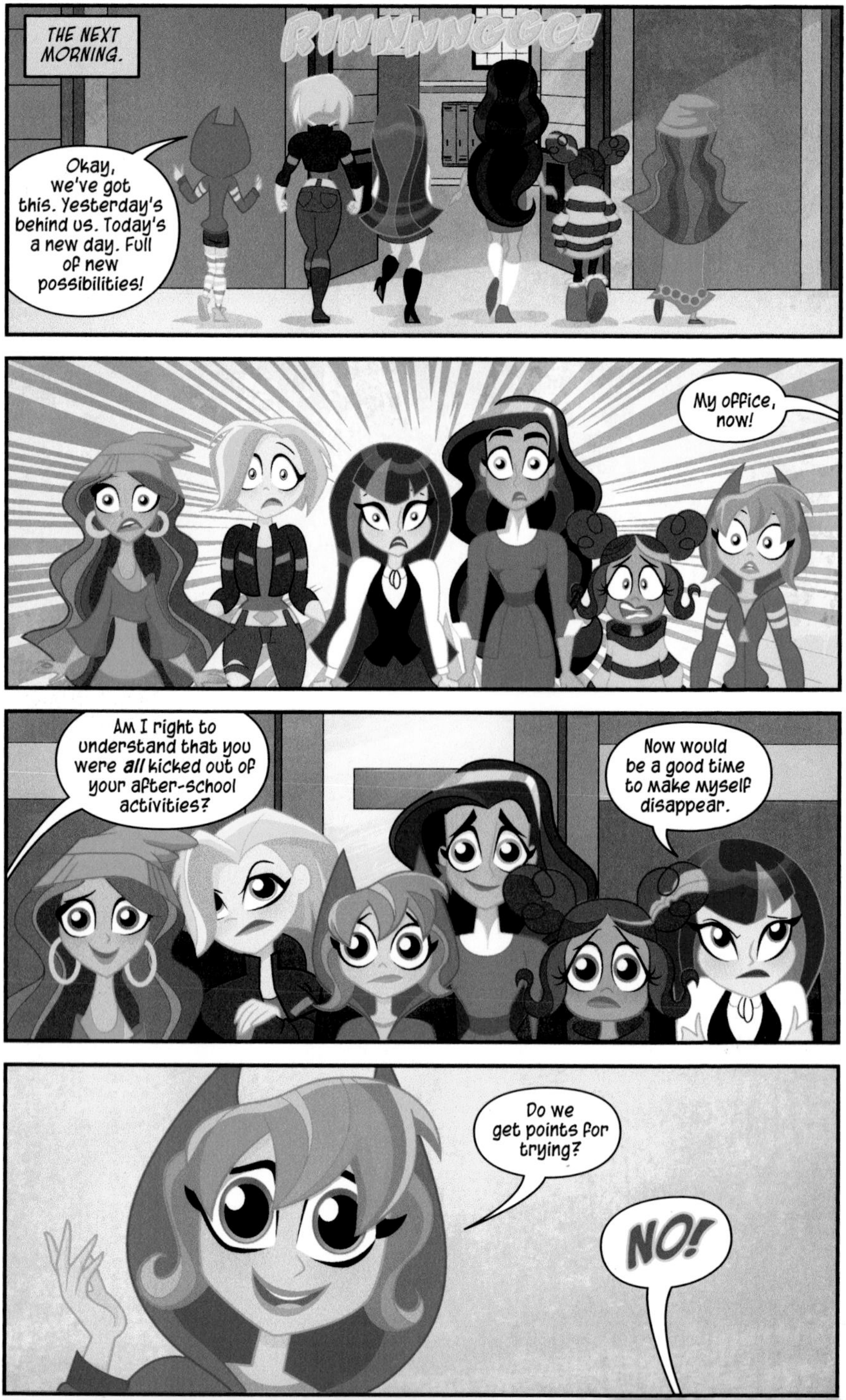
THE NEXT MORNING.
RINNNNGGG!
Okay, we've got this. Yesterday's behind us. Today's a new day. Full of new possibilities!
My office, now!
Am I right to understand that you were *all* kicked out of your after-school activities?
Now would be a good time to make myself disappear.
Do we get points for trying?
NO!

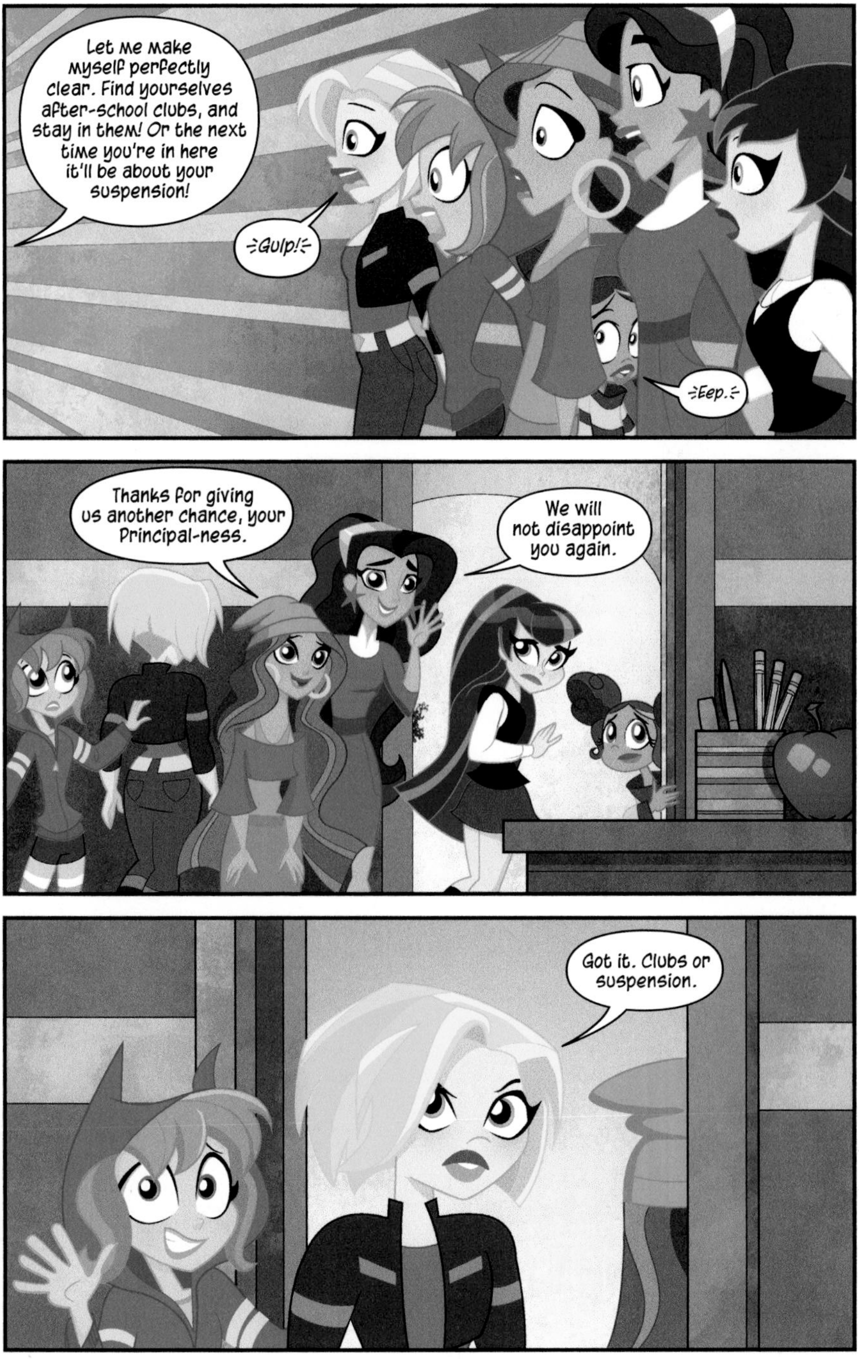
Let me make myself perfectly clear. Find yourselves after-school clubs, and stay in them! Or the next time you're in here it'll be about your suspension!
Gulp!
Eep.
Thanks for giving us another chance, your Principal-ness.
We will not disappoint you again.
Got it. Clubs or suspension.

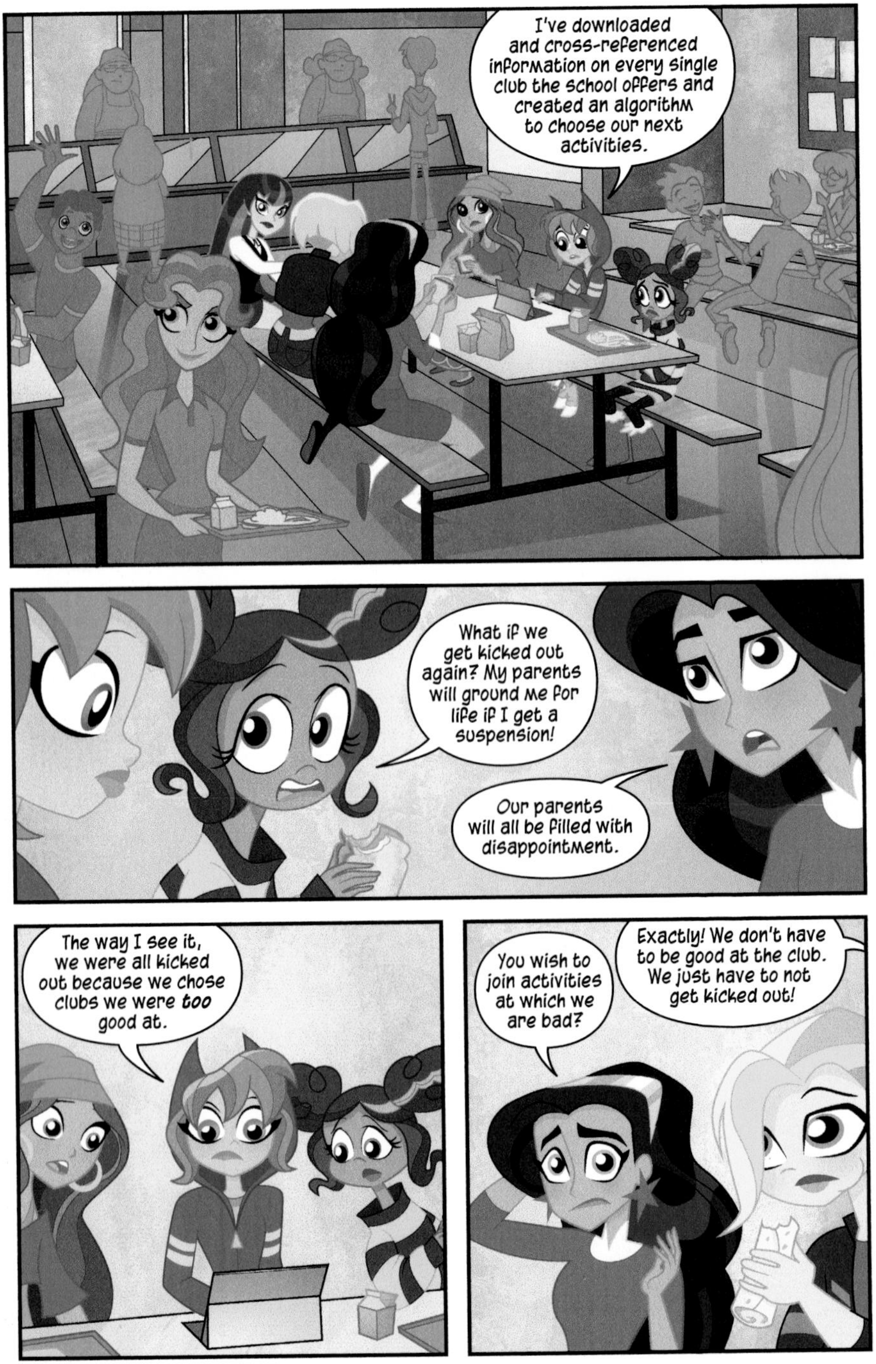
I've downloaded and cross-referenced information on every single club the school offers and created an algorithm to choose our next activities.
What if we get kicked out again? My parents will ground me for life if I get a suspension!
Our parents will all be filled with disappointment.
The way I see it, we were all kicked out because we chose clubs we were *too* good at.
You wish to join activities at which we are bad?
Exactly! We don't have to be good at the club. We just have to not get kicked out!

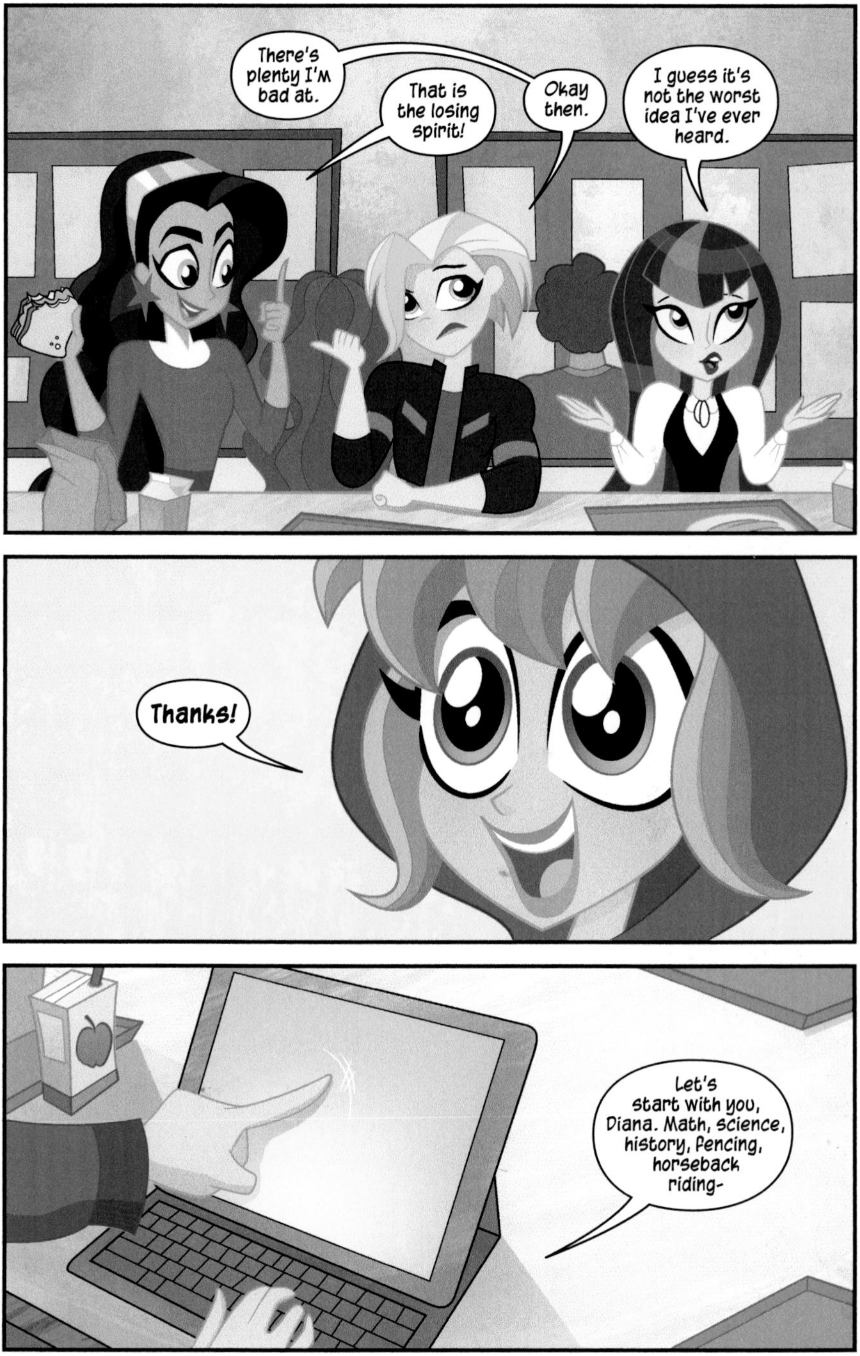
There's plenty I'm bad at.
That is the losing spirit!
Okay then.
I guess it's not the worst idea I've ever heard.
Thanks!
Let's start with you, Diana. Math, science, history, fencing, horseback riding-

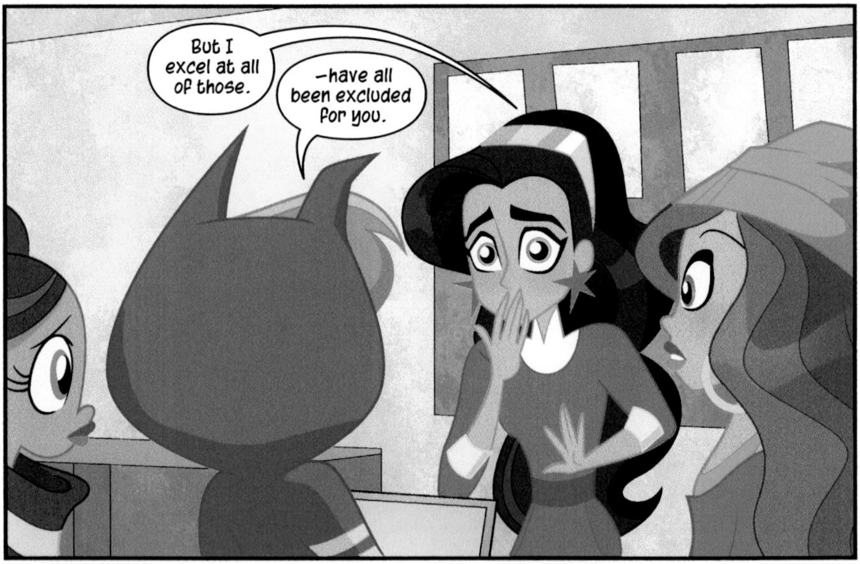
But I excel at all of those.
—have all been excluded for you.

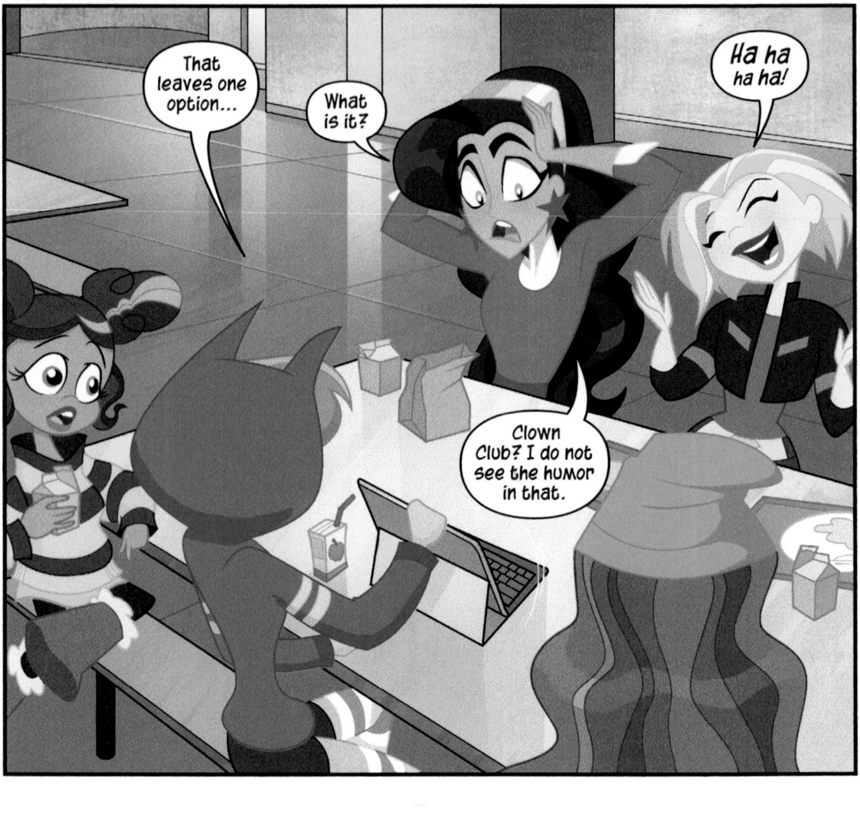
That leaves one option...
What is it?
Ha ha ha ha!
Clown Club? I do not see the humor in that.

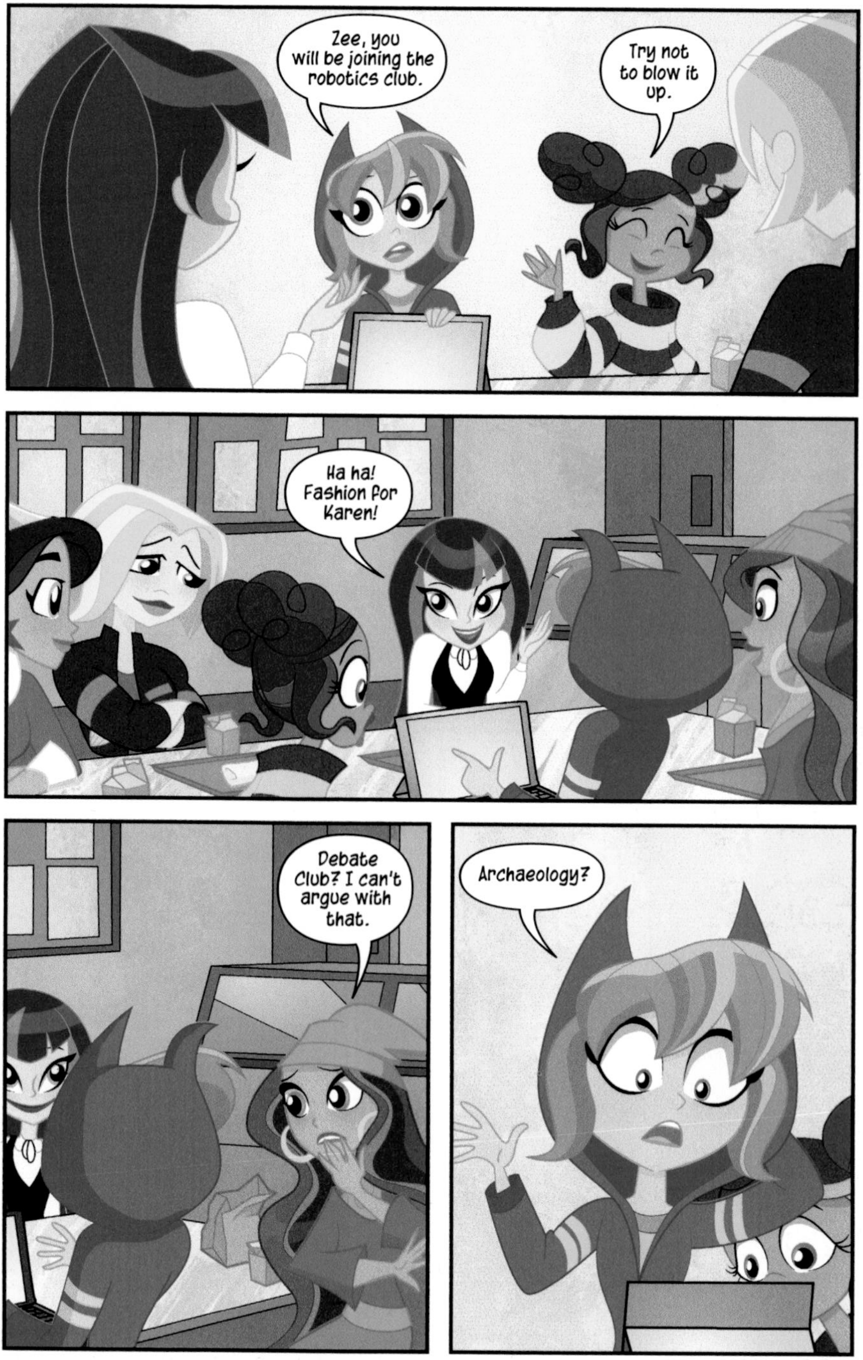
Zee, you will be joining the robotics club.
Try not to blow it up.
Ha ha! Fashion for Karen!
Debate Club? I can't argue with that.
Archaeology?

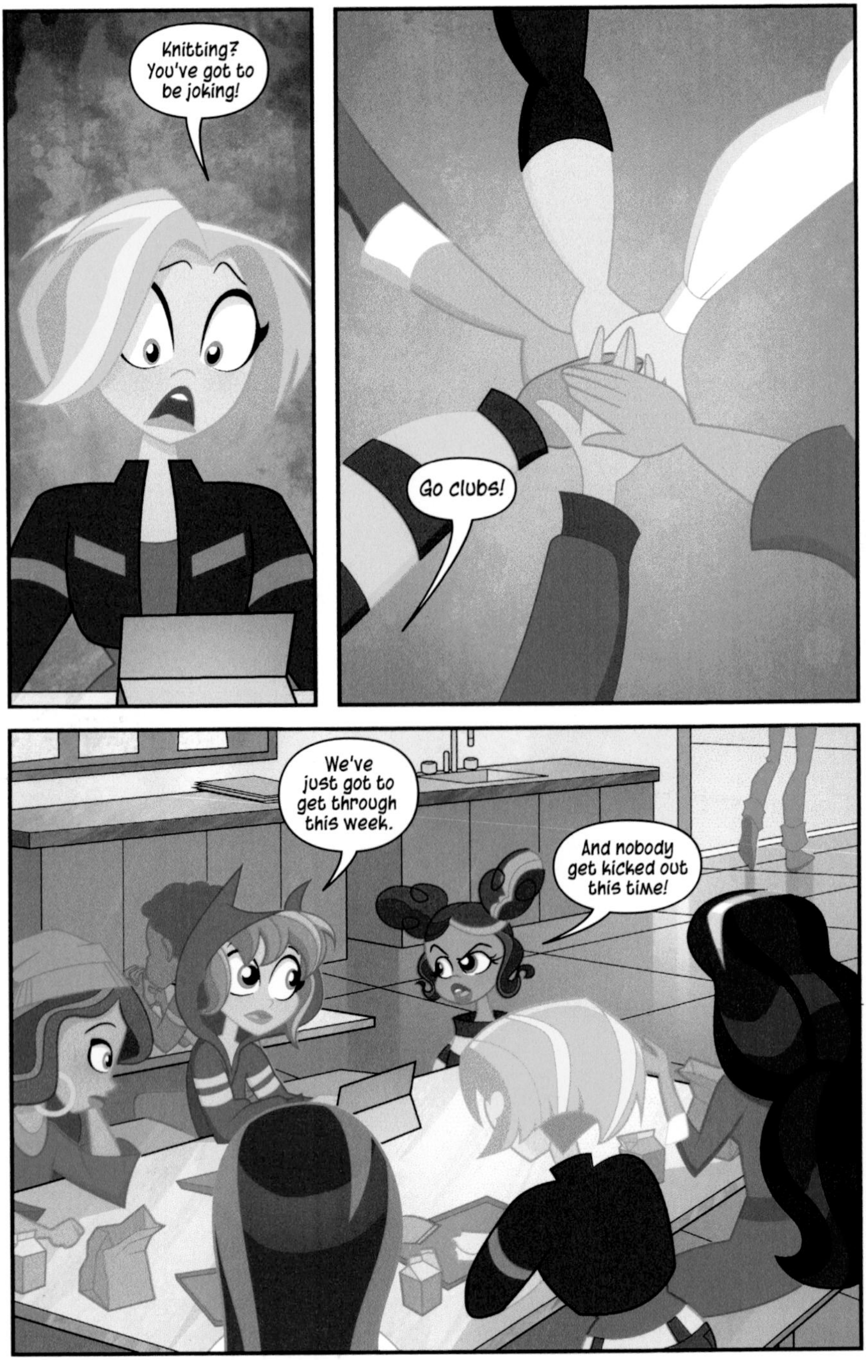
Knitting? You've got to be joking!
Go clubs!
We've just got to get through this week.
And nobody get kicked out this time!

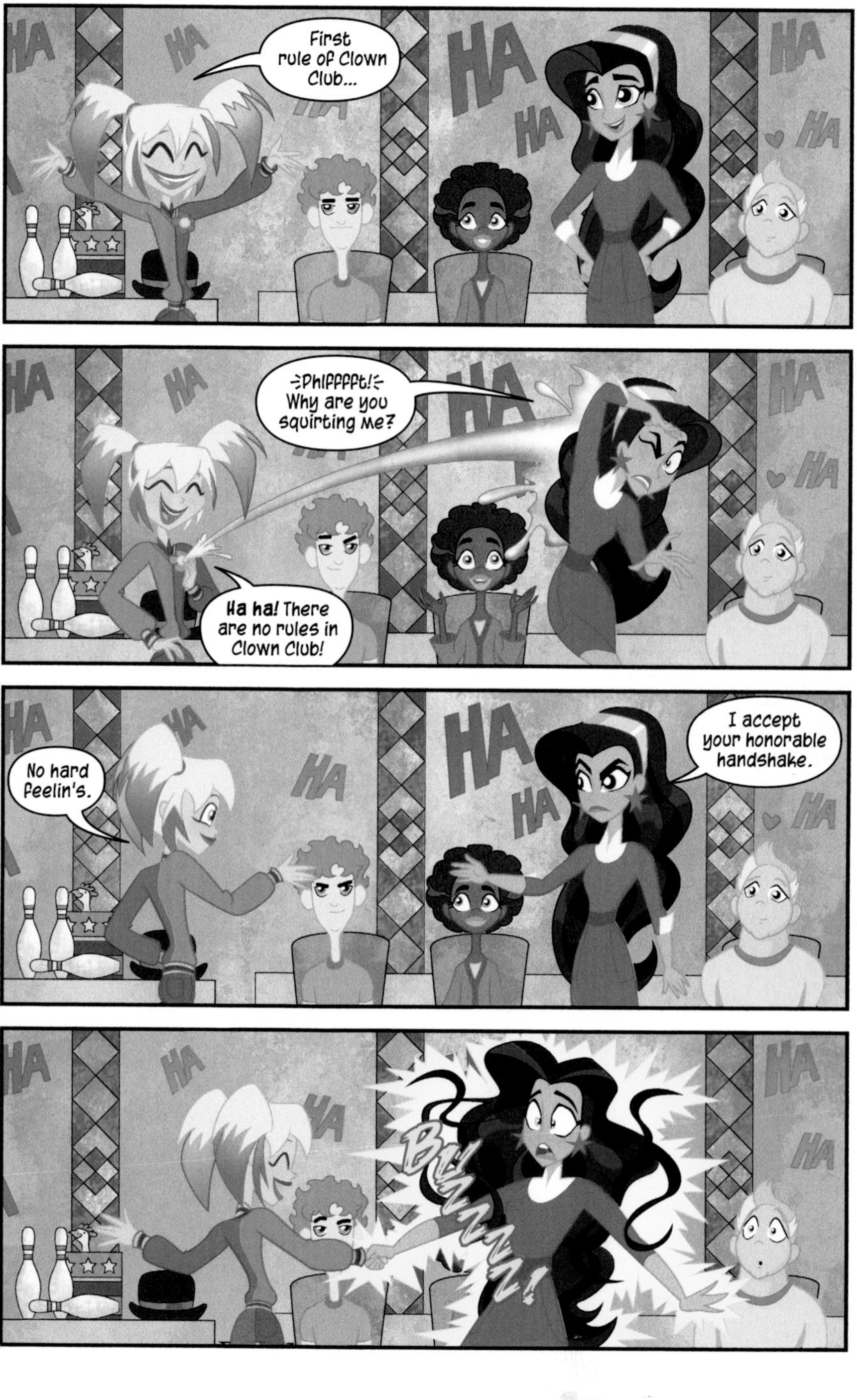
HA
First rule of Clown Club...
Phlffffft! Why are you squirting me?
Ha ha! There are no rules in Clown Club!
No hard feelin's.
I accept your honorable handshake.
BZZZZZ!

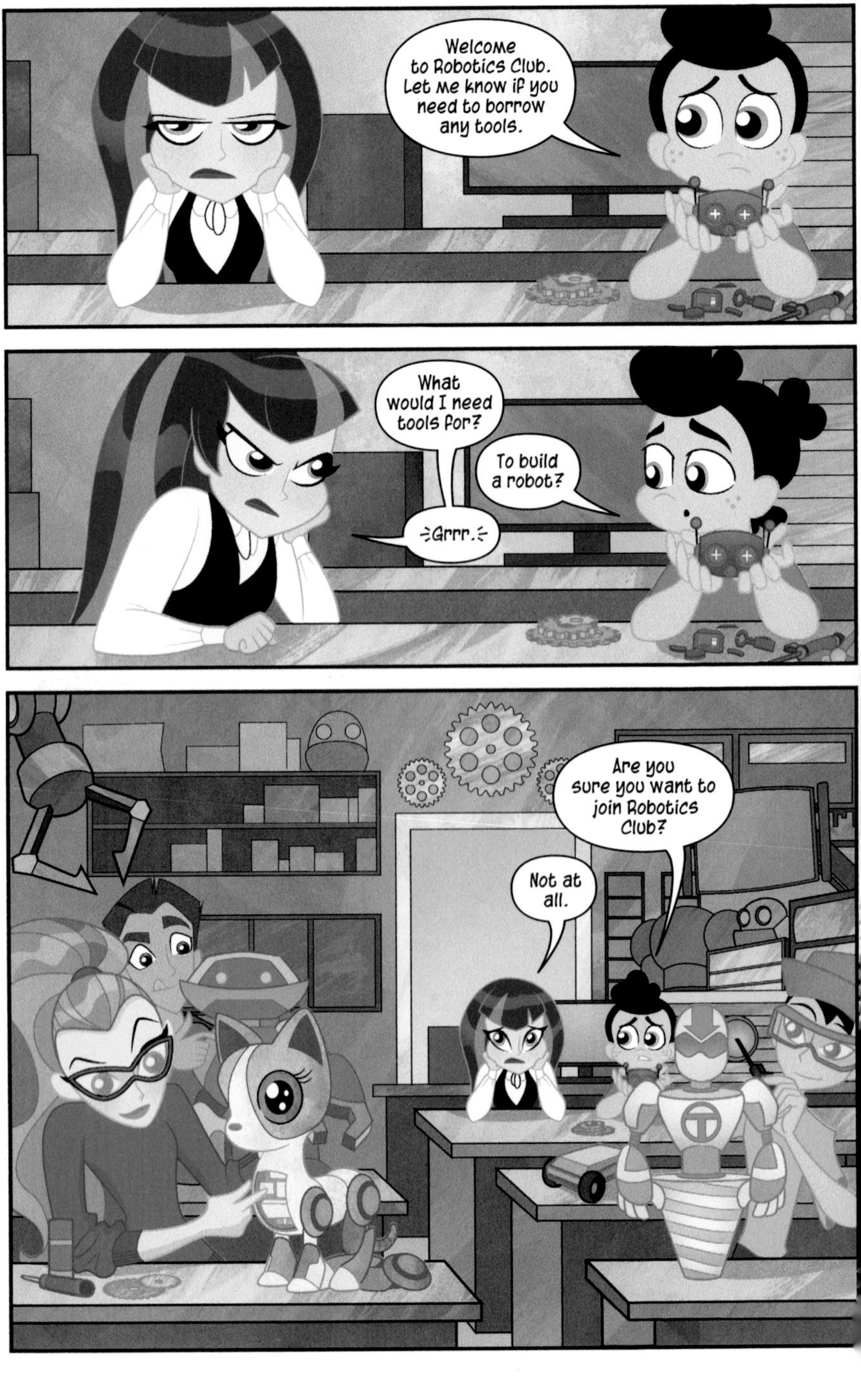
Welcome to Robotics Club. Let me know if you need to borrow any tools.
What would I need tools for?
To build a robot?
Grrr.
Are you sure you want to join Robotics Club?
Not at all.

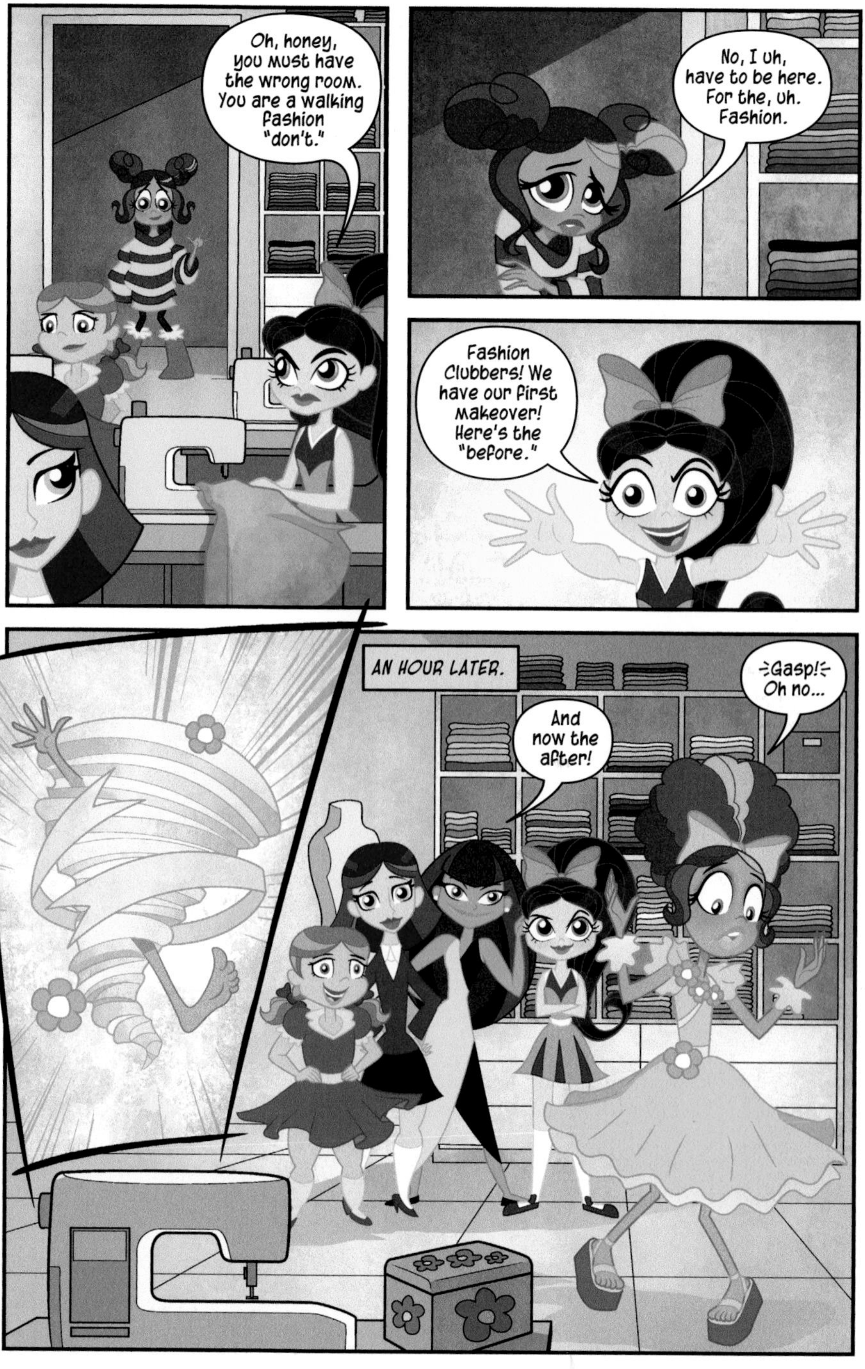
Oh, honey, you must have the wrong room. You are a walking fashion "don't."
No, I uh, have to be here. For the, uh. Fashion.
Fashion Clubbers! We have our first makeover! Here's the "before."
AN HOUR LATER.
And now the after!
Gasp! Oh no...

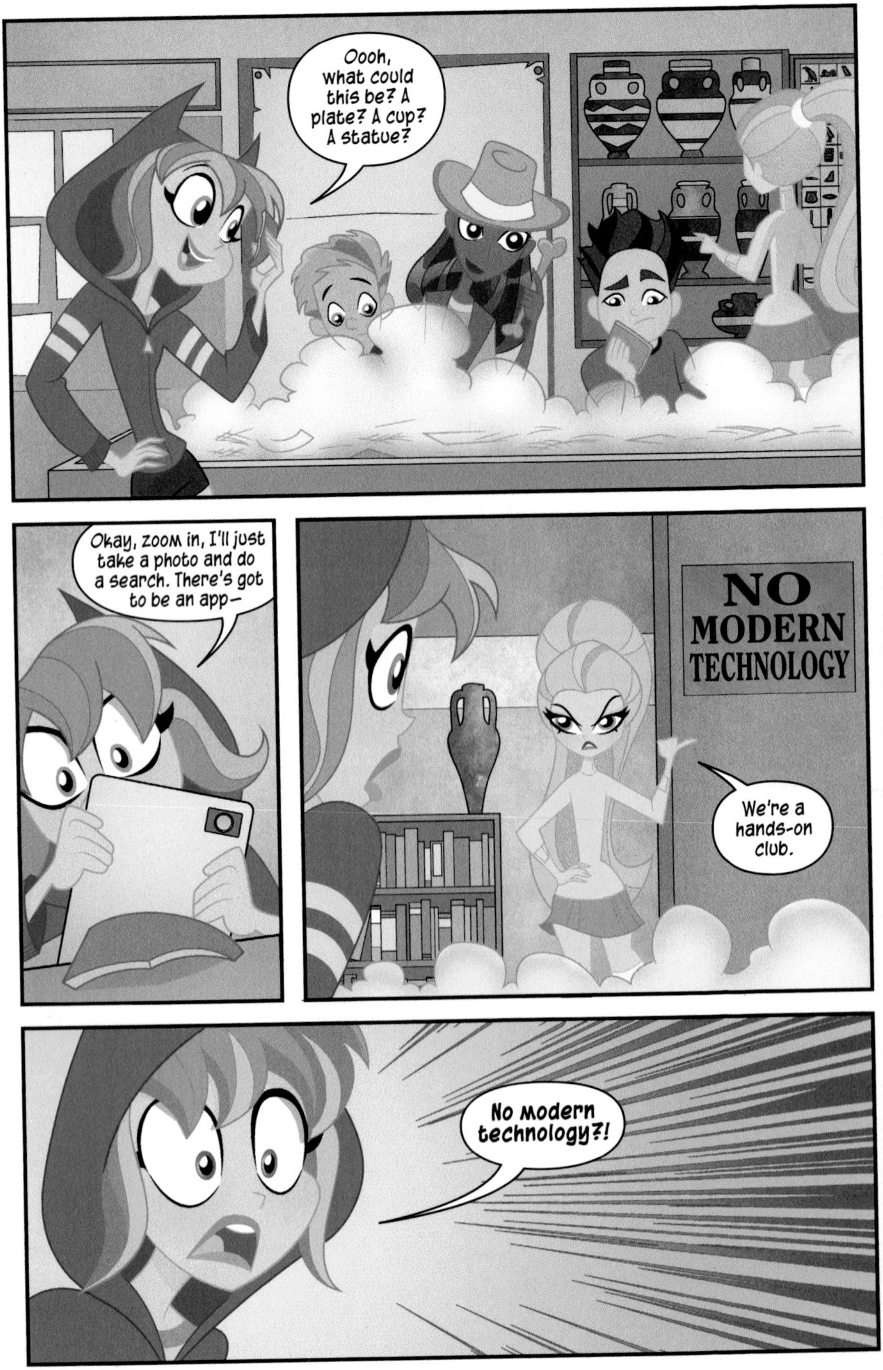
Oooh, what could this be? A plate? A cup? A statue?
Okay, zoom in, I'll just take a photo and do a search. There's got to be an app—
NO MODERN TECHNOLOGY
We're a hands-on club.
No modern technology?!

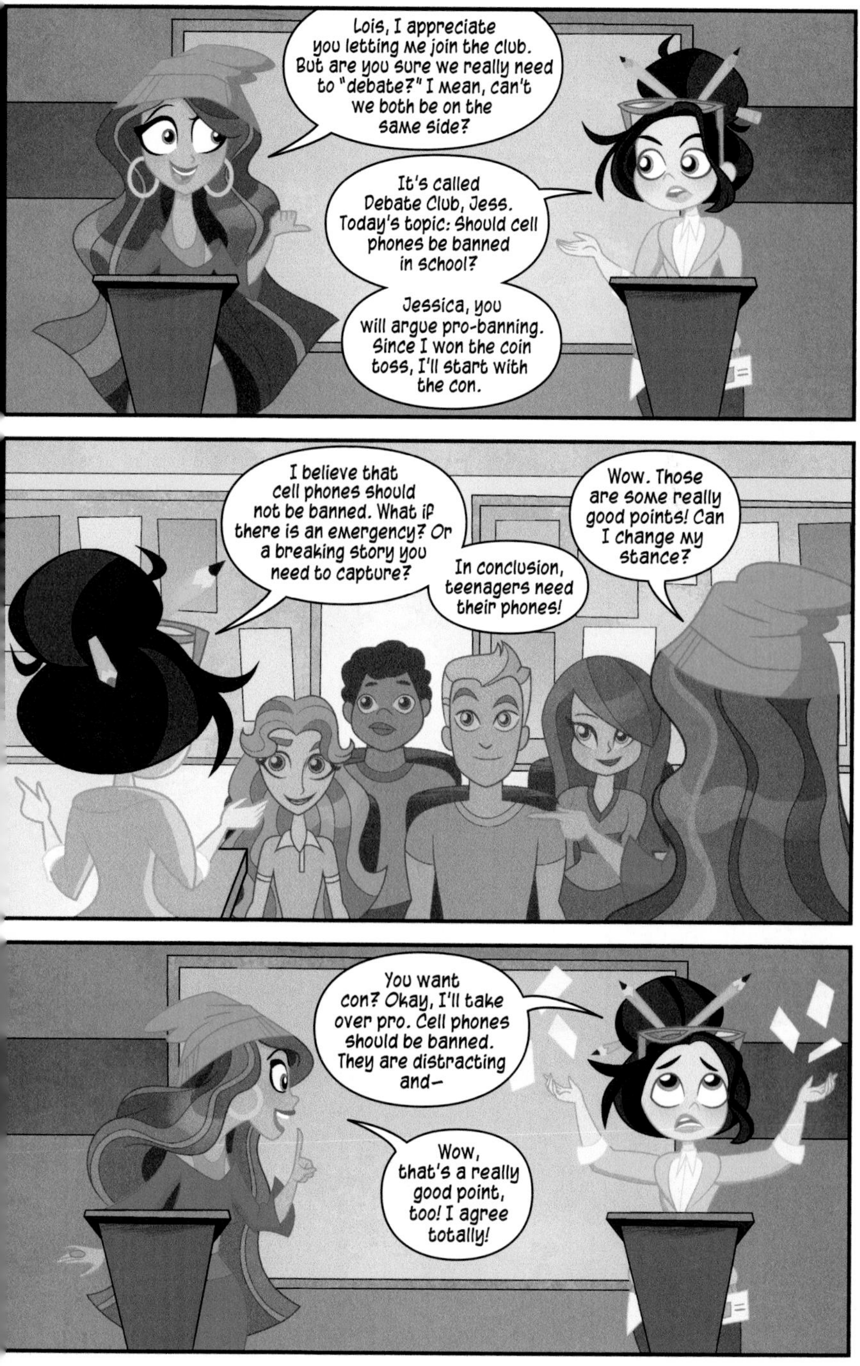

Lois, I appreciate you letting me join the club. But are you sure we really need to "debate?" I mean, can't we both be on the same side?
It's called Debate Club, Jess. Today's topic: Should cell phones be banned in school?
Jessica, you will argue pro-banning. Since I won the coin toss, I'll start with the con.
I believe that cell phones should not be banned. What if there is an emergency? Or a breaking story you need to capture?
In conclusion, teenagers need their phones!
Wow. Those are some really good points! Can I change my stance?
You want con? Okay, I'll take over pro. Cell phones should be banned. They are distracting and–
Wow, that's a really good point, too! I agree totally!

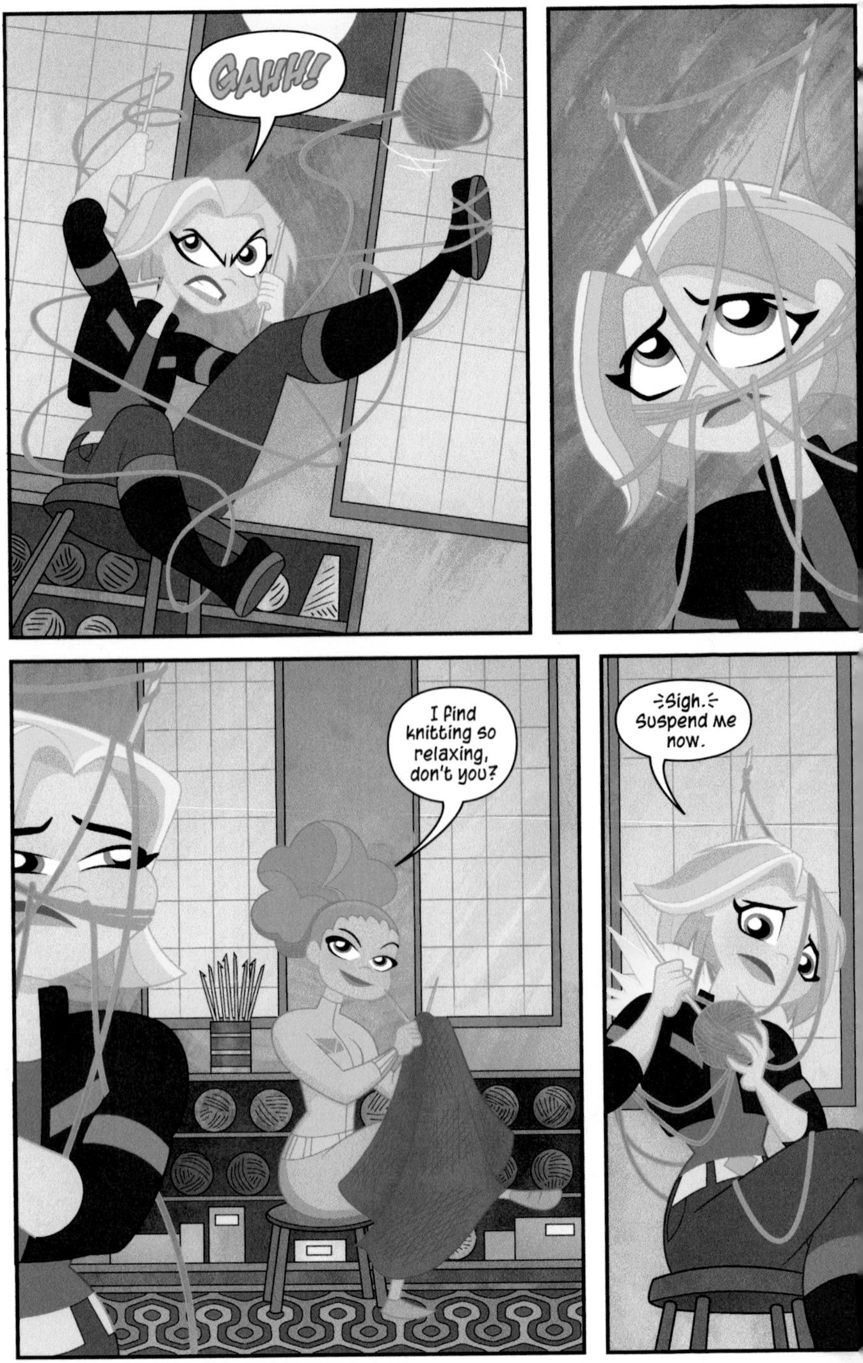
GAHH!
I find knitting so relaxing, don't you?
Sigh. Suspend me now.

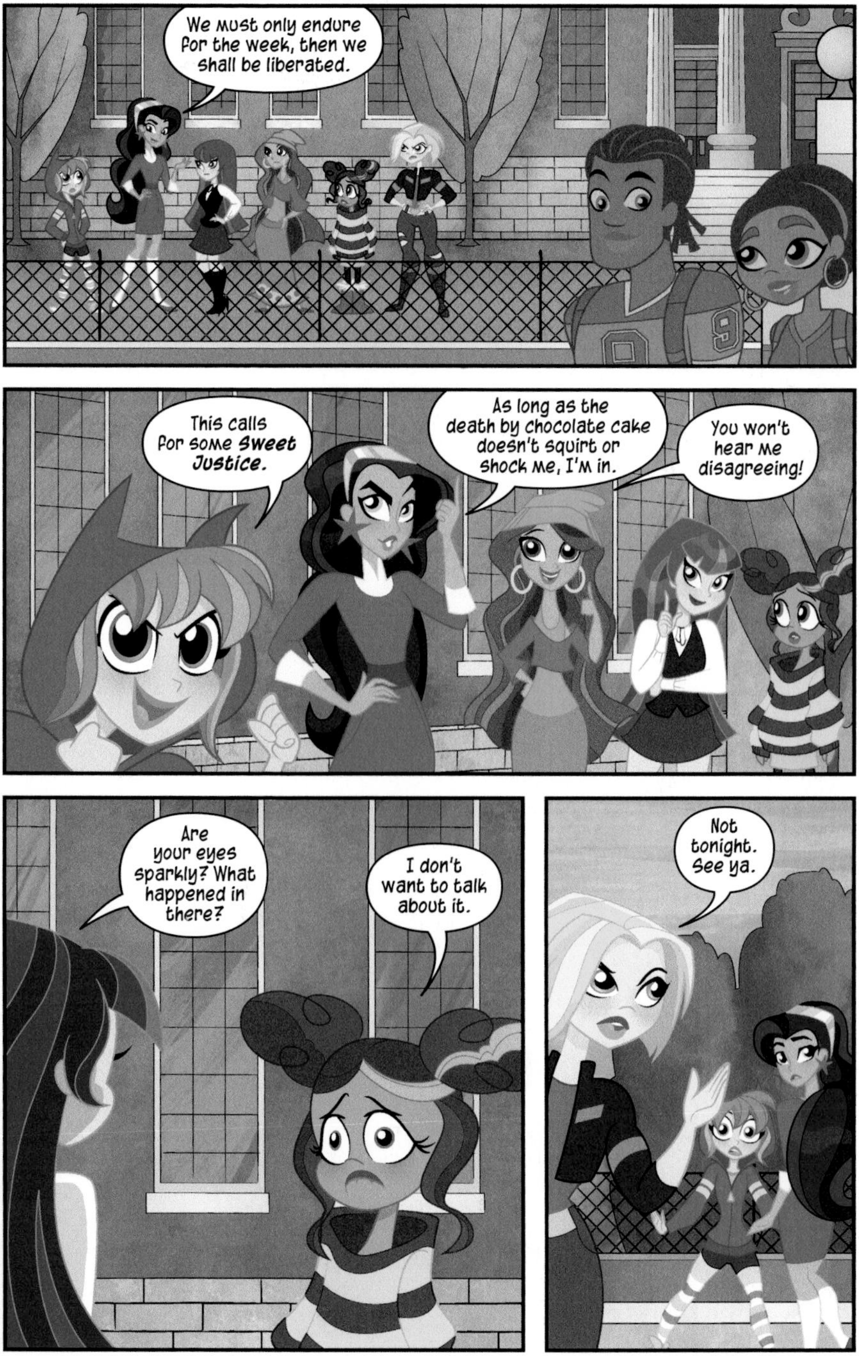
We must only endure for the week, then we shall be liberated.
This calls for some Sweet Justice.
As long as the death by chocolate cake doesn't squirt or shock me, I'm in.
You won't hear me disagreeing!
Are your eyes sparkly? What happened in there?
I don't want to talk about it.
Not tonight. See ya.

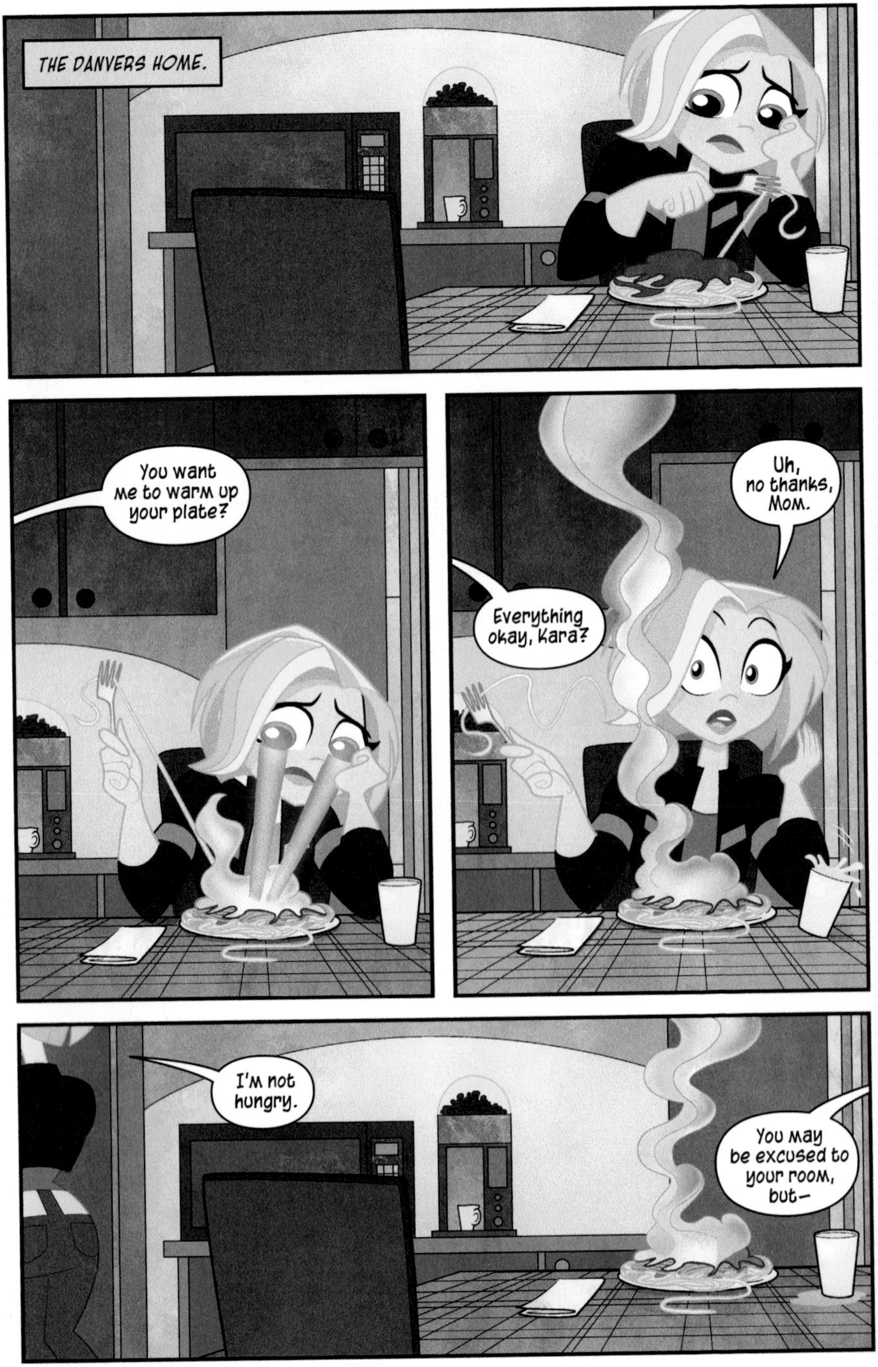
THE DANVERS HOME.
You want me to warm up your plate?
Uh, no thanks, Mom.
Everything okay, Kara?
I'm not hungry.
You may be excused to your room, but—

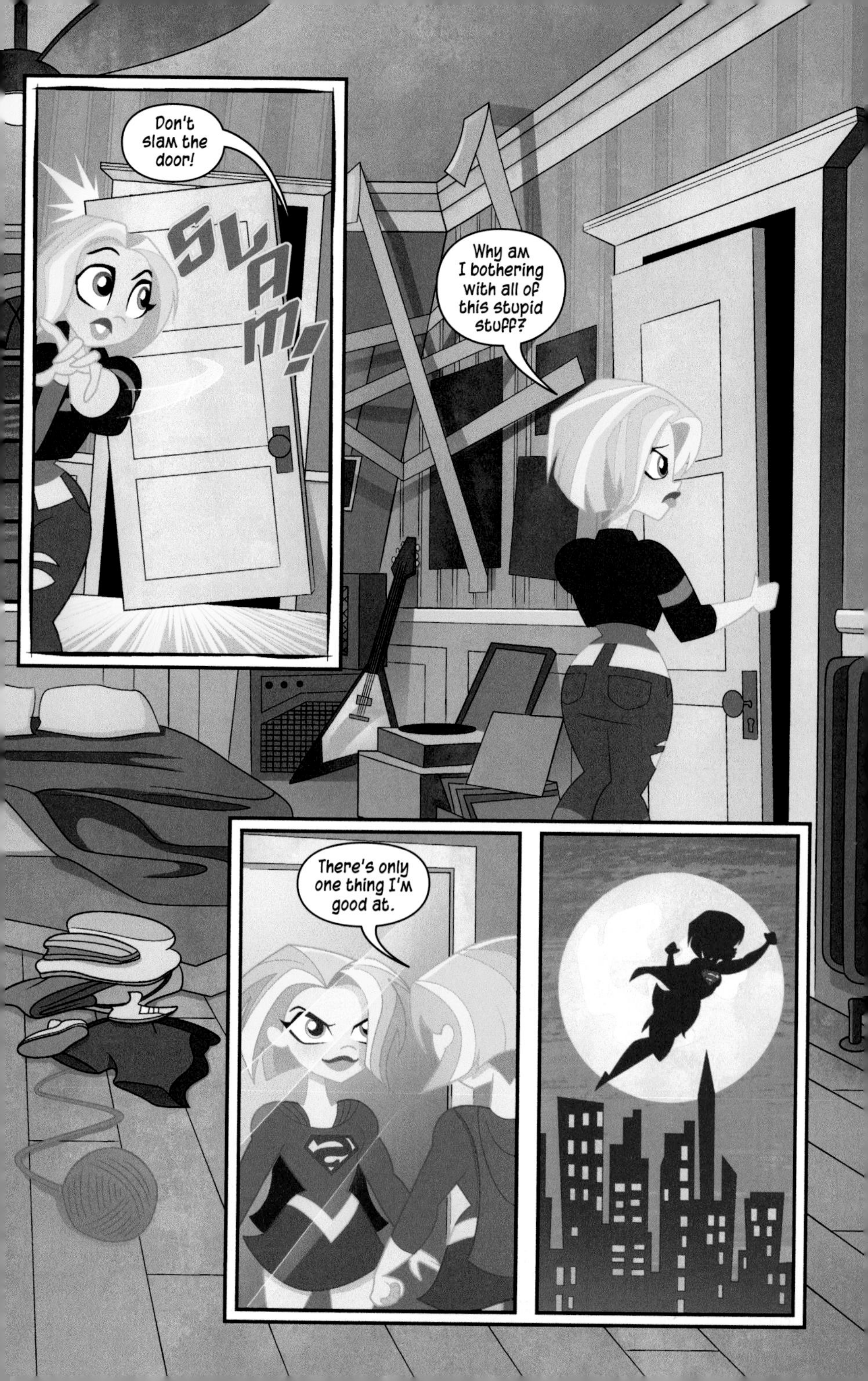
Don't slam the door!
SLAM!
Why am I bothering with all of this stupid stuff?
There's only one thing I'm good at.

chapter four
FLYING SOLO

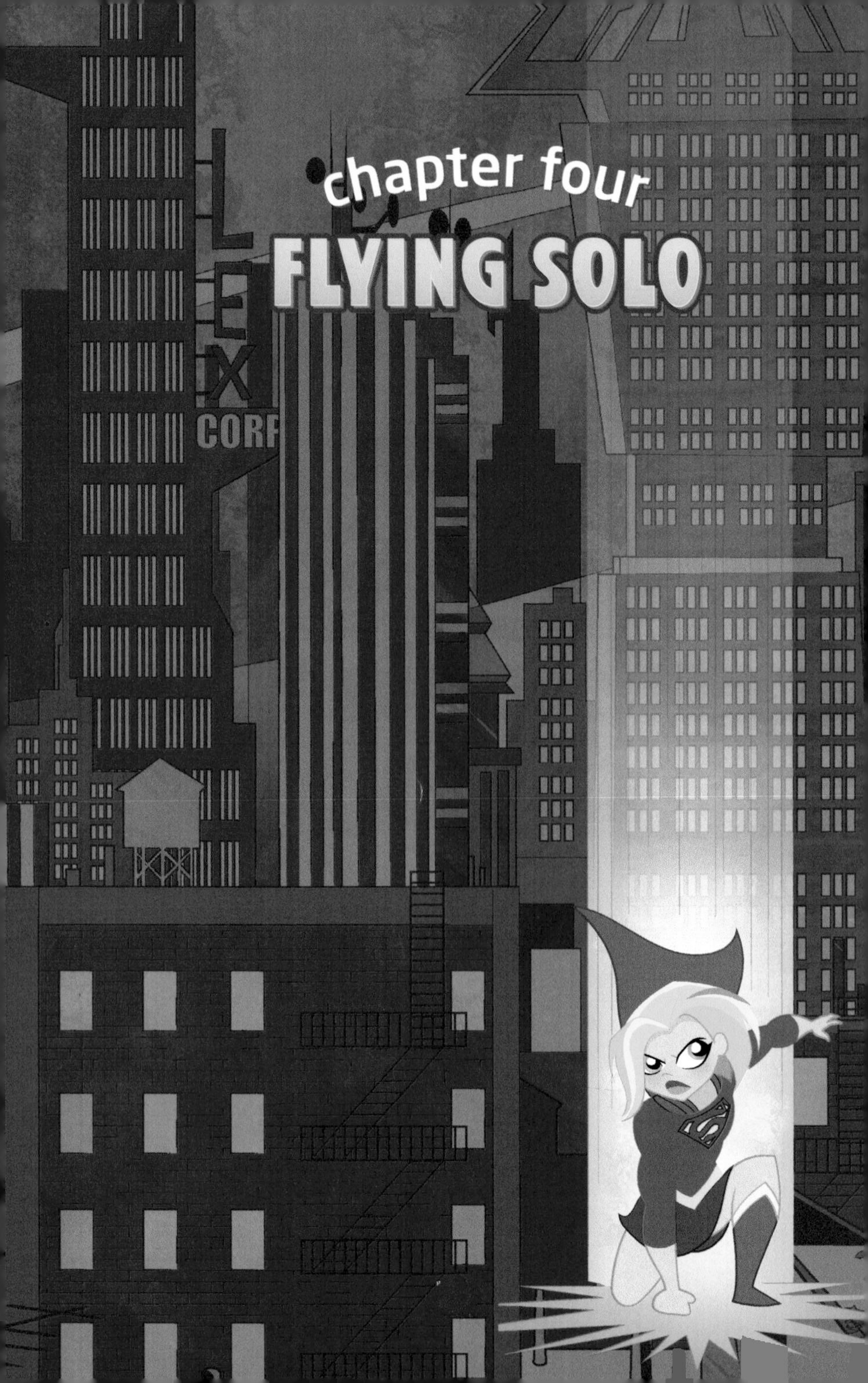
LEX
CORP

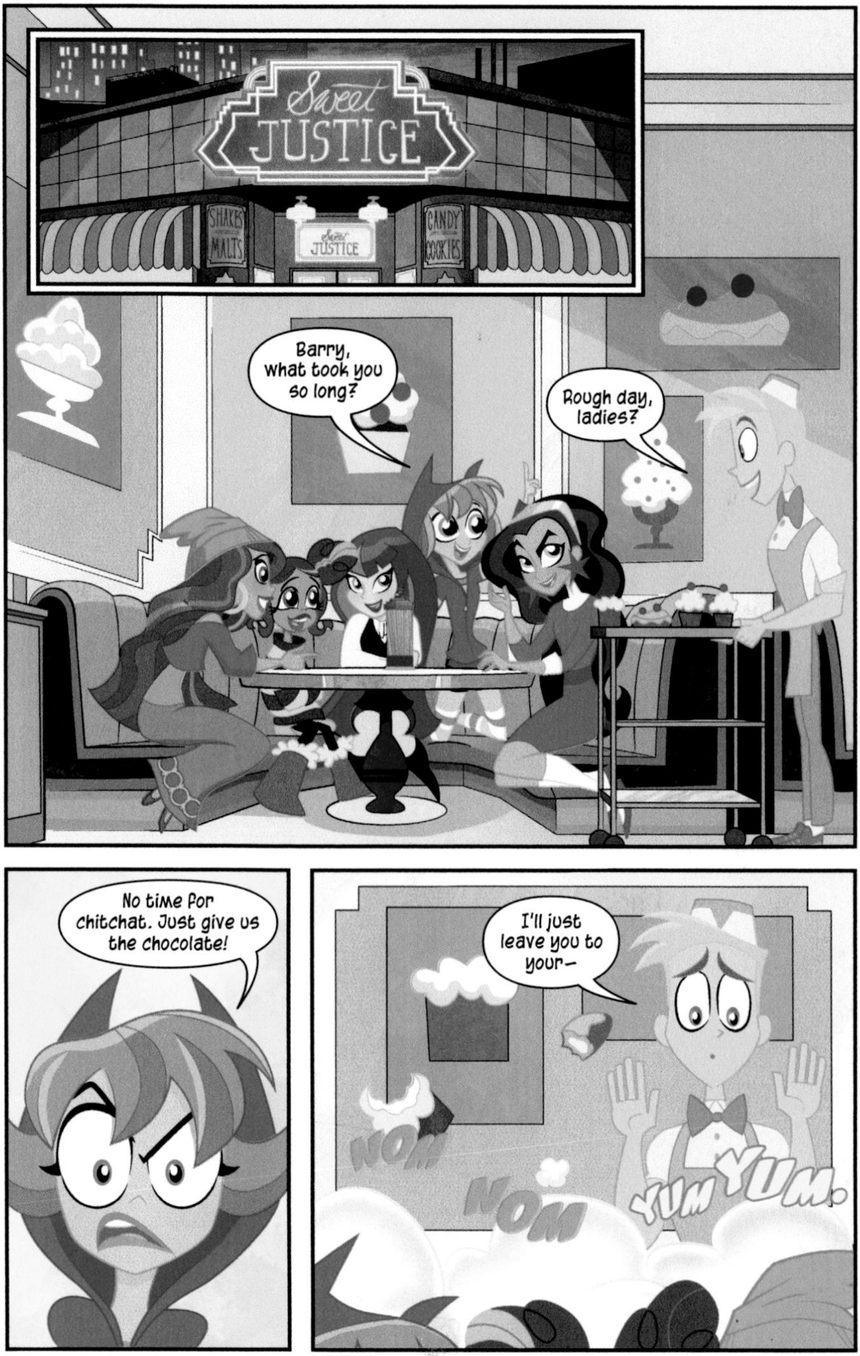

Sweet JUSTICE
SHAKES MALTS
Sweet JUSTICE
CANDY COOKIES
Barry, what took you so long?
Rough day, ladies?
No time for chitchat. Just give us the chocolate!
I'll just leave you to your—
NOM NOM
YUM YUM.

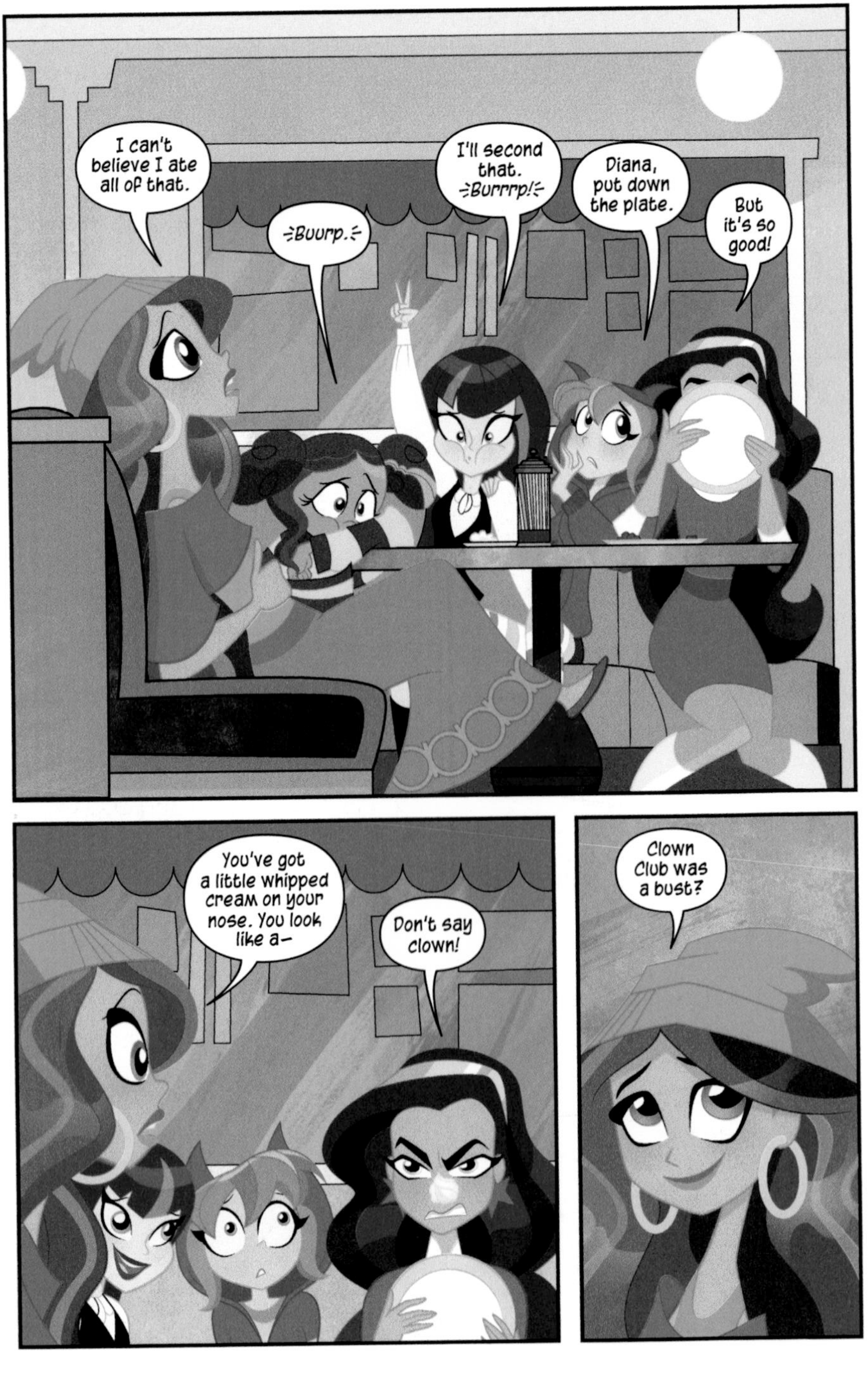
I can't believe I ate all of that.
⇒Buurp.⇐
I'll second that. ⇒Burrrp!⇐
Diana, put down the plate.
But it's so good!
You've got a little whipped cream on your nose. You look like a—
Don't say clown!
Clown Club was a bust?

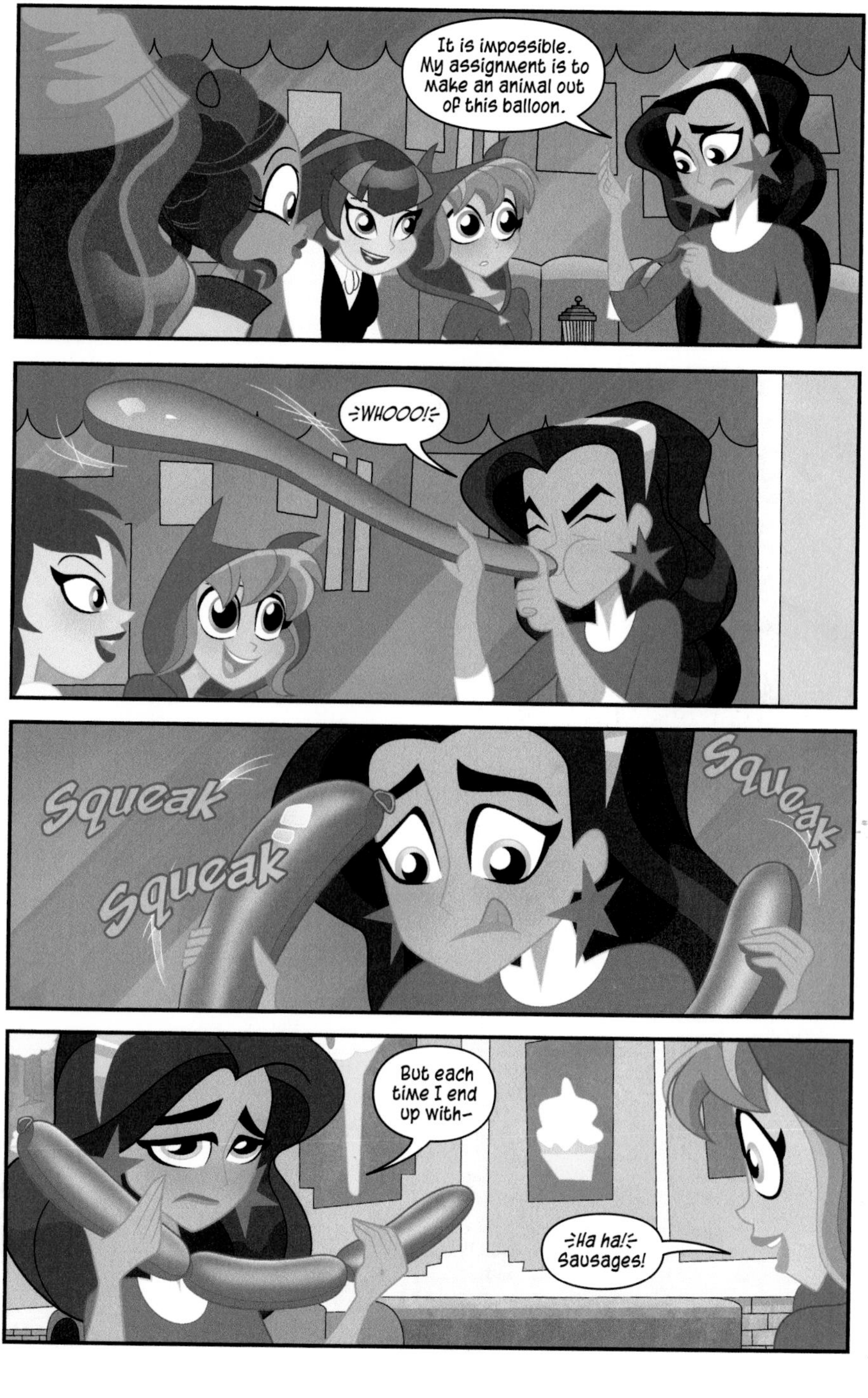
It is impossible. My assignment is to make an animal out of this balloon.
WHOOO!
Squeak
Squeak
Squeak
But each time I end up with-
Ha ha! Sausages!

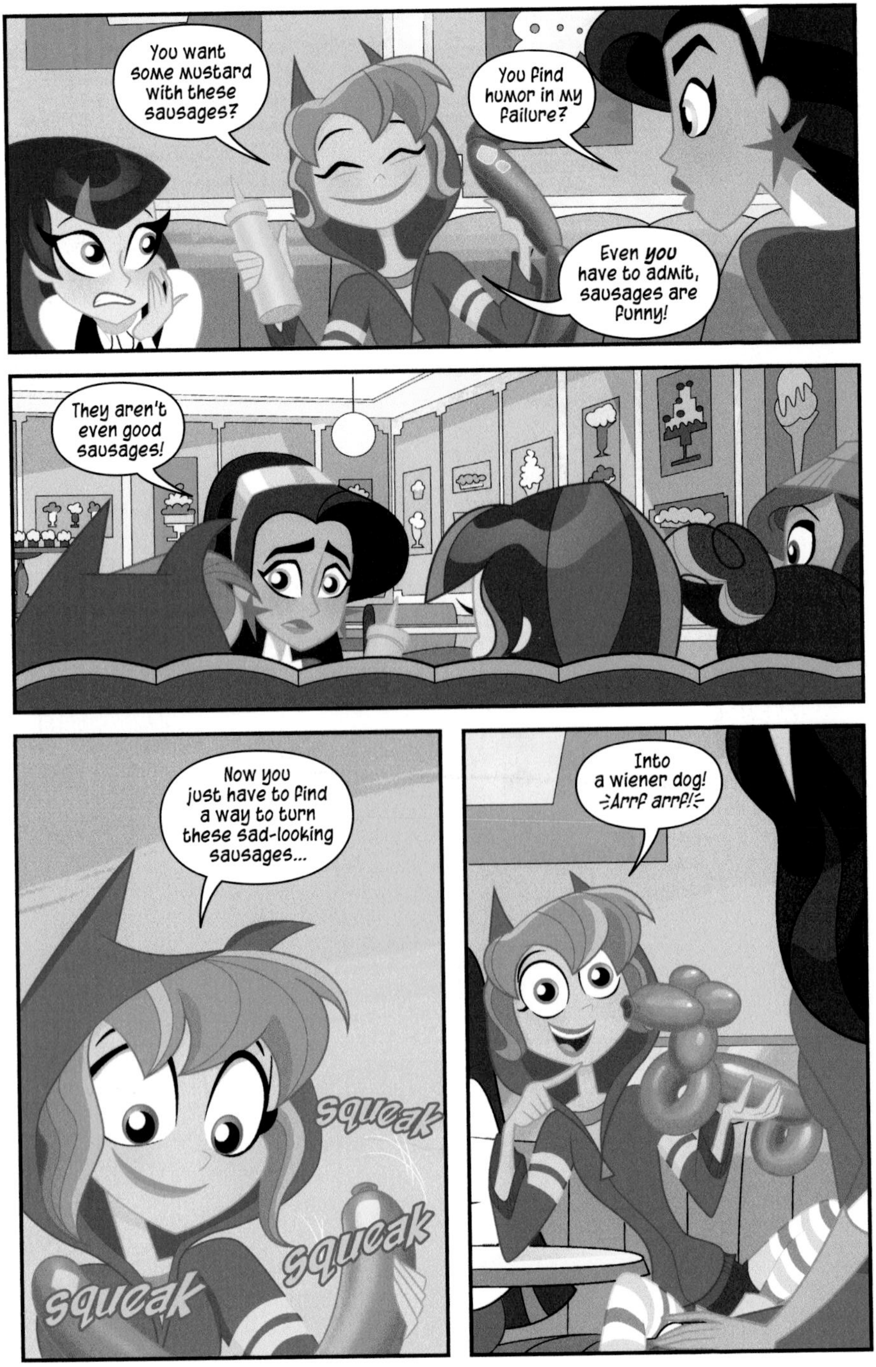
You want some mustard with these sausages?
You find humor in my failure?
Even you have to admit, sausages are funny!
They aren't even good sausages!
Now you just have to find a way to turn these sad-looking sausages...
squeak
squeak
squeak
Into a wiener dog! Arrf arrf!

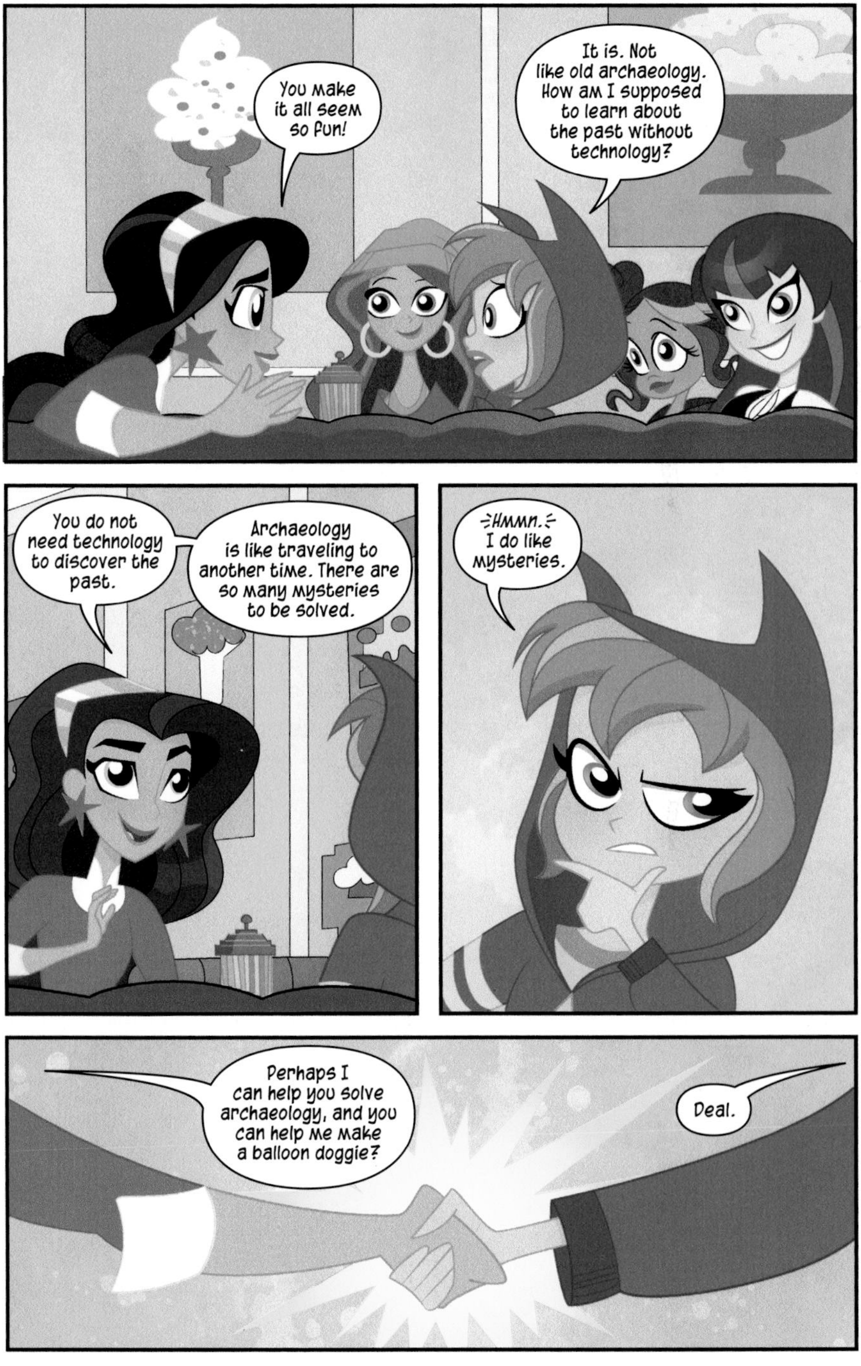
You make it all seem so fun!
It is. Not like old archaeology. How am I supposed to learn about the past without technology?
You do not need technology to discover the past.
Archaeology is like traveling to another time. There are so many mysteries to be solved.
HMMN. I do like mysteries.
Perhaps I can help you solve archaeology, and you can help me make a balloon doggie?
Deal.

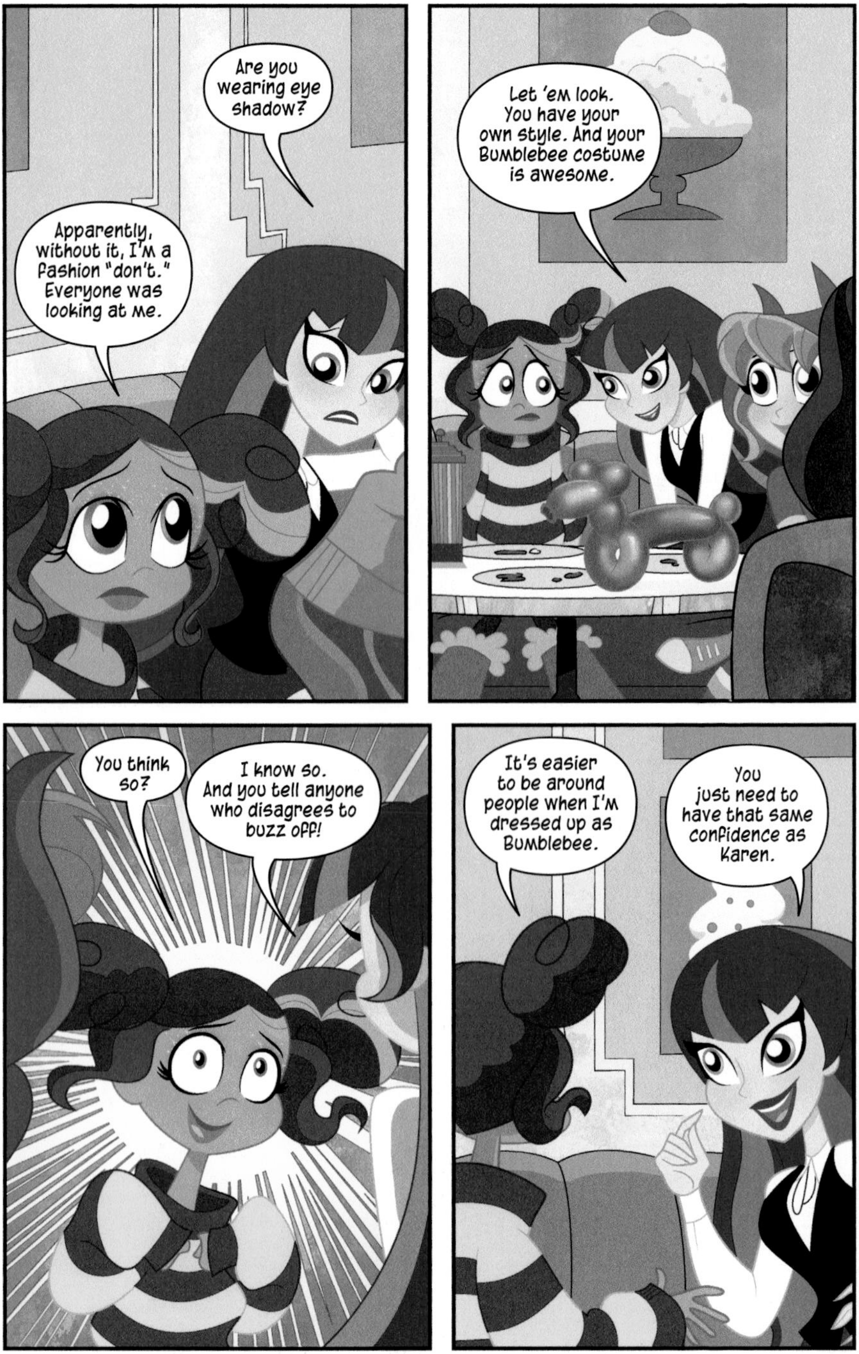
Are you wearing eye shadow?
Apparently, without it, I'M a fashion "don't." Everyone was looking at me.
Let 'em look. You have your own style. And your Bumblebee costume is awesome.
You think so?
I know so. And you tell anyone who disagrees to buzz off!
It's easier to be around people when I'M dressed up as Bumblebee.
You just need to have that same confidence as Karen.

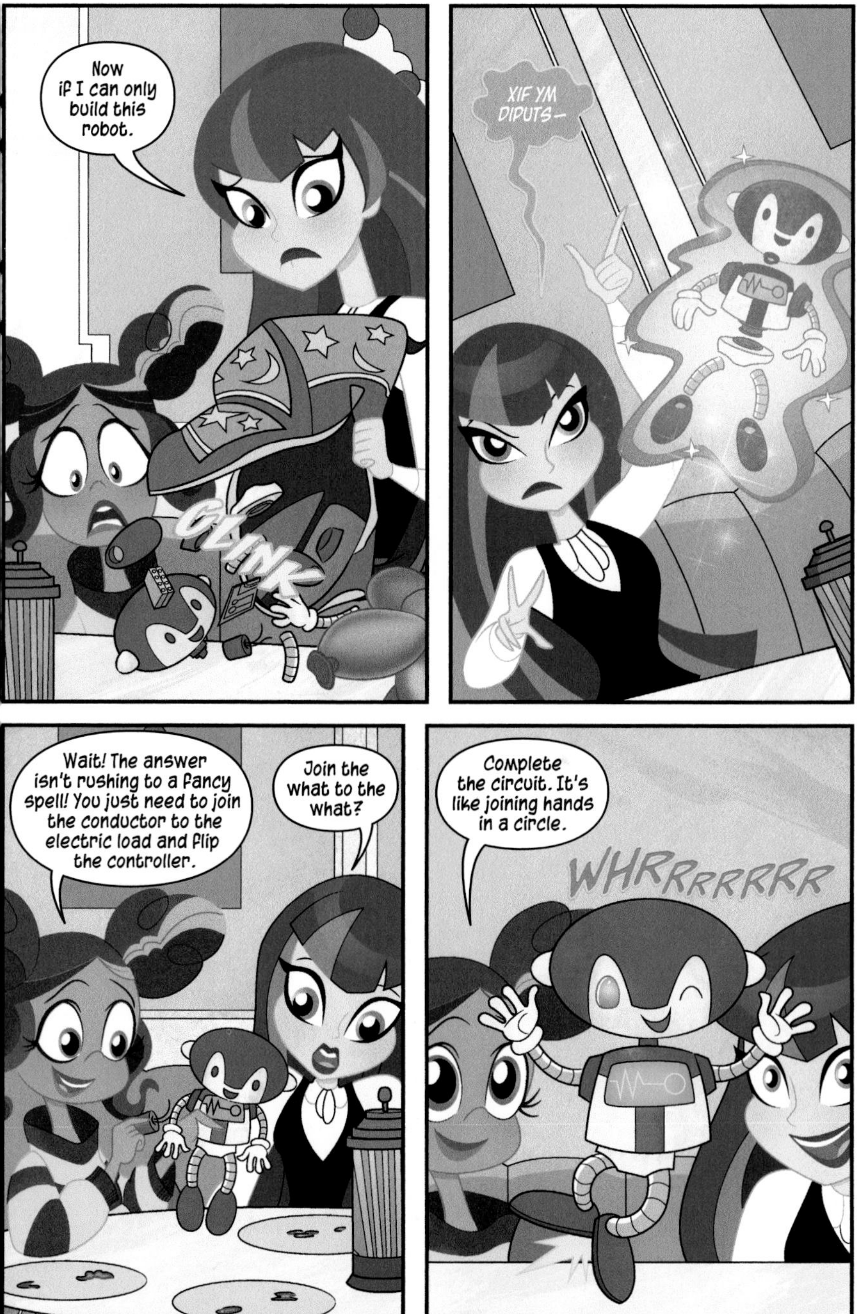
Now if I can only build this robot.
CLINK
XIF YM DIPUTS—
Wait! The answer isn't rushing to a fancy spell! You just need to join the conductor to the electric load and flip the controller.
Join the what to the what?
Complete the circuit. It's like joining hands in a circle.
WHRRRRRRR

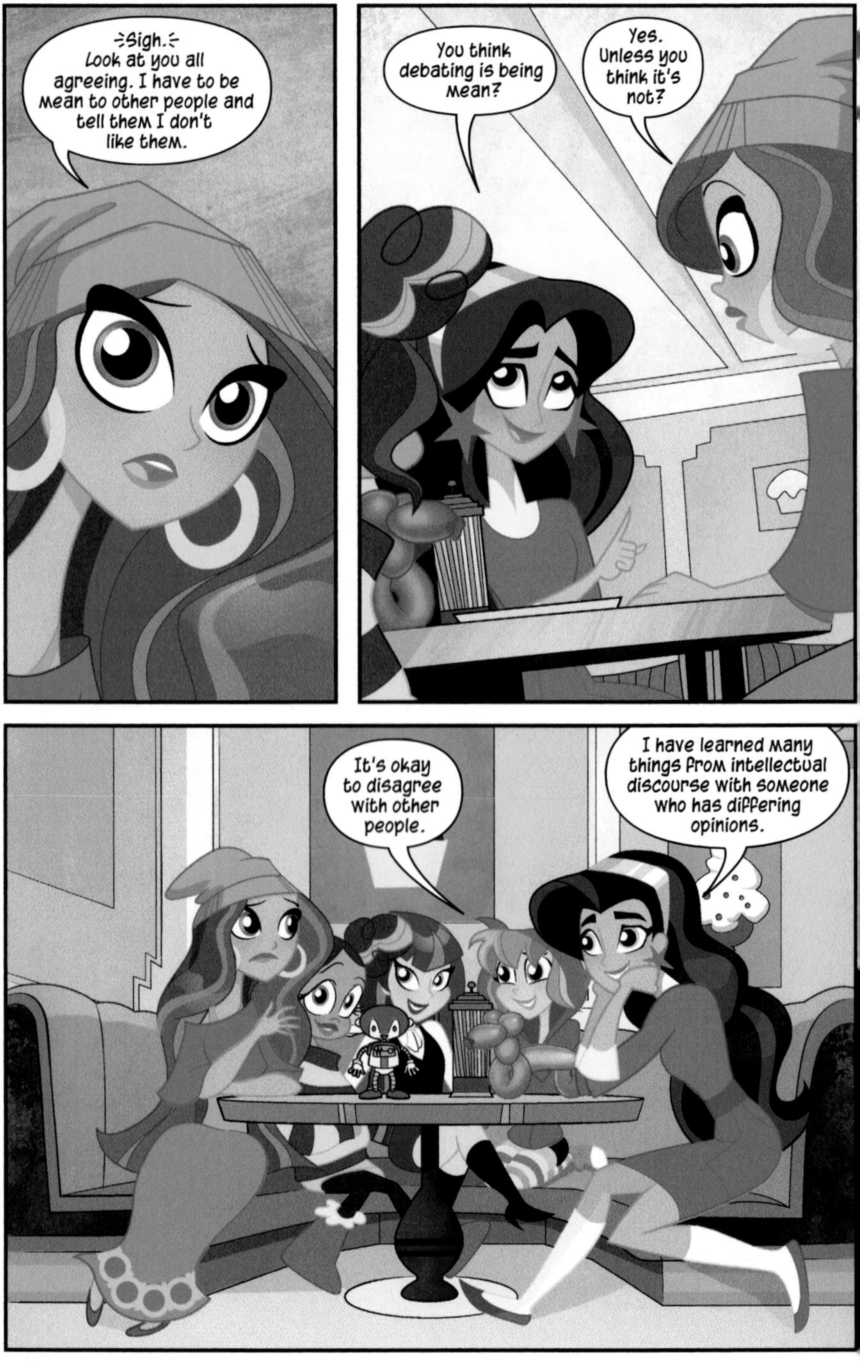

Sigh. Look at you all agreeing. I have to be mean to other people and tell them I don't like them.
You think debating is being mean?
Yes. Unless you think it's not?
It's okay to disagree with other people.
I have learned many things from intellectual discourse with someone who has differing opinions.

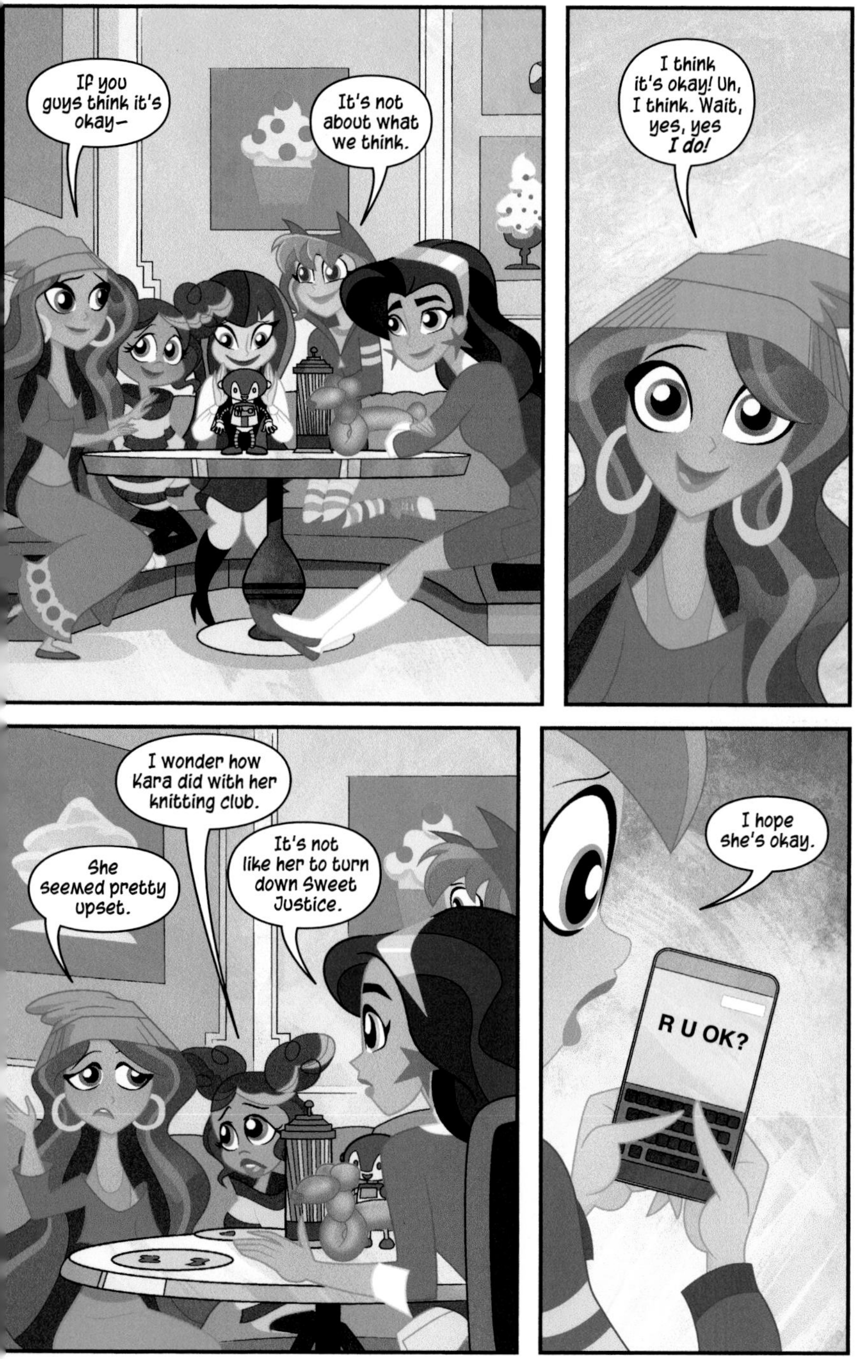
If you guys think it's okay—
It's not about what we think.
I think it's okay! Uh, I think. Wait, yes, yes I do!
I wonder how Kara did with her knitting club.
She seemed pretty upset.
It's not like her to turn down Sweet Justice.
I hope she's okay.
R U OK?

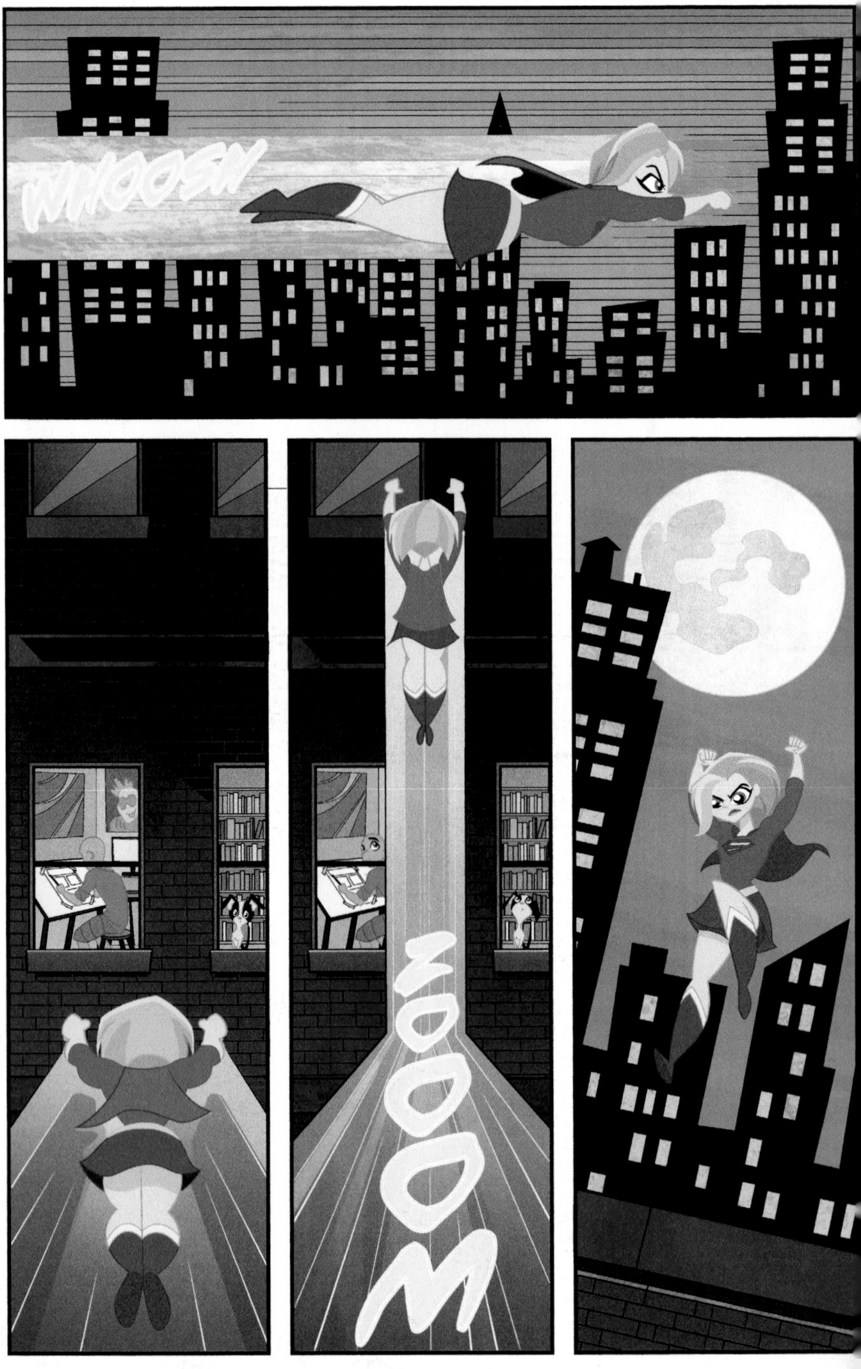
WHOOSH
ZOOOM

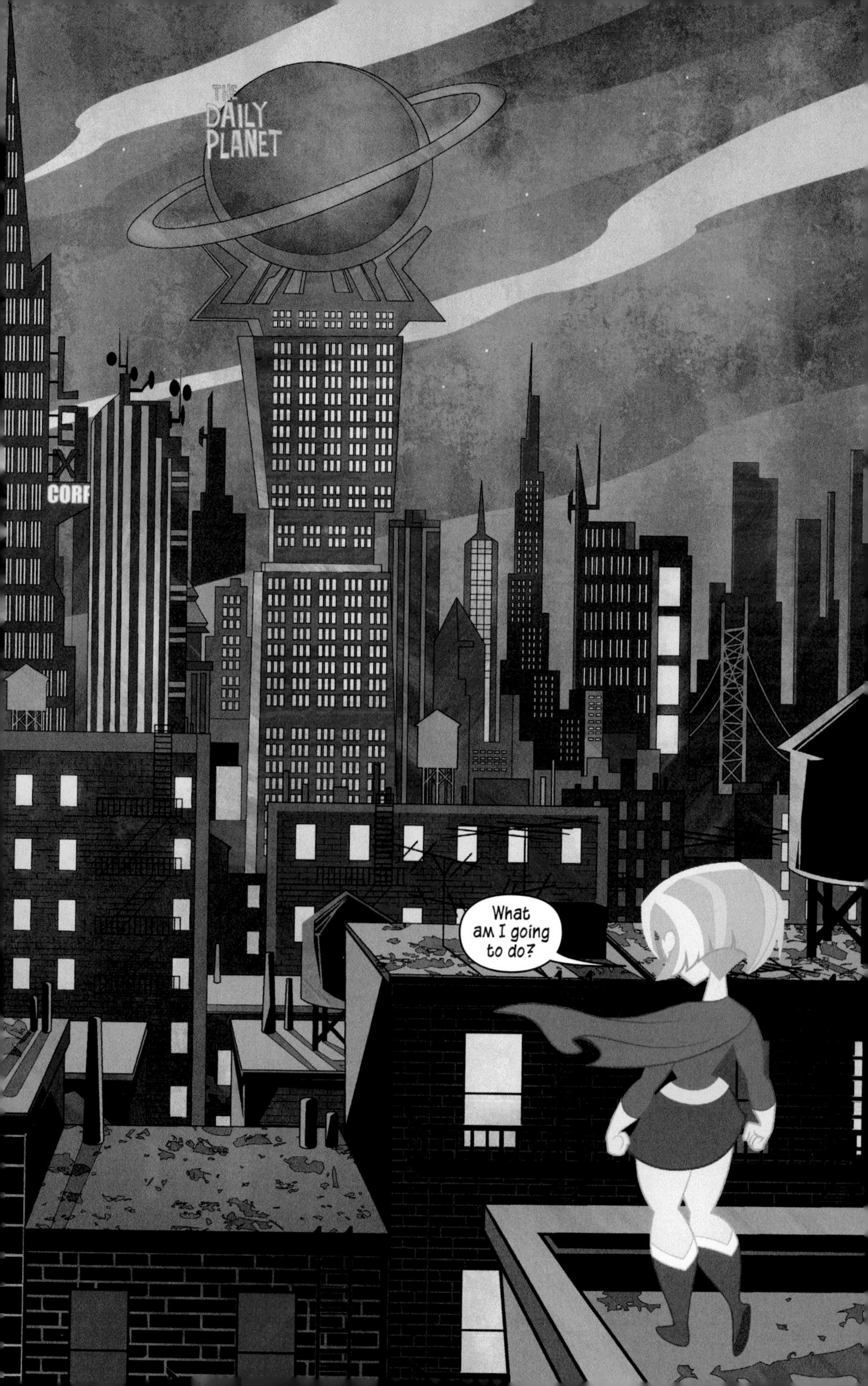
THE DAILY PLANET
LEX CORP
What am I going to do?

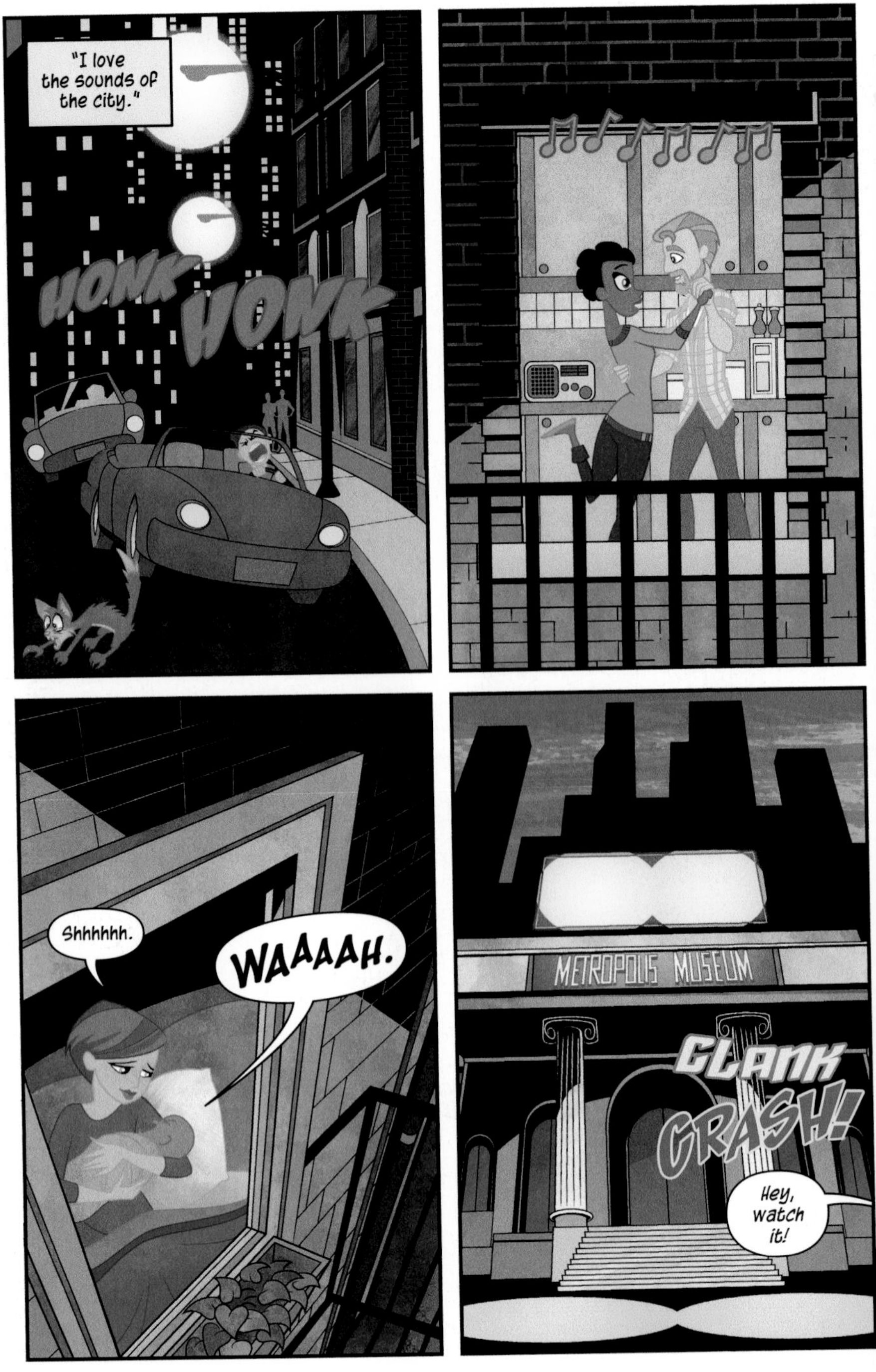
"I love the sounds of the city."
HONK
HONK
Shhhhhh.
WAAAAH.
METROPOLIS MUSEUM
CLANK
CRASH!
Hey, watch it!

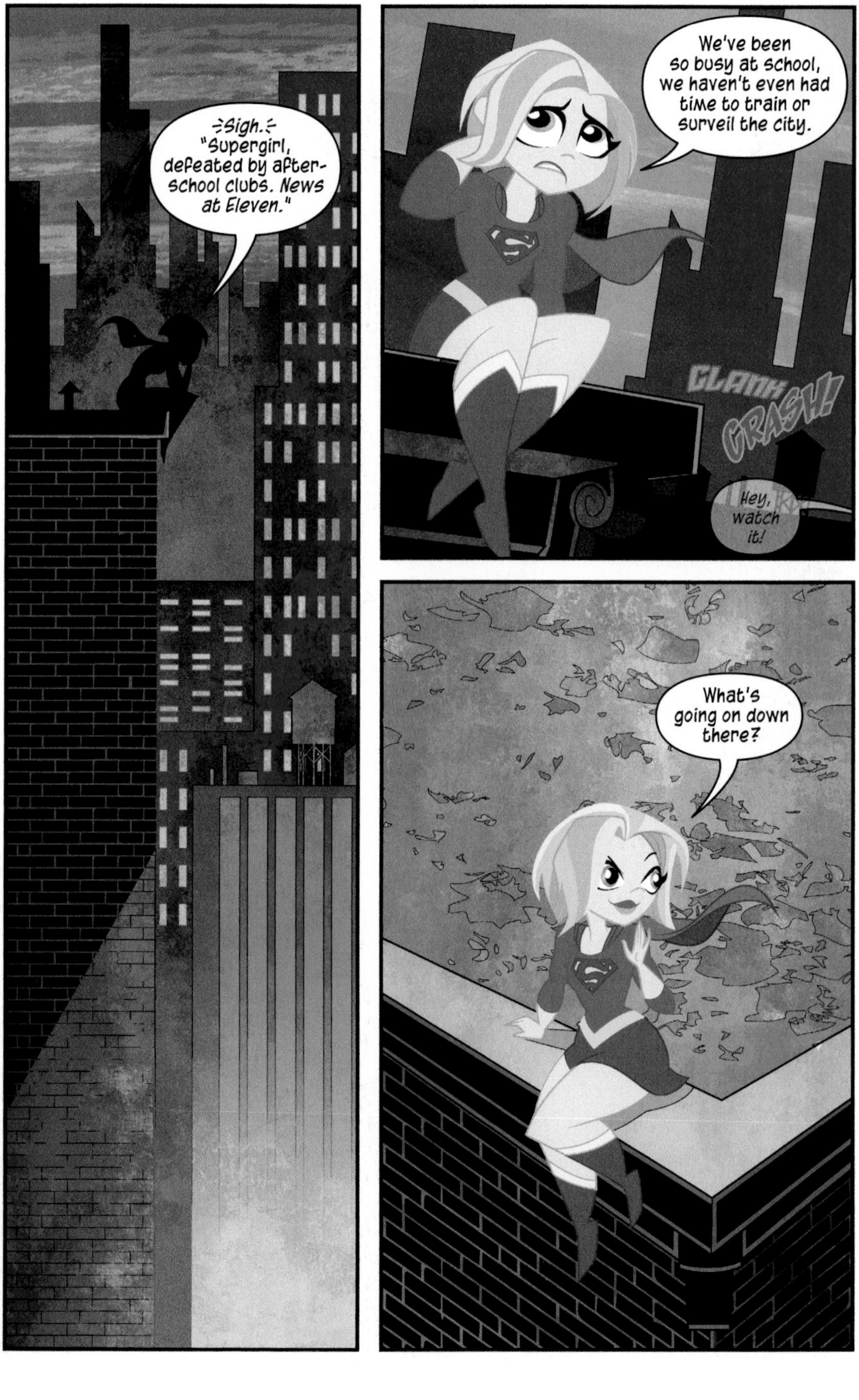
Sigh. "Supergirl, defeated by after-school clubs. News at Eleven."
We've been so busy at school, we haven't even had time to train or surveil the city.
CLANK
CRASH!
Hey, watch it!
What's going on down there?

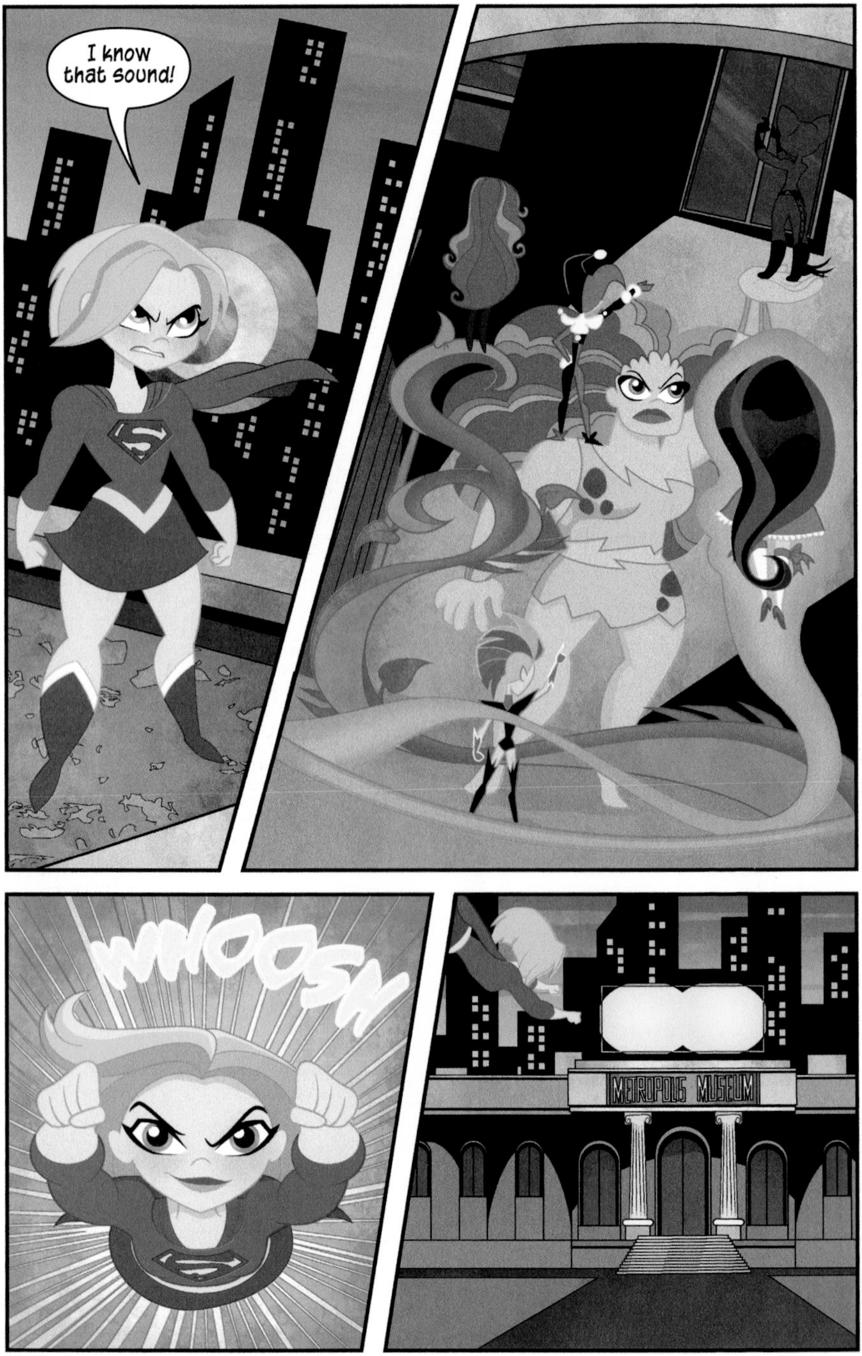
I know that sound!
WHOOSH
METROPOLIS MUSEUM

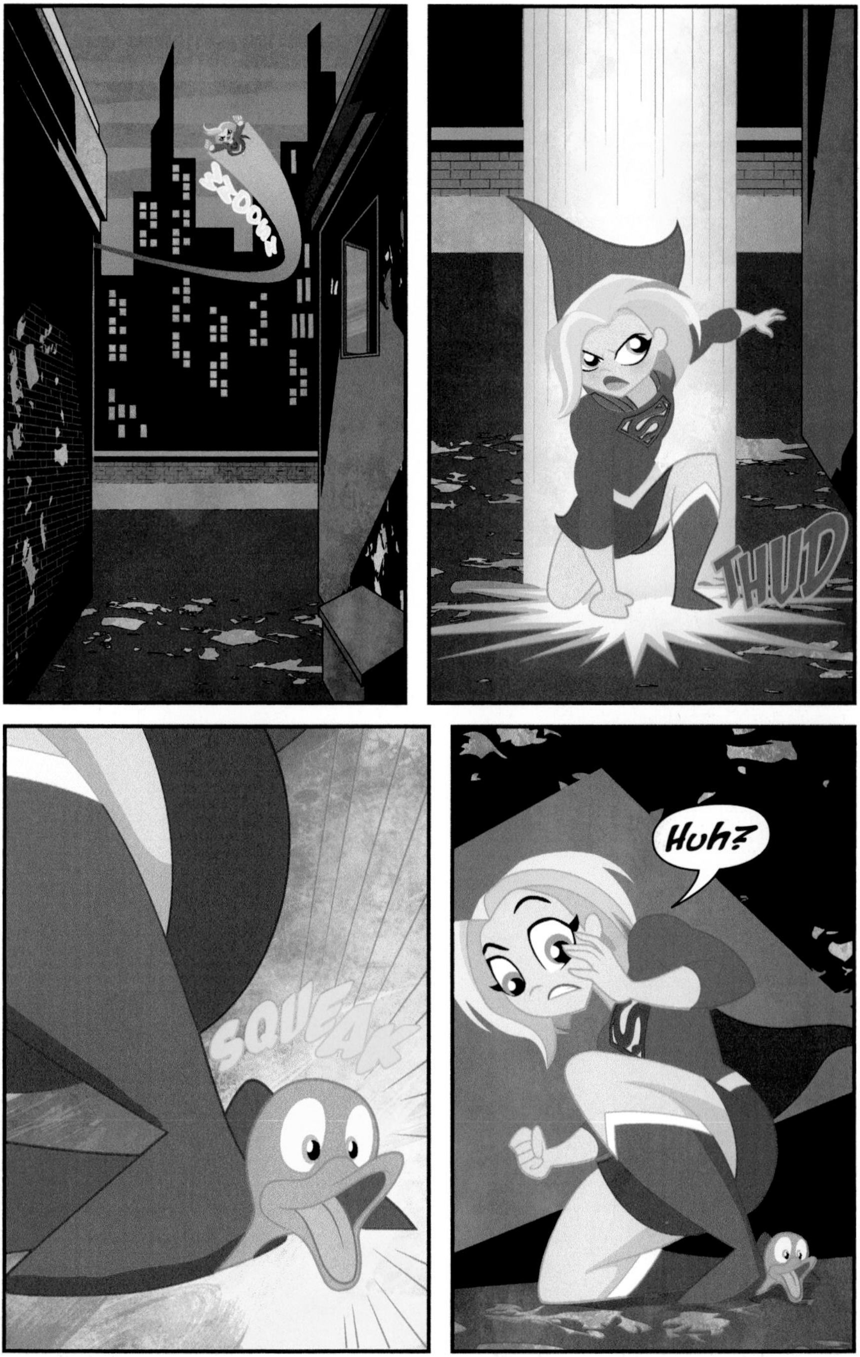
THUD
SQUEAK
Huh?

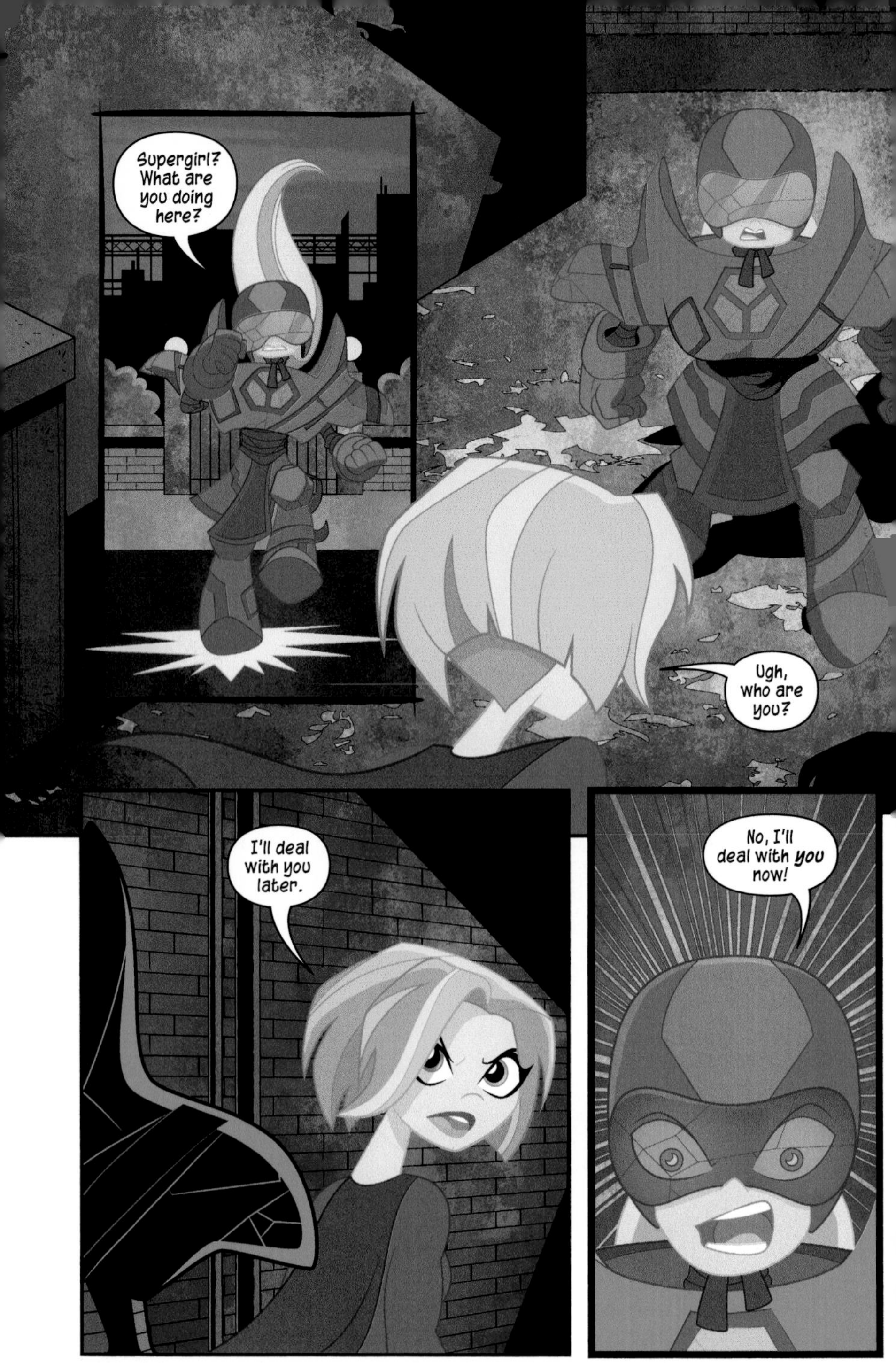
Supergirl!? What are you doing here?
Ugh, who are you?
I'll deal with you later.
No, I'll deal with *you* now!

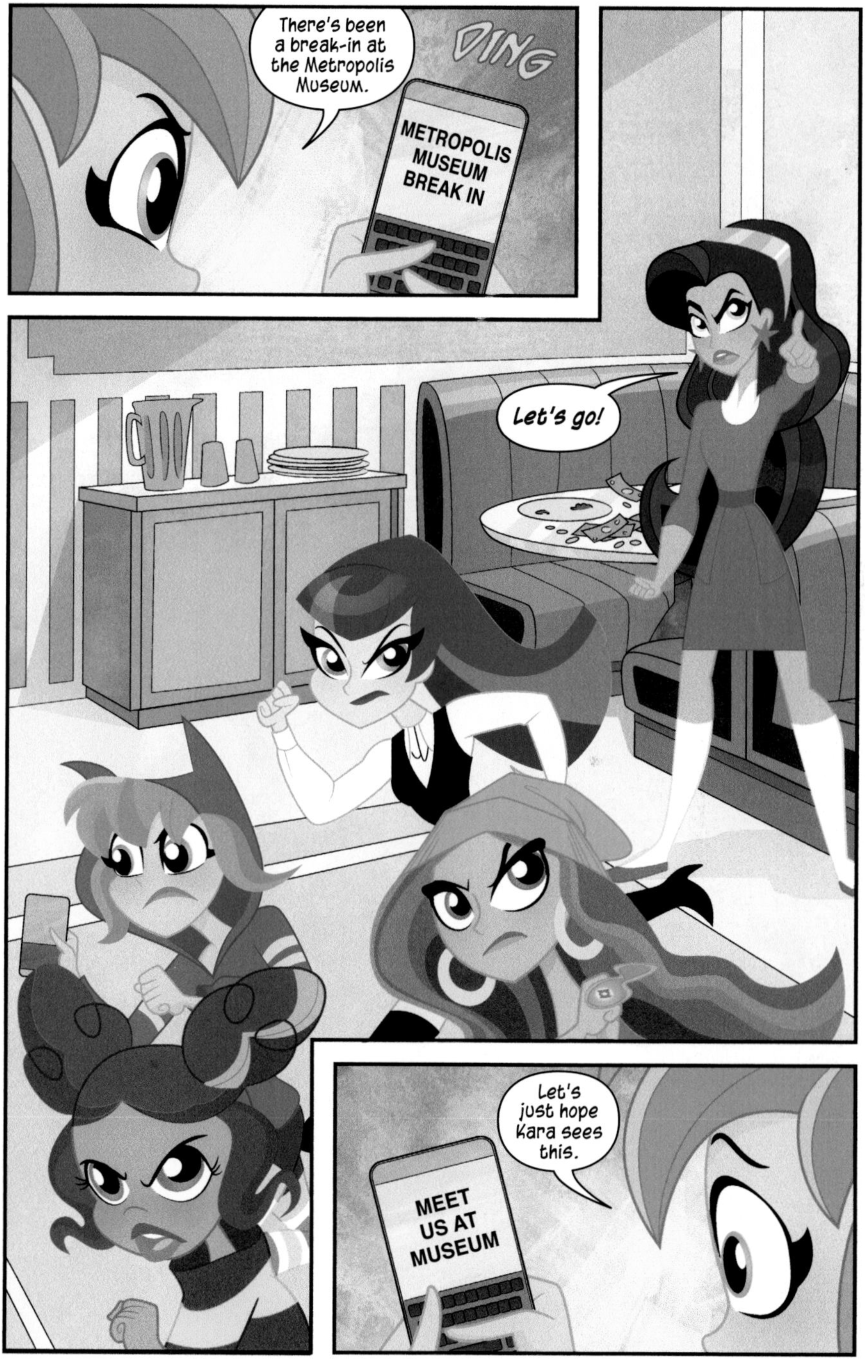
There's been a break-in at the Metropolis Museum.
DING
METROPOLIS MUSEUM BREAK IN
Let's go!
Let's just hope Kara sees this.
MEET US AT MUSEUM

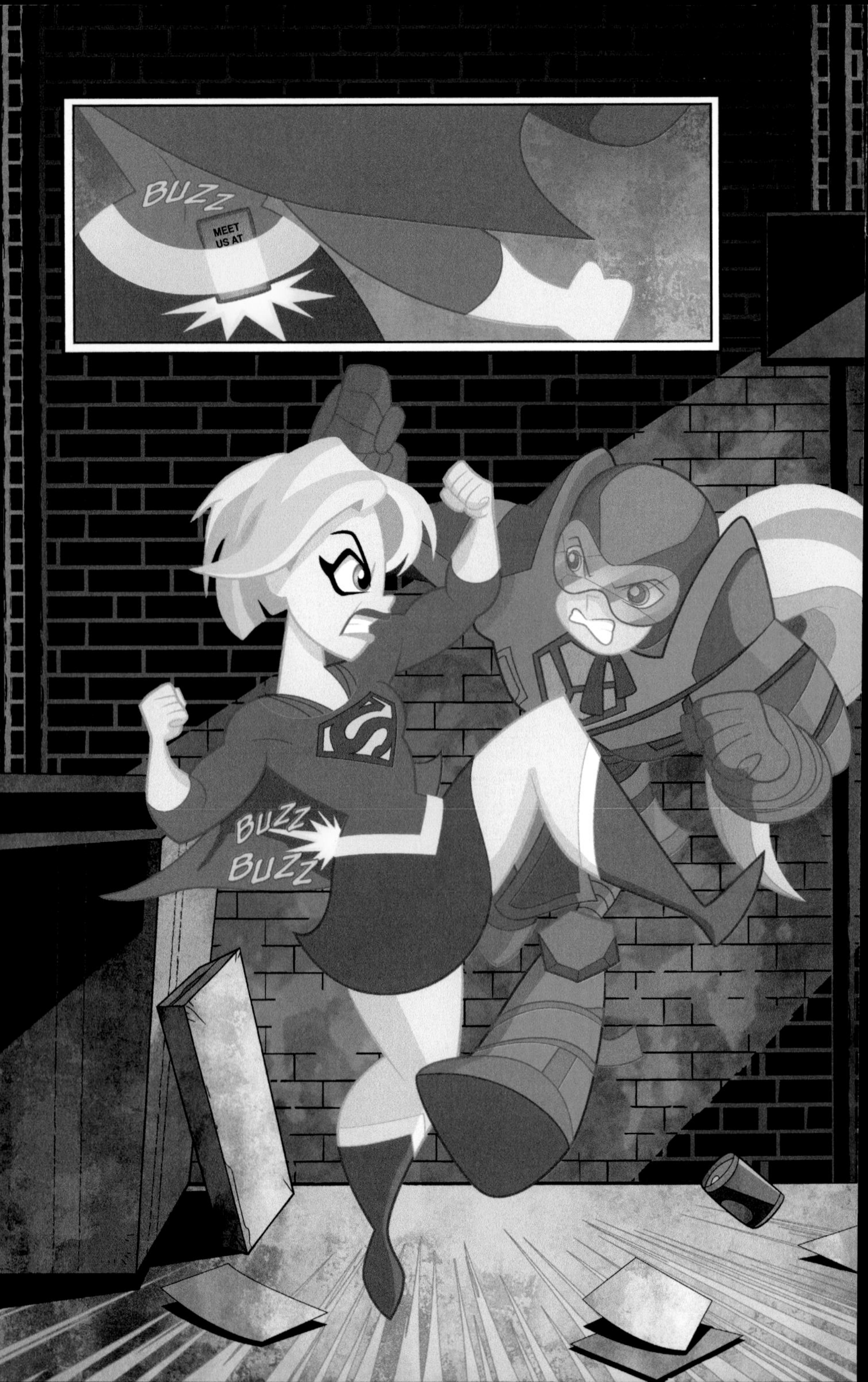
BUZZ
MEET US AT
BUZZ
BUZZ

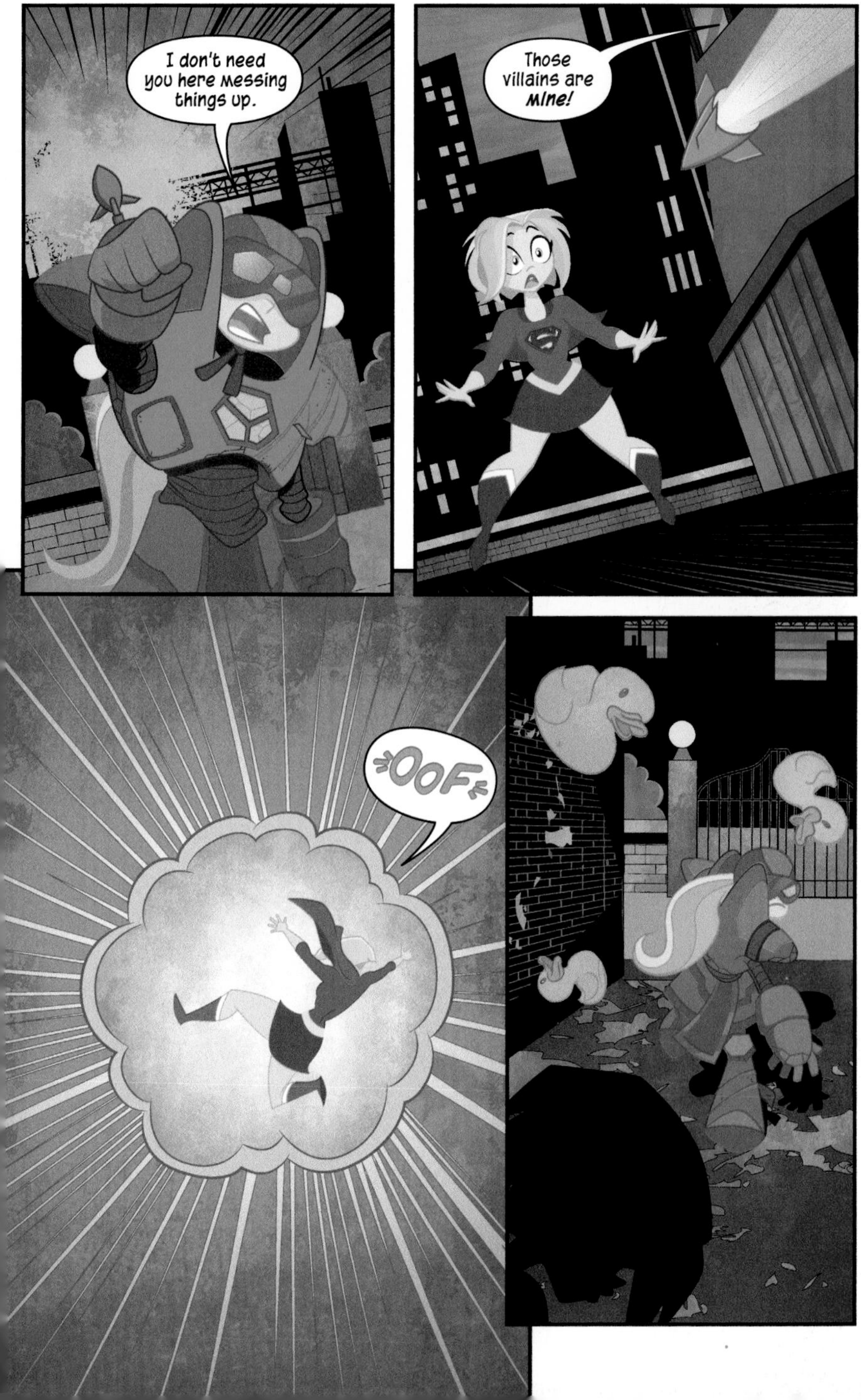
I don't need you here messing things up.
Those villains are MINE!
OOF

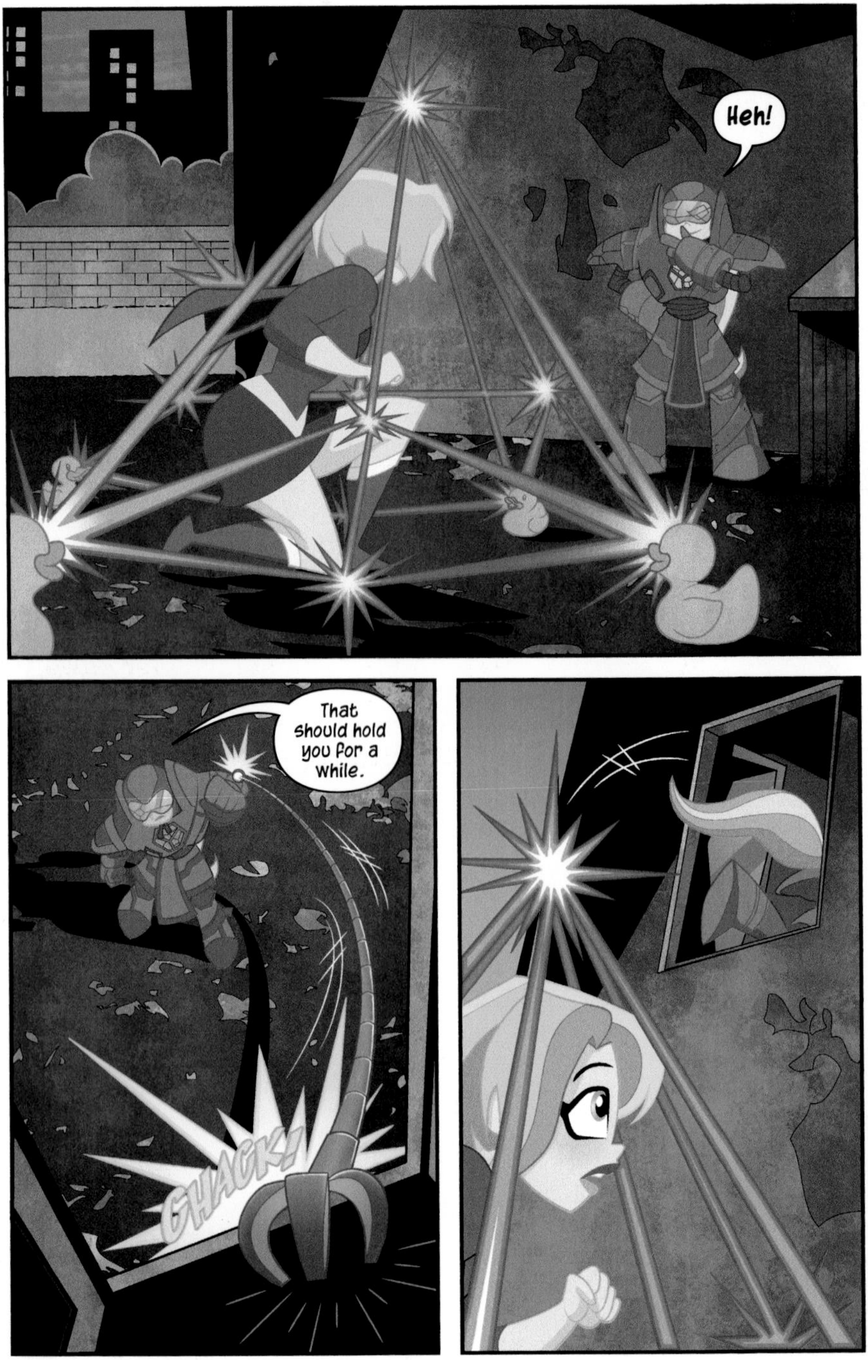
Heh!
That should hold you for a while.
CHACK!

chapter five
MUSEUM MAYHEM

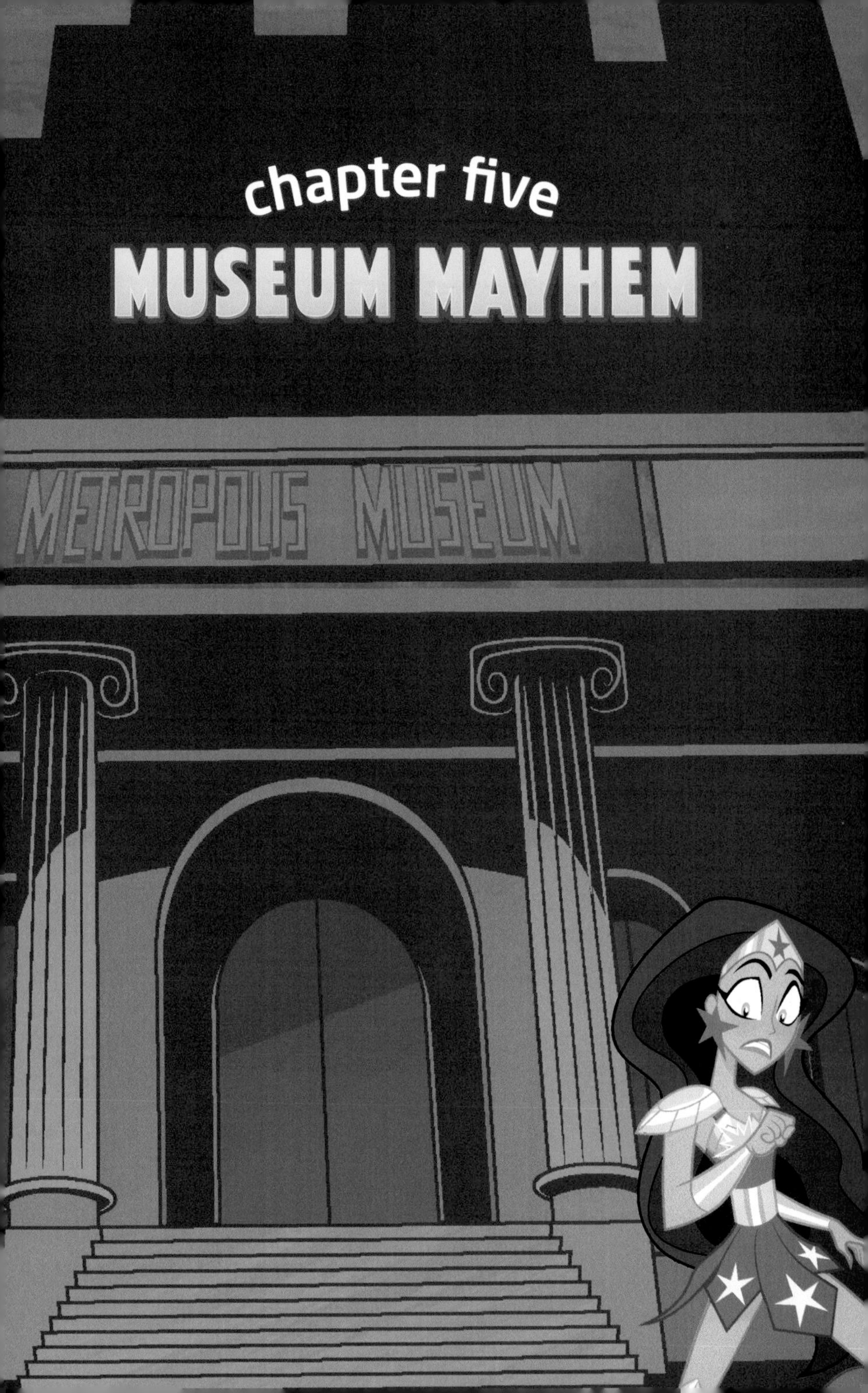
METROPOLIS MUSEUM

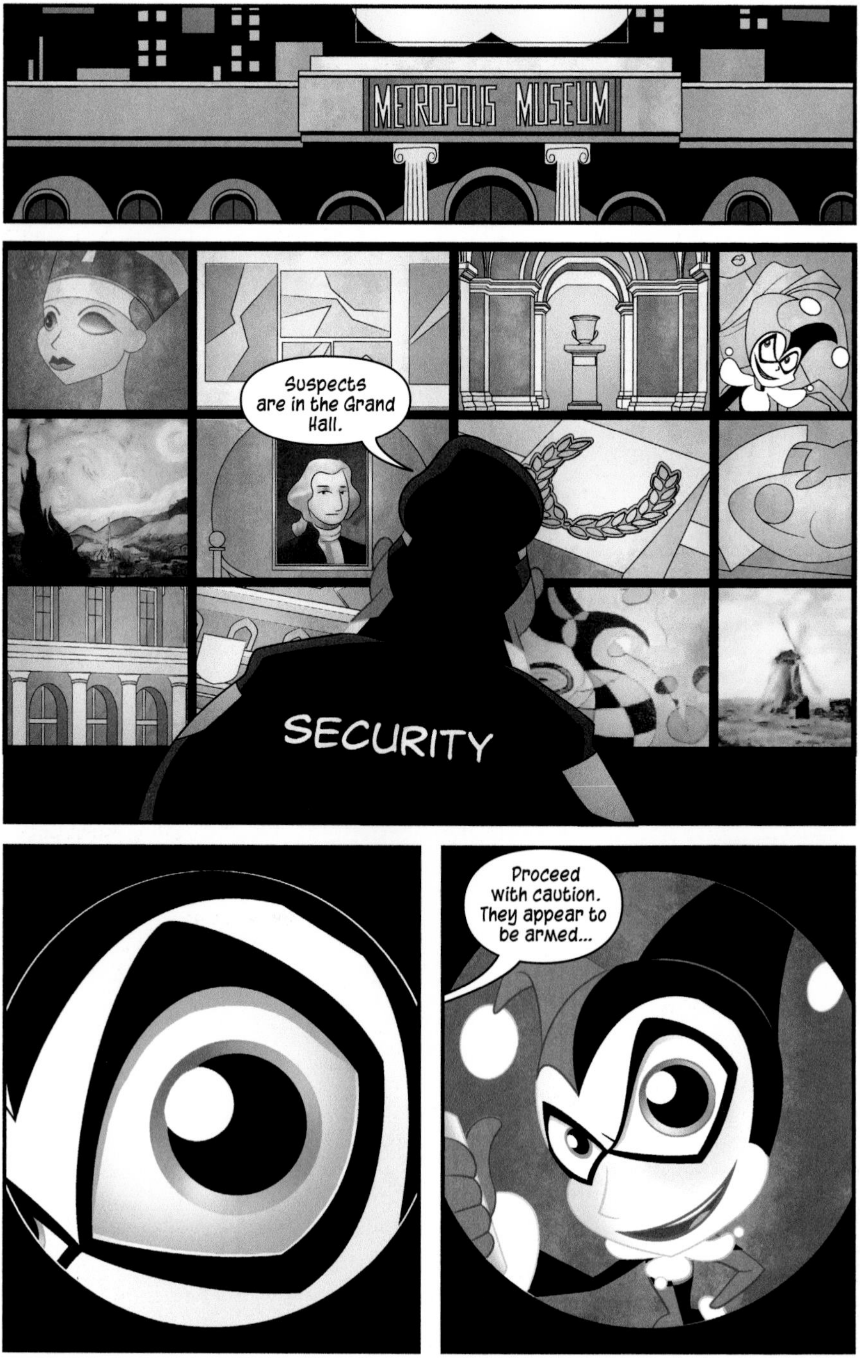
METROPOLIS MUSEUM
Suspects are in the Grand Hall.
SECURITY
Proceed with caution. They appear to be armed...

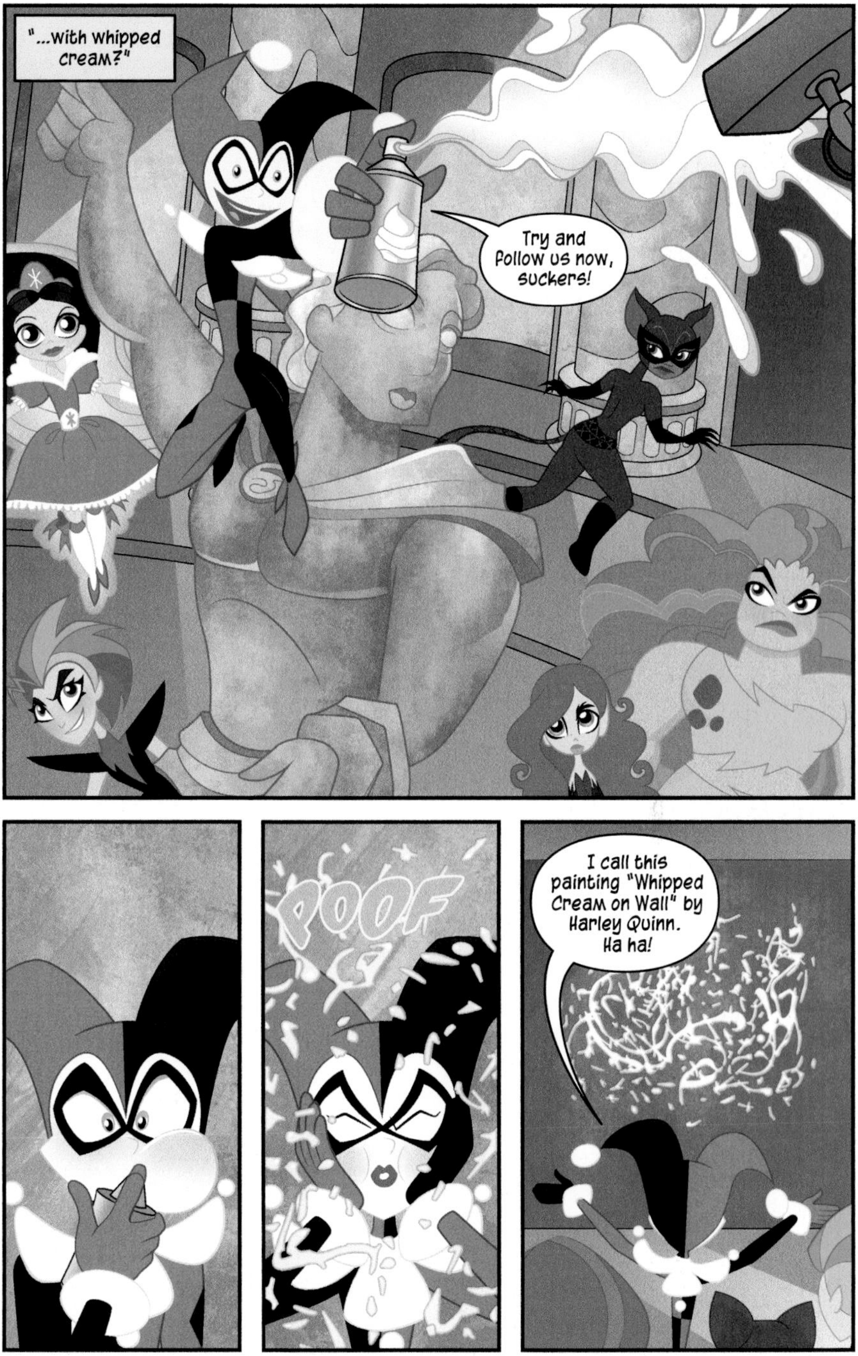
"...with whipped cream?"
Try and follow us now, suckers!
POOF
I call this painting "Whipped Cream on Wall" by Harley Quinn. Ha ha!

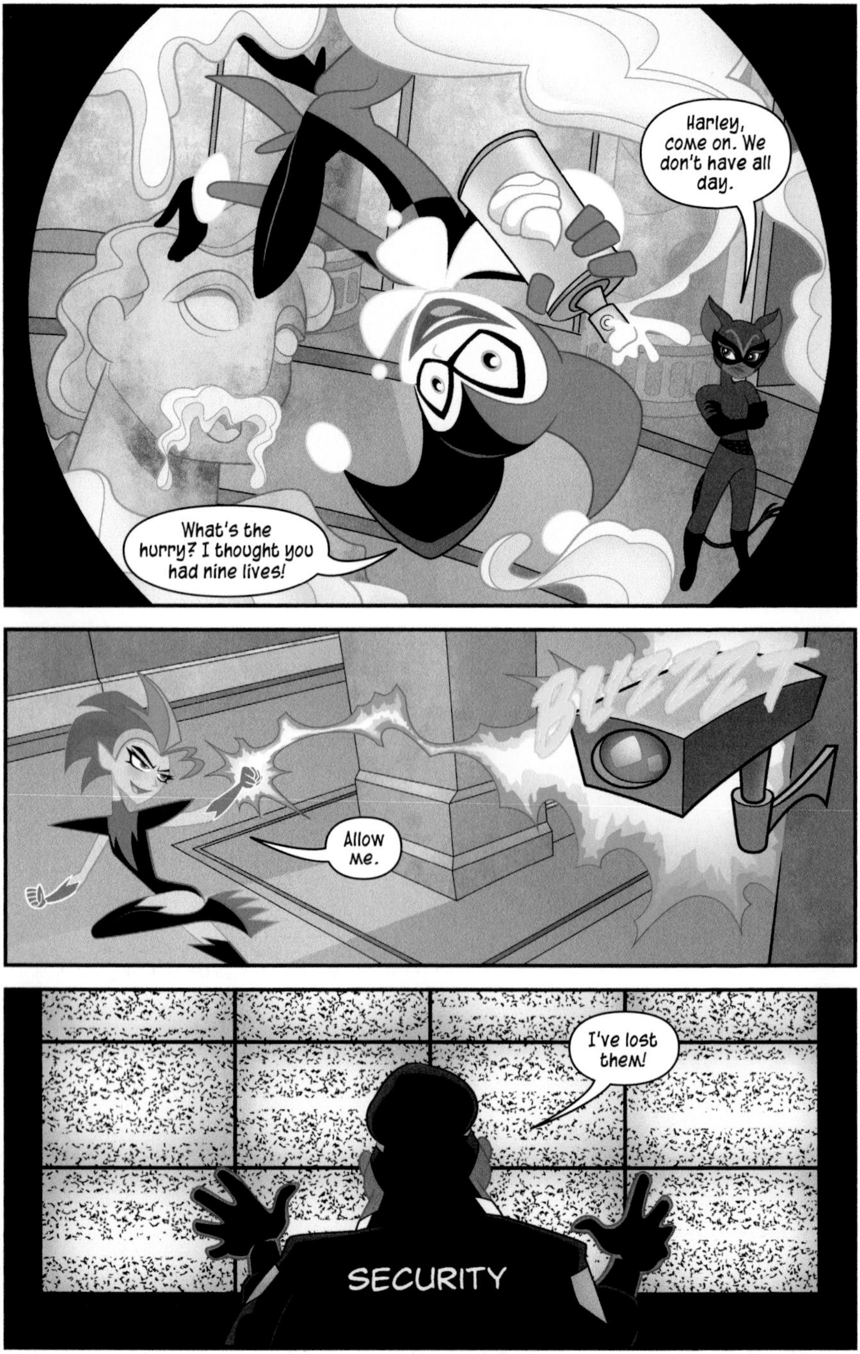
Harley, come on. We don't have all day.
What's the hurry? I thought you had nine lives!
BUZZZT
Allow me.
I've lost them!
SECURITY

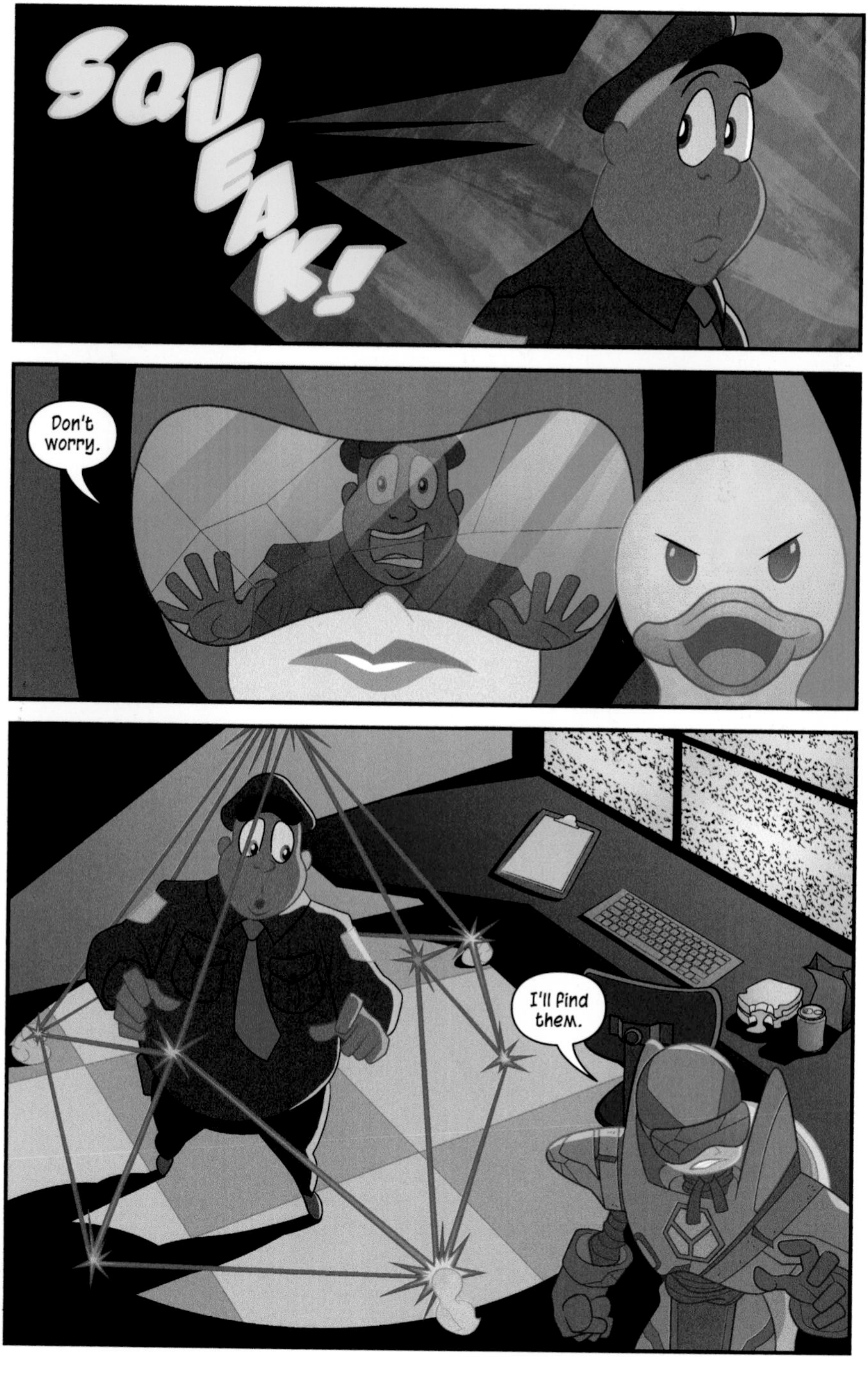
SQUEAK!
Don't worry.
I'll find them.

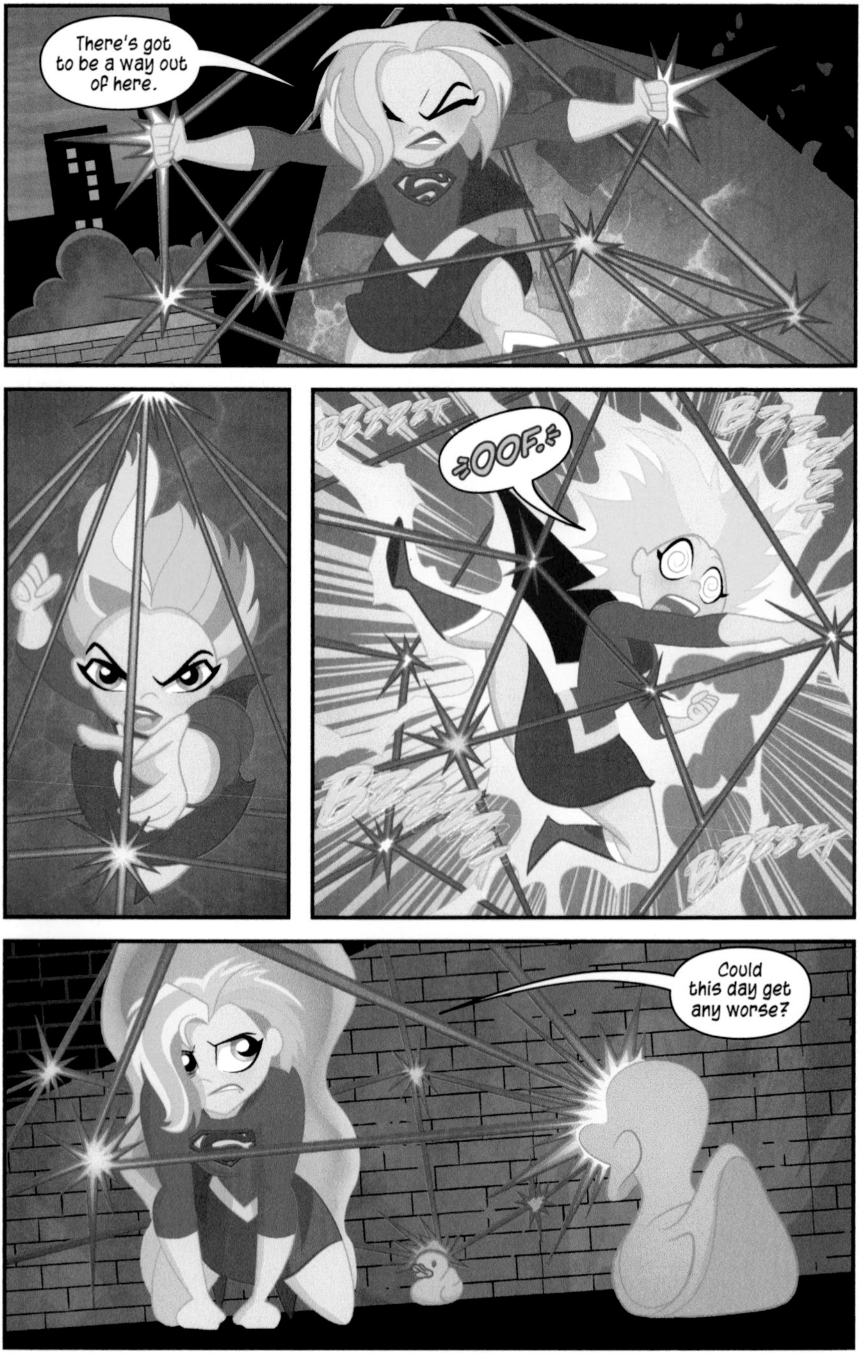
There's got to be a way out of here.
BZZZZT
BZZZZZT
OOF.
BZZZZZT
BZZZZT
Could this day get any worse?

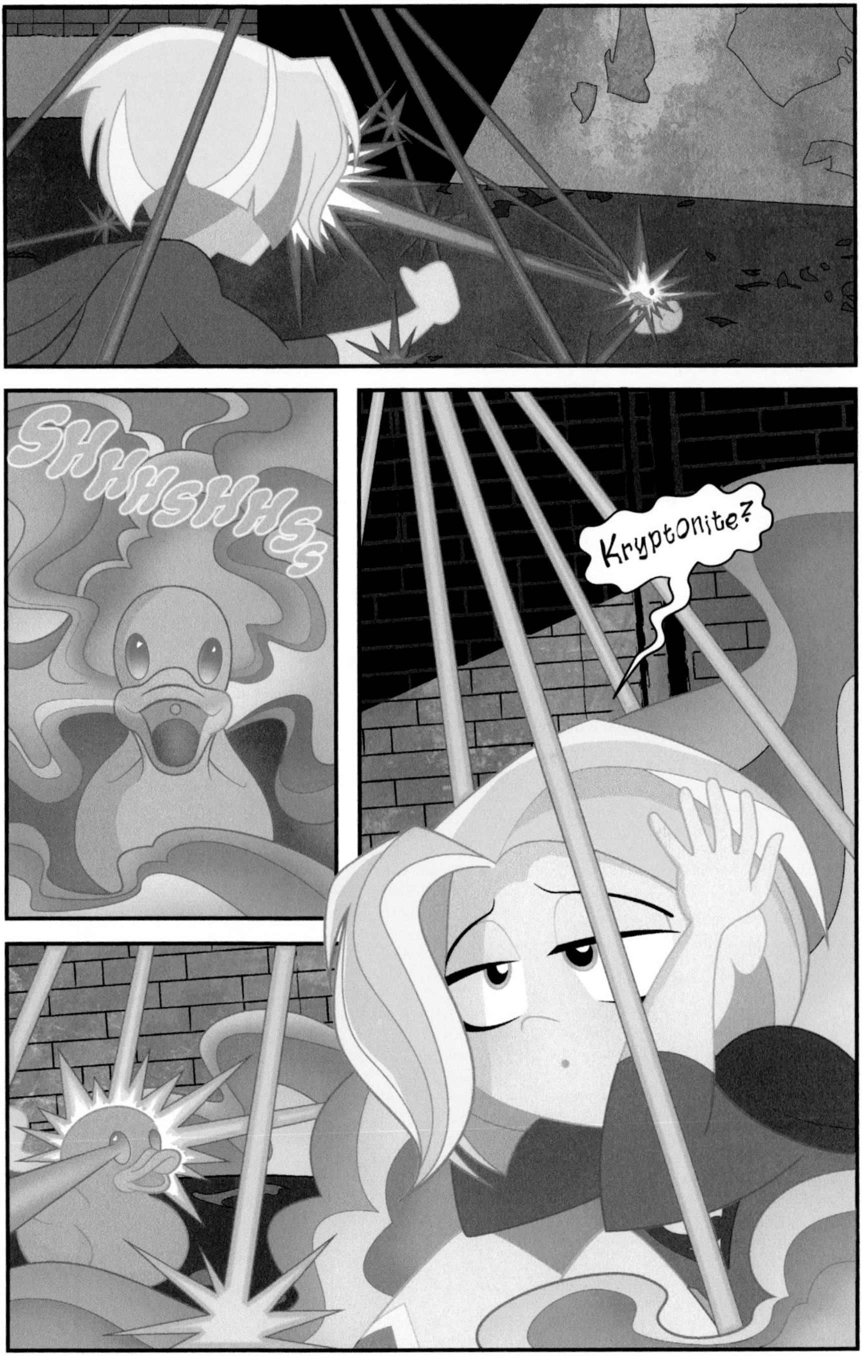
SHHHSHHSS
Kryptonite?

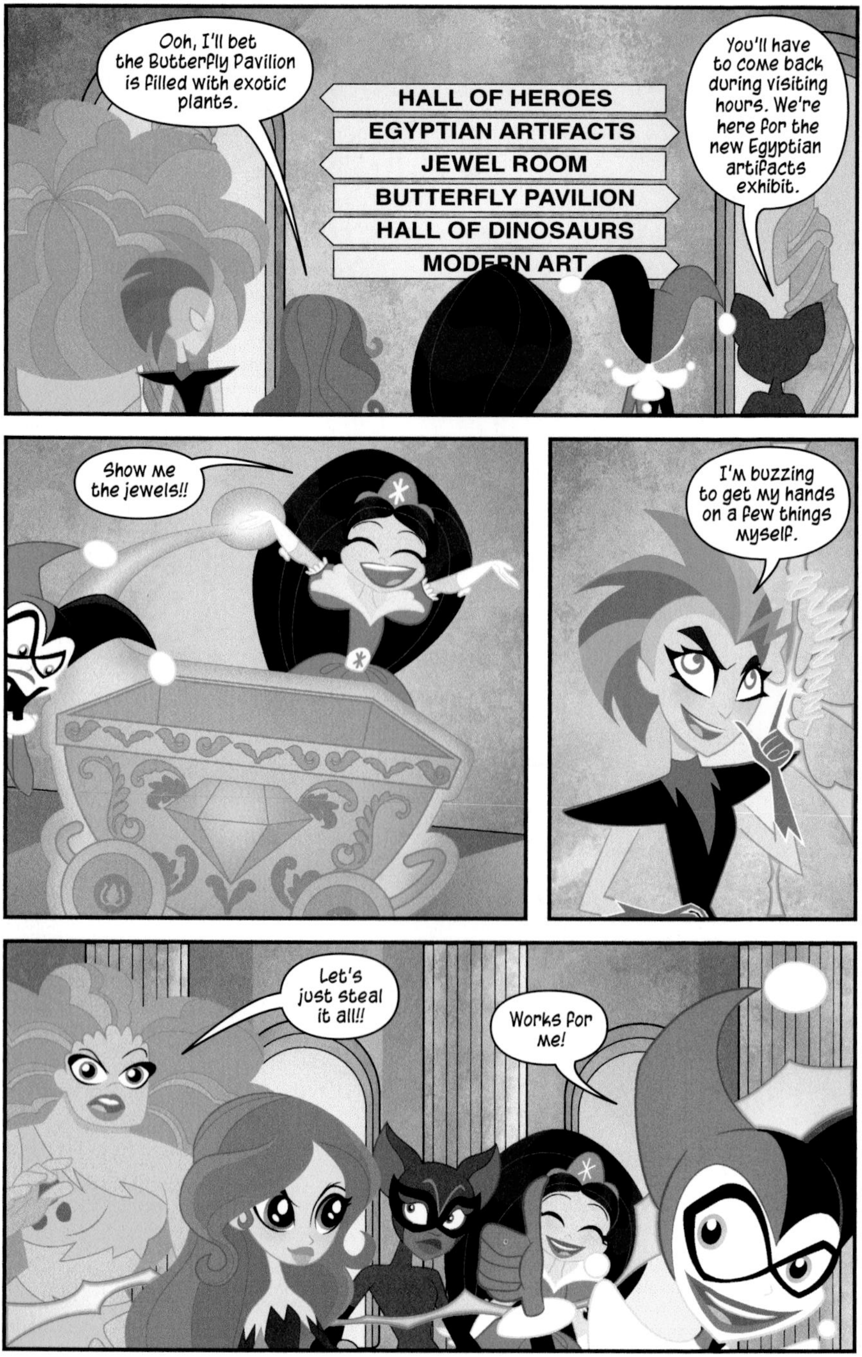
Ooh, I'll bet the Butterfly Pavilion is filled with exotic plants.
HALL OF HEROES
EGYPTIAN ARTIFACTS
JEWEL ROOM
BUTTERFLY PAVILION
HALL OF DINOSAURS
MODERN ART
You'll have to come back during visiting hours. We're here for the new Egyptian artifacts exhibit.
Show me the jewels!!
I'm buzzing to get my hands on a few things myself.
Let's just steal it all!!
Works for me!

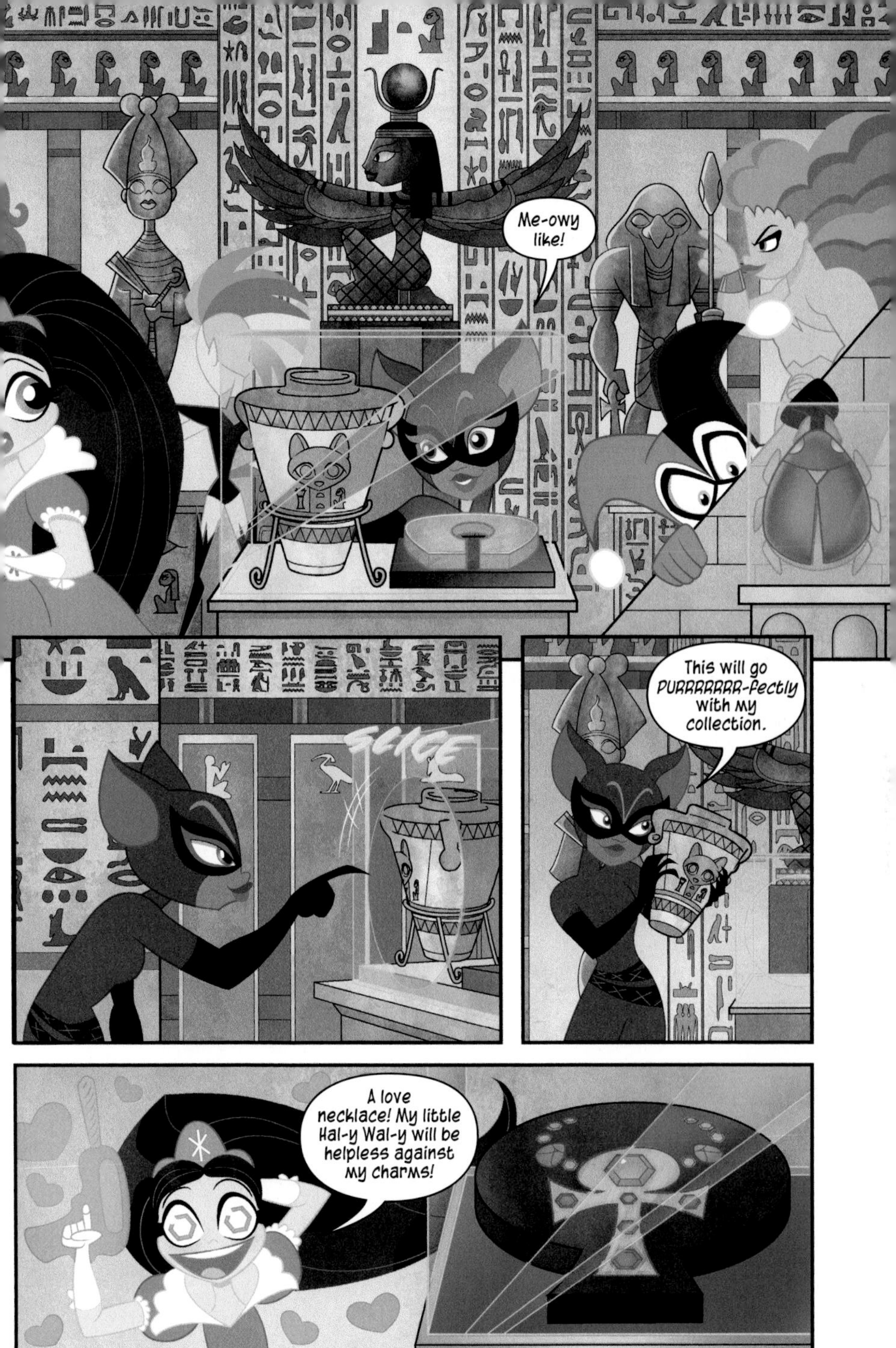
Me-owy like!
SLICE
This will go PURRRRRRR-fectly with my collection.
A love necklace! My little Hal-y Wal-y will be helpless against my charms!

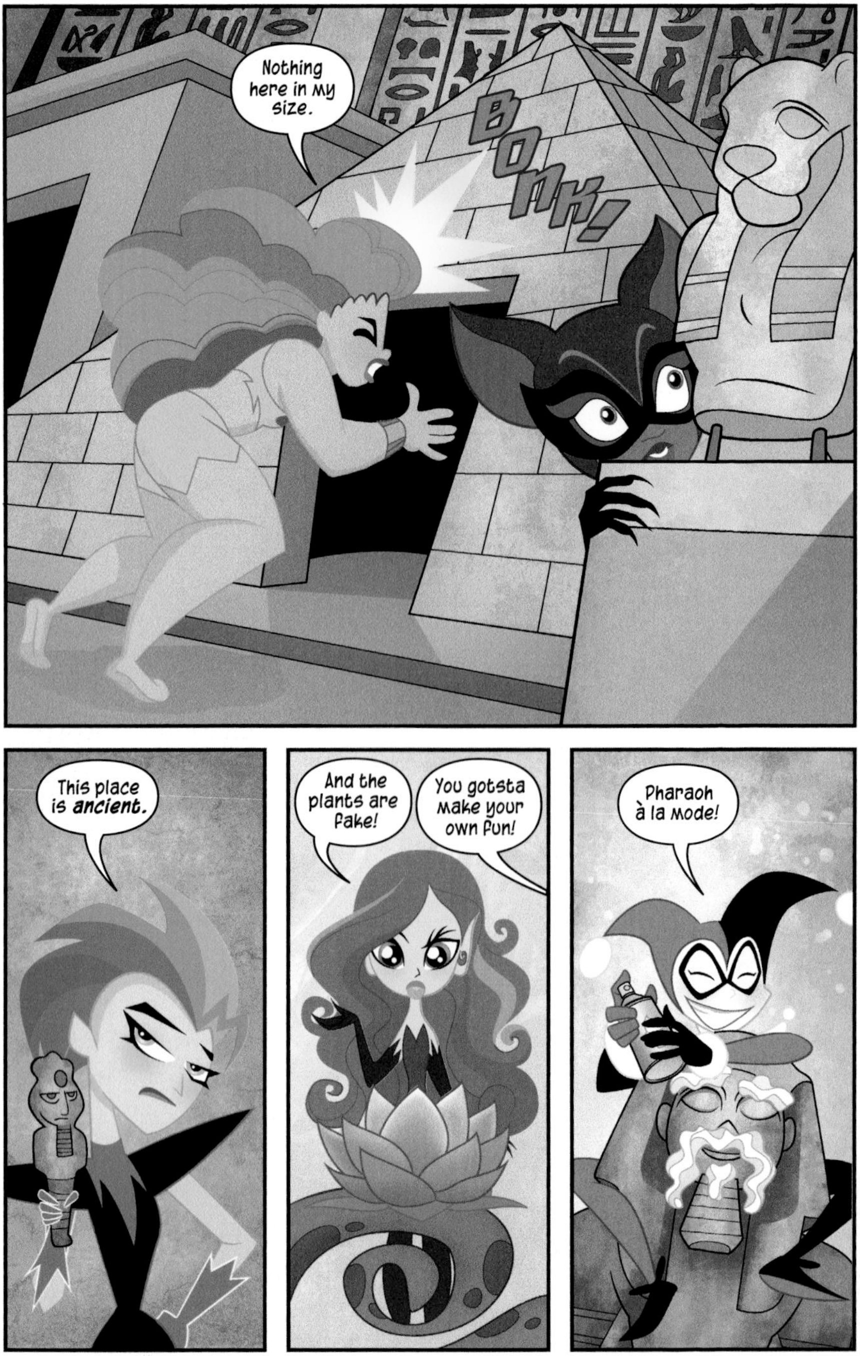
Nothing here in my size.
BONK!
This place is ***ancient.***
And the plants are fake!
You gotsta make your own fun!
Pharaoh à la mode!

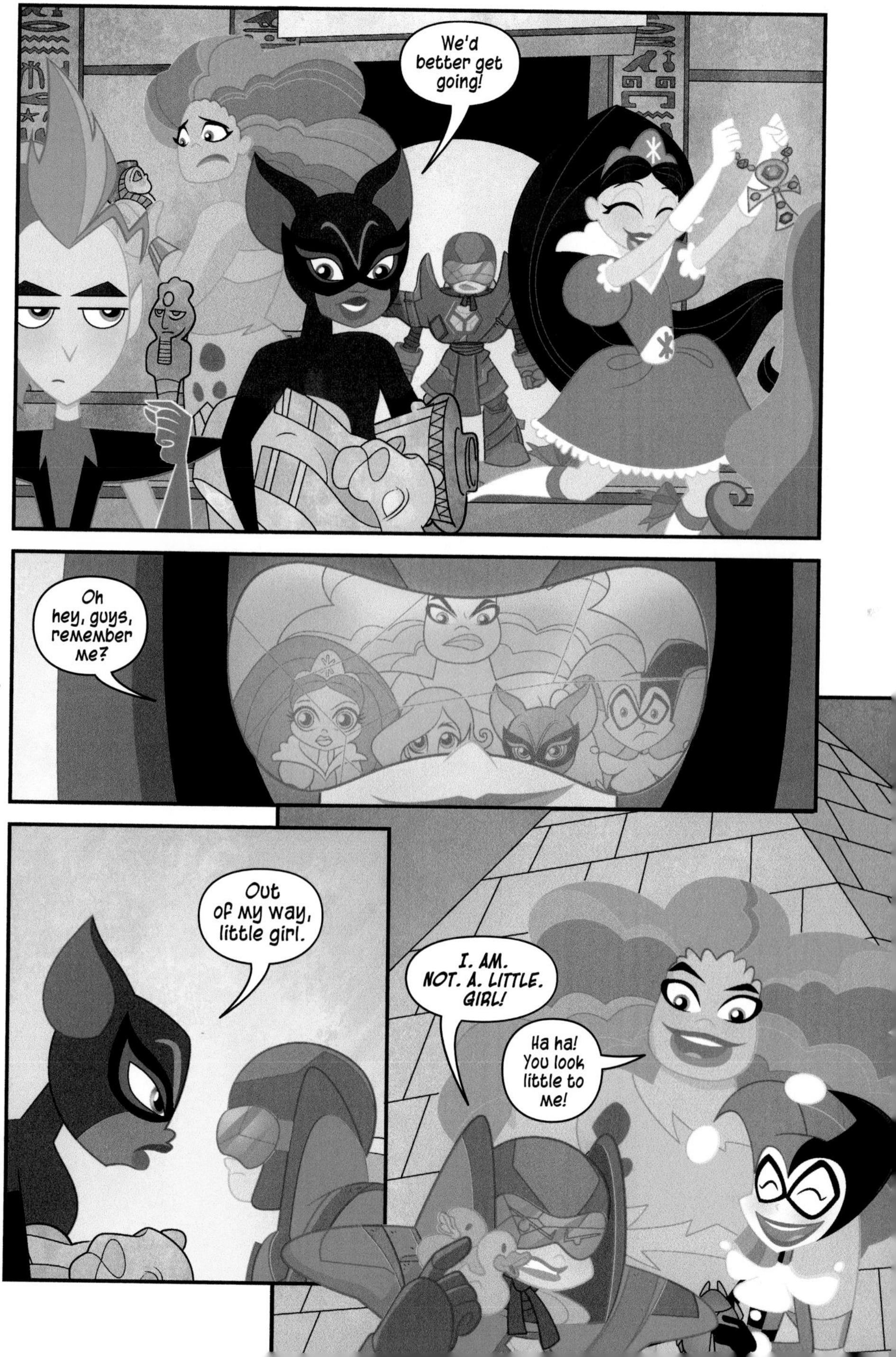
We'd better get going!
Oh hey, guys, remember me?
Out of my way, little girl.
I. AM. NOT. A. LITTLE. GIRL!
Ha ha! You look little to me!

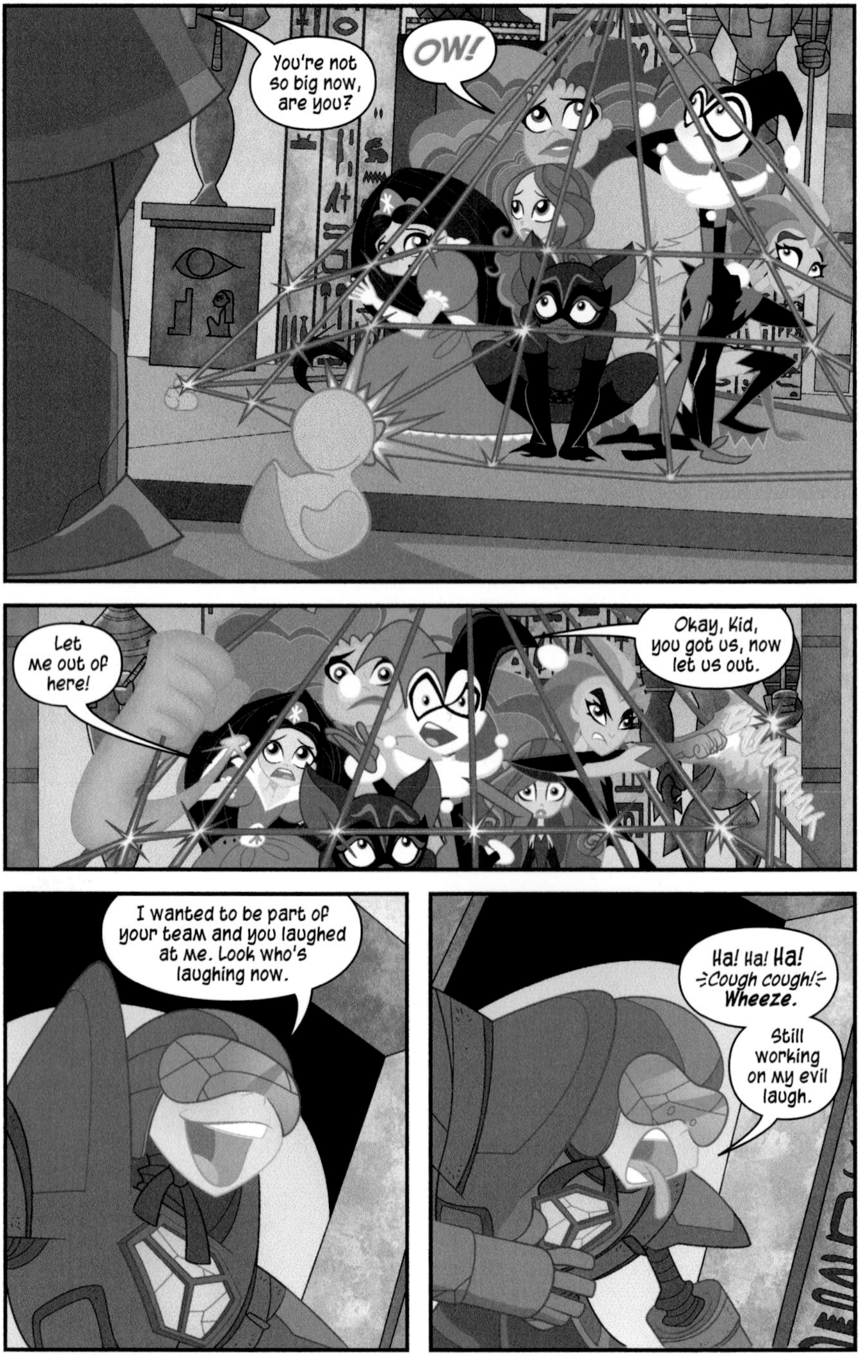
You're not so big now, are you?
OW!
Let me out of here!
Okay, kid, you got us, now let us out.
I wanted to be part of your team and you laughed at me. Look who's laughing now.
Ha! Ha! Ha! -Cough cough!- Wheeze.
Still working on my evil laugh.

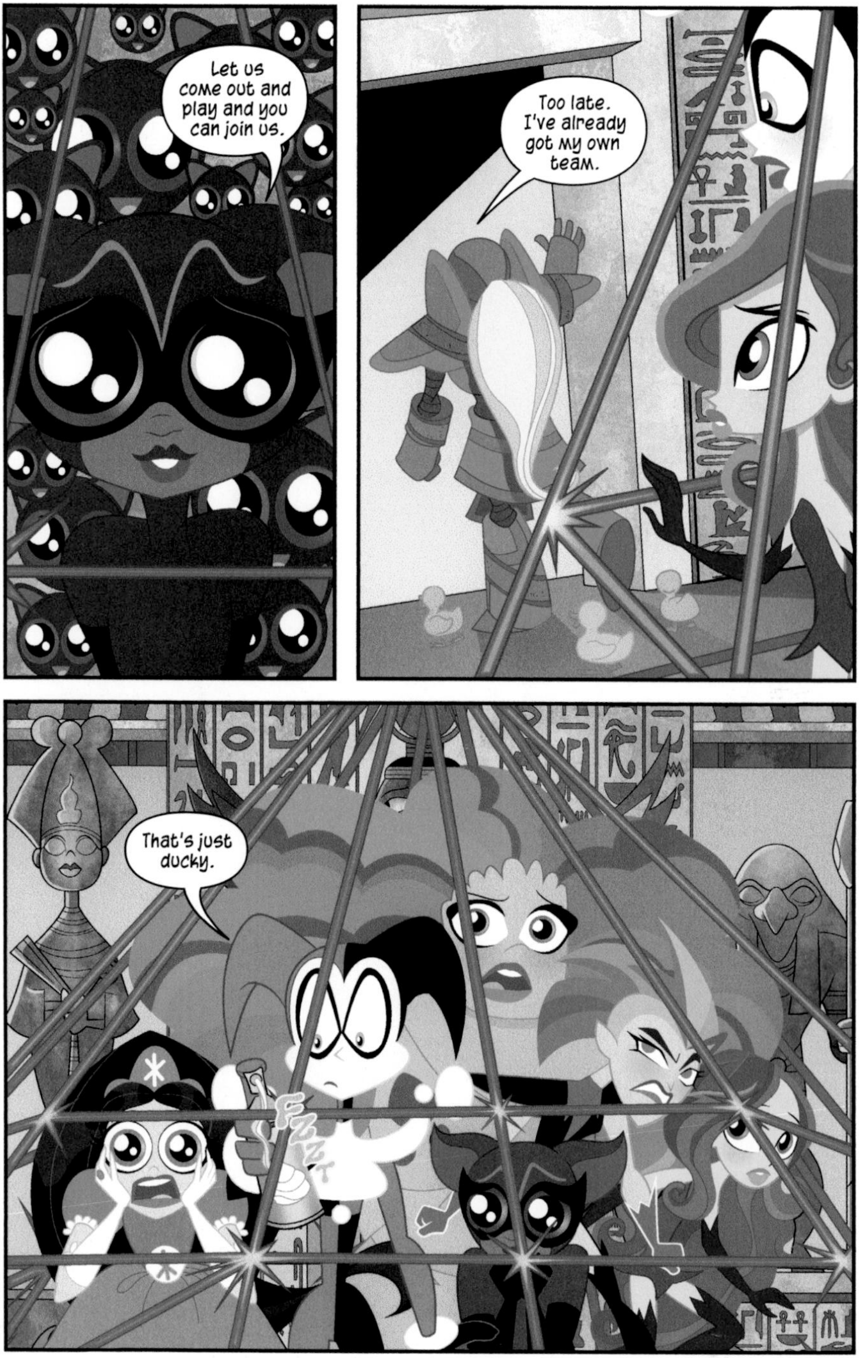
Let us come out and play and you can join us.
Too late. I've already got my own team.
That's just ducky.
FZZT

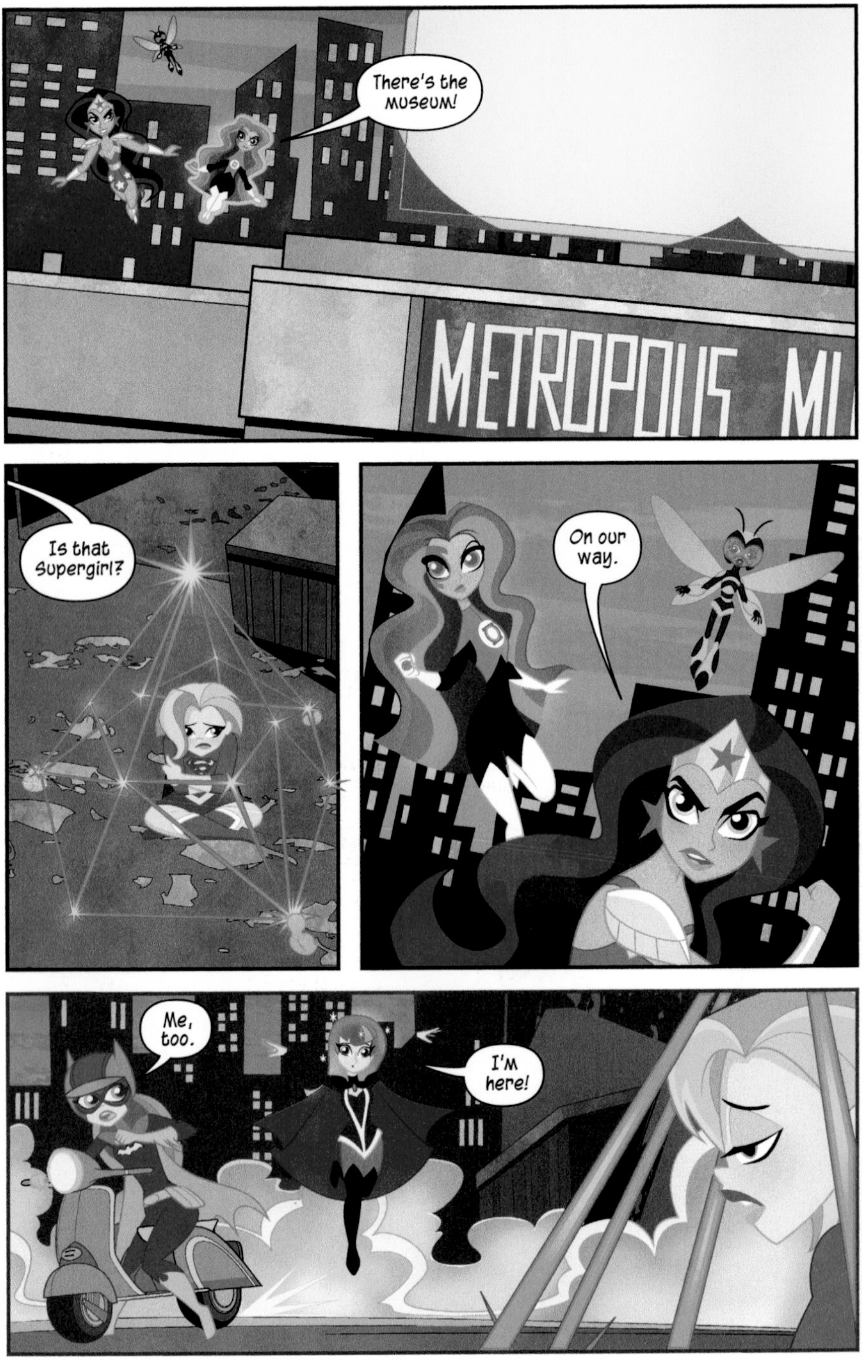
There's the MUSEUM!
METROPOLIS MU
Is that Supergirl?
On our way.
Me, too.
I'M here!

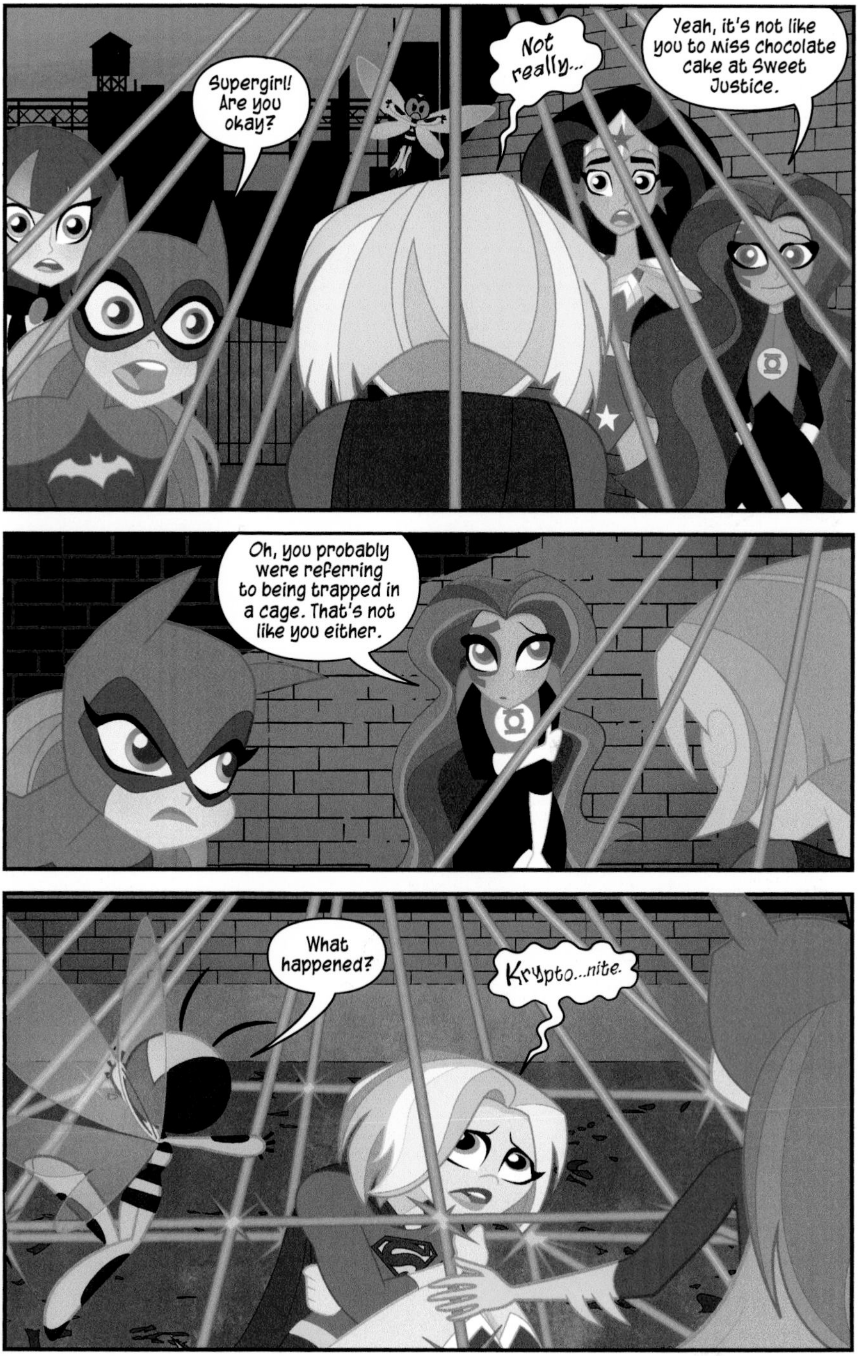
Supergirl! Are you okay?
Not really...
Yeah, it's not like you to miss chocolate cake at Sweet Justice.
Oh, you probably were referring to being trapped in a cage. That's not like you either.
What happened?
Krypto...nite.

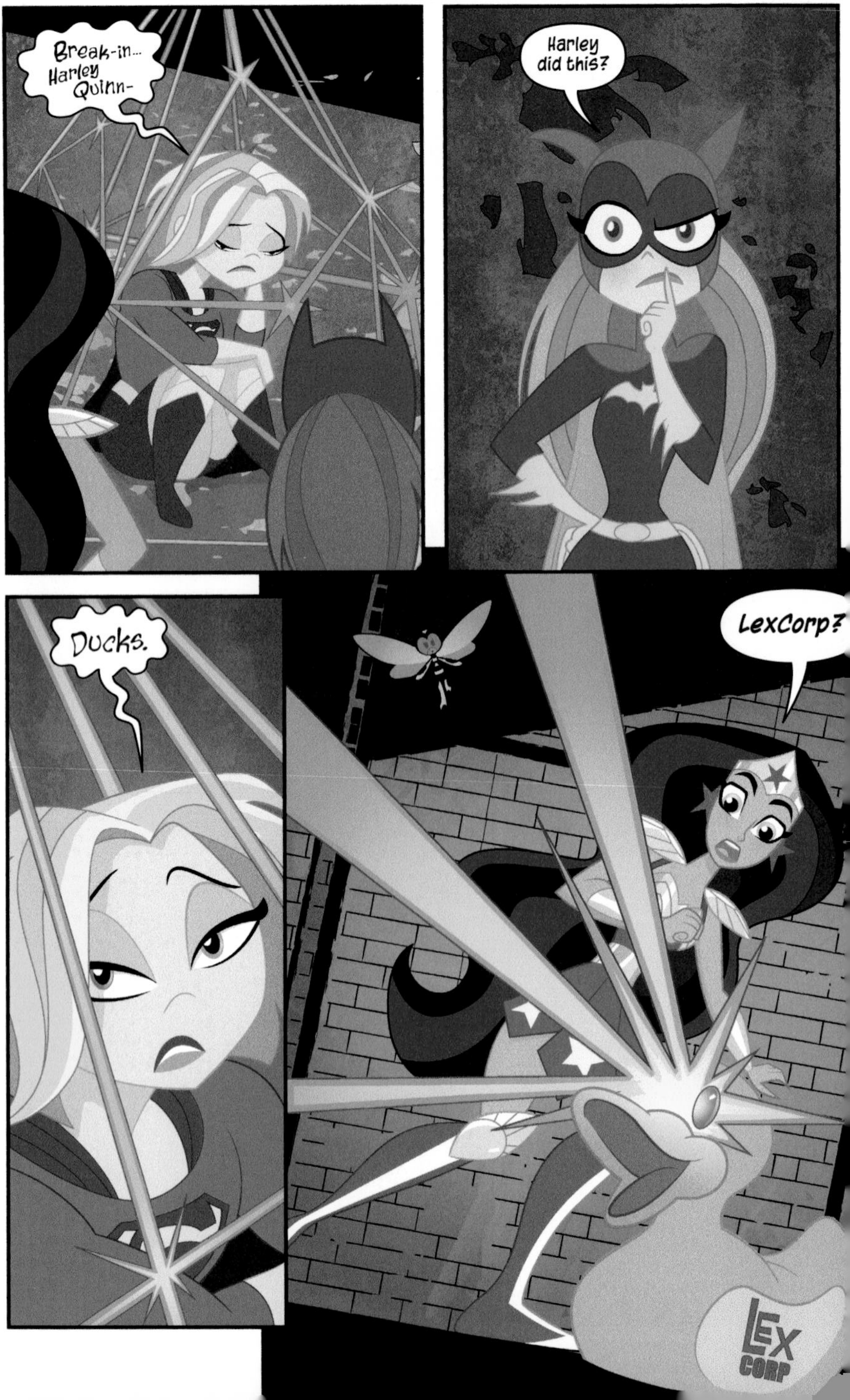

Break-in... Harley Quinn-
Harley did this?
Ducks.
LexCorp?
LEX CORP

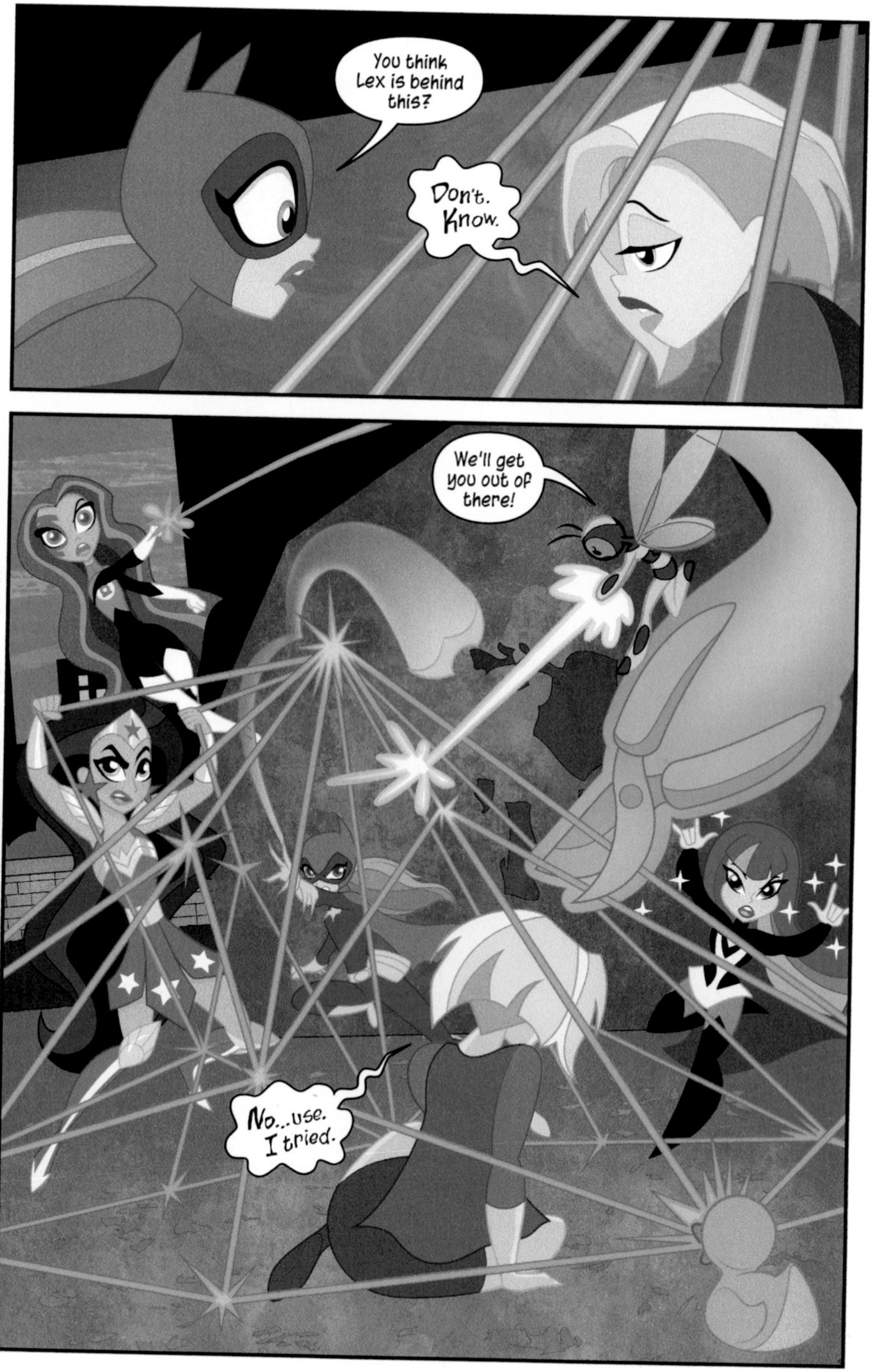

You think Lex is behind this?
Don't. Know.
We'll get you out of there!
No...use. I tried.

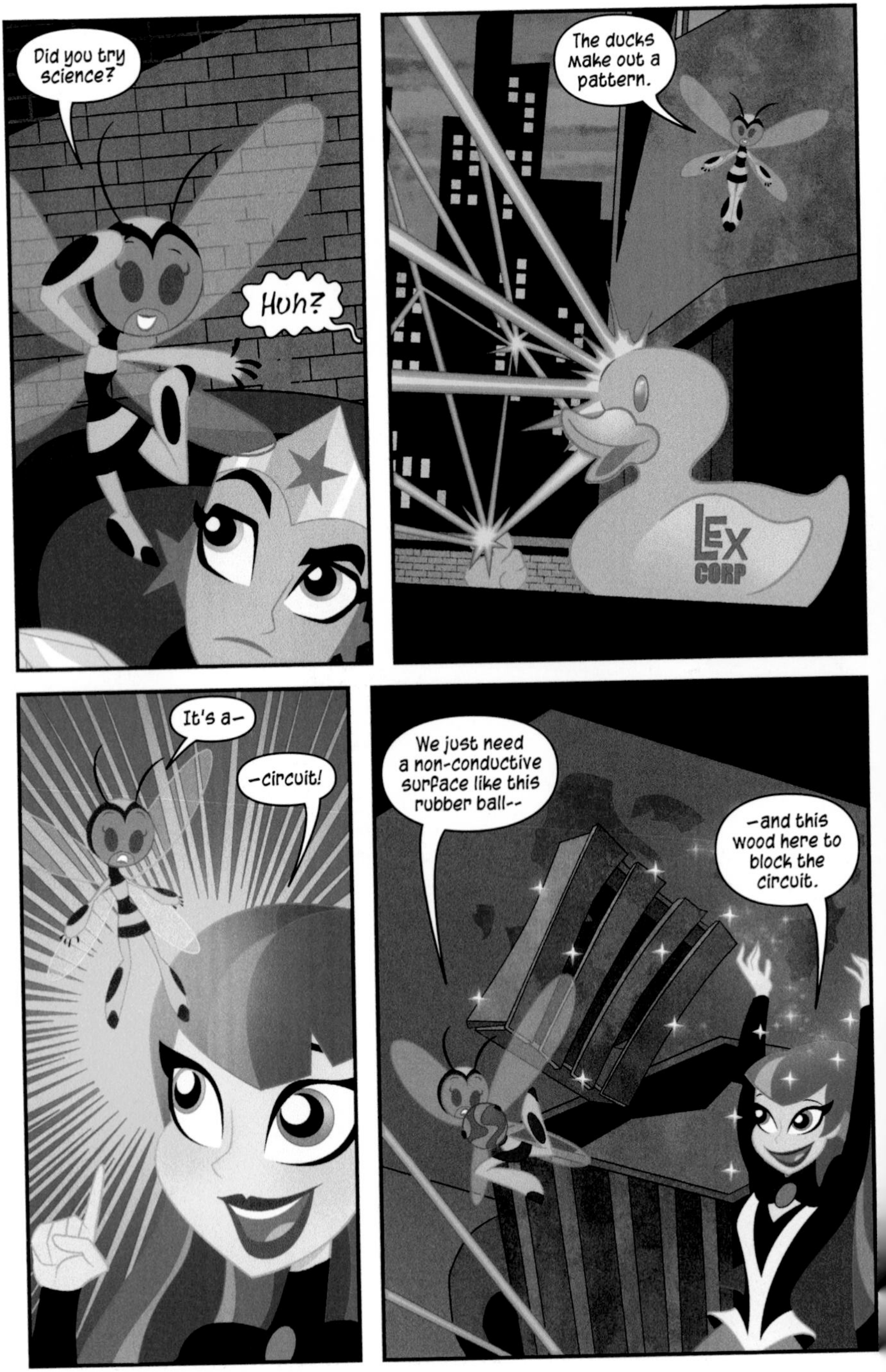
Did you try science?
Huh?
The ducks make out a pattern.
LEX CORP
It's a-
-circuit!
We just need a non-conductive surface like this rubber ball--
-and this wood here to block the circuit.

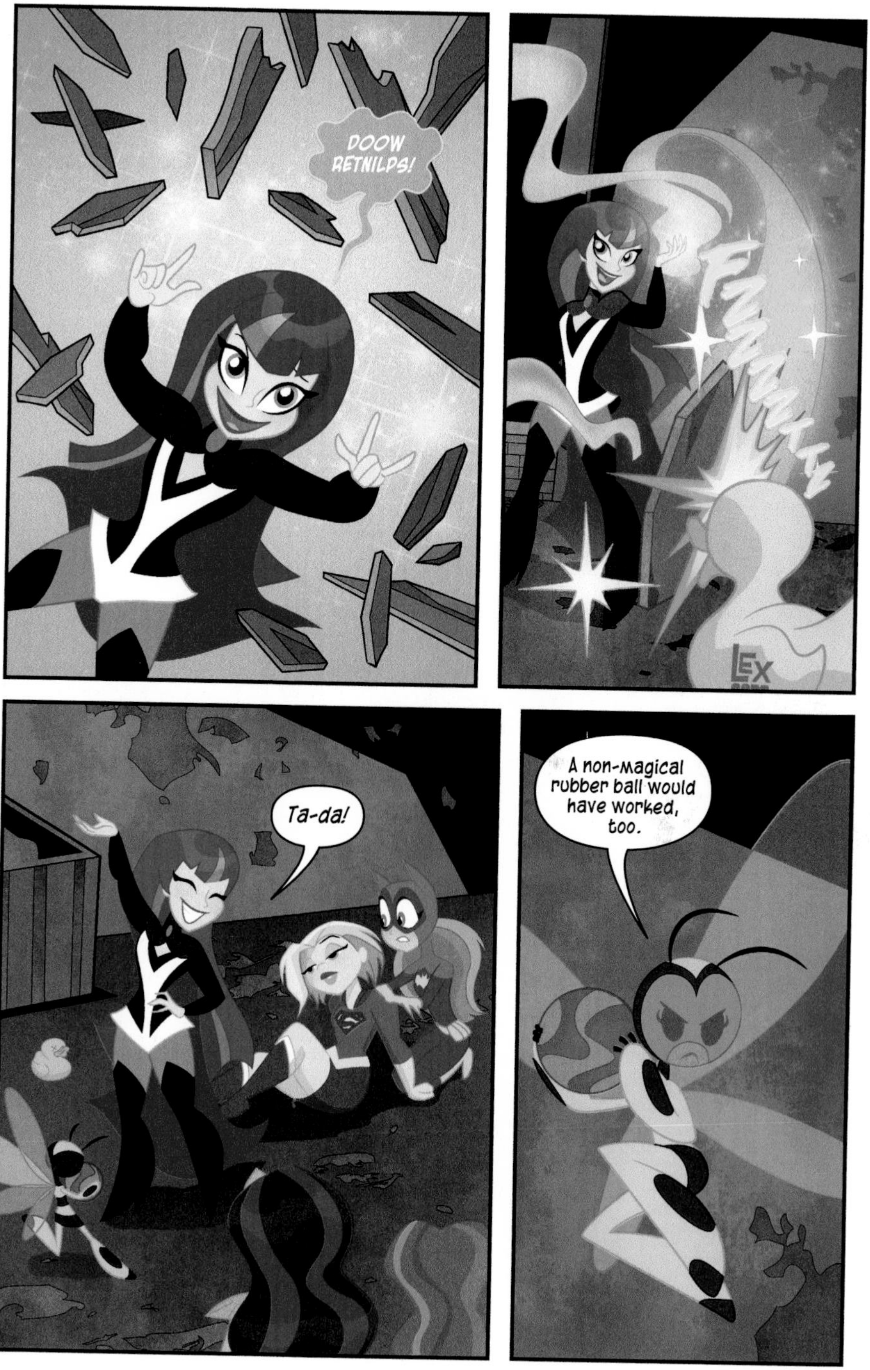
DOOW RETNILPS!
FWAAAKK
LEX
Ta-da!
A non-magical rubber ball would have worked, too.

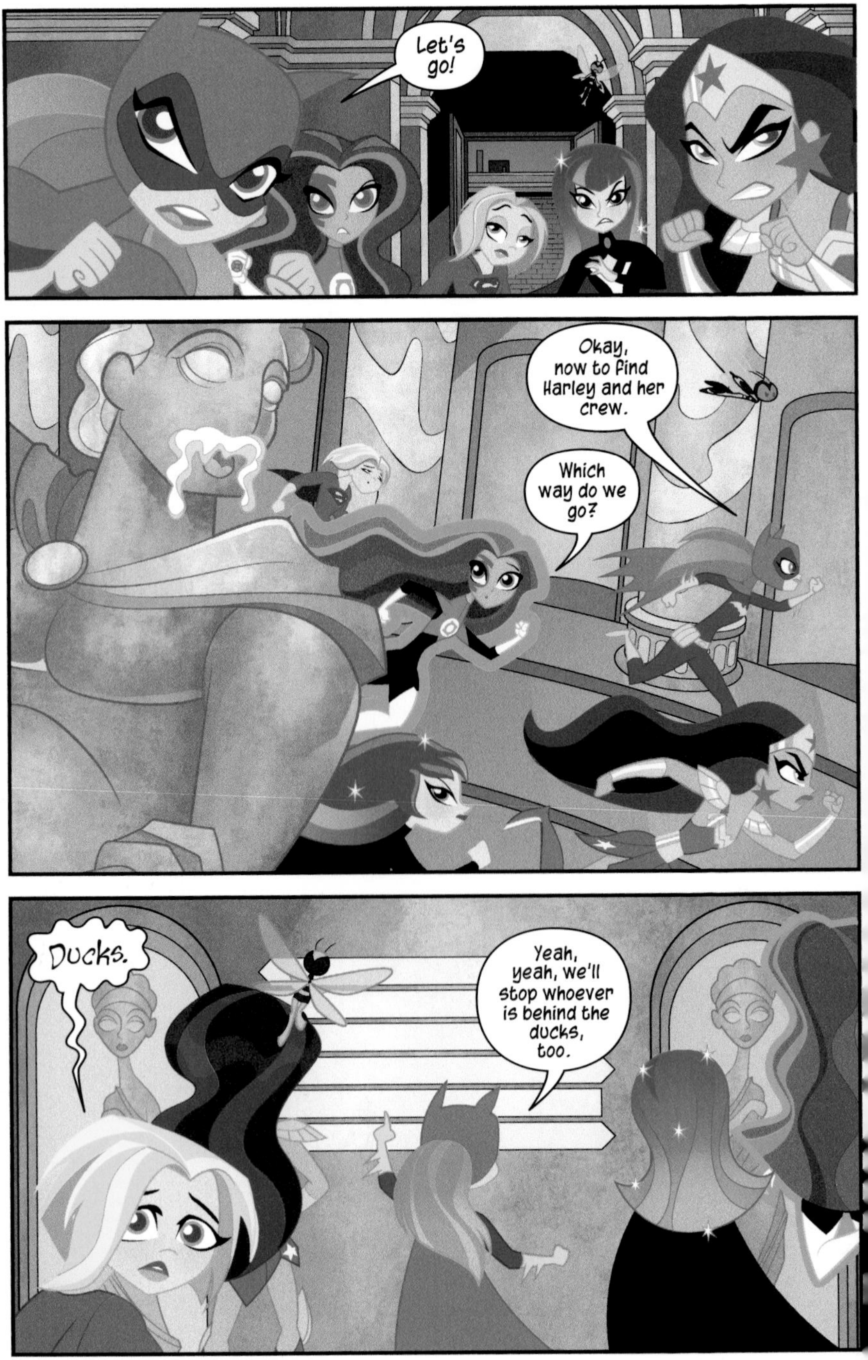
Let's go!
Okay, now to find Harley and her crew.
Which way do we go?
Ducks.
Yeah, yeah, we'll stop whoever is behind the ducks, too.

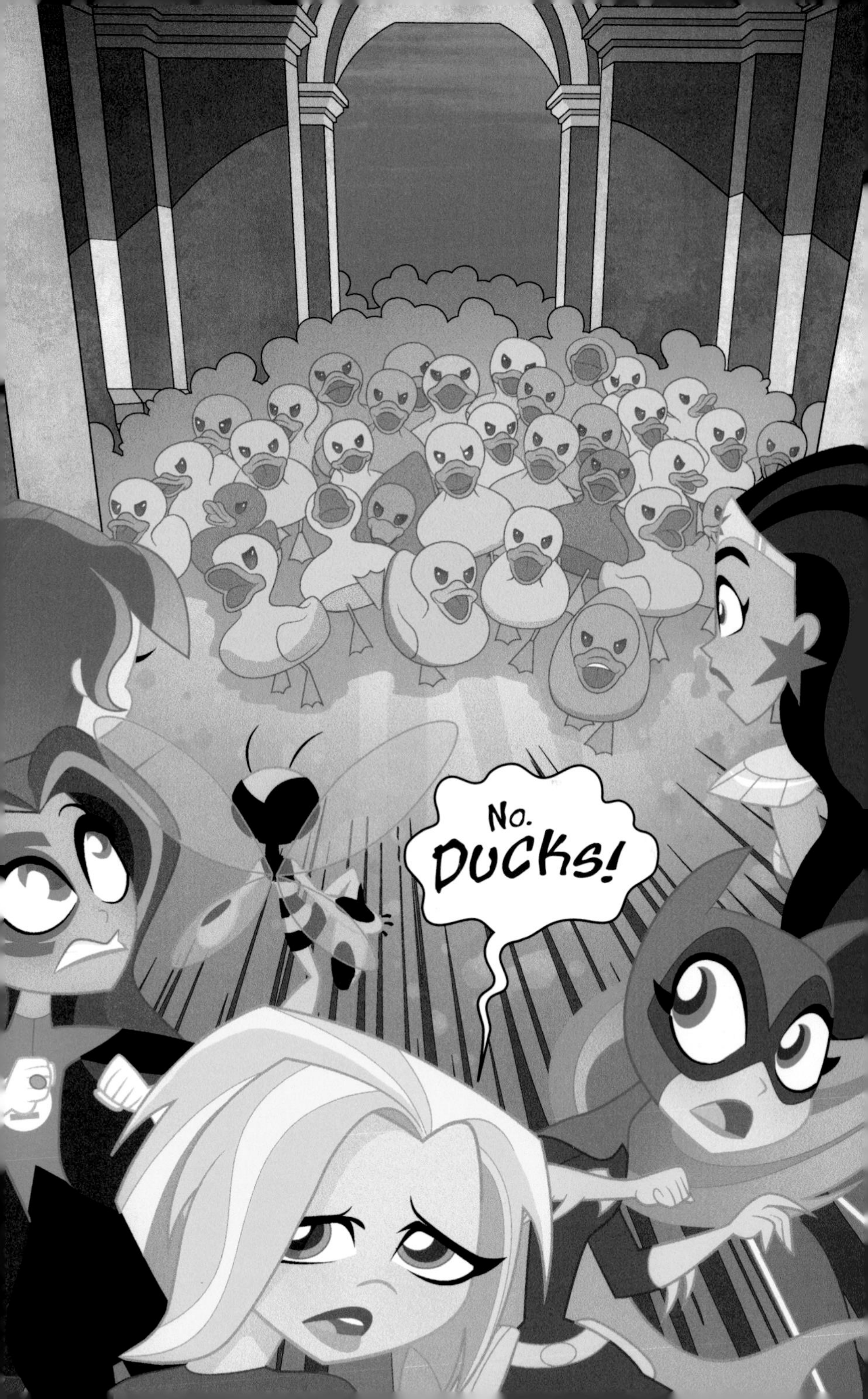
No. DUCKS!

chapter six

THE BEST CLUB IN TOWN

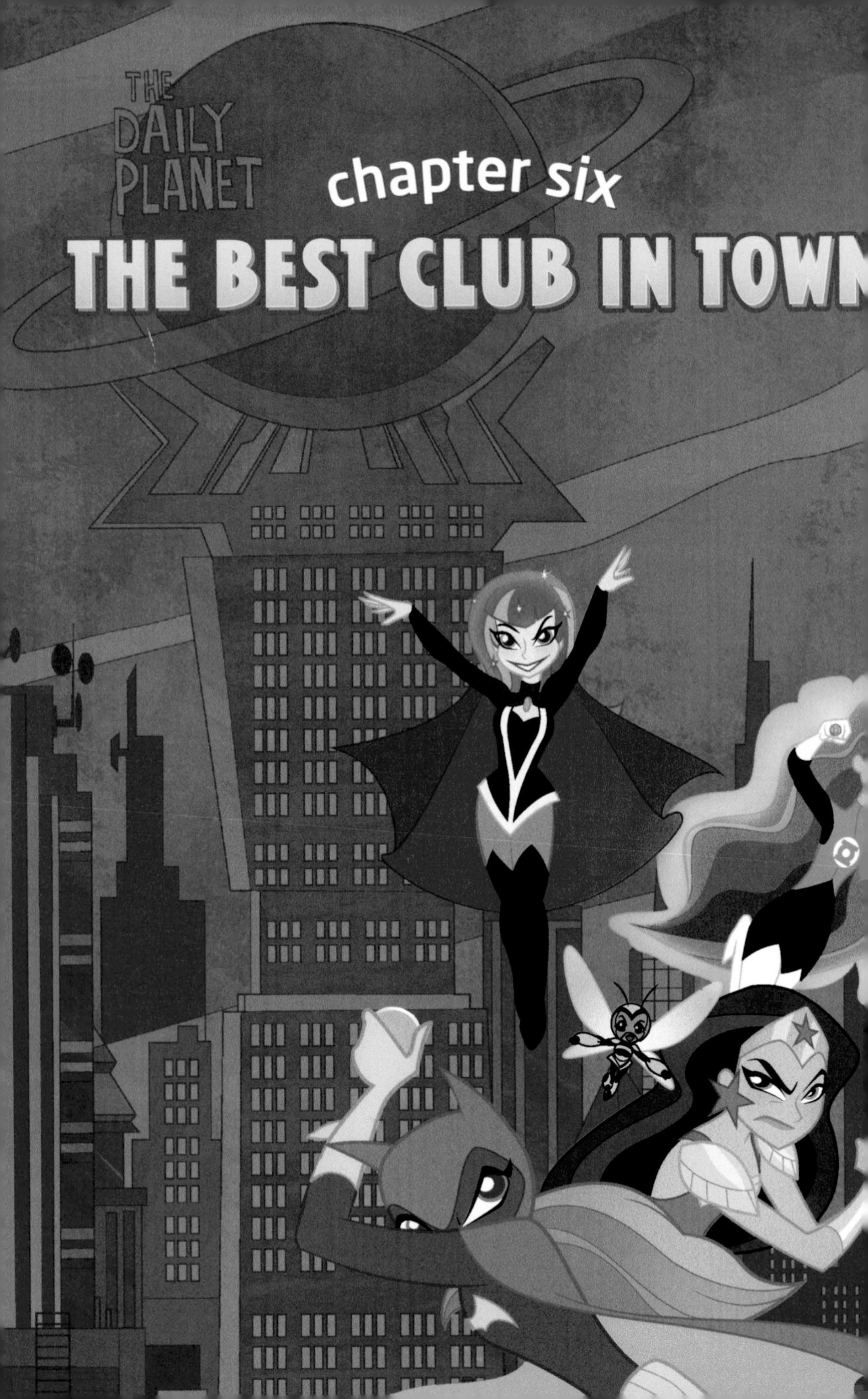
THE DAILY PLANET

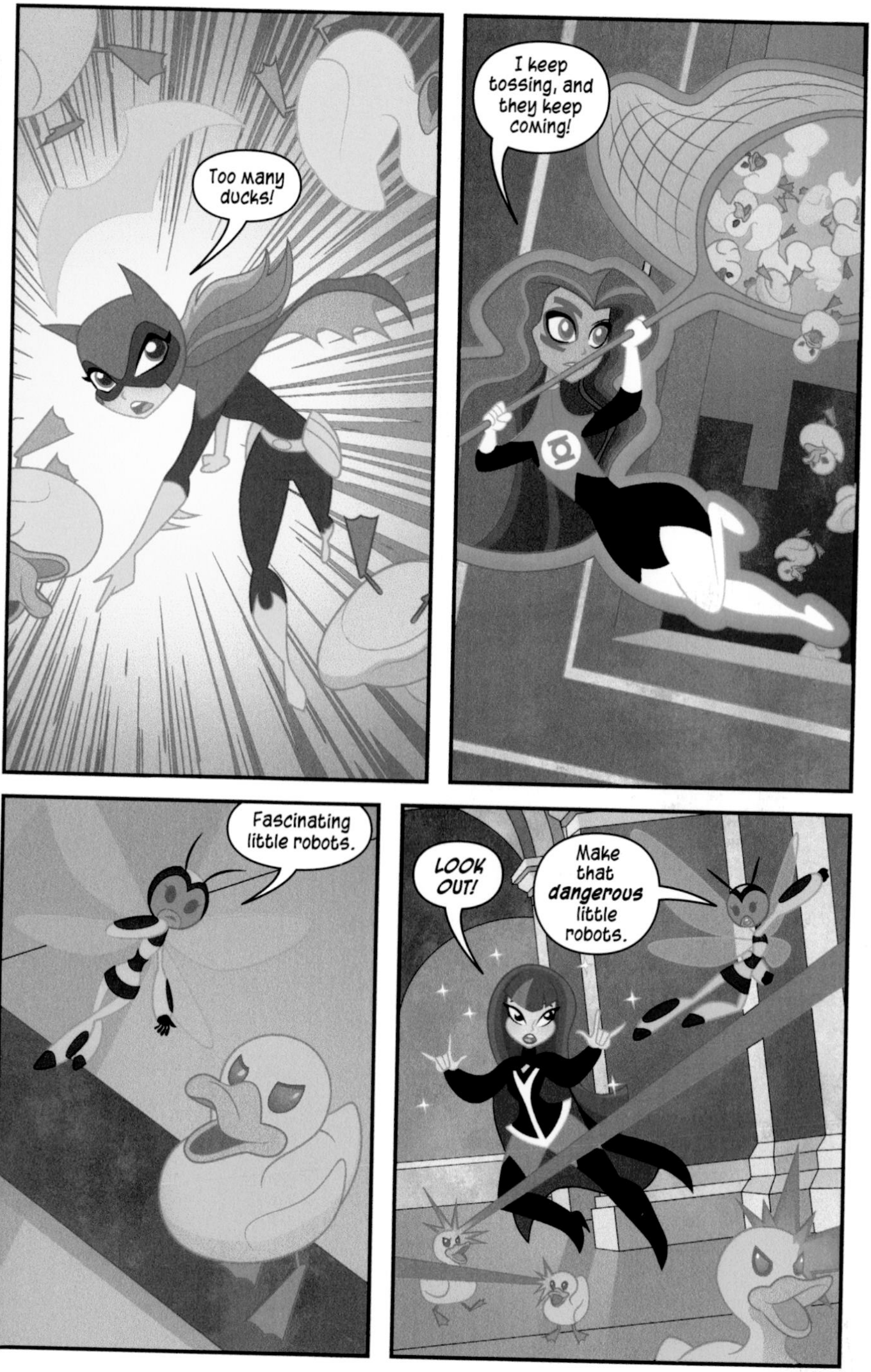
Too many ducks!
I keep tossing, and they keep coming!
Fascinating little robots.
LOOK OUT!
Make that *dangerous* little robots.

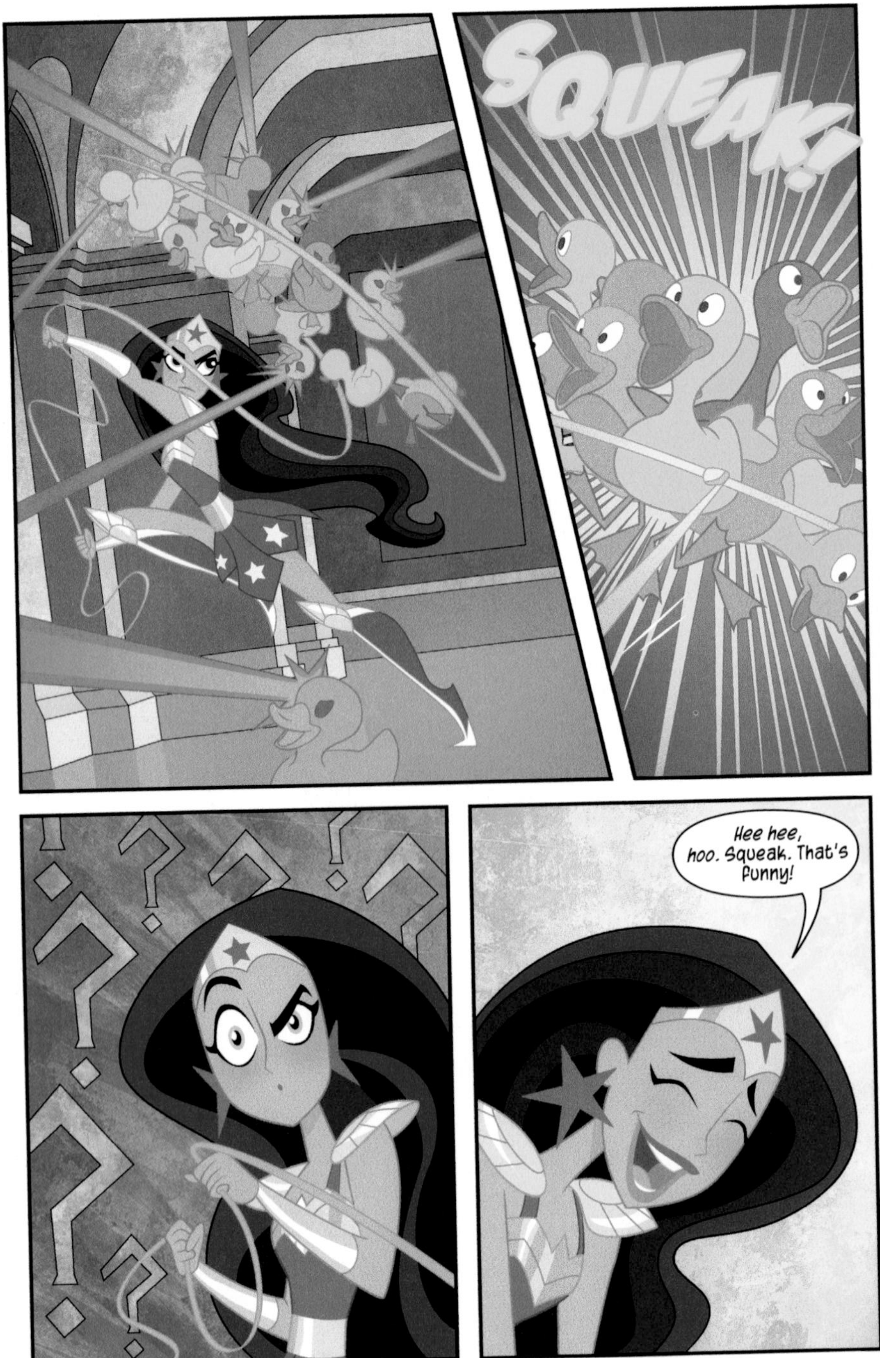
SQUEAK!
Hee hee, hoo. Squeak. That's funny!

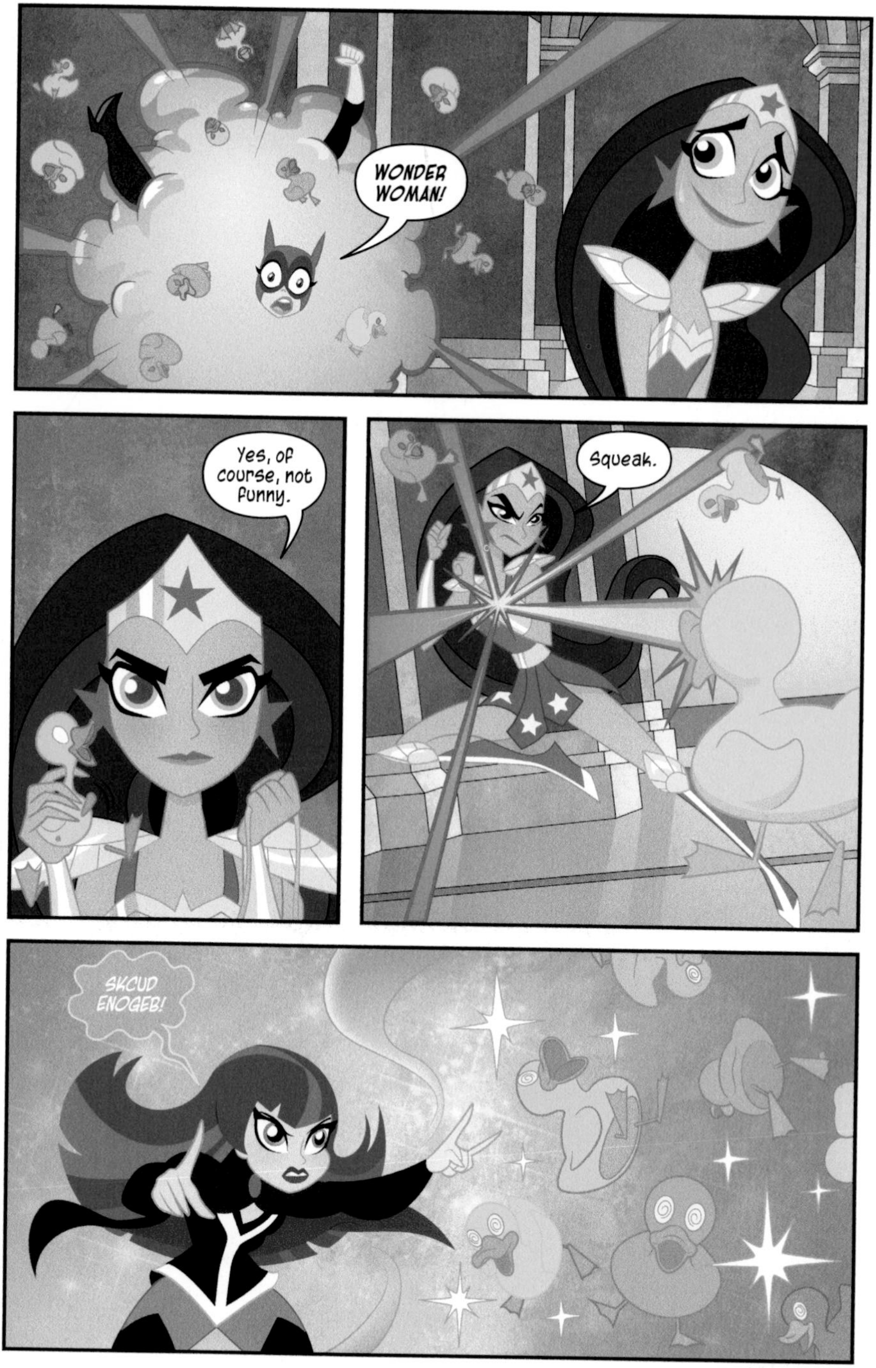
WONDER WOMAN!
Yes, of course, not funny.
Squeak.
SKCUD ENOGEB!

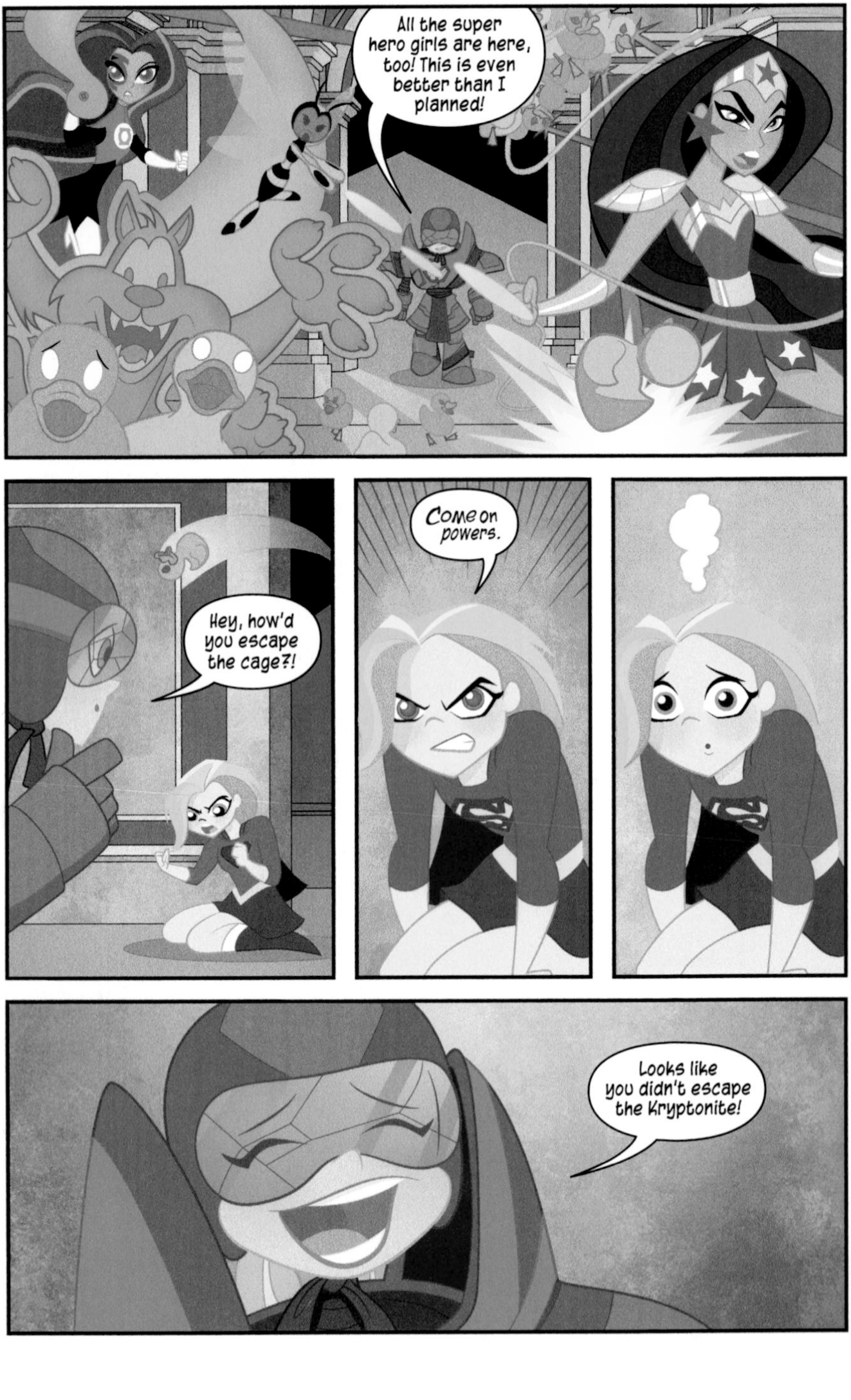
All the super hero girls are here, too! This is even better than I planned!
Hey, how'd you escape the cage?!
Come on powers.
Looks like you didn't escape the Kryptonite!

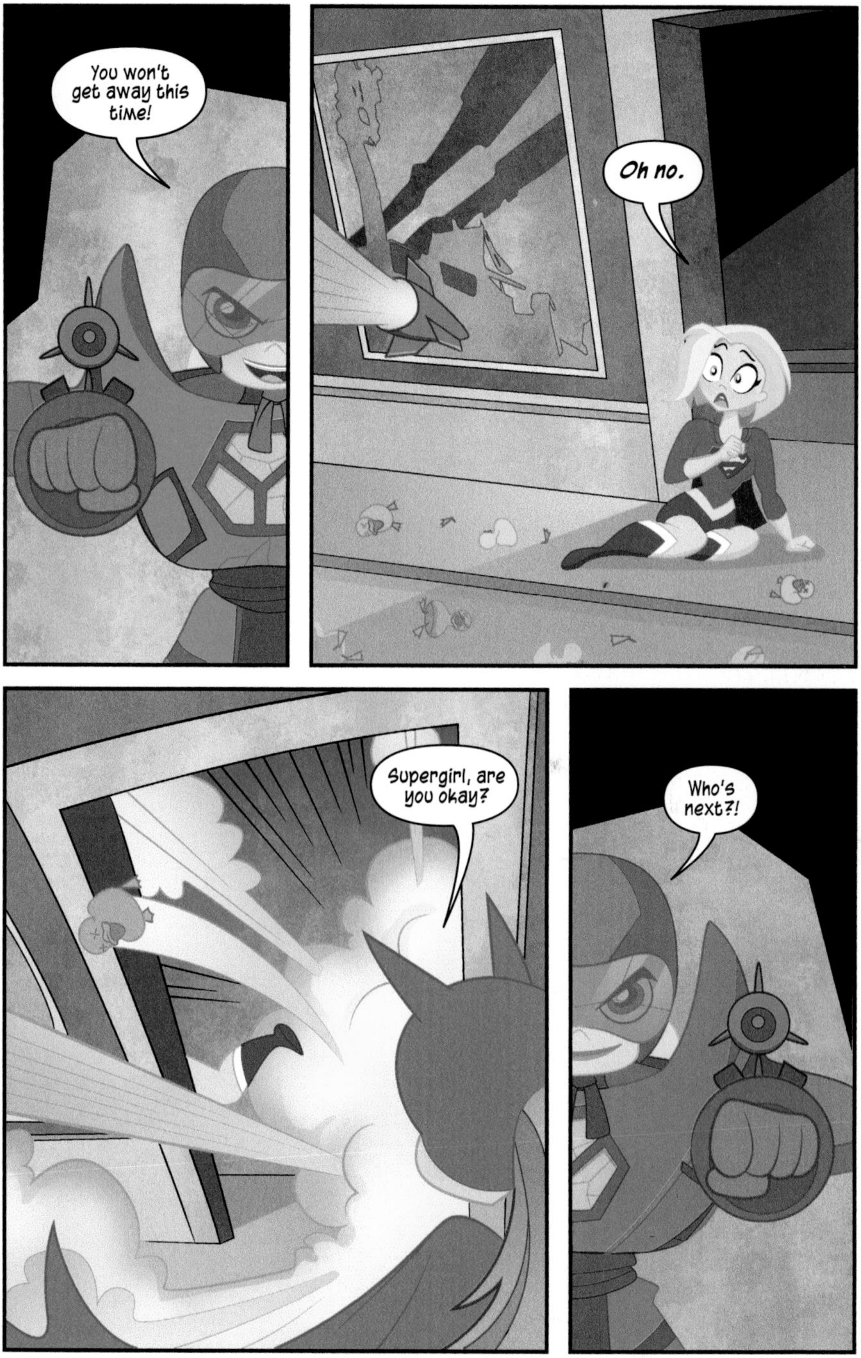
You won't get away this time!
Oh no.
Supergirl, are you okay?
Who's next?!

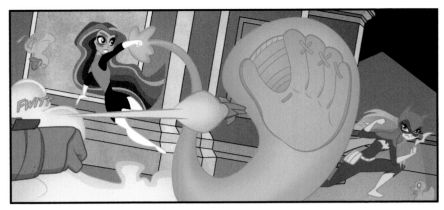

POW

Hey, you! Stop messing with my suit!

The ducks are remote-controlled!

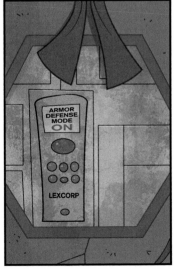

ARMOR DEFENSE MODE ON

LEXCORP

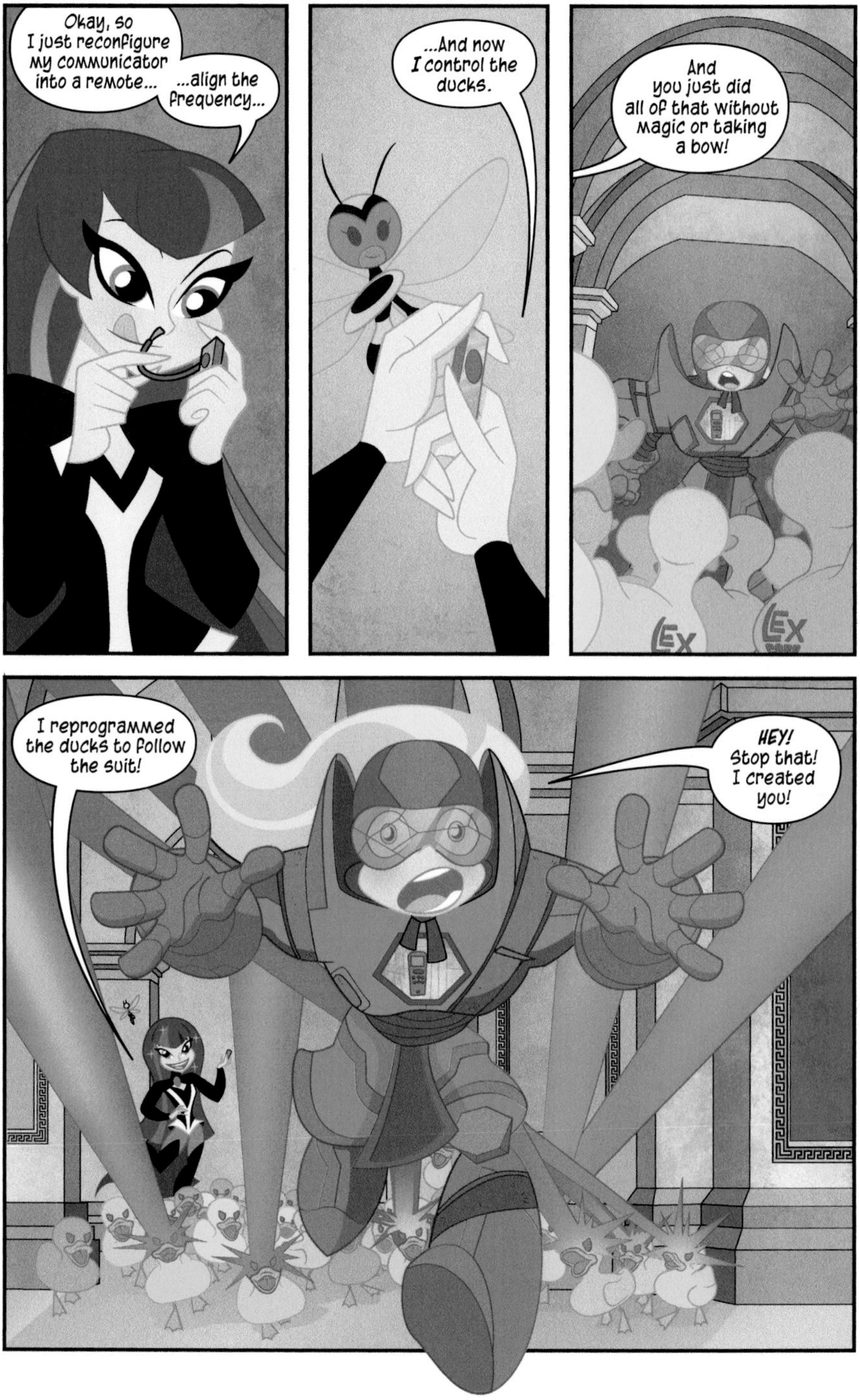
Okay, so I just reconfigure my communicator into a remote...
...align the frequency...
...And now I control the ducks.
And you just did all of that without magic or taking a bow!
LEX
LEX
I reprogrammed the ducks to follow the suit!
HEY! Stop that! I created you!

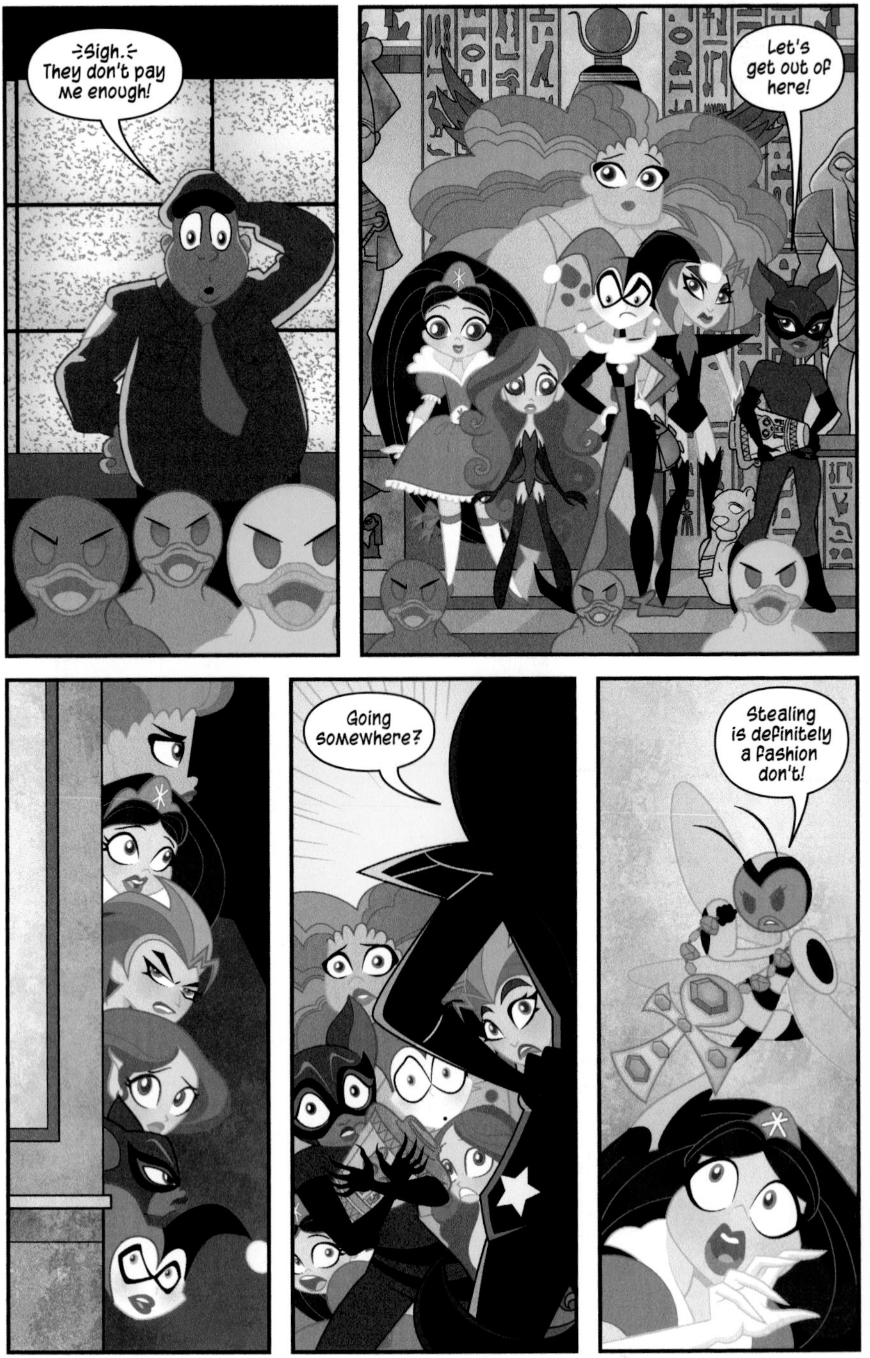

Sigh.
They don't pay me enough!
Let's get out of here!
Going somewhere?
Stealing is definitely a fashion don't!

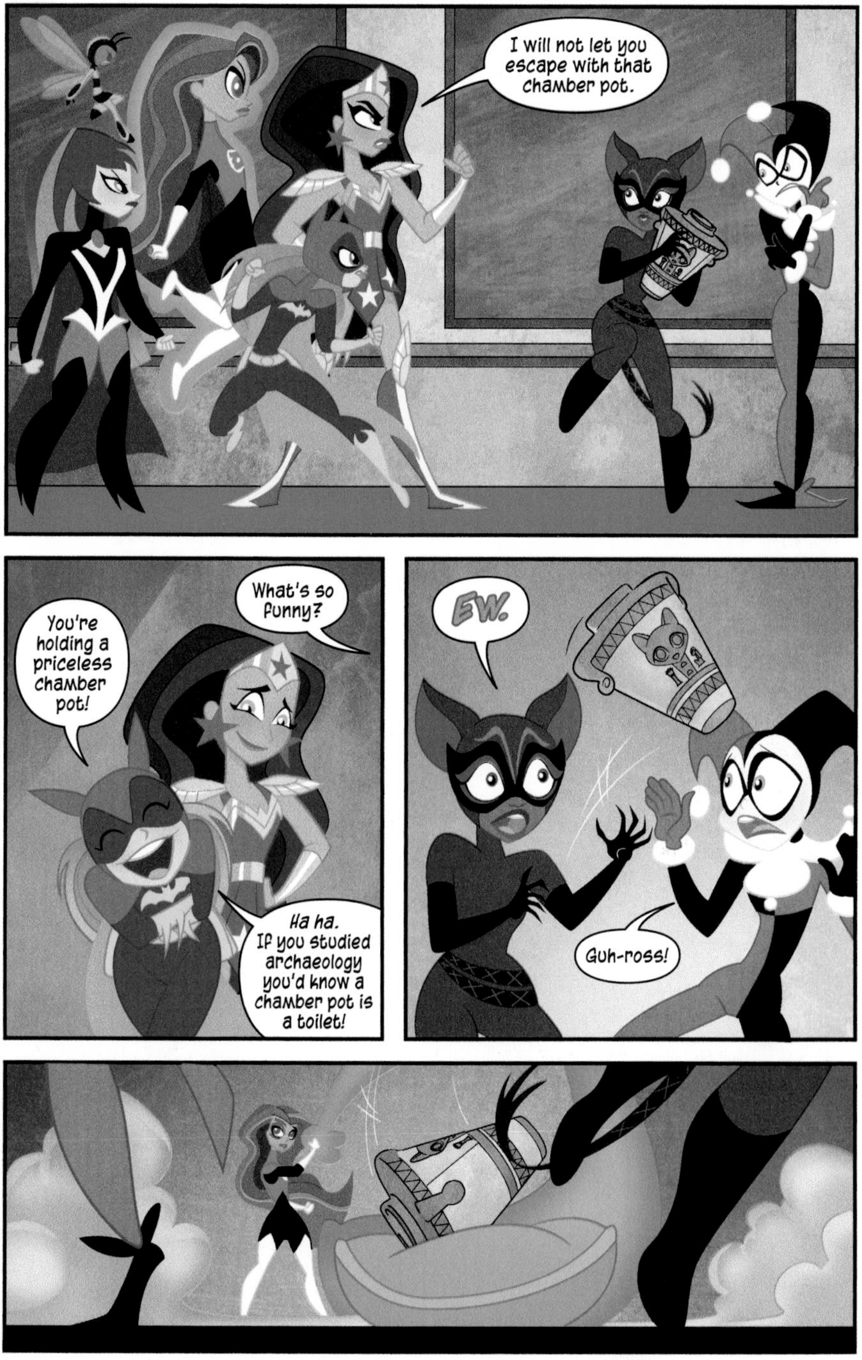
I will not let you escape with that chamber pot.
What's so funny?
You're holding a priceless chamber pot!
Ha ha. If you studied archaeology you'd know a chamber pot is a toilet!
EW.
Guh-ross!

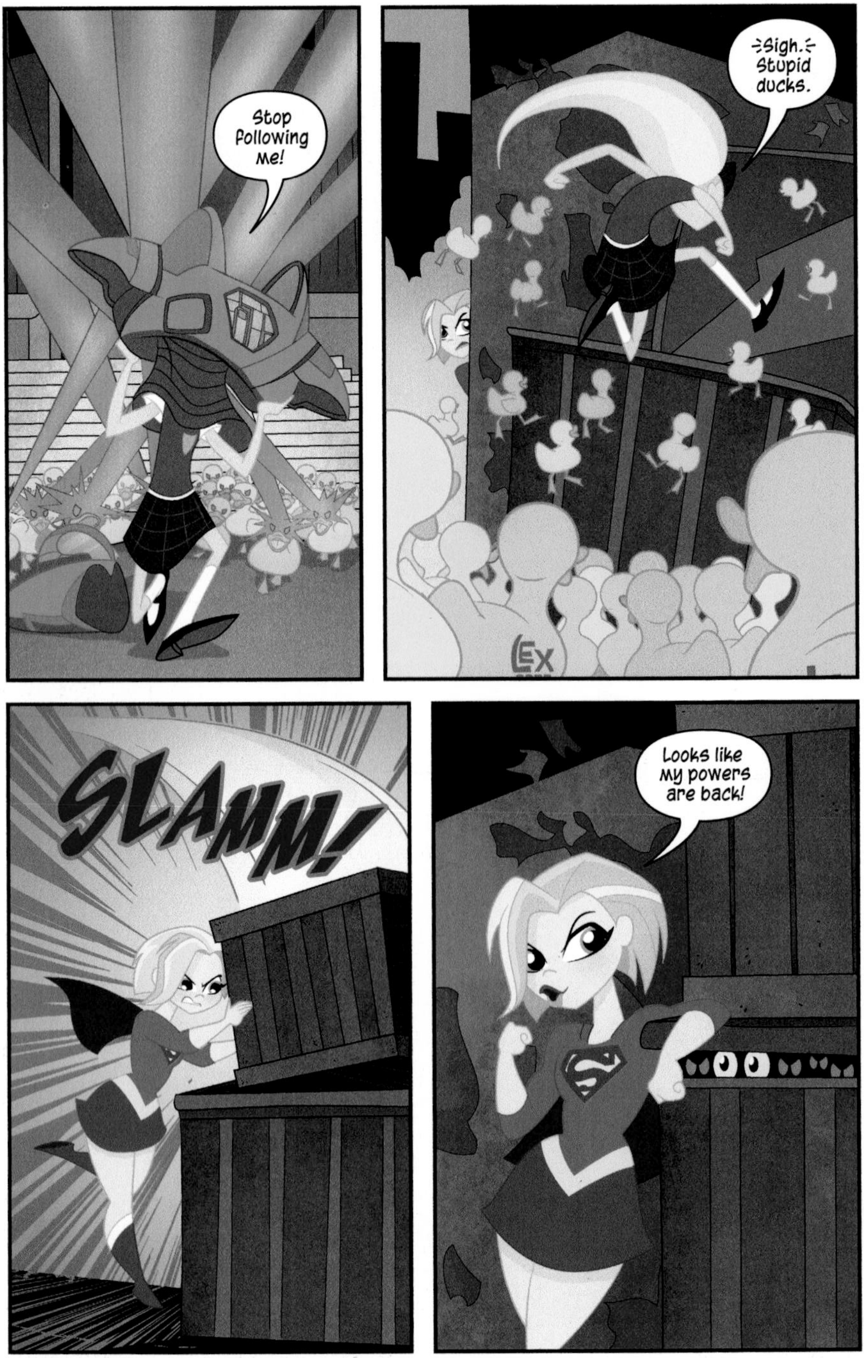
Stop following me!
Sigh. Stupid ducks.
SLAMM!
Looks like my powers are back!

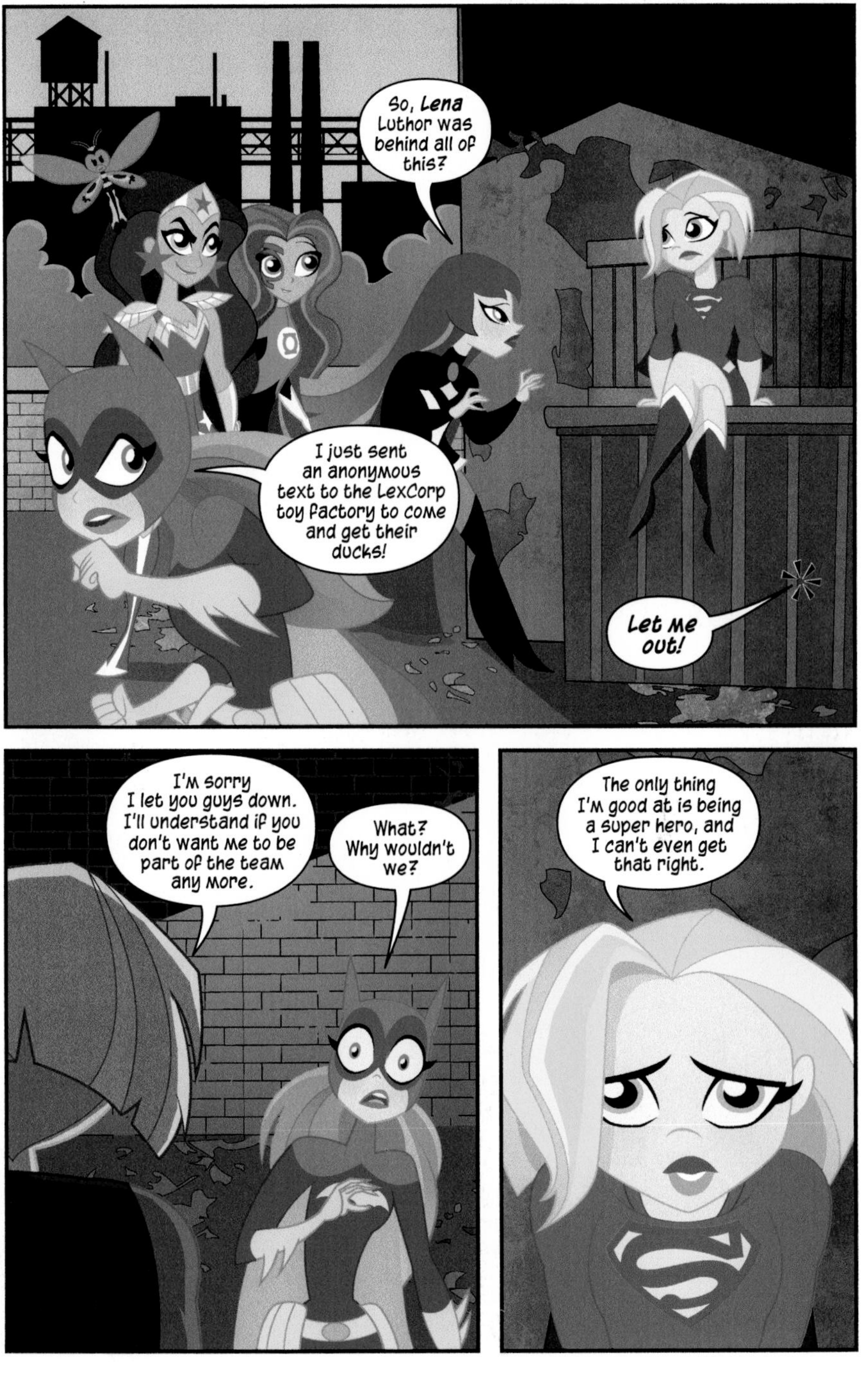

So, Lena Luthor was behind all of this?
I just sent an anonymous text to the LexCorp toy factory to come and get their ducks!
Let me out!
I'm sorry I let you guys down. I'll understand if you don't want me to be part of the team any more.
What? Why wouldn't we?
The only thing I'm good at is being a super hero, and I can't even get that right.

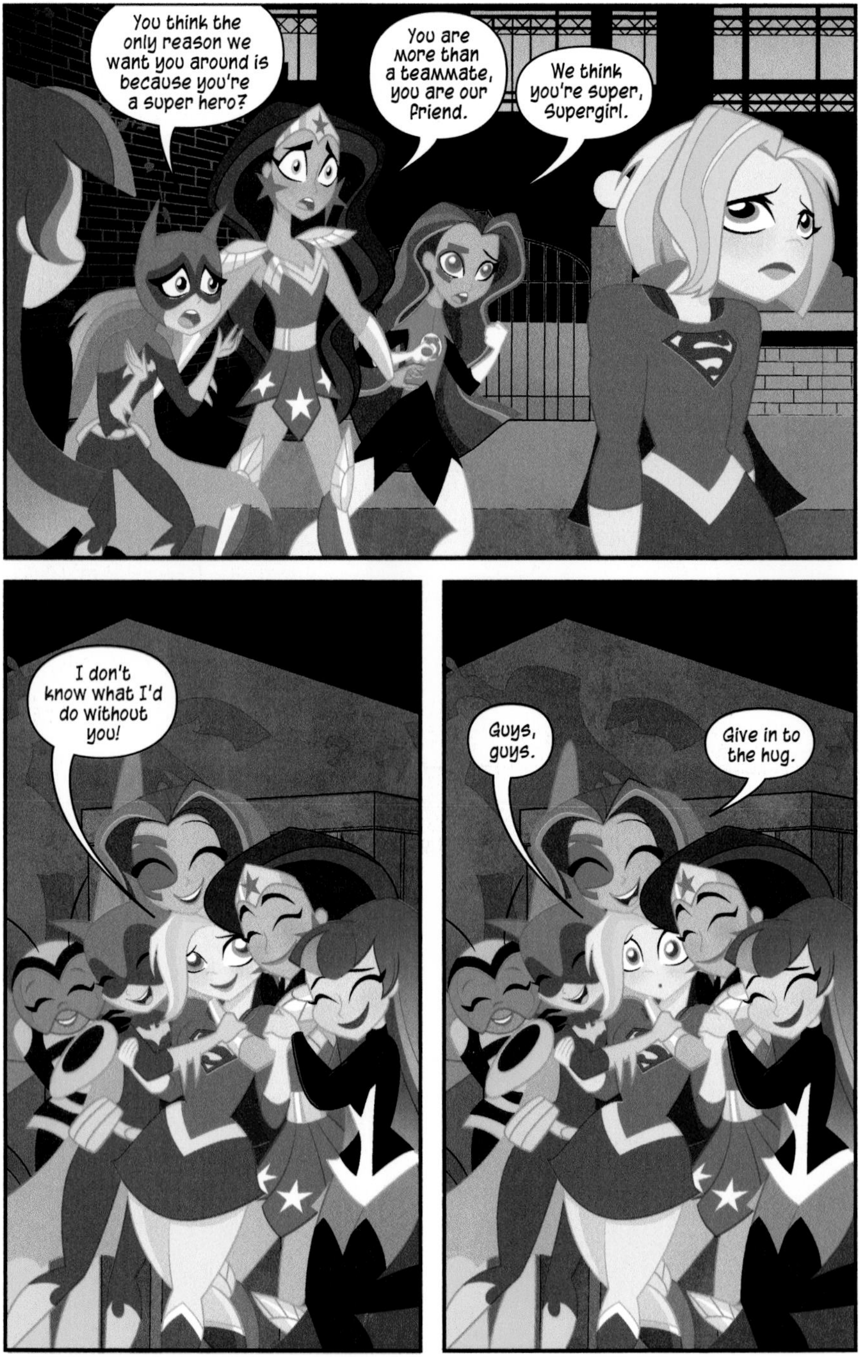
You think the only reason we want you around is because you're a super hero?
You are more than a teammate, you are our friend.
We think you're super, Supergirl.
I don't know what I'd do without you!
Guys, guys.
Give in to the hug.

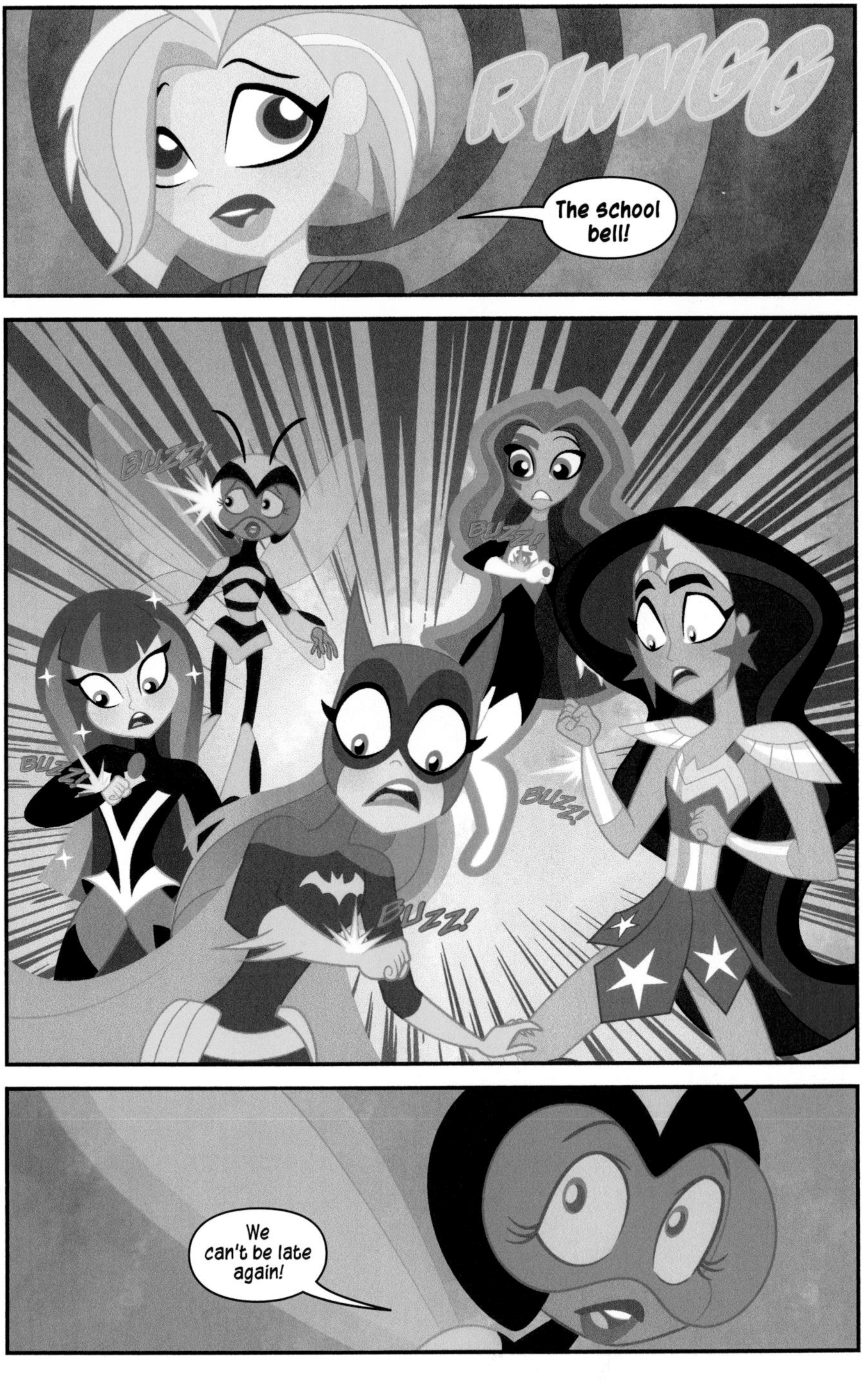
RINNGG
The school bell!
BUZZ!
BUZZ!
BUZZ!
BUZZ!
BUZZ!
We can't be late again!

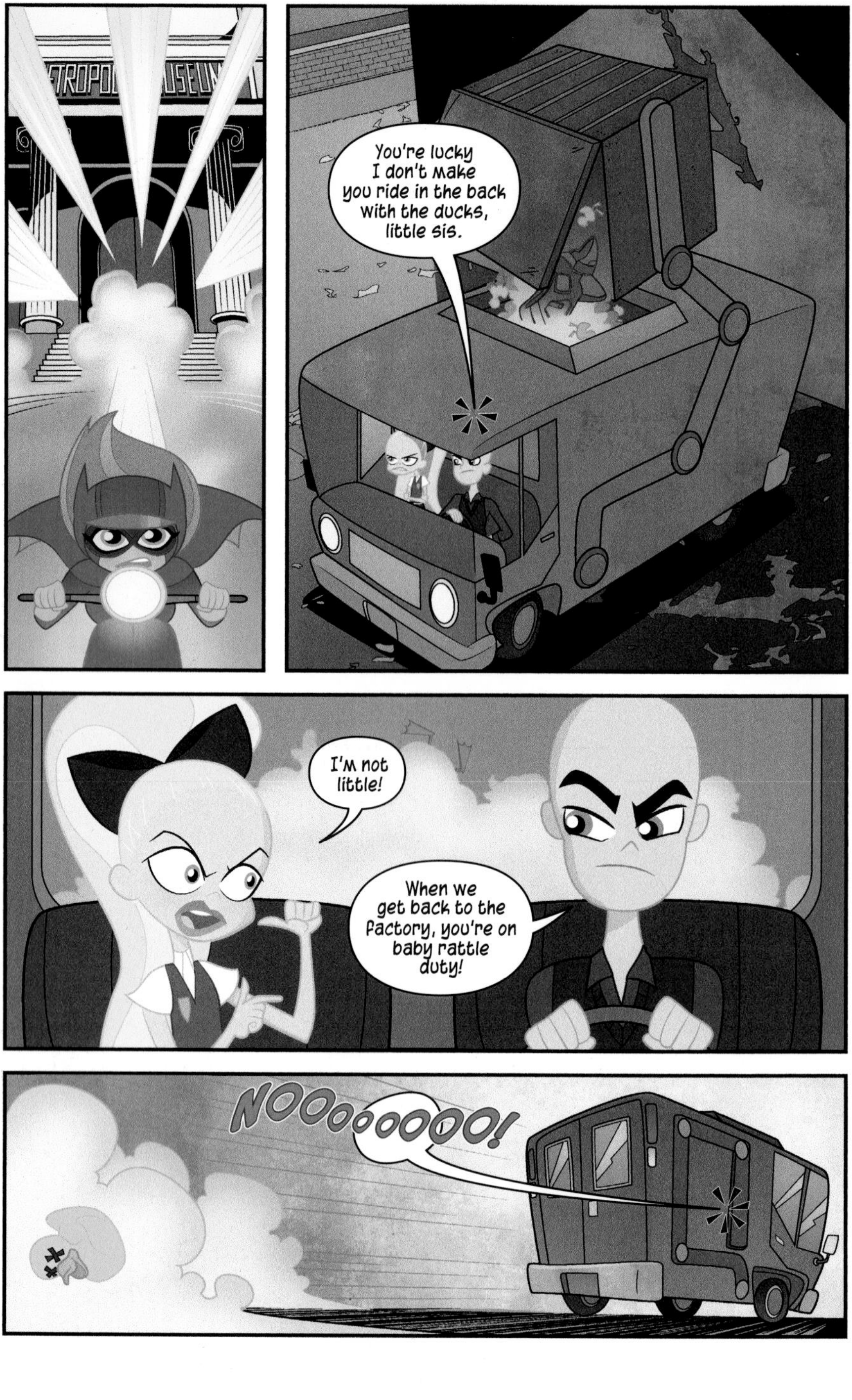
You're lucky I don't make you ride in the back with the ducks, little sis.
I'm not little!
When we get back to the factory, you're on baby rattle duty!
NOOooooOOO!

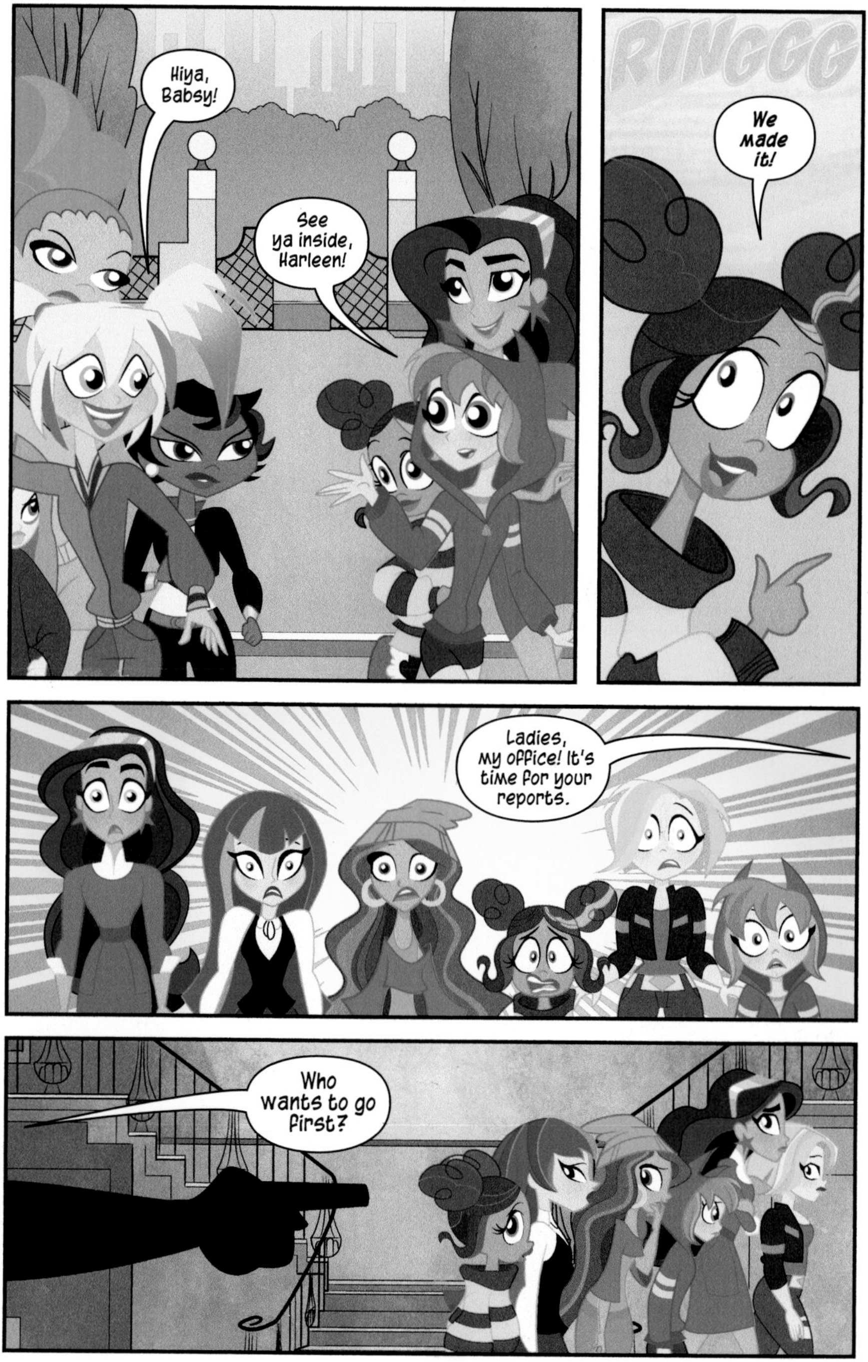
Hiya, Babsy!
See ya inside, Harleen!
RINGGG
We made it!
Ladies, my office! It's time for your reports.
Who wants to go first?

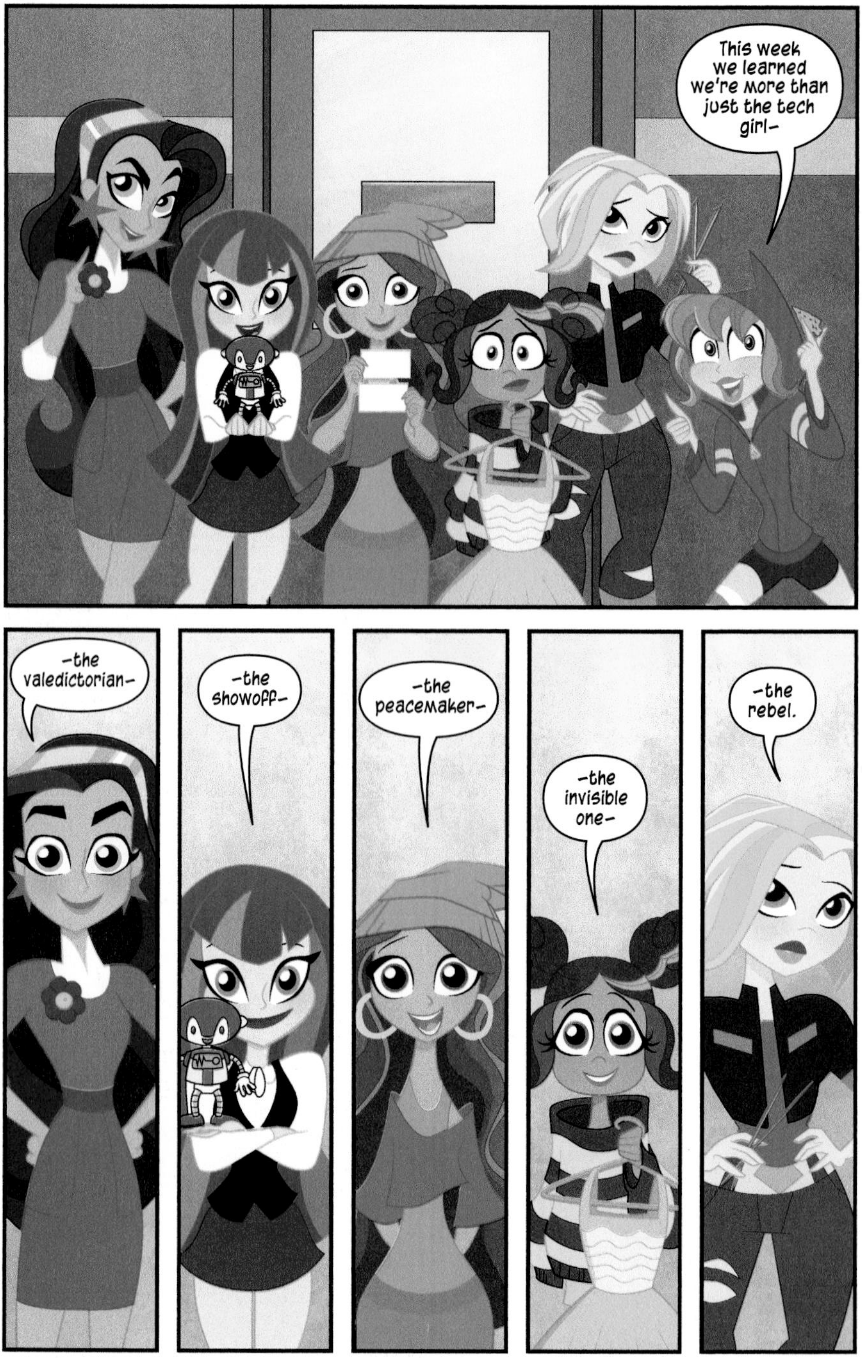
This week we learned we're more than just the tech girl-
-the valedictorian-
-the showoff-
-the peacemaker-
-the invisible one-
-the rebel.

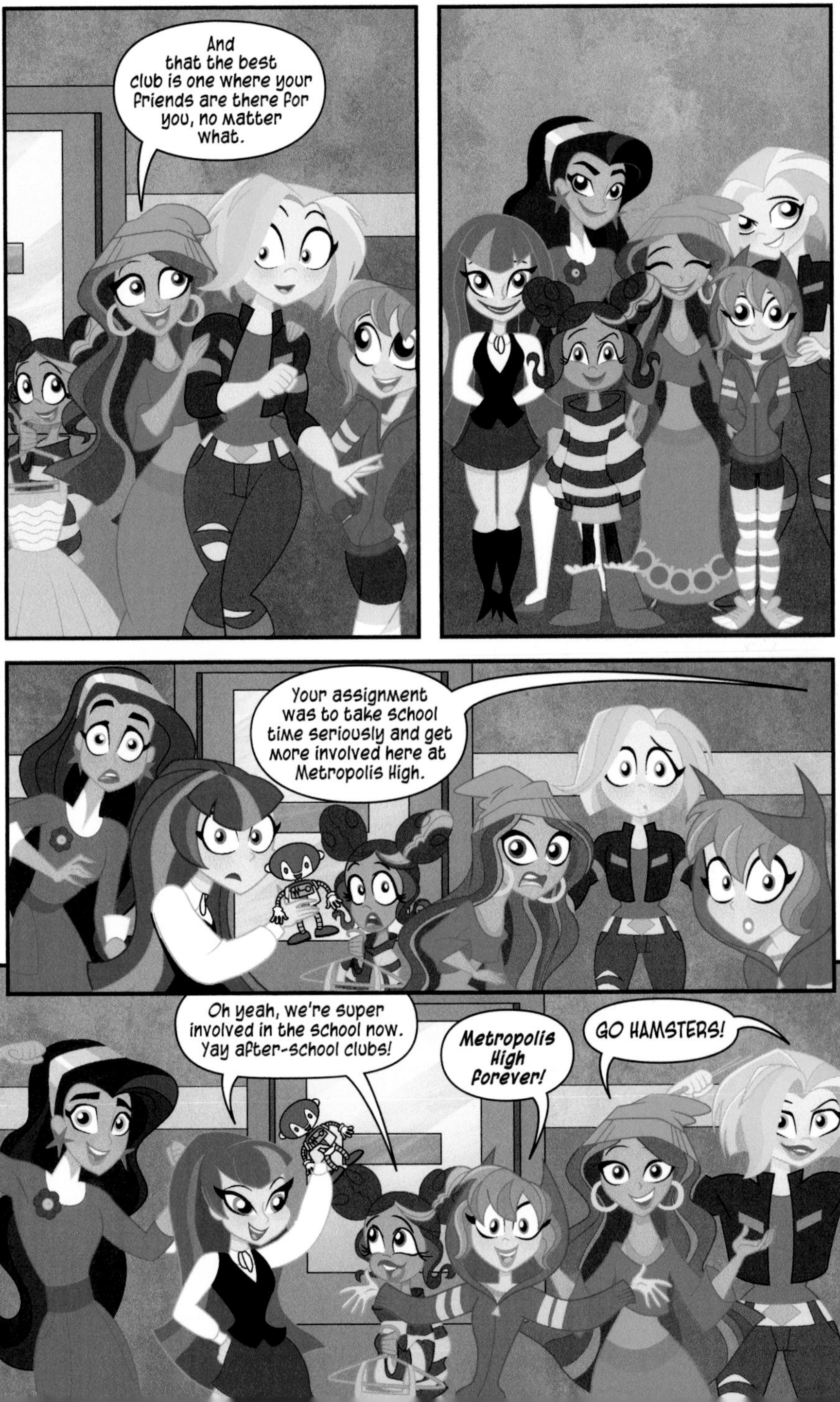
And that the best club is one where your friends are there for you, no matter what.
Your assignment was to take school time seriously and get more involved here at Metropolis High.
Oh yeah, we're super involved in the school now. Yay after-school clubs!
Metropolis High forever!
GO HAMSTERS!

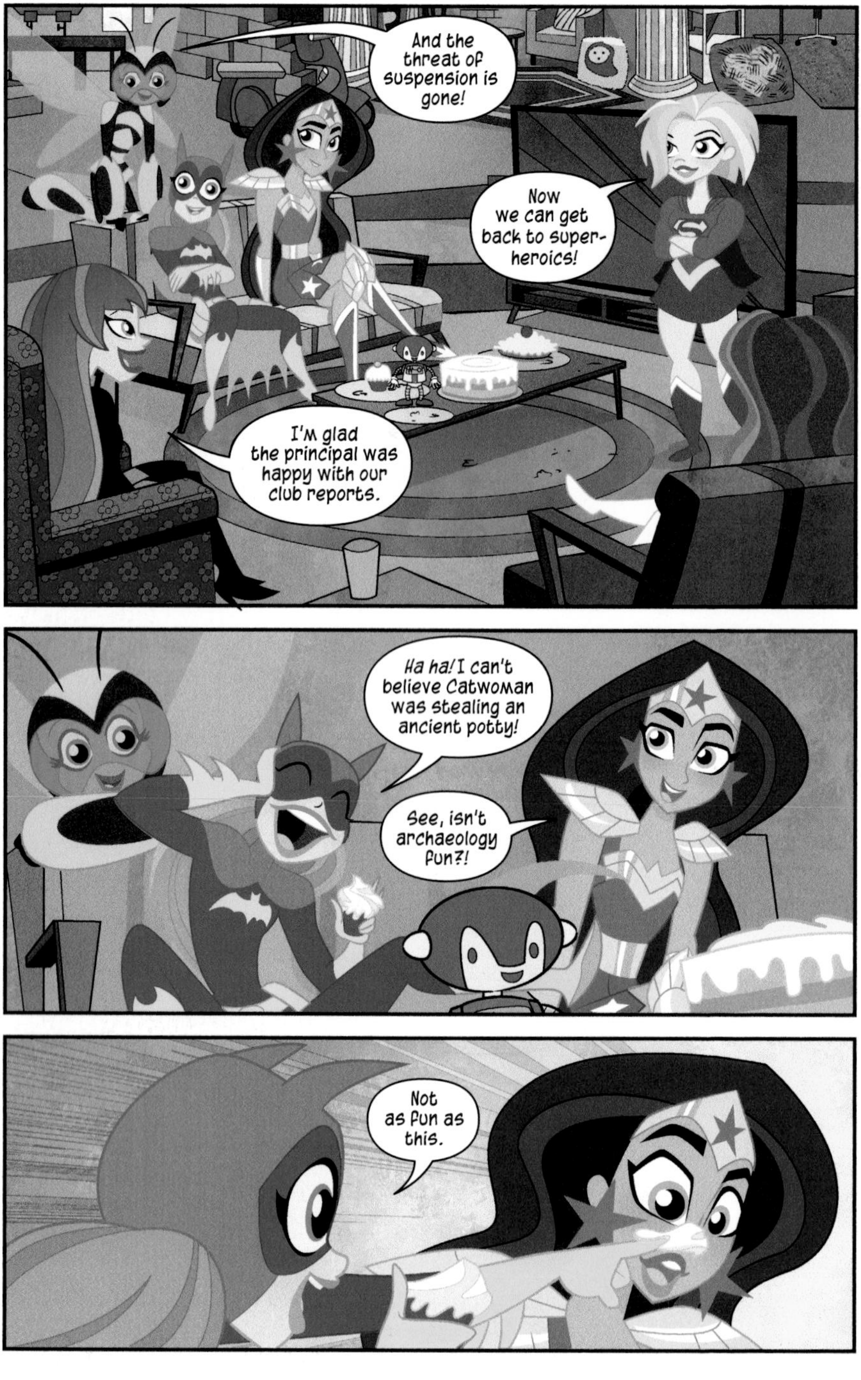
And the threat of suspension is gone!
Now we can get back to super-heroics!
I'm glad the principal was happy with our club reports.
Ha ha! I can't believe Catwoman was stealing an ancient potty!
See, isn't archaeology fun?!
Not as fun as this.

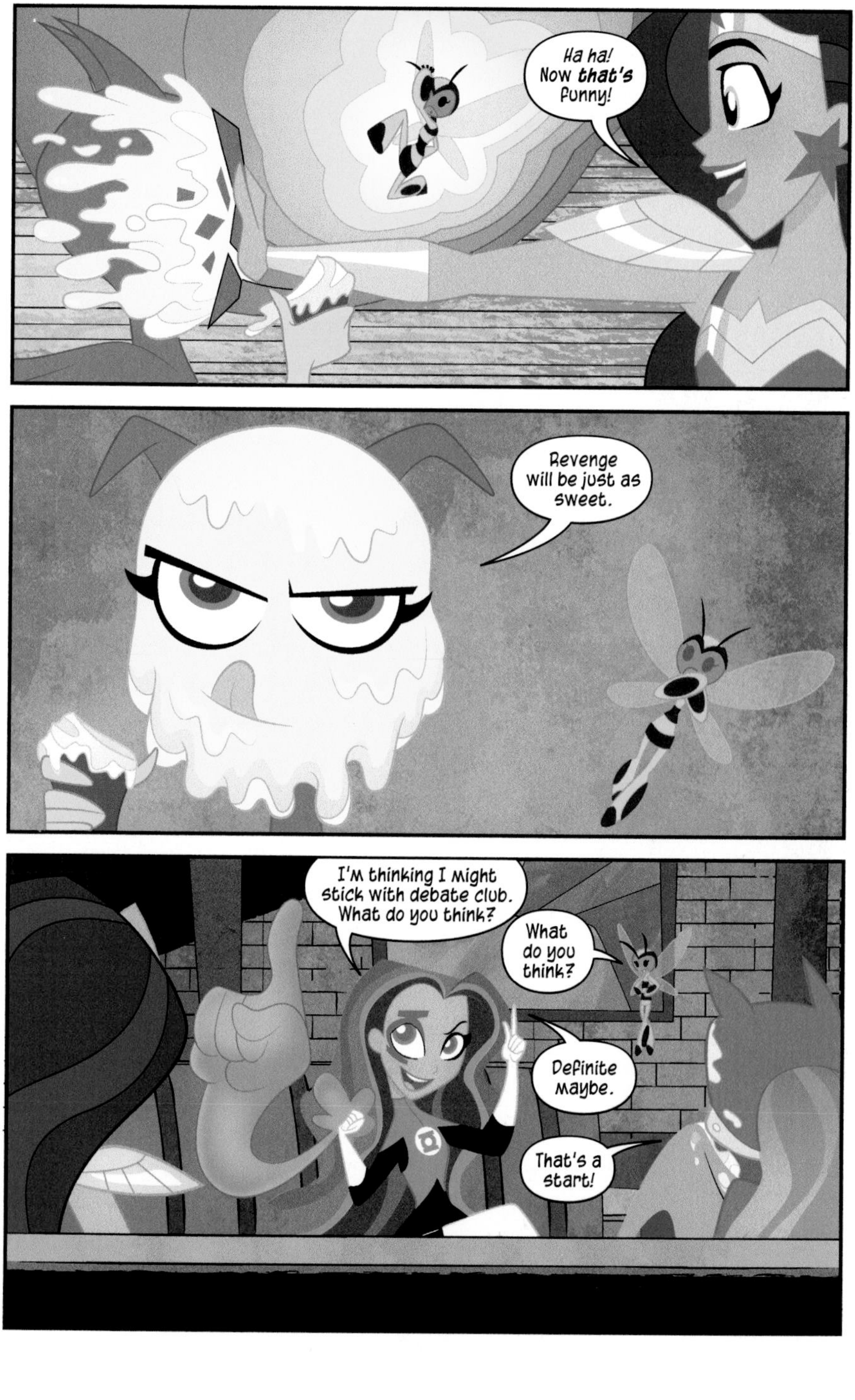

Ha ha! Now **that's** funny!
Revenge will be just as sweet.
I'm thinking I might stick with debate club. What do you think?
What do you think?
Definite maybe.
That's a start!

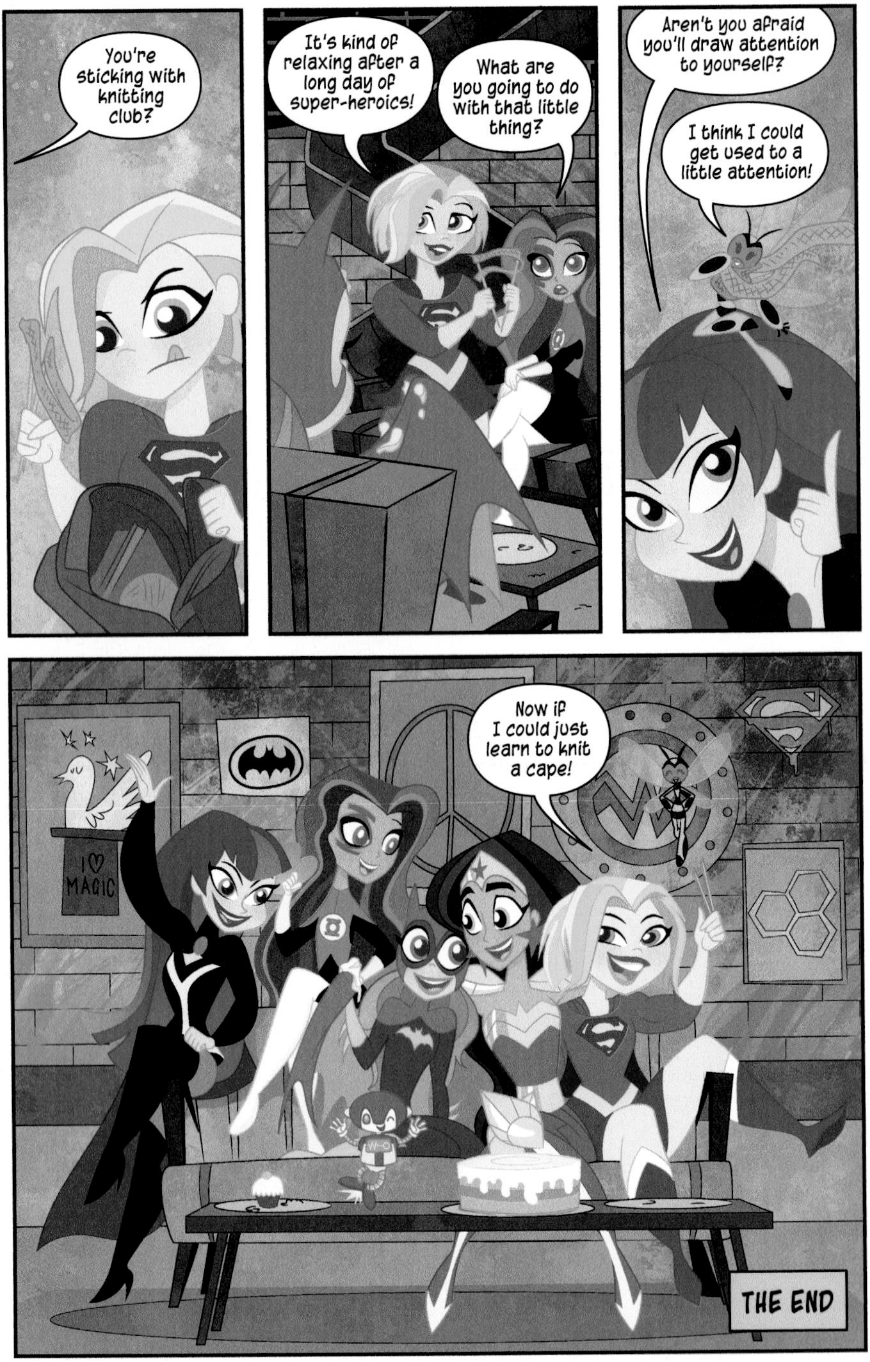
You're sticking with knitting club?
It's kind of relaxing after a long day of super-heroics!
What are you going to do with that little thing?
Aren't you afraid you'll draw attention to yourself?
I think I could get used to a little attention!
Now if I could just learn to knit a cape!
I ♡ MAGIC
THE END

Amy Wolfram is a writer for television, movies, and comic books. She is super excited to be writing DC SUPER HERO GIRLS graphic novels! If she had to pick a favorite Super Hero Girl—she'd pick them all! Best known for writing for Teen Titans for both television (*Teen Titans, Teen Titans Go!*) and comics (TEEN TITANS: YEAR ONE, TEEN TITANS GO!), Amy has also had fun writing for many of her favorite characters: Barbie, Stuart Little, Ben 10, Thunderbirds Are Go, and Scooby-Doo. When not busy writing, she enjoys crafting and quilting.

Yancey Labat is the bestselling illustrator of the original DC SUPER HERO GIRLS graphic novel series. He got his start at Marvel Comics before moving on to illustrate children's books from *Hello Kitty* to *Peanuts* for Scholastic, as well as books for Chronicle Books, ABC Mouse, and others. His book *How Many Jelly Beans?* with writer Andrea Menotti won the 2013 Cook Prize for best STEM (Science, Technology, Education, Math) picture book from Bank Street College of Education.

Monica Kubina has colored countless comics, including super hero series, manga titles, kids' comics, and science fiction stories. She's colored *Phineas and Ferb*, *Spongebob*, *The 99*, and various *Star Wars* titles. Monica's favorite activities are bike riding and going to museums with her husband and two young sons.

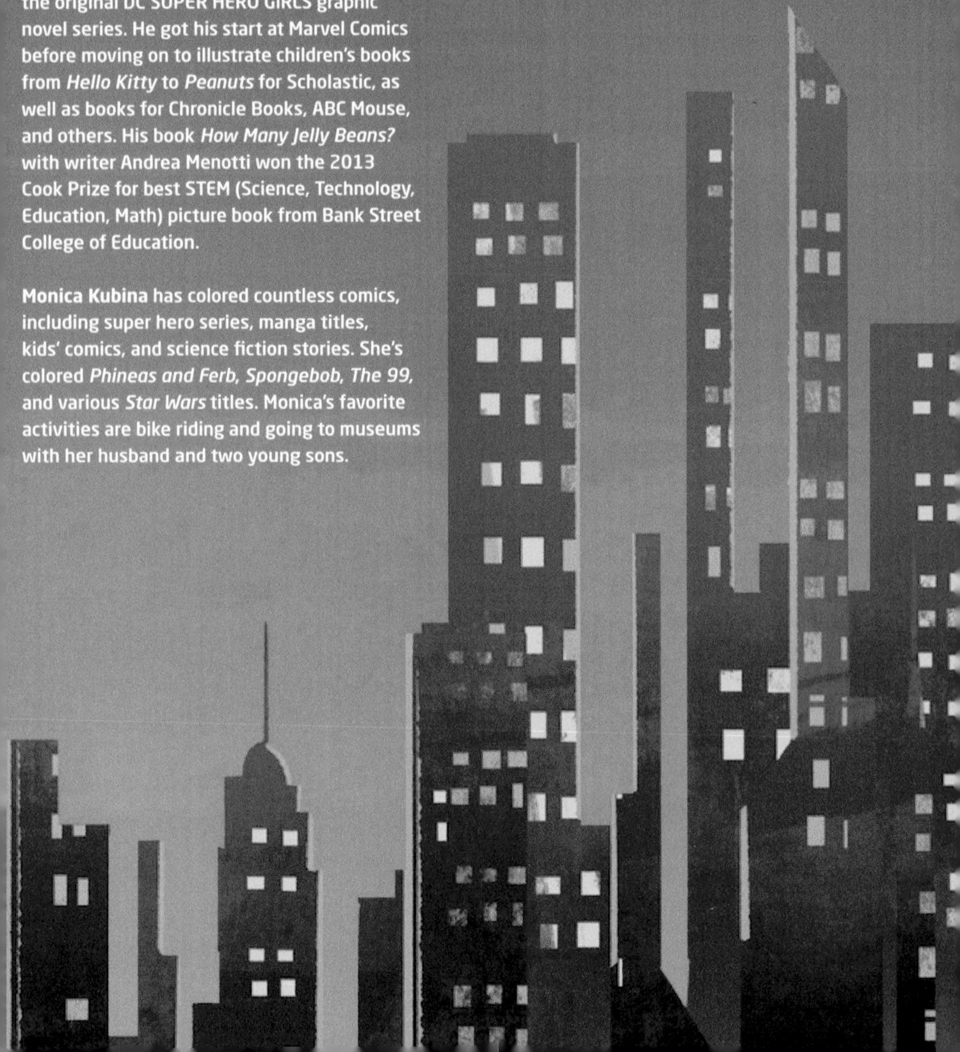

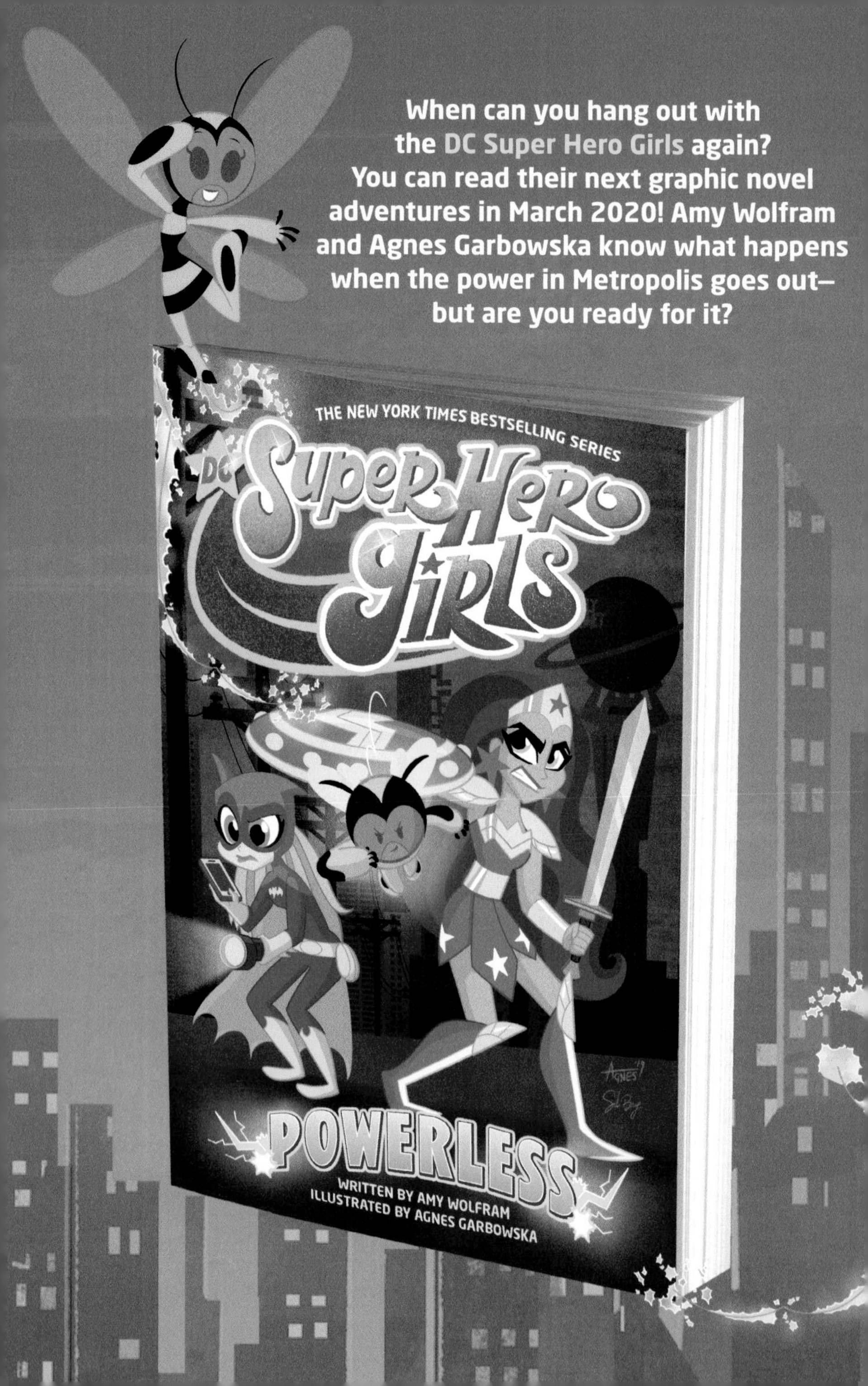
When can you hang out with
the DC Super Hero Girls again?
You can read their next graphic novel
adventures in March 2020! Amy Wolfram
and Agnes Garbowska know what happens
when the power in Metropolis goes out—
but are you ready for it?
THE NEW YORK TIMES BESTSELLING SERIES
DC Super Hero Girls
POWERLESS
WRITTEN BY AMY WOLFRAM
ILLUSTRATED BY AGNES GARBOWSKA

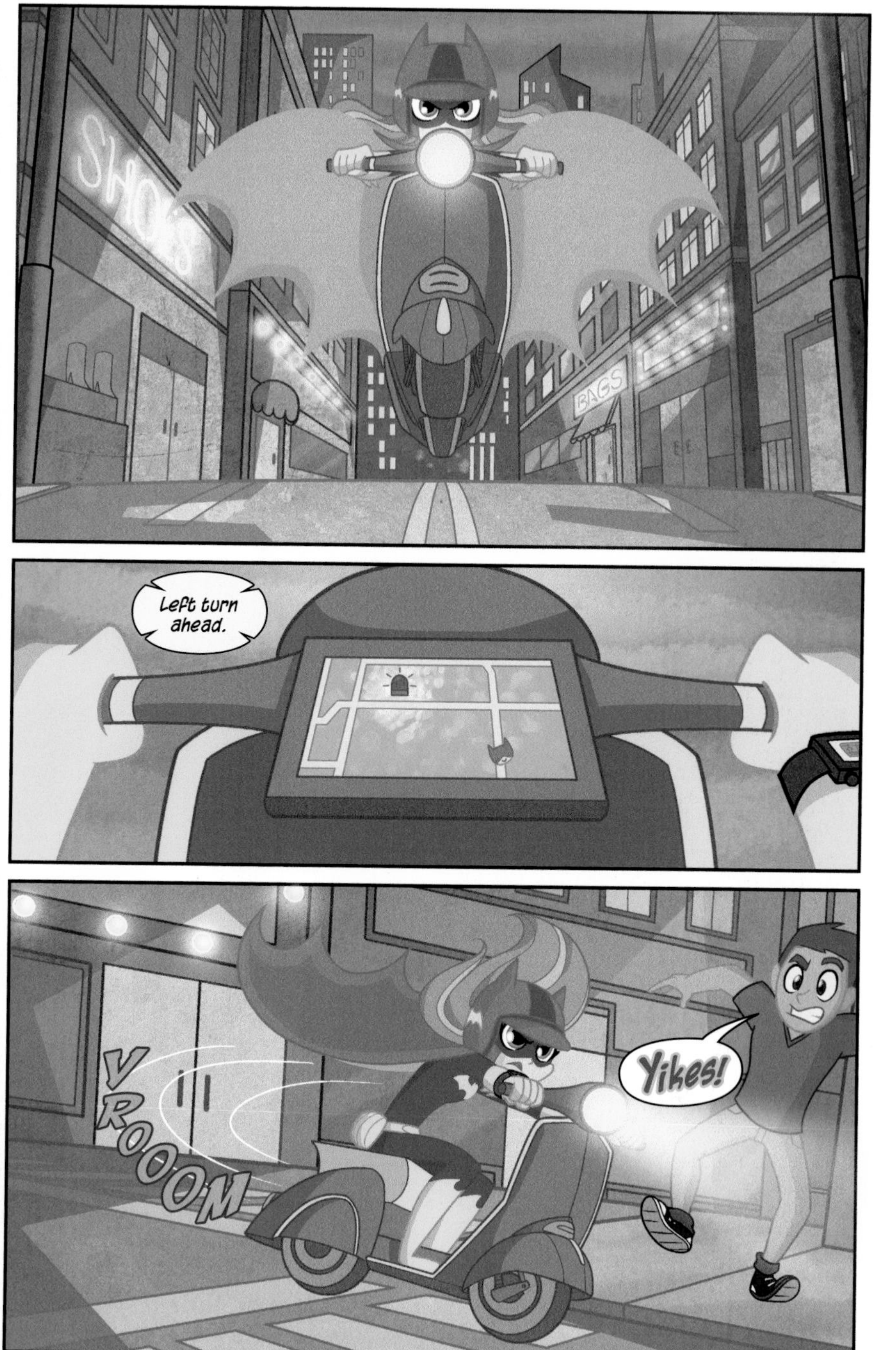
SHOES
BAGS
Left turn ahead.
VROOOM
Yikes!

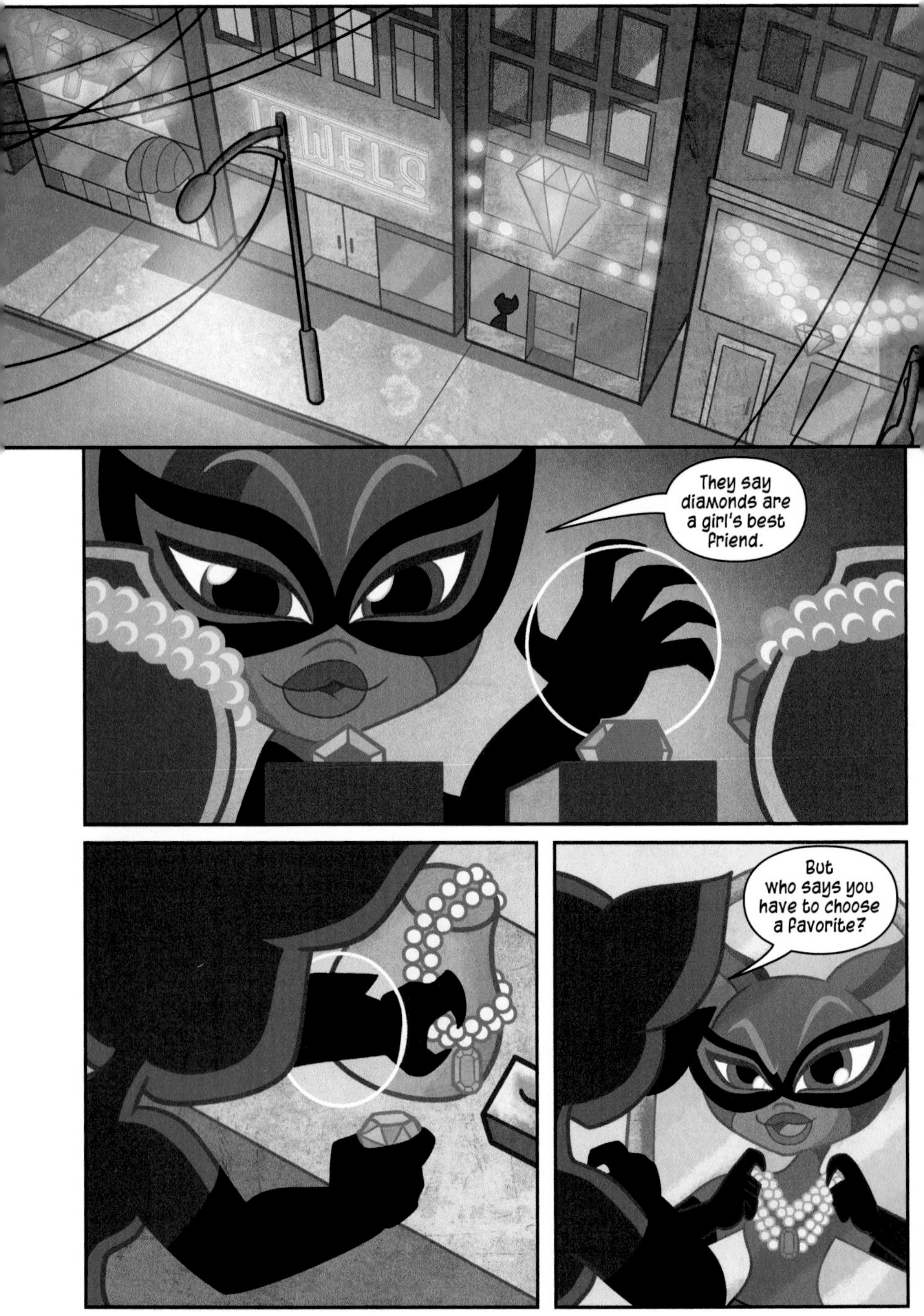
JEWELS
They say diamonds are a girl's best friend.
But who says you have to choose a favorite?

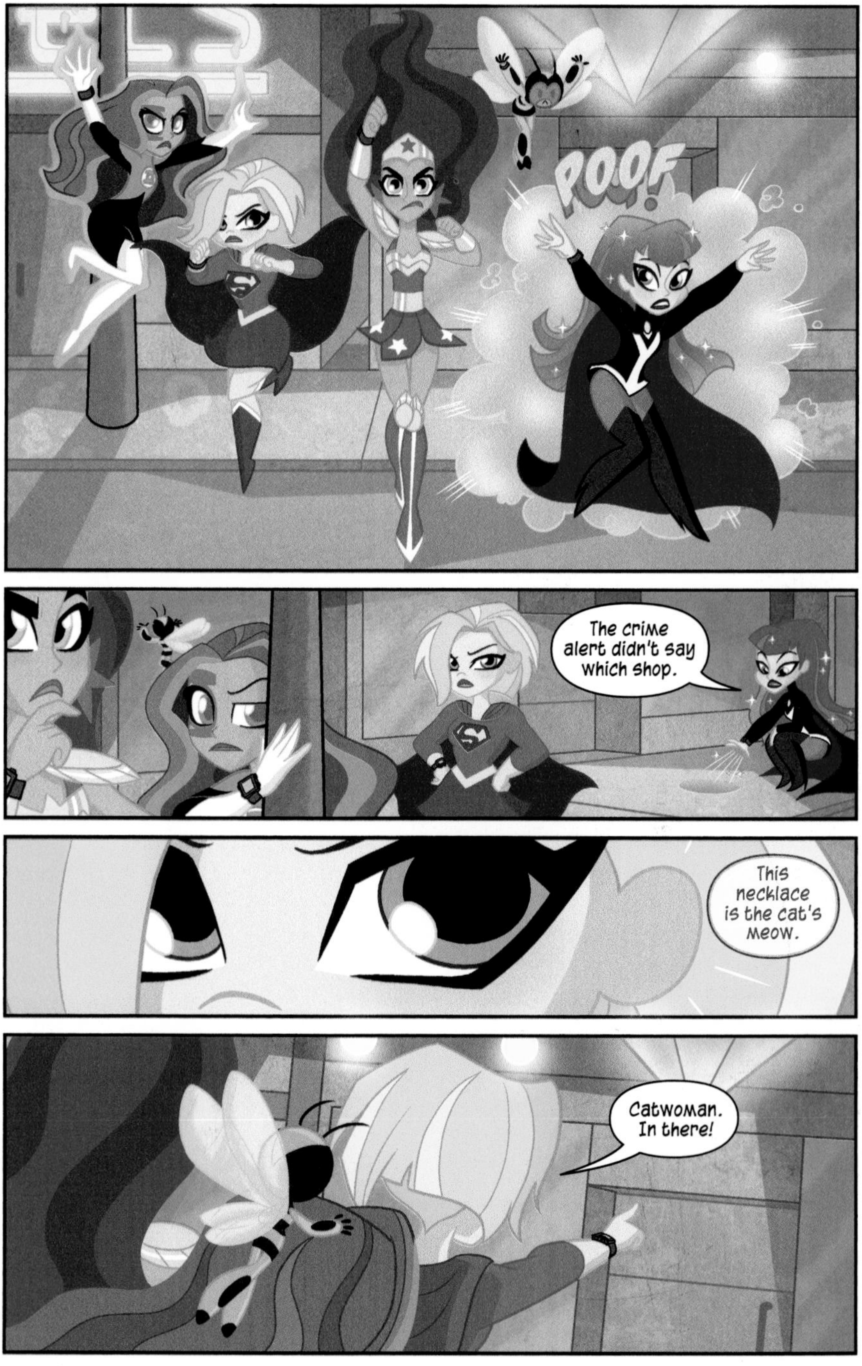
POOF!
The crime alert didn't say which shop.
This necklace is the cat's meow.
Catwoman. In there!

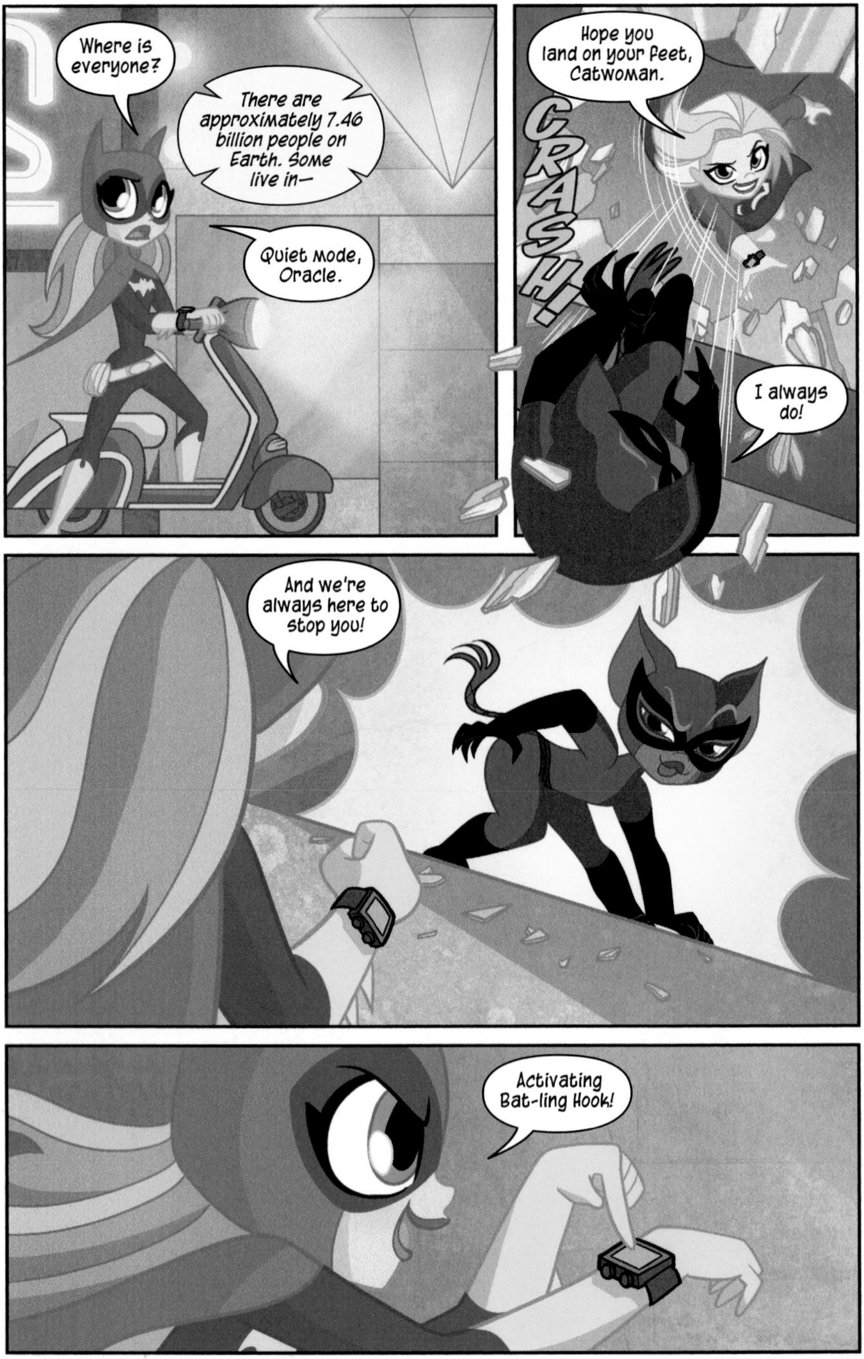
Where is everyone?
There are approximately 7.46 billion people on Earth. Some live in—
Quiet mode, Oracle.
Hope you land on your feet, Catwoman.
CRASH!
I always do!
And we're always here to stop you!
Activating Bat-ling Hook!

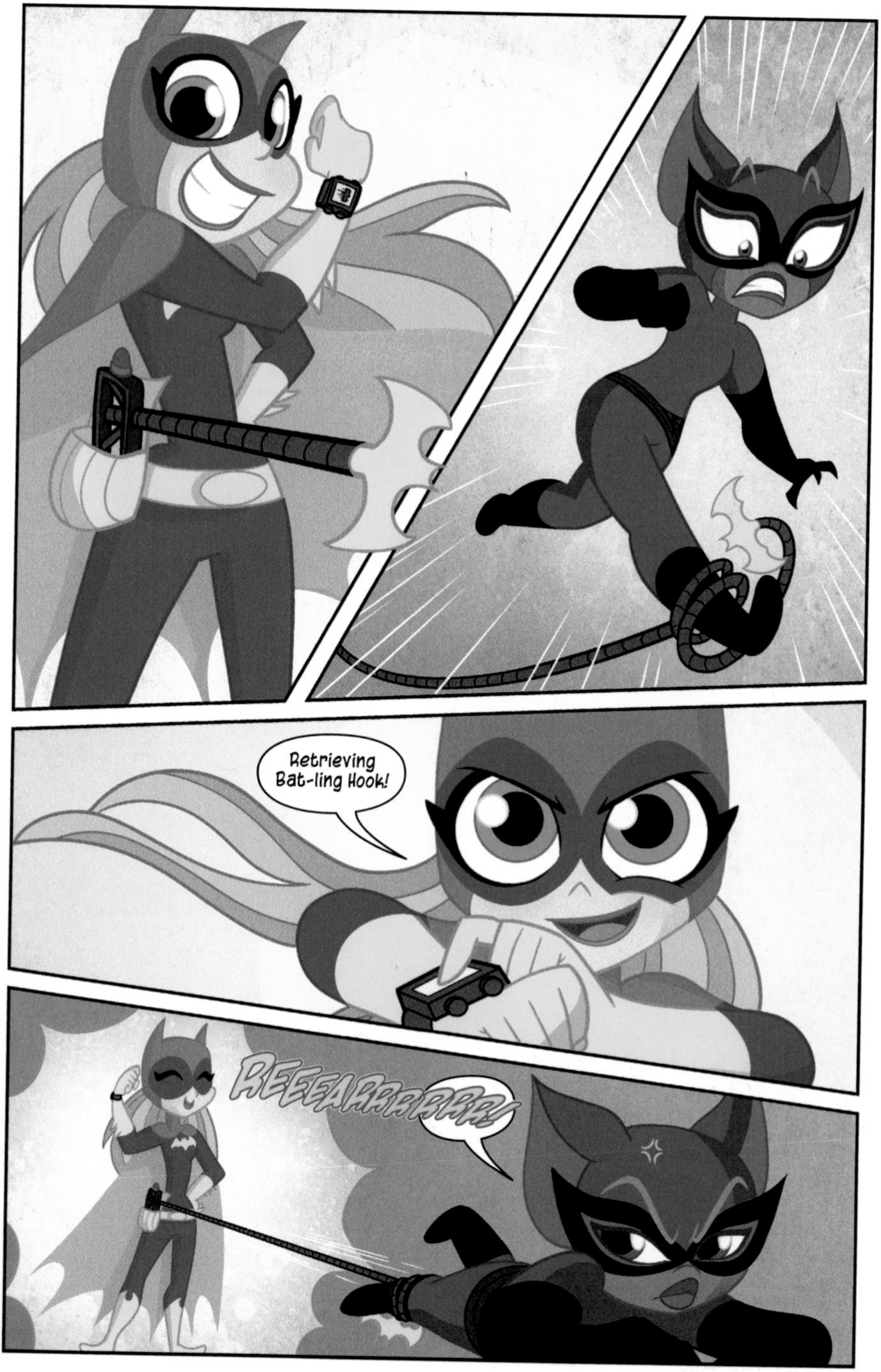
Retrieving Bat-ling Hook!
REEEARRRRRRR!

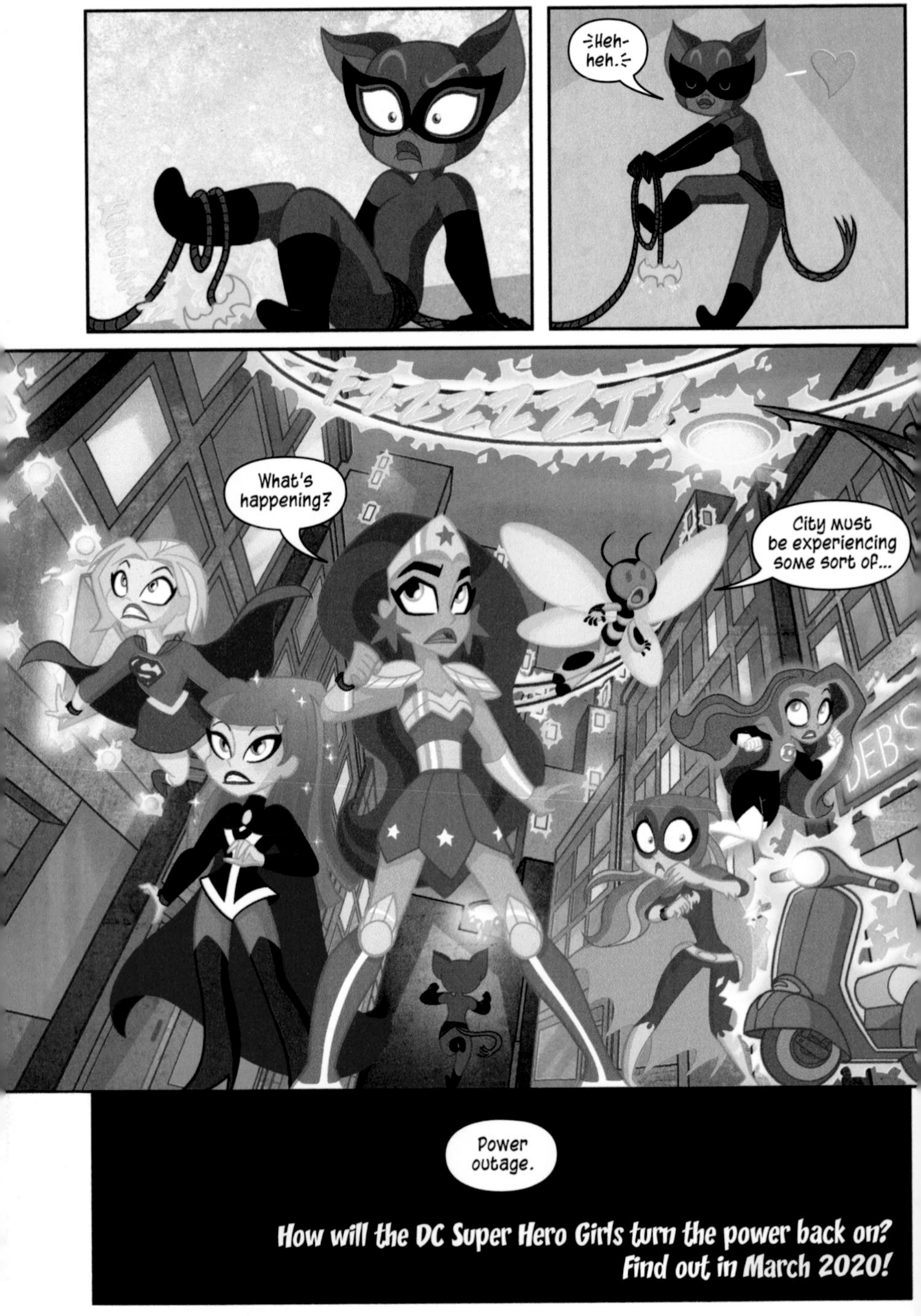

Heh-heh.
FZZZZZZT!
What's happening?
City must be experiencing some sort of...
DEB'S
Power outage.
How will the DC Super Hero Girls turn the power back on?
Find out in March 2020!

New York Times bestselling authors Shannon Hale and Dean Hale team up with artist Victoria Ying to introduce a princess who really just needs a friend.

Turn the page for a sample from Wonder Woman's earliest adventure—coming in January 2020!

NEW YORK TIMES BESTSELLING AUTHORS
SHANNON HALE
&DEAN HALE
DIANA:
PRINCESS
OF THE
AMAZONS
ILLUSTRATED BY
VICTORIA YING
A GRAPHIC NOVEL

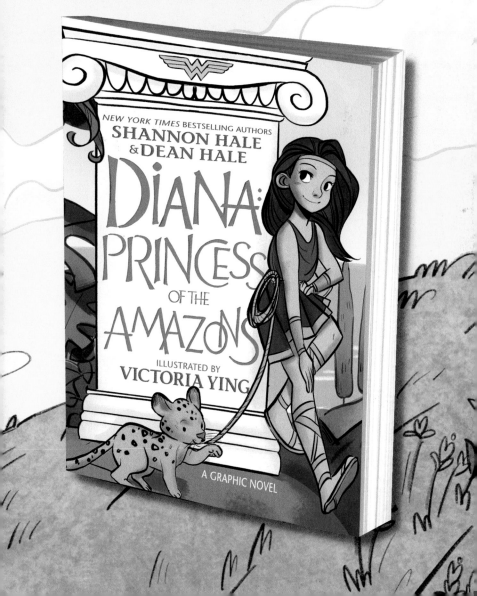

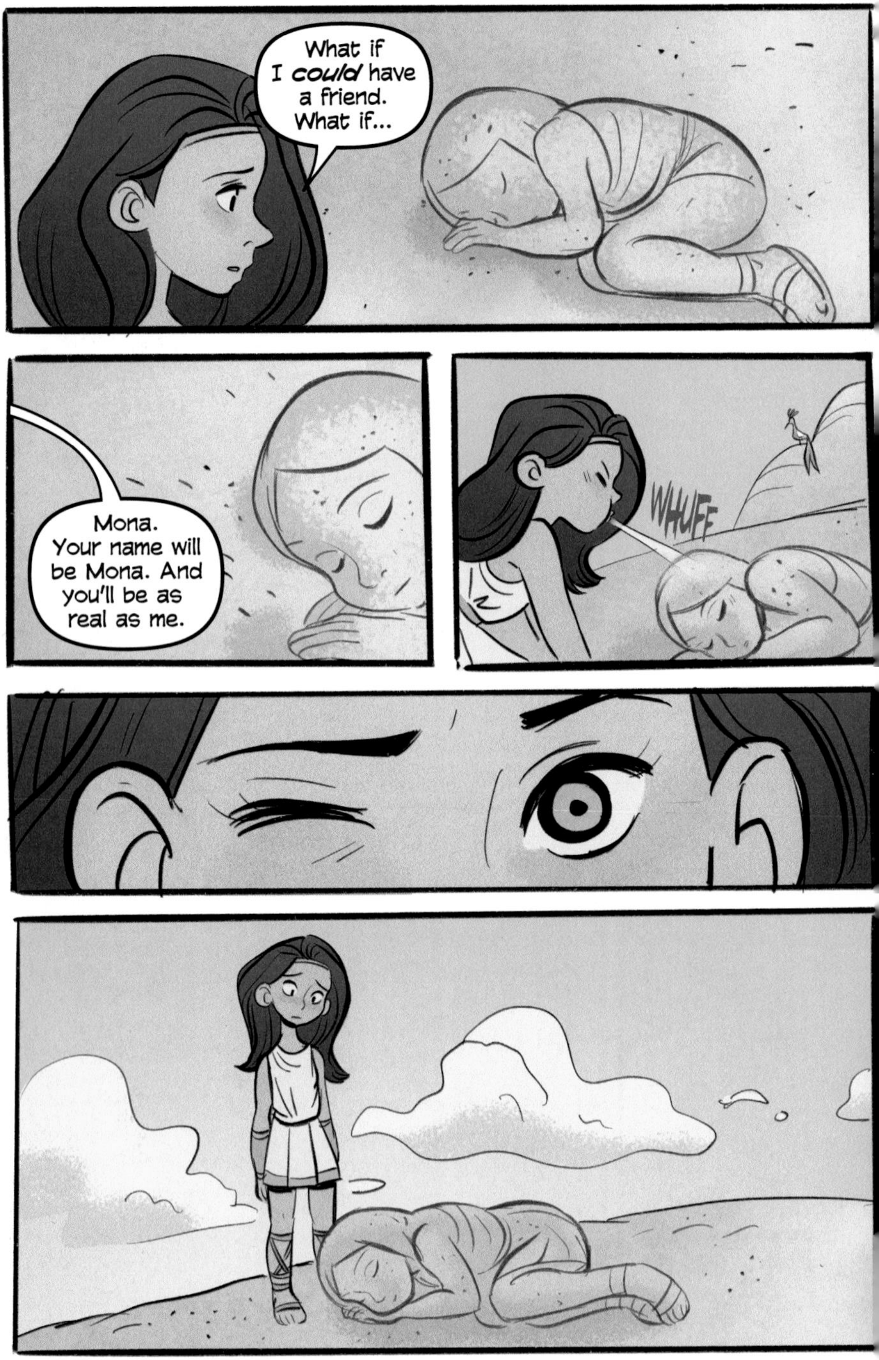
What if I *could* have a friend. What if...
Mona. Your name will be Mona. And you'll be as real as me.
WHUFF